2—

PERFECT DARK
SECOND FRONT

PERFECT DARK
SECOND FRONT

GREG RUCKA

A TOM DOHERTY ASSOCIATES BOOK

New York

TOR®

This is a work of fiction. All of the characters, organizations, and events portrayed in this novel are either products of the author's imagination or are used fictitiously.

PERFECT DARK®: SECOND FRONT

Copyright © 2007 by Microsoft Corporation

All rights reserved, including the right to reproduce this book, or portions thereof, in any form.

www.perfectdarkzero.com

Microsoft, the Microsoft Game Studios logo, Perfect Dark, Perfect Dark Zero, Rare, the Rare logo, Xbox, Xbox 360, and the Xbox and Xbox 360 logos are either registered trademarks or trademarks of Microsoft Corporation or Rare Limited in the United States and/or other countries and are used under license from owner. Rare Limited is a subsidiary of Microsoft Corporation. Copyright © 2006 Microsoft Corporation. All Rights Reserved.

A Tor Book
Published by Tom Doherty Associates, LLC
175 Fifth Avenue
New York, NY 10010

www.tor.com

Tor® is a registered trademark of Tom Doherty Associates, LLC.

ISBN-13: 978-0-7653-5474-7
ISBN-10: 0-7653-5474-8

First Edition: January 2007
First Mass Market Edition: June 2007

Printed in the United States of America

0 9 8 7 6 5 4 3 2 1

This novel is dedicated to
Gabrielle and Jennifer,
who could both teach Jo a thing or two
about kicking ass and
taking names.

ACKNOWLEDGMENTS

The trick of a second novel is doing the first, but better, which is not unlike catching lightning in a bottle . . . two times in a row. It takes nerve, grace, wit, and perseverance, and it can never be done alone. Below are the names of some—and only some—of the people who helped make the catch, so to speak.

Starting at Rare, where Joanna Dark continues to be a glutton for punishment, thanks go out to Duncan Botwood, Richard Cousins, Dale Murchie, Lee Schuneman, Tim and Chris Stamper, and especially Jim Veevaert. Additionally, the author would like to thank Chris Kimmell's frog, who was there when the going got tough, and Chris Kimmell, for having the foresight to have a frog in the first place.

Over at Microsoft, profound gratitude to the following people: Kevin Browne, Sandy Ting, Brian Maeda, Steve Schreck, Jeremy Los, Alicia Hatch, Alicia Brattin, Michelle Ballantine, Joe Bishop, and, of course, (the real) Ed Ventura. A very special thank-you to Nancy Figatner, as well.

As ever, to David Hale Smith, who continues to impress.

At Tor, a thank-you to Eric Raab. Trust us, all that hair you pulled out—it *will* grow back in. Really.

Finally, an enormous thank-you to Eric Trautmann. Weapons-grade wise-ass and storyteller extraordinaire, may your coffee always be hot, and your sights always be true.

PERFECT DARK

SECOND FRONT

Mud Bay—Approximately 1.5 km west
of Olympia, Washington
January 17th, 2021

When the pretty young woman with the dark red hair and
the sapphire-blue eyes tried to kill Zentek CEO Georg
Bricker, Georg Bricker's suit fought for his life.

It did this in several ways, activating countermeasure after
countermeasure in the spread of mere microseconds. Sensing
its owner's sudden change in heart rate, blood pressure, and
respiration, Bricker's clothes correctly concluded that his
fight-or-flight reflex had engaged, and dumped a massive
dose of designer epinephrine into his system to augment his
already natural release of adrenaline. On every out-facing surface of his suit jacket, millions of almost undetectable quills
emerged at once, each coated with an artificially synthesized
version of tetrodotoxin, the cumulative dose enough to momentarily paralyze an assailant's central nervous system.
Georg Bricker's vest, which had appeared only seconds before to be a charcoal and gray serge, like the rest of his suit,
both thickened and hardened, growing snugger around his
torso while secreting a resin that, given the opportunity, would

become hard enough to deflect all but the most determined bullet or blade.

While his suit switched into defensive mode and the pretty redhead brought her Falcon pistol to bear, Bricker's Z-sleeve—the integrated PDA grown into the lower left forearm of his suit coat—automatically switched over to panic mode. It broadcast emergency requests for assistance to all local law enforcement agencies, as well as sending a separate priority transmission to Zentek corporate headquarters in Berlin, notifying Zentek's internal security of his status, situation, and location—the last by providing Bricker's GPS coordinates. Additionally, it commenced streaming live A/V to Zentek's corporate data-hub in Frankfurt, in an attempt to record what was happening for posterity or, at least, possible future legal action.

And finally, the Z-sleeve emanated a 120-decibel oscillating screech, in an attempt both to dissuade the redhead from continuing her efforts and to alert anyone who might be nearby as to Bricker's dire straits.

As a demonstration of the integration of technology and fashion, of the inventiveness and creativity of Zentek's programmers, engineers, organics engineers, and fashion designers, it was a truly flawless display. Under different circumstances, Georg Bricker would certainly have felt a surge of pride at the quality of craftsmanship evident in his corporation's work.

As a means of saving Georg Bricker's life, it turned out to be entirely useless.

Bricker's day had begun at his home outside of Frankfurt, and it had begun poorly, with his Z-sleeve alerting him to an urgent incoming message while he sat at breakfast with his wife and son. The message was terse, stating simply that Zentek stock had jumped on the Tokyo, Sydney, and London exchanges, up sixty-three dollars and seventeen cents. In other circumstances, such a change could only be seen as good news, but Bricker knew better, and with one call to the office, his suspicions were confirmed. Beck-Yama InterNational, the hypercorporation second only to dataDyne in terms of size and power, had gone public in its takeover bid of Zentek, and the stock price had subsequently skyrocketed in anticipation of a buyout.

The news dismayed Bricker, but it did not surprise him. Since the third quarter of 2018, Zentek had been tottering on the brink of financial disaster. Attempts to revitalize the company over the past two and a half years with the latest iteration of its signature "living clothing line" and by similarly introducing the same biomorphic technology to the home market had failed to stanch the corporation's financial hemorrhaging. Zentek's problem, and Bricker knew it but was too proud to compromise the fact, was that the corporation made quality material. Cutting costs meant cutting quality of work, and the thought was anathema to him.

As early as January 2020, almost precisely a year ago, Bricker had seen the writing on the wall: unless Zentek brought to market something as revolutionary as dataDyne's null-g technology or as ubiquitous as Core-Mantis OmniGlobal's "ring rings," Zentek would go the way of the dodo.

There were board members and CEOs who would have deployed their golden parachutes then and there. Several of Georg Bricker's own corporate officers already had, in fact. But, in the same way that compromising the quality of Zentek's work wasn't an option, fleeing the company he had nurtured and guided for almost twenty years wasn't one, either. Zentek wasn't simply his company, it was his *family*, and he felt a strong and almost irrational sense of loyalty not just to the business but to his 1.2 million employees. Beck-Yama wanted Zentek not for its market share but for its trade secrets and technology. Of those 1.2 million people, at most ten thousand would find work under a Beck-Yama-controlled Zentek.

It had been in early 2020, then, that Bricker had come to an all but unheard of decision. Rather than allow Zentek to become the victim of a hostile takeover, he instead decided that some Zentek was better than no Zentek at all, and he set about looking to broker a merger with another hypercorporation.

Once he'd come to that conclusion, Bricker had truly only one choice, only one hypercorporation he could turn to. Carrington Industries was even smaller than Zentek—not to mention that Carrington's "Institute" was decidedly biased against big business. Core-Mantis OmniGlobal, while much larger than Zentek, had its own successful fashion and body-modification lines.

That left dataDyne, the monster of them all, the largest hypercorp on the planet. So big, dataDyne could swallow Zentek whole, absorbing his 1.2 million employees without so much as a pause.

His conclusion reached, Georg Bricker swallowed his pride and sent a politely worded letter—written by hand—to dataDyne CEO Zhang Li. In the letter he spoke of his admiration for dataDyne's accomplishments and business acumen, for the quality of its services and its standards of product. He spoke of his belief that Zentek shared these qualities. He concluded his letter with the proposal of a merger of the two hypercorporations, one that could certainly benefit dataDyne. All Bricker had asked was that he be allowed to preserve Zentek under dataDyne's auspices.

Much to his surprise, Zhang Li had responded almost immediately—or, more precisely, a phalanx of attorneys the dataDyne CEO employed in the mergers and acquisitions division had responded—saying that, yes, dataDyne was interested in brokering such a merger. A full accounting of Zentek's resources and assets was required, of course, and an exhaustive audit, but once these things were in hand, merger language could be negotiated to satisfy both Zentek's and dataDyne's needs.

Bricker had been relieved almost to the point of tears. Zentek's attorneys had gone to work at once, and the immense and tedious task of reconciling the one corporation with the other had begun. Work had been slow, but it had been steady, and Beck-Yama, sensing dataDyne's interest and not wishing to antagonize the world's largest—and, not coincidentally, most powerful—business entity, had backed off.

Then Zhang Li had unexpectedly disappeared from public life along with his daughter, Mai Hem, and for much of 2020 there had been nothing from dataDyne regarding the proposed merger. Bricker's attempts at contact went unanswered, and Beck-Yama once again began moving in around Zentek in a manner that could only be described as vultures circling a prospective corpse.

Only to back off again when dataDyne announced the resignation of CEO Zhang and the appointing of Dr. Cassandra DeVries to fill his position. Bricker immediately attempted to contact the new CEO, sending DeVries both his compliments and congratulations and inquiring as to the future of the merger. Since DeVries's appointment almost two months earlier, Bricker had made eleven attempts to contact the new CEO. He received no response. Not a letter, not a call, not a memo, not a word.

Bricker didn't know what to make of it.

But Beck-Yama did, and this morning announced, publicly, their intention to acquire and then dismantle Zentek.

From his home, Bricker flew to the main office in Berlin, where he presided over a meeting of the board of directors and a video conference with Zentek's division heads around the world. He declared his intention to fight Beck-Yama and did his best to rally his troops. Despite his efforts, morale remained low. Back in his office, he once more fired off an urgent letter to CEO DeVries, all but begging for a response, and now all the more certain that one was not coming. Zentek stock had jumped another fifteen dollars and seventy-one cents in the last three hours, now trading up almost seventy-nine dollars from its price of the day before.

Bricker called a strategy meeting with his CFO and the upper echelon accounting staff. Pacing restlessly back and forth past the window-monitors in his office, they discussed options, attempting to build some sort of strategy to keep Beck-Yama at bay. Of immediate concern was the stock loss, and his CFO made it plain that a buyback had to begin at once, or else Beck-Yama would hold controlling interest before the end of the day. But a buyback would cost money, and money was Zentek's problem; there wasn't enough of it to counter the billions of dollars that Beck-Yama was now spending, eating Zentek stock like a cancer. Worse, the longer the day wore on, the higher the stock price climbed. Something had to be done immediately, or else nothing else could be done at all.

Against all his principles, Bricker did the one thing left for him to do. He ordered two of Zentek's manufacturing divisions closed. In so doing, he put 68,000 of his employees out of work and freed almost 3.2 billion dollars to be redirected back into Zentek's defense. The buyback began at once, and the stock price began to stabilize. Bricker remained in his office through the night, surrounded by assistants and associates, monitoring trading on exchanges around the world. By midnight in Berlin, Zentek had stabilized, and by three in the morning—midday in Tokyo—it seemed that Beck-Yama International was once again backing off, if only for the moment.

Bricker could only guess that he'd taken them by surprise, that in his ivory tower overlooking downtown Tokyo, Beck-Yama CEO Takashi Noto had been given pause, forced to reevaluate his takeover strategy.

Bricker left the office at a quarter past three in the morning, boarded his private low-orbit transport, and flew to Seattle. He did not want to go to Seattle. He wanted to return to Frankfurt for some much needed rest and some even more needed time with his family. But he went, because he felt he had no choice. Playing at the Zee Arena that night was a concert by the performance icon Candee, the concluding stop of her forty-eight-city tour of North America. Both the tour and the arena had Zentek's name on them, and that, combined with the events of the day, made Bricker feel that it was vital he be seen in public, that he attend to show his face and thus show his faith in Zentek's future. The fact that he loathed Candee's synth-pop music only slightly less than he loathed the young star herself didn't enter into it.

In point of fact, he felt he was doing penance. He had spared Zentek from Beck-Yama for a day, perhaps two at the most, but the cost, he felt, had been too high. Sixty-eight thousand men and women out of work at his word; sixty-eight thousand men and women whose lives he had irrevocably altered, if not destroyed.

For Georg Bricker, sitting through two and half hours of

Candee's glass-shattering whining, whinging, and preening about on stage was a small price to pay.

On the ground in Seattle, Bricker was met by a null-g limousine sent by the local Zentek office and, with his security escort, was whisked quickly into the heart of the city. On approach to the venue, Bricker could see the floodlights illuminating the dataDyne Spire, where the Space Needle had once stood. DataDyne had purchased the structure in 2010, shortly after Zentek had offered sponsorship of the arena, and in characteristic fashion had then torn the Space Needle down, only to rebuild it as a much taller and more commercially successful venture.

The limousine pulled to a stop at the main entrance to the arena, and Bricker emerged, surrounded by a phalanx of Zentek security that escorted him onto the red carpet. Candee Canes—predominantly young women who strove to emulate Candee in all things, right down to her Zentek wardrobe—greeted him with shrieks of delight without having the slightest idea who he was. Their noise and their energy momentarily distracted Bricker, and for that reason, he did not note the media presence until the reporters and their cameras were upon him. He made the walk into the arena with their questions shouted at his back, flashbulbs and null-g cameras assaulting his vision from every angle.

He spent most of the first set in a private box suite with Candee's managers, agents, attorneys, and hangers-on. The view, as befitted such exclusive seating, was excellent. On the stage, Candee thrilled the crowd with precision choreography and holographic dance displays, her costume changing from moment to moment, Zentek living fabric sliding over her body to reveal calculated expanses of bare skin and perfectly toned and tanned muscle. More than once, Bricker found himself wondering how it was he had ever been convinced to sponsor such a display of near-pornography.

For the most part, however, he ignored the show in favor of the requisite glad-handing. He smiled politely through insipid conversations, nodded earnestly, and feigned interest. Twice during the first set, he ordered his suit to medicate him, each time with a buffered analgesic.

All the same, when the message from Cassandra DeVries came, it was a mercy in more ways than one.

Candee was just coming off the stage, and the crowd in the private box beginning to move en masse to join her backstage, when Bricker's Z-sleeve began vibrating. Bricker held back to examine the message now scrolling across the screen, vaguely puzzled. An unidentified caller, no ID signature, and that was unheard of; direct access to the Zentek CEO's Z-sleeve was theoretically impossible, as all calls had to be routed through Zentek Security back in Berlin. No one contacted the CEO without identifying themselves first.

When Cassandra DeVries appeared on the screen, however, any suspicions were immediately forgotten. She was an exquisitely attractive woman, even on the small screen, a porcelain blond with pale blue eyes and aristocratic features, made all the more so by her look of near reproach. Bricker's surprise immediately turned to concern at the sight of her expression, certain that she was calling to admonish him for repeatedly bothering her, certain that she was about to kill the merger altogether. He hastily pulled the earpiece for the Z-sleeve free from his collar, fitting it into his ear.

"Herr Bricker?" DeVries was saying. She spoke in German, but with an English accent.

"Yes," Bricker said. "Miss DeVries, thank you for calling."

On Georg Bricker's sleeve, the CEO of dataDyne smiled.

"I must apologize for the delay in responding," DeVries said. "I'm still getting settled into my new position, I'm sure you understand. Do you mind if we speak in English? My German's positively dreadful."

"Of course, yes—"

DeVries continued, as if not hearing him, switching to her native tongue. "And you've had quite the day yourself, haven't you? Beck-Yama can be very insistent indeed. I won't waste your time, Georg—may I call you Georg?"

"Certainly, yes, you—"

"And you must call me Cassandra. I think, given the circumstance of the day, that a discussion about the merger sooner rather than later might be a good idea, don't you? You're in Seattle? Yes?"

"At the moment, but I can—"

"No, no don't bother. The concert, yes. Listen, Georg, I'm sending my assistant to pick you up, she'll meet you just inside the lobby of the arena. Her name is Joanna, she's a lovely young lady, you won't be able to miss her, hair like copper at sunset, that one. I was in Redmond most of today on business, but I'm at my retreat near Olympia now. Jo will bring you to me, all right? We can have a late dinner—well, I'm still on Paris time, so I suppose it'll be, what, a lunch? Breakfast? We can discuss. All right?"

"Miss DeVries, *ja*, yes, absolutely. I cannot thank you—"

"Cassandra, Georg," she said, smiling brightly. "See you in about twenty minutes, then."

The screen of the Z-sleeve went dark, then reset itself to standby mode. Bricker removed the earpiece, letting it retract into the collar of his shirt. The box had emptied, Candee's entourage already making their way backstage. He shook his head, trying to clear it. The whole conversation had taken place so quickly, so abruptly, Bricker wondered for an instant if it had occurred at all.

But it had, of course it had, and here was his chance to save Zentek, and he wasn't about to keep Cassandra DeVries waiting.

▌▐║▌▐║▌▐║▌▌

The woman who met him in the lobby was as described, but even younger than Bricker had expected, not more than twenty or twenty-one at the oldest. She wore black leather—pants, boots, jacket, even, apparently, her shirt—and the shock of pale blond—almost white—at her forelock seemed all the more stark for it, even against the red hair that, Bricker had to agree, seemed to burn like copper. Her hands were empty, and she showed him her palms even as she spoke.

"Herr Bricker? CEO DeVries has sent me to bring you to her."

Bricker nodded, saying, "You are Joanna?"

"Joanna Dark, yes," the young woman said, her accent strangely exotic, as if unable to decide if it was English, South African, American, or from half a dozen other spots around the globe. "If you'll follow me, please, I have a vehicle."

The woman, Joanna Dark, turned and led the way through the doors, stopping long enough for Bricker to reach her side. She rested a hand gently on his elbow, guiding him past the still-screaming throng of Candee Canes and the waiting assault of reporters without stopping. The vehicle was the latest luxury sports model from Royce-Chamberlain/Bowman Motors, a dataDyne subsidiary, sleek and black, and exactly what Bricker expected. Joanna Dark opened the door for him, hovering protectively.

As he took his seat, Bricker glanced up, taking in the data-Dyne Spire once more. There were lights splashing along the top of the structure, more than there had been before, and Bricker could make out lances of lightning in the sky beyond, a storm moving in. Lit by one of the flashes, for an instant, Bricker could see what looked like multiple dropships, hovering in a stand-off position.

"Is that our escort?" he asked Joanna.

The redhead glanced toward the Spire, then shook her head, grinning at him.

"That's something else entirely, sir," she told him.

They flew for all of fourteen minutes, Bricker in the passenger seat, Joanna Dark at the controls. She flew them quickly, following the proscribed route along what had once been the Interstate south, before banking off and dropping to near-treetop level. The light dome in the sky around them began to fade, then disappeared altogether, and in the illumination from the null-g vehicle's running lights, Bricker could see an expanse of forest spreading out beneath them into darkness.

He glanced over to his driver and realized that the young woman hadn't looked his way once during the trip, focused entirely on her flying.

For the first time, Bricker felt a swell of nervousness.

"Where are we going, please?" he asked.

"It's a secure location, sir," Joanna Dark answered. "I'm sure you understand why I can't divulge that. We're almost there."

"CEO DeVries makes her home in Paris, does she not?"

"That's correct, sir. But dataDyne has private retreats all around the world, as I'm sure you know."

Bricker nodded, looking out his windows again. The hum of the null-g engine shifted pitch, dropping, and he realized they were coming in to land. He adjusted his position in his seat, trying to get a better look around, and still, there was only darkness, the forest at night.

Then the vehicle came to rest, and Joanna Dark disengaged

the power, shutting down the car. She was out of the vehicle before Bricker could ask any further questions, and opening his door before he realized that he was becoming very afraid, indeed.

"This way, Herr Bricker," Joanna Dark said, offering him her left hand.

Bricker hesitated.

"If you'll get out of the vehicle, please."

Bricker nodded, extended his right hand to take the young woman's left. As he got to his feet, he saw her other hand, saw the gun in it, the metal barely shining in the darkness.

DataDyne is going to kill me, Georg Bricker thought.

And that was when his clothes tried to save his life.

![barcode]

She shot him four times, square in the chest, and the vest held, but Georg Bricker found he couldn't breathe. The noise from his Z-sleeve was tremendous, and he realized, in the way that people do when they have more adrenaline than sense running through them, that anything the device might be recording certainly would be inaudible next to the incredible sound of the alarm.

He fell to his knees, and Joanna Dark lunged forward, seeking to take hold of him, and just as quickly she yanked her hand back, swearing in Mandarin. Bricker thought that odd, but as he struggled to his feet to run for his life, he thought that Joanna Dark was even odder.

For a moment, the woman had stopped trying to attack him, wobbling almost unsteadily on her feet, the tetrodotoxin assaulting her central nervous system. As she struggled to stay upright, her form seemed to shimmer, the black leather losing its shine, her features blurring. The red hair turned suddenly to black, the tiny star-shaped tattoo on the side of the woman's neck vanishing. Her shoulders grew out, broadening slightly, and at the same time, she seemed to lose height by as much as an inch, maybe two.

For a moment, just for a moment, the pretty young Caucasian woman who had just shot Georg Bricker seemed to turn into a pretty young Chinese woman.

Then Georg Bricker turned and ran for his life, crashing into woods, feeling the branches scratching at his exposed skin, snagging on his clothes. He slapped at the Z-sleeve on his forearm, trying to silent the awful screeching, and somehow managed to disable the audible alarm without poisoning himself in the process. Or maybe he had poisoned himself and his clothing had delivered the antitoxin already, along with the extra adrenaline that was making his heart pound in his ears, that was making the back of his throat taste like tin.

He ran, stumbling, and fell hard, tumbling amidst wet fir needles and broken branches. He lurched back to his feet, paused for an instant with his hands against a tree for support, straining to listen. The noise of movement through the forest came to him, quick and light, and he knew the changing woman was now making her pursuit, that she'd shaken off whatever effects the poison had caused.

Bricker resumed running, trying to think. He had no idea where he was, and while his Z-sleeve would have been more than happy to tell him the quickest route to the nearest road, he didn't dare take the time to ask it. And there was no light, there was nothing, now, as if the whole world was growing dimmer. His chest ached, burning with each breath, and he wondered how badly the shots had hurt him. Bulletproof the vest may have been, but the blunt trauma was still precisely that. The adrenaline in his veins dulled his pain reception, and he realized that he could well have been running with cracked ribs and not have realized it.

He fell again, this time harder than before, and when he

tried to get to his feet again, he discovered that his right foot wouldn't support him. When he went down the third time, the pain finally smashed through the epinephrine haze, and he screamed, his hands going reflexively to his foot. They came back slick with blood, and as he moved his eyes from his now gore-covered hands to look up, he saw the woman, a shadow in the darkness, unmoving, holding her gun pointed at his head.

"Who are you?" Bricker's voice was hoarse.

The woman moved forward, and again he saw her as she had first appeared. Even in the darkness, the tinge of red hair was visible.

"I told you," she said. "My name is Joanna Dark."

"You're not . . . you're not dataDyne. Beck-Yama? But I saw DeVries."

The woman seemed to think that was funny, and laughed at him.

"This is a hostile takeover," she told him, readjusting her aim.

Bricker swallowed, trying to find what was left of his courage, thinking that if he had a little more time, he and his suit could still escape.

"Don't I get any last words?" Georg Bricker asked.

"No," the woman who called herself Joanna Dark told him. "We've already taken care of that."

Then she fired once, into his head, and followed it with a second round, and Georg Bricker died before he had time to even consider what the young woman had said.

CONFIDENTIAL—DO NOT FORWARD

FROM: WAITS, LANDREW (VP PUBLIC RELATIONS MANAGEMENT
            TEAM) [LWAITS@ZEEMAIL.CORP.NET]

TO: ZENTEK FTE EMPLOYEES; INT SUBSIDIARIES; SENIOR MGMT TEAM

SUBJ: CEO Georg Bricker, Zentek, and our future

It is my sad duty to announce to all Zentek employees and subsidiaries that Georg Bricker, our Chief Executive Officer, died last night in the woods outside of Olympia, Washington (USA), the result of an apparent hiking accident.

Mr. Bricker was famously energetic, and his enthusiasm for outdoor activity is well known to those of us who worked closely with him, and I can emphatically state that his guiding hand on the tiller will be sorely missed.

I considered Georg more than just a colleague and mentor. He was my friend, and this news is a devastating blow to the Senior Management Team. His passion for excellence has been our guiding principle, and we are the poorer for his loss.

Mr. Bricker was born in Stuttgart, Germany in 1966, and he graduated summa cum laude from Universität Tübingen (the Eberhard Karls University of Tübingen), a student of this august institution's natural sciences program. This passion for science and nature led him to champion Zentek's efforts in the personal biowear projects (including the critically praised Z-sleeve, among countless others).

Mr. Bricker is survived by Greta Bricker, his wife of twenty-eight years, and two sons, Heinrich (22, an employee of Zentek's Fiscal Responsibility Group) and Karl (20, currently attending Freiburg University). Our deepest sympathies go out to them. The family has asked that, in lieu of flowers, donations be made to any of Mr. Bricker's favored charities (see int.node/projectshare/approved-charity-fundmatch-roster/Bricker), and naturally Zentek will, as always, match your donations.

Mr. Bricker was intently focused on the future, and that will understandably be a topic of discussion for all Zentek employees. Yesterday's widely reported flurry of stock transactions and the unavoidable cessation of production in some of our transient product divisions, coupled with the untimely passing of CEO Bricker, has created several understandable but erroneous assumptions in the unregulated media, and even here within our own offices.

To avoid unproductive rumors and speculation, it is the intention of the Senior Management Team to continue Mr. Bricker's work and ensure that his commitment not just to our products but to our loyal customers and valued employees is undiminished. It is precisely this commitment that will lead Zentek into a bold new era, one which honors its architects and betters all our lives.

For approved media statements, all employees are required to log in to the Senior Management Transition FAQ internal site (int.node/SMT_FAQ_ v2021). (As always, failure to adhere to messaging guidelines therein is grounds for reprimand, reduction in job level, or termination.)

Thank you for your cooperation,

Landrew Waits

Vice President / Zentek Public Relations, Perception Branding Team

CorruptionNet—Ratting out the Corporate Finks™ since 2010.

[FLASH!] ZENTEK CEO DEAD!

//Submitter: EyEsPy102 (node: 132.191_1_....)

Zentek CEO Bricker turned up *****dead***** yesterday. Official sources call it a "hiking accident," but then, "official sources" always say stuff like that, don't they?

The timing of Bricker's passing is certainly suspect. The Beck-Yama sharks have been circling Zentek for weeks and, thanks to hostile takeover rumors, Zentek's stock skyrocketed. But something's definitely up, since—despite stock values in the stratosphere—Bricker just downsized nearly 70,000(!) people.

Bricker's had a rep for being a generally decent guy (for a Corporate Fink™), but his death, hot on the heels of the stock shenanigans and the downsizing, has *got* to raise some eyebrows. There's something rotten in Denmark.

Everyone knows that the Z-boys have been desperate for a success, and that their necks were on the block. Bricker's always been a solid leader, but next to someone like dataDyne's new top boss, he's practically moving in reverse. So Zentek's been rocked on its heels for sure, and the biz analysts are all saying the same thing: Beck-Yama is a shoe-in to snap up what's left of Zentek.

Here's the weird part, though: The big B-Y missed out. A little bird inside the Core-Mantis OmniGlobal Mergers & Acquisitions team just leaked to *World Finance Daily* that ****they**** just gobbled up the controlling interest in Zentek. (Don't ask where I got the news; if I tell you, I have to kill you.)

Not sure what that means—or why Bricker was taken out. Was it CMO trying to snake Zentek out from under Beck-Yama, or did Beck-Yama hit Bricker, and just give CMO an opening?

Anyone with more info should post it to the FLASHNEWS forum (node 111.297.3982, subdirectory BRICKER_HIT).

\\EyEsPy102 out.

Residence of dataDyne CEO
Mlle. Cassandra DeVries
1 Rue Marinoni Paris, France
January 18th, 2021

It had been almost two months since Cassandra DeVries had gotten a good night's sleep. Almost two months of near-sleepless nights since she'd been named dataDyne's new CEO, since she had been named Zhang Li's successor. Almost two months since she had become the leader of the world's largest hypercorp, since she had found herself one of the most powerful people in the world.

If not *the* most powerful person in the world.

Almost two months since she'd murdered the CEO of pharmaDyne, Dr. Friedrich Murray.

There were good reasons for her insomnia, despite the fact that Cassandra DeVries knew that she was more exhausted—physically, emotionally, and mentally—than she ever had been before. At best, she was managing two, perhaps three hours of sleep a night; at the worst, she was managing none at all.

On those nights, after tossing and turning in futility for

an hour or more, she would give up altogether, deciding there were better uses of her time. Throwing back the hand-made silk sheets of her new antique four-poster bed, she would rise and pull on a silk robe she had no memory of buying. She would cross the expanse of her bedroom to the door and step out, and the two dataDyne Shock Troopers standing post there would each snap to attention as if expecting a surprise inspection.

Then one of the guards would ask, his voice positively deferential even behind the odd amplification of his full-face helmet, if there was anything dataDyne's new CEO required.

"Sleep," DeVries would say.

She would then begin walking the cold and nearly silent hallways of her very old new home, followed only by the whisper of transmissions passed from one guard post to the next as each accounted for her movements. Most of the time, she couldn't even hear what was being said, but on occasion she would catch a word or two, and this was how she learned of the code name she had been given.

They called her "Future."

"All posts, Future on walkabout."

"Future, second floor, south two."

"Future, third floor, north three."

"Future, third floor, west one."

Finally, DeVries would reach the very old study of her very old new house, and two new Shock Troopers—or perhaps the same two, she honestly couldn't tell—would already be in position there. One would open the door for her solicitously, closing it softly behind her as she passed within, but not before she heard the final transmission.

"Future, third floor, west two, study. In for the night."

They were her ghosts, dedicated to her safety and survival, each of them handpicked to work her private home security detail by Anita Velez, the director of corporate security. Selected by Anita Velez, kingmaker, who had stood beside Cassandra DeVries and nodded the barest approval when Cassandra had shot Friedrich Murray. Anita Velez, who had believed that Cassandra DeVries was the only possible future dataDyne could have. Anita Velez, who had, strangely enough, become the new CEO of dataDyne's only friend.

Once in the study, Cassandra would open her laptop, typing in her password, offering it her left eye for retina confirmation, making certain the friend-or-foe chip she had implanted in herself at her wrist was read properly. She would log into her office, and begin working, or, more correctly, she would resume working, because she had discovered that she was never, ever, going to be finished.

In this, perhaps, the insomnia was a blessing in disguise, because it gave Cassandra hours back in her day. Hours when she didn't need to be in the office, surrounded by her half-dozen personal assistants and secretaries and handlers; hours when she didn't need to be constantly jumping from one video conference to another, from one meeting to another, from one event to another.

Even before she'd joined dataDyne as a junior programmer in its subsidiary, DataFlow, Cassandra had known the corporation was enormous. She had known it the same way she had known that the Atlantic was enormous. She had known it as an intellectual truth, but without the emotional understanding that comes when you're floating alone in the middle of it.

DataDyne was her Atlantic Ocean, and it was Cassandra DeVries's job not only to know its depths and currents, but also the doings of all the fish in this particular sea. Upon her appointment as CEO, DeVries had spent six days in what she herself referred to as "boot camp," but which Anita Velez had called "holding court." The directors of all of dataDyne's subsidiaries had made the pilgrimage to Paris to meet with her, each of them in turn offering their congratulations, their loyalty, their gifts, and then the latest in spreadsheets, prospectuses, prototypes, and multimedia presentations. R-C/Bowman and Runyon-Adams and Patmos Casualty and Freis Construction and Dun-Chow Manufacturing and ServAuto Robotics and Ellison Electronic Security and at least twenty-seven more divisions that, until she found herself face-to-face with their respective directors, Cassandra DeVries had thought owned by other hypercorps, by CMO or Beck-Yama or Zentek.

Cassandra DeVries knew she was a very smart woman. She knew there were some people who believed she was a genius, but she had met genius, and she knew the difference. Genius was named Daniel Carrington, and she had been his lover for a time. But that had ended, because Daniel Carrington was also a zealot, and where Cassandra DeVries believed in the good dataDyne could do, he believed only that dataDyne must be destroyed. She wasn't a genius, and having seen the lengths Daniel Carrington would go to achieve his aims, she wasn't sure she wanted to be.

But she was smart, and even so, she was still being bombarded with more information than she could possibly begin to digest. As the CEO of DataFlow, her particular fiefdom of the dataDyne empire, she had been able to track all of its activities, its projects, even the majority of its personnel. She had prided herself on this ability, in fact.

DataDyne was DataFlow to the nth degree. She couldn't keep up. How Master Zhang Li had managed the corporation, let alone controlled it, she honestly had no idea. She was beginning to suspect that he never truly had.

Learning to tame dataDyne was a struggle, but it was her intention to prevail. She had killed Friedrich Murray to protect the corporation, to keep Murray's own division of pharmaDyne from bringing down all of the others with it; the fact that, in so doing, she had guaranteed her appointment as the next CEO had been incidental, at least at the moment of action.

While what she had done remained defensible to herself, and certainly to Anita Velez, it didn't change the reality that she had killed a man. The stain of it weighed heavily on her still; she wanted—needed—to make it right.

The way to do that, Cassandra DeVries had resolved, was to become the best CEO dataDyne had ever seen. The fact that only Zhang Li had come before, that she was measuring herself against dataDyne's founder and creator, did not deter her.

While Cassandra DeVries had tried to settle into her new job at the office, other people were making further alterations to her life. When Velez, who acted as her personal bodyguard during the day, escorted her from the office after the end of that first week as CEO, it wasn't until they were crossing the Seine that Cassandra realized they were heading the wrong way.

"Where are we going?" she asked Velez, glancing with some concern at the driver in the front seat, separated from them by a privacy screen of carefully crafted ballistic glass, as clear as crystal. "We're going the wrong way."

"You're going home, Madame Director," Velez said, the mirth in her voice almost hidden behind her peculiar accent, part American English, part German.

"My home's the other direction, Anita. I don't have time for this, I have a lot to do."

"Your new home, Madame Director," Velez said, and then she had smiled, something so uncharacteristic that Cassandra could only stare. "You are the CEO of dataDyne. A town house in Le Marais, lovely though it was, is hardly befitting a woman of your stature and power."

DeVries had begun to respond, then had fallen silent, because that was when the null-g limousine and the motorcade of outriding protection vehicles turned off the Avenue Anatole France and began slowing. Looking from her window, Cassandra DeVries had been forced to make a determined effort to keep her jaw from dropping into her lap.

The house—*her* house—wasn't a house at all. From the looks of it, it was a bloody palace.

Velez laughed with positive delight at the expression on Cassandra's face.

"Oh, no," DeVries said. "Oh, no, Anita, no. It's too much, it's . . . it's far too much."

The motorcade had come to a halt, and Velez exited the vehicle first, coming around to meet Cassandra as the driver opened her door. Once out of the vehicle, the circle of protection collapsing tighter around Cassandra for the twenty-meter walk from driveway to front door, Velez went silent. The protection, along with everything else, was something Cassandra was growing more and more accustomed to, and she now knew that Velez's abrupt silences at moments like these weren't due to inattention but rather the exact opposite.

They entered the house through an enormous foyer with a roof reaching almost ten meters above them. A grand staircase dominated the center of the room, then split itself and reversed for passage to the second floor. Tapestries and statues and at least five pieces of art that Cassandra was certain she had seen hanging in the Louvre made up the décor. At the foot of the stairs, standing in a perfect line, the household staff waited for introductions.

"Built in 1679," Velez told her. "Obviously, there's been some refurbishment since then. We've had teams working around the clock since your appointment to ready the location, since you have made it abundantly clear that you will not be relocating yourself to Master Li's residence in China."

"I told you," Cassandra said, her eyes still wide as she

took in the foyer, her voice low. "DataFlow is here. This is my home."

"Your home is the world, Madame Director, because that is dataDyne's home. But if you insist on sleeping in Paris more often than sleeping elsewhere, you deserve a home worthy of your position. Would you like me to show you around?"

And despite herself, and feeling very much like a princess in a fairy tale, Cassandra DeVries said, "Yes, please. Very much."

They had, quite literally, taken care of everything, right down to filling her new closets with a new wardrobe, everything hand-tailored and perfectly fitted. Her personal belongings had been packed with care, moved from across town, and unpacked with the same attention to detail. There were household attendants available for her every need, at every hour of the day. Two chefs, three maids, one butler, two under-butlers, a groundskeeper, and, of course, security. Lots and lots of security.

She was the CEO of dataDyne; anything she needed, all she had to do was ask.

But what she needed most was sleep, and the thing that no one understood, because Cassandra DeVries wasn't telling them, was that she was suffering her insomnia by choice.

When she slept, she dreamt.

And she didn't much care for the dreams she'd been having.

Velez, being Velez, knew something was wrong almost immediately.

"You look tired, Madame Director," she said to her one morning after escorting her into her office.

"I am tired," Cassandra admitted, already standing behind the desk she once had thought was far too big and that now seemed to be eternally covered in papers. As she spoke, her first assistant secretary stepped in and began projecting the daily schedule for her review from his d-PAL. The holograph shimmered and began scrolling, forming a makeshift divider between the two women as they spoke.

"New appointment for R-C/Bowman CEO at nine-fifteen," the secretary murmured.

"It's not good," Velez said. "You need your health. You cannot afford to become ill, certainly not so soon after being named CEO."

"Review candidate listing to replace Dr. Murray at pharmaDyne, nine-seventeen."

"We're closing it down," Cassandra told the secretary. "I thought I made that clear. I want pharmaDyne dismantled and folded into Patmos. R and D will reform under a new division."

"I'll schedule a call with Miss Waterberg for the same slot."

"Madame Director," Velez said.

Cassandra shook her head. "I'm sorry, Anita, I don't have time for this right now."

"Conference call with dataDyne Los Angeles in three minutes," the secretary murmured, as if to prove the point.

Velez hesitated, then nodded. "We will speak further about this when I take you home, then."

Cassandra nodded, barely hearing her, already sinking into the day's work.

"There are some sleeping aids, quite safe. I can have your physician in to see you this evening."

"It's all right."

"You said you are not sleeping, Madame Director. That cannot possibly be 'all right.' "

"I'm not going to take pills."

"There are other methods of delivery. A dermal patch, if you would—"

"No, Anita," Cassandra said, and she tried to say it gently, and with a smile. "I'm not going to take anything. I'm fine. Please, just let it alone."

Velez furrowed her brow, and it put her severe features into relief, had the effect of softening them in a way that De-Vries found unexpected. Velez was several years her senior, and Cassandra found the obvious concern in her expression surprisingly touching.

"Very well, Madame Director," Velez said. "If you need anything, you know where I am."

She wasn't sleeping, but there was only so much of that she could do without, and so, in the end, the bed won.

The bed always won.

Sun. Hot day. South of England, the drive from London to Bristol, the stop at Bath.

"To see the baths of Bath."

Eight years old. Backseat. Father driving. Mother beside him. Talking about the news of the world, football, what was on the telly last night.

Beside her, Arthur, he's six. He's her brother. Her baby brother.

Some siblings, they fight. They are close, but they do not know how to be close.

Not Cassandra and Arthur. The best of friends, those two. He's the quiet one, and she does the talking for them both, but they're always there for each other. Brother and sister, the best of friends.

Sitting in the backseat, twisting around in their seatbelts to face one another, laughing as they play snap.

"Snap!"

"Snap!"

"Snap!"

The world freezes, and Cassandra feels herself thrown back against her door, and there's something in the periphery, shiny metal and sunlight off glass and there's another car, a green car, the color of a meadow. She has no idea where it has come from. She has no idea where it is heading.

She hears her mother screaming just a fraction of a second before she hears the sound of metal ripping metal, of glass exploding from its frame. Playing cards spray in every direction. Then there's no noise at all, and she's looking at her brother, she doesn't blink, she doesn't look away, but suddenly Arthur is not there anymore.

At least, no Arthur that Cassandra DeVries, eight years old, can recognize as her best friend and her brother.

Time explodes back into motion, sound crashes back into perception, and she is upside down, right-side up, on her side, tumbling, no, she's not tumbling, the car is tumbling, the car is rolling and bouncing over and over again. More screams of metal and mothers, more cries of terror and fear, and some of them are now Cassandra's. Glass that has survived this long finally fails, and then, once again, silence.

She's on her side, still held by her seatbelt, the car finally at rest. Lying more on the rear door than in her seat. Playing cards have covered her like leaves from an autumn tree, and when she looks up, she can see the trees they could have come from, white clouds and blue sky beyond.

When she looks to her right, she can see her brother, what remains of him. He doesn't know he's dead, yet.

But she knows.

His eyes are still open, and he blinks at her, and he tries to speak.

The blood that fountains from his mouth makes Cassandra scream again.

It's the scream that wakes her up.

It was an old dream, an old nightmare, and Cassandra DeVries had thought she laid it to rest long ago. She thought she had nailed its coffin shut with the creation of AirFlow.Net, the near-bulletproof software control system she invented to guarantee the safe coordination of all null-g transport, anywhere in the world, at any given time. AirFlow.Net had brought her to the attention of Zhang Li, and that in turn made her the head of DataFlow.

That was the old dream.

Now there's a new one. It's exactly the same as the old one, but with one crucial difference. In the new dream, lying beside her isn't Arthur.

Lying beside her is Dr. Friedrich Murray, with three holes in his chest that Cassandra DeVries put there.

He meets her eight-year-old eyes, calls her a bitch, and damns her to hell.

"Wake up! Please, Madame Director!"

Friedrich Murray vanished, replaced by Anita Velez, and Cassandra realized that she was awake, that the older woman was standing beside her bed.

"Up!" Velez grabbed her by the upper arm, pulling Cassandra free from the bed and to her feet. "Hands up, hold your hands up, over your head."

The lights snapped on in the bedroom, and Cassandra

winced at their sudden ferocity, still groggy. There were Shock Troopers everywhere, standing at the door, coming toward her, one of them with a bundle in his hands.

"Can you stand?" Velez demanded. "Are you awake?"

"Anita—"

"Get your arms up, over your head. Please, Madame Director! There isn't time to waste!"

I'm still bloody dreaming, Cassandra thought, and blearily brought her arms up. The Shock Trooper lifted the bundle over her head, pulled it down, and suddenly two more Troopers were at her sides, tightening straps and pulling them so hard it crushed the breath from her chest. Cassandra was dimly aware that she was being encased in some manner of heavy body armor not unlike the suits the Shock Troopers wore.

"What do you need?" Velez was asking her insistently. "Is there anything here you need?"

Shaken, confused, Cassandra tried to speak and found she had no air for the task. She gestured with her right hand, waving toward the briefcase resting unopened on the chair in front of her dressing table. In the case was her customized laptop and the latest progress reports on AirFlow.Net 2.0 that Dr. Ventura had delivered to her office at her request. Velez turned, marking the direction, then barked an order to the first Shock Trooper.

"The briefcase," she snapped, then released her hold on Cassandra just long enough to touch the skin behind her left ear, activating her subcutaneous radio. "We have Future. Thirty seconds."

"Anita, what's going—"

Velez moved her hand from her radio to the small of Cassandra's back, and Cassandra felt the pressure rather than the warmth of the touch. She was pushed forward, not quite gently, and Velez moved with her, staying close to her right side, her customized MagSec still held in her right hand.

"Quickly. Do not stop until you're in the limo."

"My bag—"

"Will be brought, let's go."

Shock Troopers closed around them as soon as they passed the door, all of them with their weapons in hand, and then Cassandra was being hustled down the stairs, through the great hall and foyer. Velez stayed in position at her side, her hand still on Cassandra's back, guiding her, and they went through the front door and into the Parisian predawn without breaking stride. The cold hit Cassandra like a club, the winter wind slicing through the her pajamas effortlessly, the pavement stones turning her bare feet almost immediately numb.

But before she could even truly register all that, she was all but shoved into the back of her limousine, and Velez hadn't even closed the door after them before they were in motion. DataDyne support vehicles, Shock Troopers visible manning the mounted weapons, flanked them on all sides. As one, the motorcade boosted into the air, banked, and began racing over the city.

"Georg Bricker is dead," Velez said. "Murdered. There may be other attempts. We're moving you until we can be certain it's safe."

Cassandra stared, feeling vaguely ill. She had hoped to speak to Bricker in the afternoon, to finally present him with the merger agreement. She'd been hoping to do it much sooner, but there had been multiple delays in preparing the agreement, everything from files being misplaced to data being lost, a thousand small mistakes that had all been attributed to the confusion inherent in her ascension to CEO. It hadn't been until the previous morning, when she'd seen the news of Beck-Yama's stock buy, that she'd finally lost her temper and demanded that one of her assistants get the head of acquisitions and mergers on the line along with his upper echelon staff. Within two minutes, she'd had them assembled on holographic display, and without preamble had launched into her tirade, reading them the riot act. How was it possible, she had demanded, that Beck-Yama was about to walk off with the Zentek store when Bricker had offered them the same with hat in hand?

Oliver Merano, head of acquisitions and mergers and not at all pleased to be bawled out by the new CEO in front of his staff, swore on his mother's grave that everything would be ready and on the Madame Director's desk first thing in the morning. If he had to deliver it by hand, it would be ready first thing in the morning.

"It had bloody well better be," DeVries had snarled, and killed the call.

And it would have been, too, she had no doubt. The papers for the merger were most likely waiting in her office at that very moment.

Too little, too late.

"Beck-Yama?" Cassandra asked.

The flying motorcade tilted sharply, began diving back down to street level with such abrupt speed that Cassandra had to wonder if the transponder that tied every null-g vehicle to the AirFlow network hadn't been disabled. She rocked forward, then fell back against her seat as the limousine leveled off and the motion triggered sense memory, and for half an instant, she expected the vehicle to tumble, to hear the rending of steel and the shattering of glass. She made a noise despite herself, fear that died in her throat.

Velez reached out a hand, steadying her, reassuring. "Not Beck-Yama. Core-Mantis OmniGlobal has already moved to acquire Zentek, there's nothing we can do to stop them."

"Core-Mantis has never expressed interest—"

"Core-Mantis didn't kill Georg Bricker, Madame Director." Velez met her eyes, and Cassandra thought that, for the first time since she'd met her, the older woman looked honestly worried.

"Anita, what aren't you telling me?"

"There may be other assassination attempts coming. We're moving you someplace safer. We can discuss the specifics when we have you secured."

The vague sense of queasiness that had settled in Cassandra's stomach rolled, expanded, the last vestiges of her dream giving way to a suspicion that made her shiver. The world had turned, she realized, all on the hinge of one act, all upon the murder of Georg Bricker. She had gone to sleep with the hypercorporations playing their games as they always had.

Anita Velez had pulled her from her bed and into a world where everything was now in chaos. CMO would take Zentek, that was already clear. Beck-Yama, extended in their attempt to take Zentek themselves, would now have to scramble to regain their balance. The CEO of dataDyne was being rushed from her home in the small hours of dawn because there was a fear she would soon follow Georg Bricker. Those were just the changes Cassandra could see. Certainly, there were others still hidden from her, and it struck her that their effects would certainly be as dramatic as those she had already perceived. If global commerce could be equated to a game, that game was chess, albeit with sharper teeth. Like chess, success in it depended on reading the board. Not only as it stood, but as it would stand five, ten, even twenty moves along.

One move, and so many results, Cassandra DeVries thought. *And anticipating them all, that takes genius.*

"Oh my God," Cassandra said softly. "He didn't."

Velez raised an eyebrow slightly, as if surprised that her employer had done the math so quickly.

"It was Daniel, wasn't it?" Cassandra asked. "It was Carrington."

"Yes, Madame Director."

"This threat against me . . . it's credible, is it?"

"I would not be moving you if it was not."

Cassandra nodded slightly, then closed her eyes and leaned back once again. She could feel the gentle rock of the limousine, the shift as it banked once more, began decelerating. The queasiness had gone, replaced by nothing, only a numbness.

"I was in love with him," she said softly.

"I know," Velez said. "But now he is trying to kill you."

CHAPTER

2

Carrington Institute
London, England
January 18th, 2021

Joanna Dark had come to the conclusion that she was a failure.

It was something she had suspected for a while now, even before Daniel Carrington had dispatched her on her latest mission for the Carrington Institute, that of ferreting out a mole in the CI–Los Angeles office, two days prior. She'd suspected it before she'd ever met Carrington, in fact, even before her father had been murdered, but back then it had been nothing more than the ill-framed insecurities of an adolescent, of a girl growing into a young woman who was unsure of herself, her skills and abilities, and, most of all, her place in the world. The fears of a girl who had, at that time, only her father and her desperate attempts to please him. The desire to learn everything he could teach her and so become the woman he wanted her to be.

That's what it always comes back to, doesn't it? Joanna thought sluggishly. *Da, my dear old Da, ex-Marine, ex-cop, bounty hunter beyond compare, Jack Dark.*

He had tried, she knew. As much as she had, so had he. At

moments such as this, she could even admit that he had been far more a teacher than a father, far more a drill sergeant than a friend.

But he *had* taught her well, present circumstance notwithstanding. Hadn't he? Jack Dark had taught his daughter how to hunt that most dangerous prey, her fellow man. How to fight to win. How to kill if she had to. There wasn't a small arm in the world that Joanna Dark didn't know how to use. There wasn't a knife that had been made that she didn't know how to fight with. There wasn't a secret in the world that, given time and enough bashing of heads, she couldn't discover.

That was all due to her father, and if she was a failure, wasn't that her fault and not his?

"Lift on three," Jonathan Steinberg was saying. "Carefully. One . . . two . . . three. . . ."

Joanna felt herself rising, or more precisely, the stretcher she was lying on rising. Just edging into her line of vision, Jonathan Steinberg came into view, upside down, casting a brief but clearly concerned glance down at her before hefting his end of the stretcher. She felt someone likewise lifting the other end—Calvin Rogers, probably, the Institute's motor pool supervisor and pilot extraordinaire—and Joanna's view of the roof of the dropship troop compartment changed to a view of the vehicle bay of the Institute's London headquarters.

"Where's Cordell?" Steinberg was shouting. "Where the hell's Cordell, dammit?"

Joanna blinked sleepily, wanted to tell Steinberg not to worry, not to shout. It wasn't that he was being particularly loud; in fact, his voice was reaching her ears as if coming through layers of syrup. But she knew he was shouting, because Jonathan always shouted when he was upset, when he was worried, and she knew he was scared for her, and she didn't want him to be. She wanted to tell him that she was all right, that it would be all right.

But every time she tried to move her mouth to speak, she tasted her own blood, the ragged flesh of her torn lips. Just getting the air to push out the words hurt, it was hurting to breathe, and it all just seemed to be so much bother. Easier to stay quiet and to rest and to let her mind wander, meandering its way through paths of memory, recent and not.

Until her thoughts, once again, came to rest upon the knowledge of her failings and her father.

That was the heart of it, that was the proof, really. Los Angeles and Seattle, that was merely another layer. Sent on a mole hunt, sent to find and "neutralize" whoever it was who had infiltrated Carrington's operation, and Jo had known what that meant during the briefing, they all had. For "neutralize," read "kill." Find and kill the mole. And she hadn't done that, had she? That was a failure, wasn't it?

And never mind what had happened in Seattle. Never mind the fact that she'd been played like a puppet and used like a punching bag by some mercenary, by one of Leland Shaw's legendary Hawks. Roarke, something or other Roarke, and he'd worked her over but good. She had the broken ribs and the shattered knuckles and the half-dozen lacerations on her face, arms, and hands, to prove it.

He was probably the son of a bitch who had shot her, too.

"Jo? Joanna Dark, can you hear me?"

Joanna blinked once again, felt her eyes dry against the inside of her lids, knew she'd been staring at nothing. She refocused her eyes, saw Jonathan's expression of concern eclipsed as another man leaned into her field of view, frowning. She didn't recognize him at first, the brown eyes and the brown face, and she wondered if she was going to have to fight again, and she hoped like hell not. She didn't think she could anymore. Then the recognition trickled in even as the man's sure hands ran along her side, pulling back her jacket and then tearing open her shirt. She gasped despite herself when his gloved finger pressed against the edges of her bullet wound, knowing that the palpation had been gentle, and still it was enough to make her want to howl.

"She's torn it right open," the man said softly, and it was his voice that connected him to a name. Cordell, Dr. Montgomery Cordell, the Institute's physician. ER doctor and super-surgeon all in one, the way Carrington only ever hired the best of the best.

What would the Old Man do when he realized just how much of a failure she was? Joanna wondered.

Steinberg was saying something, Cordell working on her. She was vaguely aware that the stretcher had been laid on the floor of the vehicle bay, that they'd stopped moving her long enough to apply some much needed triage. A snake bit into her left arm, and she watched Cordell hand an IV bag to Steinberg, saw Steinberg's expression looking all the more concerned.

He was saying something to her. Something about . . . pies? Something about pies?

Why the hell was he talking to her about pies?

She tried again to get the air to speak, was about to force it out despite the pain, when Cordell put an O_2 mask over her face. She gave up again. She'd figure it out later. Steinberg was all-American, sandy blond hair and blue eyes, a former US Army Ranger that Carrington had recruited to both build and train his covert action team. Times like this, when she knew she wouldn't have to own it later, Joanna could even admit to herself that she thought he was handsome in a dashing, bring-it-on kind of way. Her father would have liked him. Jack Dark would have called him "all right" and said it was a pity Steinberg had been a drag-ass Army grunt rather than a real-deal Marine.

There it was again: Jack Dark. Dead but not, because there wasn't a day that didn't seem to go by without Joanna thinking about him. It wasn't grief any longer—at least, not purely the grief. She'd worked past that. She missed him, she always would, but now, when she thought about her father, the thoughts weren't always ones of sadness, but rather of guilt.

She had, after all, gotten her father killed, had abandoned him to that bitch daughter of Zhang Li's, Mai Hem. Everything Joanna had gone through to save him, and in the end Jack Dark had died anyway.

They were moving her again. Joanna realized they'd shifted her off the stretcher, onto a null-g gurney, that she was being floated out of the vehicle bay. Probably taking her to medical. Or maybe taking her to the Old Man, so he could fire her and call her worthless and tell her that she didn't belong here. She hoped not. She didn't know where else she would go.

Steinberg touched the back of her hand, repeated whatever he was trying to tell her about pies. Or maybe lies. That would make more sense, Joanna thought. There had been a lot of people lying to her lately. *Everyone* in Los Angeles had lied to her, and a lot of those people had then tried to kill her. Maybe he was trying to tell her something like that. Or maybe he knew what she was thinking, and he was telling her that she was lying to herself. She hadn't killed her father, after all—Mai Hem had.

Technically, Joanna couldn't argue the point. As an issue of factual record, certainly, Steinberg was right. Joanna had gone to China, had managed the unheard-of act of infiltrating Zhang Li's private fortress-slash-mansion. She had alternately snuck and killed her way past layer upon layer of security until, ultimately, she'd found herself within the mansion and in the presence of the CEO of dataDyne himself.

Zhang Li had been, in almost all ways, horrific, an old and withered man with more stims and biomaintenance devices grafted to his body than Joanna had imagined possible. That he could move around on his own power seemed miraculous to her, and that he did so without obvious agony was unbelievable

Somehow, Joanna had found herself coerced into a virtual battle with Zhang Mai, Zhang Li's daughter. But Zhang Mai was better known to the world by her DeathMatch VR gamertag of Mai Hem, and that had been their field of battle. DeathMatch VR was dataDyne's premier virtual entertainment system, a game system that allowed players all around the world to link up and fight in infinitely customizable environments, with an infinite variety of weapons, all for the pleasure of some virtual bloodletting. That was how Joanna and Mai Hem had fought, as much for Zhang Li's pleasure as his daughter's, battling on a customized DeathMatch system.

Customized in that, while the bloodletting was virtual, its results were very real. When you died playing on Zhang Li's set, there was no reboot and try again.

Joanna had fought, and Joanna had won, but Zhang Li had saved his daughter at the last minute. When Joanna had finally found and then freed her father, when they were making their escape, that had come back to haunt them both. Pinned down by dataDyne guards, unable to reach the dropship with which father and daughter could make their escape, Jack Dark had made a run at Mai Hem, drawing fire. As Joanna had commandeered the dropship, Mai Hem had dropped Jack Dark.

So, yes, Jonathan was technically correct, if that was, in fact, what he was saying, if he was saying that Joanna was wrapped up in lies and not, for instance, a fan of pies, or the lord of the flies, or whatever the hell it was he kept trying to tell her. Yes, he was correct, Mai Hem had killed her father. And, eventually, Joanna had taken her revenge. She had killed Mai Hem, and then she had killed Zhang Li, and that really should have been the end of it.

But none of that changed the fact that Joanna Dark felt that it was her fault.

He was her Da, he was her life, and she had left him to die.

||||||||||||

They were in her rooms, now, Steinberg and Rogers carefully lifting her from the gurney and onto her bed, while Cordell supervised. She heard the doctor thanking them both, telling them to go, and Rogers left, but Steinberg didn't, and again Joanna wanted to tell him not to worry, that it would be all right. She could feel the tug on each of her legs as her boots were removed. When they rolled her to get her out of her jacket, she gasped again, the sound of it bouncing back with odd amplification from the O_2 mask over her face.

Cordell went to work on the bullet wound, cleaning it up, applying liquid skin and biostaples. He used clothing shears to cut her out of her shirt, and when he did it, Joanna saw Steinberg turn away, and she thought that was almost cute. Then Cordell wrapped her ribs and applied more liquid skin to her lacerations. He changed the bag on the IV, hanging it from a peg on the wall. He gave her an injection in the left shoulder, and it made her whole body feel suddenly, delightfully warm, and wonderfully heavy. He covered her with her blankets, then moved to speak to Steinberg, and whatever it was he had injected her with, she found it easier to hear their words, but no easier to add her own.

"I won't ask what she went through," Cordell said. "Most important thing now is for her to get some rest. Aside from the litany of injuries, she's clearly exhausted. When was the last time she slept?"

"Three days ago," Steinberg answered, keeping his voice soft. "Not counting brief bouts of unconsciousness."

"Which explains her concussion."

"What do I tell the Old Man?"

"You tell him that she's used up for the time being, Mr. Steinberg. Our fair Miss Dark is many things, but right now, the thing she is most is wounded. I'm concerned about the bullet wound. In and of itself, it wasn't too serious. Whoever worked on her initially did a good job of it."

"That would have been Dr. Hwang."

"He's CI–Los Angeles, isn't he? He did a fine job, but clearly she refused bed rest, because the fine job he did, she promptly undid. When she tore the stitches, she expanded the wound, and she may have opened herself to infection. So aside from the blood loss, the exhaustion, the broken rib, the multiple lacerations, the minor fractures—"

"There are other breaks?"

"It looks like she went fifteen rounds with a gorilla, Mr. Steinberg." Cordell's response was mild, almost admonishing. "Minor fractures in her right hand—she leads with her right, doesn't she?—as well as her left foot. I'm guessing she kicked something, or someone, possibly while barefoot. There are contusions, avulsions, she could audition as a practice patient for first responders in training, they'd love her."

"But she'll be all right?"

"As I said, yes, she will. If—and I really cannot stress this enough, Jonathan—if she gets the rest she needs. Frankly, I can't imagine her *wanting* to be up and about, the state she's in."

Joanna heard Steinberg laugh softly. "Doc, clearly you don't know her very well."

"No, I don't, but I know our lord and master, and I'm relying upon you to convey to Mr. Carrington that she is to be removed from any active duty for the near future."

"How long are we talking about?"

"If I had it my way? Six weeks. Knowing Carrington, I'll settle for four."

"I'll let him know."

"See that you do. I'll be back to check on her in the morning."

There was a rustle, the sound of the door sliding back, and Joanna knew Cordell had left, and she thought that perhaps Steinberg had, as well. Then the young man moved back into her field of vision, crouching down on his haunches beside the bed. With more difficulty than she thought it would require, Joanna rolled her head to the side to look at him. Steinberg brought his hand up, hesitated, then brushed the hair off her forehead. He frowned.

It's really going to be okay, Joanna thought. *I'm fine, really. Just a failure, that's all.*

But, again, the words were too much effort, so she just gave him a smile, the best one she could manage. Even hidden behind the oxygen mask, he seemed to see it, and it made him chuckle softly, made him shake his head with amused resignation.

"Can you hear me?" he asked her softly.

With effort, Joanna nodded.

"You can close your eyes now, Jo," Steinberg told her. "You're home. You're safe. You can close your eyes now."

Eyes, Joanna Dark thought, and if she hadn't been so exhausted, and so hurt, she would have laughed. *Not lies. Not flies. Not pies.*

Close your eyes.

She closed her eyes, and she slept.

Carrington Institute
Operations Center
London, England
January 18th, 2021

Even with the anger simmering in his chest, Jonathan Steinberg waited until he was certain—absolutely certain—that
Joanna Dark's eyes were truly closed, that she was finally allowing herself to lower her guard and to rest, before he moved
to leave her room. Once her features had relaxed, the gentle
rise and fall of her breathing assuring him that she was truly
asleep, he rose, fighting his urge to linger.

That she'd so tenaciously refused to succumb to unconsciousness hadn't surprised him, even if her unfocused and
unwavering stare at nothing during the flight back from London had left him more than a little unnerved. There wasn't
much about Joanna Dark that did surprise him at this point,
and it wasn't because he knew all her secrets or even knew
her that well at all, having made her acquaintance less than a
year earlier. It was simply the fact that Joanna Dark, in that
brief time, had surprised him so frequently and in so many

ways that his capacity for it had been exhausted. Perhaps if she suddenly sprung a second head and another three sets of arms, Steinberg could manage it.

But then again, perhaps not.

He was a soldier, and he was an experienced one. Before joining Carrington's crusade against the hypercorporations of the world, dataDyne in particular, Jonathan Steinberg had served the United States, had fought in conflicts in both Africa and Central Asia. He'd been an Army Ranger, had taken fire in Afghanistan, fought house-to-house in Kinshasa and Dar es Salaam. He'd battled with rifle, bayonet, and fist. He knew combat, and he knew killing, and he knew the men and women who did both. He'd seen the good ones and the bad ones, the lucky ones and the fools. He'd seen enough violence to know that the difference between those who were alive at the end and those who weren't came down, as often as not, to dumb luck as much as skill and experience.

Joanna Dark was, quite simply, the best killer he had ever seen.

That she was so good and not yet twenty-one wasn't something he much cared to think about. That Daniel Carrington was unrelentingly eager in his desire to use her abilities was something he enjoyed contemplating even less.

How she had become so, he didn't know. It couldn't have been easy, and it most certainly hadn't been pleasant. Carrington maintained that she was a natural, gifted in the art of combat in much the same way that Picasso had been gifted in the art of painting. Maybe he was right, but Steinberg—whose whole career had been shaped by outside training—found himself wondering more often than not how much of Joanna Dark had been nature and how much had been nurture.

Maybe she could do what she did so well because of her

nature. But he knew as a certainty that the only reason her eyes had never closed for more than a blink all the way back to London was nurture. That was training, that was conditioning.

That was the legacy of Jack Dark.

Jonathan Steinberg had never met Jack Dark. He never would meet Jack Dark. And as he left Jack Dark's daughter to finally sleep and rest and begin to recover, Jonathan Steinberg was glad he never would.

It would save him from having to punch the son of a bitch right in the face.

Steinberg left Joanna Dark's rooms in the residence building, turned left down the hall, ignored the elevator, and went straight for the stairs, descending them three at a time. He wasn't quite running, and he wasn't quite walking, and he knew he was sincerely and deeply pissed off, but he was having trouble determining exactly whom he was pissed off at. Not Joanna, certainly, and maybe even not Jack Dark—or at least, not more than he normally was. He wasn't even angry at Leland Shaw's Hawk, Roarke, who had done everything he could to put Jo down, to literally reduce her to nothing but a stain on the pavement.

Steinberg didn't think he'd ever seen a fight like the one between Joanna and Roarke, the two of them trading blows atop the dataDyne Spire in Seattle as lightning lit the sky above them, as citizens oblivious to the truth of their world queued up for a concert below. Joanna, already wounded and off her game, versus Roarke, stimmed to the gills with combat enhancers and leaking data from a neural dump. Roarke fighting to escape and Joanna fighting for time, and it was as brutal a thing as he'd ever witnessed, and it had killed him that witnessing it was all he could do.

But Joanna had triumphed, the way she seemed to triumph: she had survived, and more, she had won.

As Steinberg walked out of the building and onto the Institute's grounds, he allowed himself to admit that he was angry at the Old Man. It wasn't the assignment, although, once again, Carrington had handed Joanna a job knowing full well that once she took it, she'd see it through to the end, no matter what the cost to herself, and of course Carrington had done so because he had suspected—if not, in some way, already known—that the cost to the agent involved would be damn high.

No, the thing that was burning Steinberg, that was eating his liver and making him mutter obscenities he'd picked up back during his Army days, was that Carrington had done it and then hadn't bothered to welcome the girl home. Wounded as she was, beaten as she was, and the Old Man couldn't be bothered to heft his bulk the two hundred meters or so from his personal quarters to the residence or—God forbid—the vehicle bay, to check on his new favorite agent's status, to tell her, "Job well done."

Steinberg was so consumed with these thoughts that he was halfway toward Carrington's office before he realized that something was wrong. Or not wrong, perhaps, but *off.*

It was well into morning, with the sky still feigning nearer to dawn, gray and heavy. He had been cutting across the lawn, feeling as much as hearing the frost-encrusted grass crunching beneath his boots, and that was the trigger. That sound—it was the only sound he was hearing. While the Institute was never a noisy place, even at the best of times, the silence was so total as to be almost oppressive.

Steinberg came to a stop, puzzled. After a moment he began to turn in place, a slow three-sixty sweep, taking in the details around him.

His first thought—and his anger at Carrington flared the

hotter for it—was that the Old Man had ordered an all-stations drill, a full defense deployment, perhaps for training purposes. Along the perimeter wall, Steinberg could see the Institute guards in full turnout gear, apparently armed to the teeth. The ECM "Tangleweb" countermeasures had been broken out as well, the small canisters with their strange radar dishes and odd little launch tubes now positioned on every rooftop he could see. Even the Institute's air defense systems had been deployed, the Stingray SAM batteries now sitting aboveground, instead of in their holding containers beneath the lawn.

But it wasn't a drill. Paranoid though the Old Man could be, he'd never order a full-on drill like this without telling Steinberg—his director of operations—that he was doing so. Not a drill.

Which meant only one thing, really.

It meant that the Carrington Institute was expecting an attack from a rival hypercorp.

Steinberg broke into a run, making for the Operations Center, and becoming more and more alarmed by the thought of what he might find there.

It wasn't an ops center any longer; it was a war room.

For a moment, just standing in the doorway, Steinberg could do nothing but take in the scene. He knew the Ops Center well, had spent more time than he cared to admit within its shielded and countermeasured confines, staring at holographic displays and multidepth plasma screens until tears streamed from his eyes with fatigue. He'd stood beside the Old Man for hours on end, watching as Institute operations and Institute operatives all around the world had undertaken their missions, some with more success than others.

He'd never seen the room like this, not with every display humming, every terminal manned. Seven separate displays were tracking live video, flicking from one feed to another, images sent from the different Institute campuses around the world, from Moscow to Milan to Chicago to Seattle to Barcelona, on and on, over and over. On at least two other screens, Steinberg could see corporate news feeds, one of them dataDyne's "premier" subscriber service, the other from Beck-Yama's mouthpiece. At least a dozen other displays, all of them holographic, ran cascades of code, machine and programming languages that Steinberg could never hope to understand.

Daniel Carrington stood in the midst of it all, almost dead center in the room, wearing his tweed and leaning heavily on his cane. As Steinberg tried to track everything that was happening in the room around him, the Old Man turned to face him with the ponderous deliberation of a tank acquiring a new target. Past him, Steinberg could see Stanley Grimshaw, the Institute's computer guru and Carrington's handpicked combat hacker, working frantically at his multitude of keyboards and monitors.

"Where the hell have you been?" Carrington demanded.

"I was with Jo," Steinberg said, making his way toward Carrington and dodging a technician who was running from one station to another. "What the hell is going on?"

"You were with Jo."

"Yes, I was with Jo, we landed over an hour ago. Cordell says she's going to be fine, but—"

"The whole time?" Carrington asked. "You were with her the whole time? In Seattle?"

"If you mean was I monitoring her the whole time, yes, I was. Was I with her on the Spire, no, obviously not. But you know that, I sent you the preliminary report—"

Carrington pivoted, used his cane to whack the back of Grimshaw's seat. "Show it to him, Grim."

"Monitor three," Grimshaw said.

One of the monitors flickered, the image on it shivering, then redrawing, and Steinberg saw that it was a video capture, some red carpet someplace at night. Lots of young women dressed in Zentek style, heavily made up and projecting attention-grabs from their dataDyne d-PALs or their CMO ring-rings, holographic turnarounds of one of the superstarlet sex bombs that Grimshaw himself seemed to spend so much time online searching for nude photos of. Steinberg couldn't remember the name, sure it was something stupid, something like Licorice or Bubblegum.

"This was Seattle, last night, at the Zee Arena," Grimshaw was saying. "Candee's last show on the North American tour. This was taken at roughly the same time Lady Dark was supposed to be whacking it out with that Hawk Team mofo atop the Spire."

The view on the screen swung around, away from the fans and to the entrance of the arena, catching the sudden burst of flashbulbs as two people emerged, one guiding the other, a man and a woman. Steinberg recognized both instantly.

"Okay," he said. "That's impossible."

The image froze, and he heard Grimshaw's fingers dance quickly on his controls, the beep of the computers. The screen redrew, zooming in.

"Georg Bricker, CEO of Zentek," Grimshaw said.

"I know who it is," Steinberg shot back. "But that's not her with him."

"Sure as hell looks like her, Jonny-boy. Even when we go to the close-up, voila."

The image redrew a third time, now focused entirely on the red-headed young woman escorting Bricker from the arena. The woman who looked identical to Joanna Dark, or at least, identical to Joanna Dark when she hadn't been alternately shot at, stabbed, beaten, and blown up.

"Even got the tat right, perfect dimensions, right down to the micron," Grimshaw was saying. "And believe me, I checked."

"You've never been that close to Jo's tattoo," Steinberg muttered, moving closer for a better look.

"And *you* have?" Grimshaw shot back.

"That's *not* her," Steinberg told Carrington. "It's just not, Daniel. It's a physical impossibility for Jo to be in two places at once. If you want proof, just go to her room and *look* at her. This fake here doesn't have a scratch on her."

"Georg Bricker was found dead in the woods outside of Olympia roughly three hours after this footage was taken." Carrington turned his head slowly, showing Steinberg his profile. "CMO completed their hostile takeover of Zentek as of seventy-three minutes ago."

"So this fake, she's CMO. They're the ones who kick ass in body modification and cosmetics."

"It's possible, certainly. That's not our problem at the moment."

As if taking Carrington's words as a cue, alarms started shrieking all around the room, every monitor simultaneously flashing the words "intrusion attempt" in pulsing red letters. Steinberg nearly jumped, but Carrington didn't move a muscle except to deepen his frown. To his right, Steinberg heard Grimshaw swearing, then begin shouting out commands to the technicians throughout the room.

"Dammit, they're trying again!" Grimshaw said. "Brody, monitor the firewall, c'mon, quick quick *quick*!"

"They're through the first gate!" someone shouted.

"Second gate!"

"C'mon, c'mon!" Grimshaw urged. "Come and get me, you low-baud bastards. Come and get me."

Carrington leaned forward, whispering into Steinberg's ear, just loud enough to be heard over the din of the still-screaming alarms.

"This will be attempt number seventy-six to breach our network."

Just as quickly as it had begun, the alarms, the flashing, all of it ceased, and Steinberg watched as Carrington pulled back, straightening up. He flashed a small, hard smile, utterly devoid of amusement.

"And stay out!" Grimshaw said, and he sounded out of breath, and more than a little punch-drunk. "Okay, everyone, reset infrastructure. Let's see if we can chase it back this time. Move move *move*!"

Carrington put his free hand on Steinberg's arm, turning him away from the monitors, from the image of the Joanna doppelganger, guiding him toward the back of the room, out of Grimshaw's earshot. He was walking slowly, and the frown was still in place, and Steinberg wondered if Joanna wasn't the only one who'd been going without sleep.

"Someone has poked the bear, Jon," Carrington said to him, softly. "Someone has poked the bear, and made it look like we were the ones doing the poking. And now they're poking back, and it will get a lot worse before it gets better."

"Which bear?" Steinberg asked.

Carrington waved back to the various monitors without bothering to even look their way. "Take your choice. CMO. Beck-Yama. DataDyne. One of them—if not all of them—thinks we took Bricker out."

"Jo's a new operative, she's not that well known—"

"She's known enough, Jon. Certainly she's known to Anita Velez, and we have every reason to believe she's known to Core-Mantis, as well."

"Another reason to think it was Core-Mantis who did this."

"They're certainly the ones making the obvious profit from it," Carrington agreed.

"You think dataDyne's going to hit us? You think Velez, DeVries, they're viewing this as your opening salvo?"

"I don't know."

The words came out with unexpected difficulty, filled with obvious distaste and ringing with frustration. Steinberg wondered how many times in his life Daniel Carrington had been forced to utter them before. He didn't imagine they'd been said easily, or often, if ever.

"It's a dataDyne strategy to attack the opposition's information networks before launching a conventional assault," Carrington said, after another moment's thought. "It's their playbook, but it could be misdirection. After all, if we know it's a dataDyne tactic, it's reasonable to believe that both Beck-Yama and CMO know it, as well."

The thought of dataDyne dropships coming over the wall, of Shock Troopers falling from the sky like raindrops, made Steinberg wince. "You really think we're about to be hit?"

"I don't know," Carrington said for a second time. "But I'd rather we be ready in case we are, wouldn't you?"

"What do you need me to do?"

"Prepare to repel boarders."

Steinberg nodded, began heading for the door.

"Jon?" Carrington called out, his tone softening. "How's Joanna?"

For a moment, Jonathan's burgeoning anger subsided. Then, Carrington added, "Can she fight?"

The anger Steinberg had been carrying before flared, irrational, but just as intense, and he needed a moment to assure himself he could keep it from his voice when he answered.

"She can barely stand, Daniel."

Carrington rubbed a hand over his beard and mustache, as if absently reassuring himself that both were still on his face.

"Pity," he said, and turned, making his way back to Grimshaw and the other technicians engaged in the Institute's information defense.

The alarms had just begun declaring intrusion attempt number seventy-seven as Steinberg left the Operations Center to ready the Institute defenses.

Home of Former dataDyne CEO
Zhang Li (Deceased)
38 km SW Li Xian, Sichuan Province
People's Republic of China
January 20th, 2021

The change was wearing off by the time Chun Fan returned home to the rest of the Continuity, and she was consequently in exquisite agony by then. Her brothers and her sisters helped her to her room, and two stayed with her for the last hour of the reversion, listening to her screams of ecstatic agony as the final vestiges of the Chrysalis leaked from her body.

Chun Fan knew what a masochist was, but she didn't think she was a masochist. A masochist only loved pain, after all, and Chun Fan was not so simple. She loved the pain, she could admit it, but at the same time, she hated it. Just as she could, at once, both love and hate the woman she had pretended to be when she put Georg Bricker out of the misery he called his life. So she screamed, thrashing on her bed, flailing her arms and legs even as her limbs, like the rest of her, reverted to what they had been before leaving China.

Cell by cell and bone by bone, her body returned to its original form, and instead of looking like Joanna Dark, she once again looked like Chun Fan, eldest of the Continuity, Zhang Li's chosen children.

The physical demands of the change were such that Fan spent much of the following day in bed. Ke-Ling, two years younger than Fan's nineteen, and thus the second-eldest of the family, brought her updates of their progress while she recovered.

"CMO took Zentek, just as we planned. The intrusion attacks on Carrington's main campus started two hours and forty-seven minutes after you popped the German, just as the news went public. We're up to assault number—dig this—114, and I'm sure we're giving their chief programmer fits, though he also probably thinks the reason we've failed is that *he's* so damn good. Quon and Zi-Zi both want to go all the way in and just crash their optical now, but I've been sitting on them."

Fan rolled onto her side in the bed, reached for the cup of tea her brother was offering. It was still too hot to drink comfortably, but she took a gulp anyway, forcing it down, before asking, "What happened to the Bitch?"

"Velez moved her right away, we're not sure where. I'm guessing to the 'secret' house they just finished in New Zealand, but Tai-Hua thinks maybe they're in Buenos Aires."

"You don't know? Baby brother, what would our father say?"

Ke-Ling cracked a broad grin at her, showing his tattooed teeth. "He'd say it is the battle that defines us, and the stakes must be high for the battle to be worth anything at all."

"Contact our friend in Paris, use my handle, see if he doesn't let it slip."

"You don't want to do it yourself? The next packet is ready for upload, I figured you'd want to be the one to send it."

"Bring me a deck, then," Fan said, finishing her tea. "And a rig, I need to practice. Jo-Jo is back at the Institute, yeah?"

"We're pretty sure, yeah. She was picked up in Seattle roughly the time you were leaving with the dead man. She's going to be hard to track once she finds out."

"Well, that's fine, because we don't *need* to track her." Fan returned her brother's smile with one of her own. "She'll come here. She already knows the way."

Ke-Ling nodded, leaned down, and kissed Fan gently on the lips. "There's one more thing."

"Hmm?"

"The CMO woman, she'll be here in the morning with the payment."

"Just make sure I'm up."

He put a hand to his heart, as if wounded by the thought of any dereliction of duty. "But of course. I'll get you that deck."

"And a DeathMatch rig, Ke-Ke. I need to practice."

"You don't need to practice. You're better than Zhang Mai ever was."

"So was Joanna Dark," Fan said. "And she's the one I'm going to have to beat."

▌║▌║▌║▌

Fan stayed in bed, handling the upload to Paris, then switching to the DeathMatch rig and booting up her favorite combat simulation, loading the arena with as many virtual Mai Hems as the program would allow. She armed them all to the teeth, then gave herself a combat knife. She switched the feedback safeties off, so she could feel the sting every time she was hit. Then she proceeded to murder Zhang Li's dead daughter eighty-four times in succession before finally succumbing to a rocket attack and being virtually splattered all over the virtual interior of the Sistine Chapel.

She did a second game immediately thereafter, this time loading the custom bot she'd programmed with her brothers and sisters, the one of Joanna Dark. She gave them each identical load-outs and used the baseline arena setting for their battle. Again, she kept the feedback safeties off.

The Joanna bot was a good one, loaded with all the moves recorded off her during her actual battle with Mai Hem here, in the mansion. There were tweaks, too, information culled from other sources; there'd been a treasure trove of information in the pharmaDyne security servers, showing her in a rooftop fight with some junkie who'd also had some good moves, but no artistry. That was one of the things Fan loved about fighting Joanna Dark; she was pure art. Watching her fight was like reading poetry, like listening to opera, like watching Shakespeare. Fan adored it, adored her, the woman who had killed Zhang Mai not once, but twice, even if it was only the second one that really counted.

How could Fan not have loved her for that? For killing her rival, for killing the arrogant, preening, self-centered bitch who had put herself between Fan and her father, Zhang Li. Of course Chun Fan loved Joanna Dark. She had to.

Just the way she had to hate Joanna with a murderous strength as powerful as her love. Because, while Joanna Dark had killed Mai Hem, she had also killed Zhang Li. And when someone murders your father, well, you're supposed to hate them.

Fan felt supremely confident that Joanna Dark would understand that.

It was a good battle between Fan and Joanna, lasting almost two and a half minutes this time, longer than normal. Jo clipped her with a blast from a SuperDragon early on and managed to score two hits to Fan's chest with a MagSec, but Fan's body armor held, and she was on Joanna then, and they went hand-to-hand. Joanna was strong, too, and had more reach than Fan, but she didn't have the weight, and finally Fan was able to flip Joanna into one of the support pillars, smashing her forehead against the sharp edge. There was a gratifying crack of bone, and it was enough to send Jo reeling for a second. Fan pivoted low, taking the other woman's knees out from behind, and when Jo went down, Fan was ready, and grabbed a handful of that beautiful, wonderful, silky red hair.

Then Fan proceeded to bash Joanna Dark's face into the ground over and over again, reducing her pretty features to soup.

The woman from CMO was named Portia de Carcareas, and she was exactly the type of woman Chun Fan detested, because she was all image and no soul, no substance. Like all of the women from CMO, Chun Fan was certain. The ones who always reminded her of Zhang Mai and the way she would slut around the mansion wearing a dress that seemed made of equal parts masking tape and Mylar. The high-and-mighty Mai Hem had thought it made her sexy, had made her irresistible, but Fan knew the truth; it made her look tawdry and cheap, and everyone who ever saw her in it just thought she was a whore, bringing dishonor to their father's name. The fact that Zhang Mai lasted as long as she had as their father's "only daughter" was due to her proficiency in DeathMatch VR and her subsequent popularity with fans of the "sport"—nothing else.

At least Portia de Carcareas had the courtesy and sense to not dress like a whore, even if, in the final analysis, that's what she was. Likewise the drivers of the three null-g Overlanders that came with her, all women as well, ferrying the Continuity's payment for services rendered.

That was CMO's thing, Fan knew. The public face of the

company was that of Shane Eddy, ruggedly handsome, quick-witted, and given to extravagant media stunts. Most recently, he had issued an open invitation to all the other hypercorp CEOs to join him in a snowmobile race from one edge of Antarctica to the other, the stakes being, of course, controlling interests in each of their companies. All had declined, leaving Eddy to race alone; the last Fan had heard, he was approaching Amundsen-Scott-GloboProComm Wireless at the South Pole.

But Shane Eddy didn't run Core-Mantis OmniGlobal, and Chun Fan and her brothers and sisters in the Continuity were perhaps the only people outside of the CMO upper echelon who had discovered that fact. Eddy was a show pony, a figurehead, and the hypercorporation was run, instead, by a close-knit clique of women who called themselves—in internal communications only—Harmonia's Daughters.

"The who?" Fan had asked upon being informed of the discovery.

Her youngest sister, Shuang, explained. "It means they think of themselves as Amazons, you know, the warrior women."

"The ones who cut off their. . . ."

Shuang giggled. "Yeah. They were supposed to be all savage and sexy and the Greek men were scared of them so much they would pee themselves rather than fight them."

"So why don't they just call themselves Amazons?"

"Well, the Amazons were supposed to be the children of the god of war, Ares, and this super sexy water nymph named Harmonia. So maybe they thought it sounded better?"

"How do you know all of this?" Fan had asked.

Shuang had shrugged, the movement almost entirely hidden beneath the folds of the red and gold silk dress she liked to wear. The dress was far too big for her, tailored to a woman twice her age. Shuang was only twelve, but she tried to convince all her other siblings she was actually fourteen, as if it made a difference.

That was Core-Mantis OmniGlobal, third largest hypercorporation in the world, and, if things went according to Fan's plans, soon to become second largest. A company run by women who wished they were Amazons. It didn't mean that men weren't employed by CMO, but it meant that ultimately, men held no real power in the corporation. If something was important to CMO, it was handled by a woman.

It pleased Fan that Carcareas had brought other women with her, because she knew it meant Core-Mantis was taking their transaction seriously. It meant that they valued everything the Continuity could offer them. All the more important because of what Chun Fan intended to offer them next.

Fan greeted the convoy of vehicles in the outer courtyard, with Ke-Ling accompanying her. There'd been snowfall recently, and it clung to the trees and the buildings, to the ancient stone sculptures, some of them from as far back as the Chin dynasty. The air was crisp, and the noise of the approaching Overlanders carried through it, echoing off the mountainsides around them. Cold, but not so cold that the water in the reflecting ponds and the little streams that crisscrossed the outer garden had frozen over.

Before their father had died, simply getting this far into the mountains and beyond the first wall would have meant running a gauntlet of security and guards, everything from snipers to antipersonnel mines and laser grids. These days there were no guards, because Fan and her brothers and sisters didn't need them. Just the networked security system with their personalized tweaks. If they needed to kill someone, it would be done with the press of a keyboard, not the pull of a trigger.

The lead Overlander came into view, followed by three others, all of them painted black, with the CMO logo laser-etched on their hoods. The first vehicle passed through the gate, then pulled over when its driver saw Fan and Ke-Ling standing there, waiting, and as it came to a gentle landing on the ground, the remaining cars in the convoy pulled to a stop in a line, their null-g engines idling.

From the corner of her eye, Fan could see the distortion fields beneath each of the waiting vehicles, the warping of space that always made her feel a little dizzy, a little nauseated. She avoided looking at them directly, instead focusing on Carcareas, who was now exiting the lead vehicle.

"Signora Carcareas." Fan bowed.

"Lady Chun," Carcareas said, returning it. She'd come dressed for the weather, winter in the mountains of Sichuan, boots and a skin-tight black thermal suit that hugged each and every one of her elegant curves. A fur-lined coat, tailored well enough that it accentuated her shape rather than hid it, capped the ensemble. No weapons visible, but that meant nothing, and, in truth, Fan didn't really care. Carcareas wouldn't raise a finger against her, or her brother, or any of her family, she knew; not unless one of the Continuity did so first.

Carcareas was taller than them both by only a few inches, and certainly older, but Fan wasn't certain by how much; CMO specialized in body-modification more than any other hypercorporation, everything from performance-enhancing implants to drug therapies and cosmetic alterations. She could have been sixty rather than thirty, there was no way to tell. Whatever her age, she was beautiful, with olive skin and thick black hair, and pouting lips that promised sensuality and passion.

"Allow me to introduce you to my brother, Ke-Ling."

"A pleasure." Carcareas indicated the waiting Overlanders. "I have your payment, exactly as you insisted."

"All of it?"

"Seventy-two million, two hundred and ninety-four thousand, six hundred and two dollars. In cash."

At her side, Fan heard her brother chuckle softly, and she had to struggle to keep her expression serious. It was a ludicrous figure, for several reasons aside from the ridiculousness of the actual number. The truth was, Fan had come up with it literally from thin air. After all, who knew what the actual market price was for killing not just the CEO of a hypercorp, but the hypercorp itself? As far as that went, Fan was certain she had given Core-Mantis OmniGlobal one hell of a bargain.

"Very good," Fan said. "If you would like to direct the drivers to the inner courtyard, we can unload it there."

Carcareas nodded slightly, then dipped her chin and spoke inaudibly to her ThroatLink. After a moment, she raised her head again, smiling once more. "Shall I follow you?"

"This way." Fan turned, waiting for Carcareas to come alongside her, then began walking along one of the many paths that would lead, eventually, to the inner courtyard. "We trust you were pleased with our results?"

"Very much so," Carcareas said. "Everything occurred exactly as you said it would, and the information you provided was entirely accurate. We were able to access the Zentek servers in Berlin exactly as you directed. It was as if their security simply ceased to exist. The directors are very impressed."

"We are pleased."

There was a moment of silence as the three walked together, cresting one of the paths high enough that they now had a view over the inner wall, to the inner courtyard. The Overlanders were coming to a stop near the massive fire pit at the center of the garden. Smoke and waves of heat rose from the flames, and as they looked down, Fan could see almost a dozen of her siblings emerge from the mansion, moving to greet the vehicles.

"Have them open the cases once they're unloaded, please."

Carcareas murmured to her ThroatLink, and while they watched, the drivers of each of the Overlanders exited, began removing case after case after case of the currency. Each was opened as it was set on the ground, and Fan watched as another of her brothers, Wei, moved from one to the next, checking their contents.

"It's all there, I promise you," Carcareas said. "We wouldn't wish to jeopardize our relationship with the Continuity."

"It has served us well, hasn't it?"

"It has. To such an extent that I have been instructed to inquire about another . . . arrangement."

Fan again had to hide a smile, feigning curiosity. "Oh?"

"Beck-Yama's attempt to acquire Zentek has left them momentarily cash poor. They are overextended and vulnerable—"

Fan raised her right hand, holding up two fingers, and Carcareas fell silent.

"Ke-Ke, please give Signora Carcareas your d-PAL."

Ke-Ling stepped forward, offering the slender, credit-card-sized PDA to Carcareas.

"What is this?" Carcareas asked Fan.

"Beck-Yama International."

The other woman's eyes widened momentarily, and then she recovered from her surprise and took the d-PAL from Ke-Ling's hand. Fan waited while she activated the PDA, began quickly scanning the terabyte upon terabyte worth of files that Ke-Ling had prepared, alternately projecting and scrolling data.

"Most of this is encoded," Carcareas said after nearly a minute. "You've encrypted it."

"Did CMO do your eyes, as well, Signora?" Fan asked mildly. "The ThroatLink is a surgical procedure, of course, and I am assuming you've had the pheromone secretion therapy. Did they do your eyes, too?"

Carcareas stiffened, glaring at Fan, and Fan met the look with the mildness she had put in her questions now on her face. Carcareas relaxed, flicking off the d-PAL and handing it back to Ke-Ling.

"Two augments," Carcareas admitted. "Series Four: the Spectrum, and the Memory set."

"So you see why we might wish to encrypt the data when your eyes can literally record everything you see. It would have been poor business on our part to do otherwise."

"So what did I *not* see?"

"Everything you needed to successfully bring Beck-Yama to its knees. Back-door access to its quantum optical systems, location of their datacore itself. All the financials. Passwords. Work-arounds. Troop deployments."

"What you gave us on Zentek."

"Yes."

"How do you keep getting this information?"

Ke-Ling laughed again, and this time Fan allowed herself to join him. Carcareas tried to keep smiling, but it was clear to Fan that it wasn't because she was amused.

"It's all there for the taking, Signora," Ke-Ling said. "You just have to know where to look."

"We know where to look," Carcareas said. "We have the best programmers and hackers in the world working for us—"

"No," Fan said, still laughing. "No, you don't, or rather, you did, and you will again, if you meet our price. But the best don't work for CMO. You're looking at them right now. Right here, and right down there."

Fan pointed again to the courtyard, where her siblings were now assisting the Core-Mantis drivers in their process of unloading. There were a lot of cases, silver metal shining in the daylight.

"If you want the best, you have to pay for it."

"How much?" Carcareas asked.

Fan furrowed her brow, as if thinking, though in fact she was simply buying time. The figure had been determined over a week before, during the final stages of the Continuity's planning.

"Two point three billion dollars," Fan said. "And three cents."

Carcareas snorted.

"In cash," Fan added.

"That's ridiculous."

"Do you think so?"

"Two point three billion dollars in cash?" Carcareas said. "I'm not certain there's that much currency in circulation."

"Actually, there's over eight hundred billion American dollars currently in circulation," Ke-Ling offered, helpfully.

"See?" Fan said. "Not so difficult after all."

"It's far too much."

"No, it isn't, and you know it. We are willing to give Core-Mantis OmniGlobal the ways and means to bring Beck-Yama International to its knees. You and your sisters will have gone from being the third-largest hypercorporation to being the second in the space of a week, and large enough to seriously consider challenging dataDyne for its top position."

"And that's where you're heading with this, is it?" Carcareas asked.

"DataDyne must die." Fan said it as a matter of fact, nothing more, as devoid of malice as she could manage.

"Why?"

"That is not your concern, Signora. It is enough for you to understand that the corporation of our father *was* our father. He was a genius, and a visionary. Without him, there can be no dataDyne."

"Two point three billion?" Carcareas asked.

"And three cents," Ke-Ling said.

"And three cents."

"Correct," Fan said.

"I'll have to take this to the directors."

"The offer is valid for twelve hours." Fan looked down at the inner courtyard once more, saw that the last of the cases had finally been unloaded, opened, and checked. "We appear to be finished."

"So we do." Carcareas considered, pulling on her lower lip with her teeth for a moment. Then she turned to face Fan and her brother, and offered them a bow once more. "Thank you for your time and your offer. I'll see you receive a response as soon as possible."

"Ke-Ling will escort you out," Fan said. "If you want, you can have sex with him before you leave."

Carcareas stared, and Fan turned away, following the path down to the inner courtyard, the sound of her laughter bouncing off the stone and the snow.

"Did you?" Fan asked her brother when he finally joined her and the others by the fire pit. The Overlanders with their drivers had departed, and once again, they were alone in the home of their father.

Ke-Ling grinned, then looked over at the line upon line of

open cases, each filled with currency. "What should we do with the money?"

Fan laughed once again, feeling elated, full of anticipation and desire, of love and hatred. She leaned forward and grabbed her brother's shoulders, kissing him on the forehead.

"The same thing we're going to do to the world, Ke-Ke," she told him. "Burn it. Burn it all."

Beck-Yama InterNational's Zentek Takeover Bid Fails

The Beck-Yama Giant Stumbles

By Pieter von Beck, Staff Writer, *World Financial Times-Independent*
London (FT-I)

Hypercorporate powerhouse Beck-Yama InterNational suffered a series of setbacks this week, culminating in a staggering 22% drop in stock value and a 13% decline in overall liquid assets. Industry analysts and angry shareholders have scrambled to sift through public disclosure forms to divine the source of Beck-Yama's current woes, which seem to center around the disposition of beleaguered and foundering competitor, Zentek.

"They started off well in the Zentek takeover process," said Wall Street analyst William Bassett, senior partner at the financial management firm Bassett-Wallace-Green. "But they were slow off the mark when [Zentek CEO] Bricker passed away, which allowed Core-Mantis OmniGlobal to move in and claim the prize."

Other analysts point out the series of unfortunate system failures and other IT infrastructure problems that slowed Beck-Yama shortly after Zentek came into play. Insider reports indicate widespread network failures, which many theorize were the work of an aggressive hacker effort—a large-scale denial-of-service attack—which crippled Beck-Yama at the critical moment.

Beck-Yama's official position, as portrayed in a flurry of media alerts and press releases, is that the system failures were "unrelated to our ongoing expansion efforts, and the unfortunate interruption of Beck-Yama's plans to partner with Zentek in a long-term, synergistic relationship."

Whatever the cause, Core-Mantis OmniGlobal's stock has skyrocketed with the official announcement of the takeover of foundering Zentek. CMO stock has shot up almost 31%, and global public-perception and approval ratings have climbed to levels that, as of this writing, have only been attained by dominant hypercorporation dataDyne.

Industry experts predict that the Zentek fiasco is far from the last word in the current fencing match between CMO and Beck-Yama. "CMO has to quickly and efficiently fold Zentek into their current organizational structure, and even more rapidly bring Zentek products to market, in order to show the Zentek brand has long-term equity and consumer appeal—a considerable challenge, given Zentek's dismal showing in the marketplace in recent years," said Bassett. "And Beck-Yama will not take the Zentek acquisition lying down. Look for fireworks between them in the near future."

Independent World Financial News

Corporate Watch: Beck-Yama InterNational

Beck-Yama CFO Suffers Fatal Heart Attack

Dateline: Tokyo, Japan
22nd January 2021

Chief Financial Officer for Beck-Yama InterNational (*WORLDAQ: BYI*) Shin Matsuo died this morning, the victim of a severe heart attack while dining in Tokyo, in the famed Ginza district.

Mr. Matsuo had been dining in the private banquet facility of Kyubei, a popular and long-established restaurant, when he collapsed, complaining of severe chest pains.

Several bystanders rushed to assist Mr. Matsuo, and one woman—seen in the accompanying photographs—stayed by his side through the ordeal, and attempted mouth-to-mouth resuscitation. This unidentified Samaritan was seen applying first aid until a Beck-Yama First Response Care Team arrived.

Emergency responders attempted to stabilize Mr. Matsuo but were unsuccessful. He was pronounced dead at Beck-Yama/Jutendo Hospital at 3:40 a.m. local time, of an acute myocardial infarction.

Chief Public Relations Officer of Beck-Yama InterNational/Tokyo Sazaki Nobekazu issued a statement this morning, confirming Mr. Matsuo's death and issuing a request for information leading to the location of the unknown young woman who attempted to assist.

"Beck-Yama InterNational appreciates the efforts undertaken by this young woman and wishes to reward her for selfless actions," said Mr. Nobekazu. "In addition, we are offering a modest reward to anyone who can place us in touch with her."

The unknown young woman is described as being in her early twenties, with a slim, athletic build and red hair (possibly with a streak of white or blond). Anyone who can identify her is requested to contact a Beck-Yama InterNational Public Relations liaison via the corporate Web site.

dataDyne Executive Safehouse
37 km ENE of Nelson, New Zealand
January 22nd, 2021

The safehouse had been built in what, Cassandra DeVries had to believe, was one of the most beautiful, isolated, and defensible places she had ever been in her life. Facing roughly northeast, built into the mountainside, it afforded a view—once again through bulletproof glass as clear as cut crystal—of the South Pacific and its vibrant blue waters. Trees, heavy with leaves and lush with life, grew on all sides, and were she to actually make the three-quarter-mile walk down the stairs from the house to the beach, she'd have found fine sand baked by the warmth of the sun.

The house, too, was without compare. Larger than she'd expected, given Velez's descriptions and the accordant haste with which it had been constructed, with plenty of open space to work or relax. An indoor pool, three sun decks—one on each level—four bedrooms, not including her own master suite. And once more, everything in her closets had been made for her, chosen in her styles, her colors. The sheets on the bed, once again, were silk.

It would have made a grand spot for a secluded vacation, for a little time away from the office, and perhaps she could even have convinced herself that was what she was having, but for two things. The first was the security, of course. At least 160 Shock Troopers were on duty at all times. They patrolled the perimeter in constant motion, directed by a command post buried inside a hardened room that had actually been dug out of the mountainside. They stood on post in twos or fours at every access point, at every door into the house, at the ends of each and every causeway. They patrolled the water in null-g hydrofoils that traversed from beach to wave and back again in perpetual sweeps. They manned sniper positions in the nearby mountainside. They worked anti-aircraft and missile defense platforms on all sides.

If it wasn't Velez at her side during her every waking moment, Cassandra had at least two Shock Troopers in Velez's stead. Things had progressed to such an extent that, when she needed to use the toilet, the bathroom was swept and cleared of possible threats first.

That was the first thing.

The second was that she couldn't actually escape "the office." She *was* the office, and though she was secured in her safehouse, the work still found her. The papers still arrived. The video conferences—now with her location carefully concealed and interference buffers riding the communication wave to keep her position from being triangulated—still occurred on schedule. The calls continued.

It struck her, as she emerged from her morning shower on her third day at the safehouse to find Anita Velez once again handing her a towel, guarding her even as she bathed, that her fury at Daniel Carrington had nothing to do with his possible desire to end her life. No, she was furious at him for an altogether different reason. He was costing her time—time she could not afford to waste.

Because, while the work continued, it continued at a much slower pace. Security demanded it. Papers had to be screened. Calls had to be rerouted. And personal meetings were out of the question, at least according to Velez.

She was growing so frustrated and so angry, she had half a mind to grant the proposal Velez had put before her during their flight from Paris.

She had half a mind to tell Velez to go ahead and kill Daniel Carrington.

████████████

From the time she'd left her home in Paris to the time she was loaded aboard her personal low-orbit transport, less than eight minutes had elapsed. The motorcade had come to a screeching halt, null-g engines laboring with their effort, at the dataDyne airfield adjacent to Charles de Gaulle, and as quickly as Velez had bundled Cassandra into the limousine, she was being bundled out of it and onto her aircraft. They were moving again even before she was in her acceleration couch, and she had only just managed to get her harness fastened before the transport switched from null-g to booster.

They'd launched into the dawn above Paris with Cassandra looking out the port-side window to see two more transports, identical at least on the outside to the one she was riding in, taking to the sky. Velez, buckled into her seat opposite, was using a headset to speak to the pilots, and that was when the decision was made to head to New Zealand. Glancing out the window again, the dataDyne CEO watched as the other two transports peeled away, each of them pursuing a different flight path.

She's honestly worried we'll be shot out of the sky, Cassandra thought, and that made the sadness, the anger she was feeling all the more acute. That she should now have to fear Carrington this much, that she should now literally be afraid for her life because of the one man she had ever given her whole heart—it was almost unbearable.

And if Anita Velez had stopped to consider that at all, Cassandra knew, the older woman would never had done what she did next.

They were cresting orbit, the daylight again turning to darkness, the stars suddenly coming visible, when Velez unfastened her harness and half-stepped, half-floated to the seat beside Cassandra's. She reached into her jacket, removing an envelope, and handed it over.

"I am requesting your authorization for this," Velez said.

The envelope was unsealed, and Cassandra removed its contents to find two perfectly typed pages, what Velez had labeled a "conops," or concept of operation. Cassandra knew what it was, because she had seen it before, though she reread it anyway, just to make certain. The document outlined a mission Velez needed CEO approval to undertake, and in the document, the CORPSEC director had carefully listed, point by point, the logic underlying the proposal and the net gain for both dataDyne and Cassandra herself, should it come to successful completion. As a proposal, it was immaculate, both in content and presentation.

The main thrust enumerated Carrington Institute operations against dataDyne and the resulting costs to dataDyne in both personnel and material. According to Velez's research, Carrington Institute operatives had been responsible for the deaths of upward of 375 dataDyne employees, most of the deaths the result of firefights with CI operatives. The document then went on to point out, succinctly, the fact that this pattern of behavior was no doubt going to continue, all the more so given Daniel Carrington's involvement with the situation that had brought Cassandra to power. The conclusion regarding Carrington himself was declarative and simple: he meant to destroy dataDyne, no matter the cost.

The proposal, finally, concluded with the simple request:

> *For the reasons listed herein, and given the high probability of continued aggressive action from the Carrington Institute, its agents, and Daniel Carrington himself, it is concluded that the Carrington Institute presents a clear and present danger both to dataDyne as a whole and to Dr. Cassandra DeVries, CEO.*
>
> *Thus, it is respectfully proposed that an operation be undertaken to neutralize this threat: to wit, destroying the Carrington Institute's ability to fight; destroying the Carrington Institute's will to fight; and destroying the Carrington Institute's ability to potentially recover and assume these actions once more in the future. It is thus concluded that the most efficient and tactically precise means of effecting this goal is the neutralization of Daniel Carrington as an adversarial force with extreme prejudice.*

Cassandra read it twice over, the first time with a growing anger that made the second reading necessary. The changes to the document since the last time she had seen it were minor. Finished, she turned to face Velez.

"No," Cassandra said, and she handed the document and the envelope back.

"Madame Director—"

"No, Anita. I will not give authorization to assassinate. My answer remains the same. The discussion is closed."

But it wasn't, not for Velez, and for the first time, Cassandra saw the other woman lose her temper.

"This should have been authorized the same day you became CEO, Madame Director! You are being foolish, you are being sentimental, and you cannot afford to be either, not any longer! This man"—and Velez held the envelope up in her fist, as if holding Carrington by the throat—"wants to destroy you, me, and dataDyne, and he has made that intention plain. He has the means, he has the will. He is our enemy, and we cannot suffer him to continue unopposed!"

"I said no!"

Velez sat back, looking hurt, looking bewildered, as if she had discovered, suddenly, that the person she had been speaking with all along hadn't understood a thing that had been said. "Why? Why won't you do this? Why won't you protect yourself? Why won't you protect us?"

"I have my reasons."

"Madame Director, this is a defensible, inevitable action. He has brought it on himself."

"I have the blood of one man on my hands," Cassandra snapped. "I don't need the blood of another!"

Velez had stared at her, and for a moment Cassandra felt a pang of sympathy for the hurt she was seeing in the other woman's eyes. Then, without a word, Velez replaced the proposal in its envelope and the envelope in her coat, and returned to her seat.

They said nothing else to one another for the rest of the flight.

That had been four days ago. Four days of the beautiful safehouse, of Cassandra DeVries's beautiful prison. Four days of working in an office with her secretaries speaking to her from holographic monitors while Shock Troopers stood by, still as statues and serious as the grave.

"Madame Director," Velez said. "Something's happened."

Cassandra turned from where she was standing behind

her desk, saw Velez waiting in the doorway, the two Shock Troopers there standing at rigid attention. Cassandra held up her hand, motioned Velez to come forward, then turned her attention back to the most insistent of her secretaries.

"I'm putting you on hold," she said.

The holograph flickered, the secretary looking suddenly pained. "Madame Director, this needs your attention immediately."

"In a moment," Cassandra said, and she muted the call, pulling her earpiece free from her ear. "I should just get one of the subcutaneous, I swear. I'm spending more and more time on the bloody phone."

"Something's happened," Velez said again. "The situation is getting worse."

"I haven't heard anything."

"Have you looked at the markets today?"

"Not for an hour or so, I've been buried."

"Matsuo had a heart attack on his way home from work yesterday."

"Matsuo? He was CFO of Beck-Yama?"

"Yes."

Cassandra didn't speak for a moment, reading the expression on Velez's face, and seeing in it all her sudden suspicions. There was more coming, Cassandra knew, but already she knew she didn't need to hear it. She knew where this was going.

"You have proof he's behind it?" Cassandra asked softly.

Velez removed her d-PAL from its sleeve at her hip, handing it over. "Replay newsfeed, Tokyo local, archive one."

In Cassandra's hand, the d-PAL chimed, responding to Velez's voice. From its projector bloomed a video image, the angle slightly skewed and the recording choppy. Voices speaking in Japanese crackled.

"Private video, recorded on a hovercam," Velez said.

"You can see it. Outside the Beck-Yama building near the Ginza."

The image shimmered, focus resolving, and Cassandra found herself looking at a cluster of people, men and women, most of them in suits, all rushing toward the same spot, forming a circle of spectators. The camera moved closer, rising, and over the shoulder of one of the bystanders, she was now seeing Beck-Yama CFO Matsuo lying prone, on his back, one hand to his chest. The pain and fear in his expression was unmistakable, a sheen of perspiration shining across his brow. On his right side, a woman was holding his hand, trying to comfort and calm him. The mysterious Joanna, Carrington's new favorite toy.

First Bricker, now this, Cassandra thought. *Is that what she is to him? His blunt instrument?*

"No doubt it's her?" Cassandra asked.

"None. You can see . . . here, when she gets up."

In the holograph, EMS had arrived, Beck-Yama medics pushing through the cluster, roughly moving Joanna out of the way. She righted herself, then got to her feet, her expression almost convincing in its concern, and for a moment she looked directly into the camera, and Cassandra imagined there was mirth in her eyes, and felt sickened.

The holograph winked out, the d-PAL in her hand chiming once more. Cassandra handed it back to Velez.

One of the secretaries was waving for Cassandra's attention from his holograph, and without looking at him, she reached over and killed all her open calls with a push of a key. The various images winked out.

"It's not good, is it?" Cassandra asked quietly.

"No, it is not, Madame Director." Velez frowned, then added, reluctantly, "Based on this new information, I am afraid I am not comfortable in allowing you to return to Paris.

I'm going to require that you remain here for a few days longer."

"He's just . . . he's out of control, Anita."

"That is how it appears, yes, Madame Director."

Cassandra sat down heavily in the unused chair at her desk, ran her hands through her short blond hair, tugging at it.

"Do you have the proposal?" she asked Velez, suddenly.

It took Velez a moment to realize what Cassandra was saying, and then she dipped into her coat, removed the same envelope she'd presented her CEO with four days earlier. Cassandra tore it open, pulling the sheets free and laying them on her desk, grabbing the nearest pen. She scanned quickly, crossing out words, writing in new ones, then initialing each of her changes. Without a pause, she added, at the bottom of the document:

Agreed upon and implemented, this day, January 22nd, 2021.

Finished, she handed the pages back to Velez.

"I won't let you kill him," Cassandra said. "But it's about time someone put a stop to his little Joanna, don't you agree?"

Her father used to say that pain was God's way of letting you know you weren't dead yet, and by that logic, Joanna Dark could only conclude that she was still alive. From the catalogue of her aches and wounds, very much alive, indeed.

It wasn't the first time she'd awoken since returning to the Institute, but it was the first time she'd opened her eyes to find herself feeling, finally, rested and able to face the world. Prior, she'd simply awoken long enough to be tended by Cordell or Steinberg, to eat the food they'd brought her, to drink the water they'd given. Neither had had much to say, and it was probably just as well, because she'd been so damned tired, she wouldn't have been able to carry a conversation on a forklift.

This time, though, she was awake—truly, finally awake—and for a time, Jo simply lay in her bed, listening to the silence around her, taking a slow inventory of herself. She began with her feet, confirming they were still at the end of her legs, and experimentally wriggled her toes. They responded without delay or discomfort. She tried moving her legs next, just slightly, feeling the lurking presence of her childhood fears once again, remembering the time she had spent as a small girl unable to move at all due to a spinal cord defect. But her legs responded as her toes had, albeit with more stiffness and the dull throb that told of bruises and strain along her quads and hamstrings.

It was her torso that really hurt, she determined. The bullet wound still burned in her flesh, and she knew she was breathing shallow, trying to keep from straining her injured ribs. At some point while she'd slept Cordell had removed her IV, and her arm where the needle had been inserted presented a different soreness, somehow more subtle that the rest.

She blinked, realized she'd dreamt of her father again. Unpleasant, still rife with her guilt, but at least not as bad as some of the other ones she'd had about him recently. Those weren't dreams, in her opinion—no, those qualified as nightmares, the kind where she woke up screaming. Jack Dark, decomposing flesh sagging and putrid hanging from his face, pointing his finger at his daughter and telling her that she had done this to him, that she had let Zhang Li's bitch daughter Mai Hem kill him.

This most recent dream—at least as much of it as she could remember—was less directly accusatory, but its thrust had been the same, if perhaps more subtle. A memory of six, maybe seven years ago, only thirteen, as her father taught her how to shoot. Nothing particularly remarkable about it, except in the dream Joanna was twenty-one, not thirteen, and suddenly she couldn't shoot to save his life. That had been what he'd said, berating her on the firing range in her dream, growing more and more frustrated with her.

"You can't shoot to save my life," Jack Dark had said.

No mystery in what that was about, no sir. But at least he wasn't decomposing in front of her as he said it.

She gave it almost half an hour, just lying there, before finally attempting to sit up, and it went well right up to the moment Joanna swung her feet off the bed and onto the floor. It was the move that did it, the unconscious shift of her torso as she'd turned her hips, and both the bullet wound in her side and the broken and cracked ribs in her chest announced their displeasure. The pain wrapped her like a hug, searing around her middle, and she lost what little breath she had for a moment, and had to catch herself with her right hand on the headboard to keep from toppling, an act that made the pain, for a moment, crescendo, but that, thankfully, kept her from toppling face first onto the floor.

Okay, Joanna thought. *We'll try that slower.*

Slower, it turned out, was the way to go, at least for the time being. Very slow, in fact, so that it took her nearly an hour to shower and change into fresh clothes. Getting her boots on was the hardest part, because it required her to bend, and every time she did so her vision would swim with dots of white light. In the end, she managed to get the boots on her feet, but abandoned the idea of lacing them up.

Finally, Joanna ventured out of her rooms and into the ominous silence of the Institute grounds.

She found Daniel Carrington in the Operations Center, where he was overseeing some fifteen other Institute staffers as they worked their duty stations. The atmosphere inside the larger room was thick with the combined smells of body odor, electronics equipment, and half-eaten meals, and the always-dimmed lighting of the room only amplified the palpable sense of tension. Tired and battered as she felt, she thought everyone else—right up to and including Carrington—looked worse.

"Sir?"

Carrington and Grimshaw both turned, their expressions almost identical in fatigue and frustration. If pressed, Joanna would have said that Grimshaw, who never took particular pride in his appearance or his hygiene, looked marginally the worse of the two.

Still, the hacker managed to flash her a wan smile before turning back, wordlessly, to his battery of consoles.

"You're up finally," Carrington said, eyeing her with a look so full of doubt, Jo wondered if he expected her to collapse once more there and then. "Jonathan seemed to think you were going to be out of commission for a while."

"Shows you what he knows." She gave him her cockiest grin, then snapped to attention and gave him a salute. "Reporting for duty, sir."

Carrington stared at her, assessing, and Jo hoped she was selling herself well. Before entering the room, she'd taken a minute to steady herself, to straighten up and put on her best face, trying to banish her multitude of hurts for the meeting. Carrington could be as overprotective as he could be apparently reckless, and the last thing Jo wanted was for him to send her back to bed. Something was clearly going on, after all; she had determined that much on the walk over, and the atmosphere in the Ops Center had confirmed it. That Carrington himself appeared so grave told her one thing more.

Whatever was going on, it concerned dataDyne.

And that meant that Jo wanted—*needed*—to be a part of it.

Carrington grunted, gesturing vaguely with his free hand, and Joanna dropped the salute. He came forward, using his cane, and Jo waited until he was almost in reach before asking the question that had been burning her since she had entered the room.

"What do you need me to do?"

The old man made a noise, almost another grunt, but this time, Jo could hear the amusement in it. He put out a hand, taking her arm at the elbow and giving her an almost grandfatherly squeeze.

"That's my girl," he said. "Though it would seem, at least to some, that you've already done more than enough."

"What's that supposed to mean?"

"It means, Joanna, that you have apparently done me one better. I invented the null-g engine. You, on the other hand, have apparently mastered instantaneous teleportation. Or translocation. Or some manner of material manifestation. Or something."

Joanna felt her brow furrowing in confusion and hoped the look she was giving Carrington was all the response he needed.

He chuckled again, softly and entirely without mirth. "Aye, and if you're bewildered, just imagine how I'm feeling at the moment. While you were fighting it out with Roarke in Seattle, Joanna, you were simultaneously escorting Zentek CEO Georg Bricker from the Zee Arena some 315 meters below you."

"Uhm."

"And while you've been sleeping in your room the last handful of days, you've also found the time and the means to journey to Tokyo, where you apparently induced a heart attack in Shin Matsuo, Beck-Yama InterNational's chief financial officer. You're not moonlighting for Core-Mantis now, are you Joanna?"

"Okay," Jo said. "What?"

"Someone has taken upon themselves to shift the balance of power amongst the hypercorps, Jo, and they're making it look like you're their agent of change. Bricker is dead, Zentek is gone, and Beck-Yama looks poised to collapse within the next eight to twenty hours. In both instances, Core-Mantis OmniGlobal has been—or looks to be—the group to benefit."

"CMO? Not dataDyne?"

"And yet another reason for my continued frustration. CMO. At the rate things are progressing, by this time tomorrow they'll be second only to dataDyne in size and power. A distant second, but second nonetheless."

"But I've never even *dealt* with CMO! Just this last time, in Los Angeles, and before that, during Initial Vector, when I was following Hayes, but . . . but I've never even spoken to one of their agents!"

"There was Carcareas."

"She was meeting with Dr. Murray's psycho, I never spoke to her! I barely got a look at her, and I *know* she never got a look at me!" Jo stopped herself, realized that her voice had been rising, and that just that much effort was making her chest ache. "How are they doing this? Why me?"

Carrington scowled, started to speak, then stopped, and Jo thought he was rephrasing his answer in his head.

"To the first, obviously it's some technological means of which we've been unaware. Or, possibly, a complete cosmetic redesign of an agent—Core-Mantis, perhaps, someone else, perhaps—remade to appear as much like you as possible. The second, however, that's the question of true issue, Joanna. Because you are now linked to me, at least in the eyes of our most dangerous adversary, dataDyne. You are known to both Dr. DeVries and her head of security, Anita Velez. And while I have every reason to believe that what they know is limited only to the fact that you work for me and nothing further, that is more than enough. Regardless of what CMO, Beck-Yama, anyone else may think, certainly dataDyne believes that it is you committing these murders, and that you're committing them at my behest."

She could feel herself flushing, feel the sense of outrage rising as all the implications of what Carrington was telling her took hold. The sense of violation was as acute as it was sudden. Joanna had grappled, and grappled hard, with the knowledge that she was a killer, that the gifts she had been given, however they had come to her, were ultimately to that end. That someone would use her face to hide their own murders made her feel raw, and it made her feel used.

Whoever was responsible, dataDyne, Core-Mantis, even Alfie at the tobacconists down the lane, it didn't matter. She had to stop them, and more, she had to make them pay.

Even as Jo concluded that, she knew, absolutely, that it was what her father would have had wanted of her.

"DataDyne," Jo said after a moment. "How much do they actually know about me? Do they know that I killed Zhang Li, for instance? That I killed Mai Hem?"

"To the last I would say that they certainly do not. If they had, their entire mind and power would have turned long ago to the task of apprehending and punishing you."

"Punish," Jo said. "You mean kill."

"That would have been the inevitable result, yes. But do not doubt for a moment that they would not have . . . extracted as much information from you as possible before granting that mercy."

Joanna's snort was filled with contempt.

Mercy, she thought, *and dataDyne. Two words that could never be made to go together, not even if you tried bonding them with an arc welder.*

Carrington scratched at his beard, musing. "As to the

broader question, what does dataDyne know about Joanna Dark, I would hazard not much more than I have already said. Grim has gone to great lengths to erase any and all public information about you, no matter where that information might have resided. As I said, Velez and DeVries know of your part in Operation: Initial Vector, that you infiltrated pharmaDyne Vancouver. They know you're one of my operatives, and they've certainly concluded that you are a trusted one. As to *who* you are, I'd guess that they know next to nothing. Your first name—because they heard me use it, to my folly—but there are many Joannas in the world, I shouldn't think. But the number of people who know you as the daughter of Jack Dark are certainly limited to a handful, and I'd daresay, all of them people in my employ."

"What did you say?" Jo asked.

"Hmm?"

"Why'd you call me that? Call me 'the daughter of Jack Dark?'"

Carrington looked genuinely puzzled. "Because you are. Have I committed some offense, Joanna? If I have, I must beg your forgiveness . . . I'm approaching my thirty-seventh hour without sleep, and fear the fatigue may be betraying me."

She stared at him, wondering how sincere the words were, wondering if she wasn't simply transferring her own fears onto the man. Her father had warned her of Daniel Carrington, after all—had told her that she couldn't trust him, should never trust him. But he had never given her a reason, and in Jack Dark's absence, Daniel Carrington had come to fill his place—to an extent—in Joanna's life.

Jo shook her head and grinned, dismissing the comment, trying to downplay the awkwardness of the pause. She turned to take in the battery of displays, the dancing holographic images and the vivid plasma screens.

"All right," she said. "Guess I should start with CMO, right? They're the obvious suspects."

"The Institute's in lockdown, Joanna, every campus, all across the world. Nobody's going out, not until I'm certain dataDyne won't be landing an advance assault force on our front lawn."

"Okay, that's everyone, but that's not me."

Jo gnawed on her bottom lip, thinking. One of the holographs was projecting an image of her, captured from the footage of Shin Matsuo's heart attack. A wire-frame had been overlaid on the image, and call-outs floated at the periphery, drawing lines to various points on the image's body, declaring percentage matches, offsets. According to the readout, the woman hovering at Shin Matsuo's side, giving him mouth-to-mouth, was a 99.4 percent match with Joanna Dark.

"CMO's been the one to gain the most," she said. "They've got to have an idea who's behind this if they're not behind this themselves."

"You're not listening to me, Jo," Carrington said. "I'm not authorizing any action. You're staying here."

She turned away from the image of herself, of her doppelganger, and found that Carrington was watching her, his stare heavy. She recognized the look, because she'd seen it before, but never actually directed at her. In the past, it had always been leveled at Jonathan. It was the look Carrington pulled out when he was ending debate, when he was taking the last word on a subject.

It made her angry.

"That's *me* up there," Jo said, sweeping a free hand toward the holograph without thinking, and feeling the consequent lance of pain bending around her chest. She swallowed it, struggling to hide her discomfort. "That's my face!"

"But it's not you, Jo."

"You can't ask me to just sit here and wait around while some CMO harpy is killing in my name!"

"So you think I can make a precarious situation better by sending you out to do the same? You're not thinking, Jo. You're publicly linked to two high-profile deaths, dataDyne and Beck-Yama are certainly looking for you, and if your imposter *is* out of CMO, then they're undoubtedly trying to track you as well, just to keep from having two of you in the same place at the same time. I'd be daft to send you out there with your lack of subtlety."

Indignation made Jo's voice climb. "I can be subtle!"

"Not when you're angry you can't, and you're clearly livid at the moment. No, Jo, I can't allow it. Even if the situation was different, if I wasn't in fear of an imminent dataDyne attack, I still couldn't. No, the last thing I need right now with a fake one of you out there killing is the real one doing the same thing."

"You can't make me stay here!"

"I can't?"

"No!"

Carrington frowned slightly, as if considering the merits of her argument, but only for a fraction. Then he said, "Tie your boots, Jo."

Jo balked. "What?"

Using the tip of his cane, Carrington indicated her feet. "Your boots are untied, you could trip and hurt yourself. Tie them."

"They're fine."

"I'm just asking you to tie your boots, Jo," Carrington said with convincing paternal care.

"I don't need to tie them," Jo said, and it sounded incredibly lame, even to her, a child's petulant refusal.

"You mean you can't tie them."

Heat crept suddenly up her neck, and Joanna could feel it

leaching into her cheeks, and she knew Carrington could see it, and it made her all the more furious. She shrugged, trying to convey that he was the one being unreasonable, not her, then moved for the nearest chair.

"No," Carrington said. "Do it standing up, Jo."

She stopped, and now she knew her cheeks were flushed, and she only hoped the subdued lighting of the Ops Center was concealing it from the old man's sight. Grimshaw had looked up from his work, was watching the interaction curiously. She hoped he hadn't actually heard what had been said, was reacting to the sight rather than the sound.

Gritting her teeth, Joanna bent forward and reached for her right boot. Instantly, her ribs began shrieking their protest. She kept herself from gasping with the pain, tried to continue the motion forward, slowing without wanting to, and then the bullet wound joined the chorus of protests, and she knew she was biting her lip to keep from making a sound.

"Stop," Carrington said, and Joanna froze. "Don't, please. I have never relished watching another's suffering, and watching yours is all the more distasteful."

He moved forward, and she felt his hand, light on her shoulder.

Carefully, her whole body burning with the sense of failure and humiliation, Joanna straightened up once more, meeting Carrington's gaze. His expression had softened to something approaching pity, and Joanna hated that all the more.

"I can do it," she told him.

"No," Daniel Carrington said. "But you'd willingly kill yourself trying."

She broke the stare, looking down, and found herself staring at her untied boots.

"You're confined to the Institute grounds for the duration of the lockdown, Jo," Carrington told her gently. "Now, please . . . go to your room."

Feeling as sullen as the child Carrington seemed to think she was, Jo turned and left the Ops Center. As she stepped through the doors and back out into the hall, she could have sworn she heard someone laughing, and it took her a half-second longer to realize that it had been imagined, and that, in her imagination, the one who had been doing it was Jack Dark.

Laughing at his daughter's continued failures.

Carrington Institute Grounds
London, England
January 23rd, 2021

As the man responsible for the Institute's security, Jonathan
Steinberg also knew its weaknesses. Where the gaps in the
surveillance net lay, where the floodlights wouldn't quite il-
luminate, where the sensors were overwhelmed by ambient
sound and natural movement. Given that they were, as far as
he was concerned, at a state of war, he'd done everything he
could to fill those gaps. But there were still holes, albeit
small ones, the places where no matter how hard one tried,
something or someone could slip through.

As he approached Joanna Dark, as she was preparing to
get over the wall on the northwestern side of the lake, he
comforted himself with the thought that the security had
been designed to keep people out and not to keep people in.
He told himself this was how she'd managed to get this far
without his spotting her.

Yeah, Steinberg thought. *Right.*

She was wearing street clothes, having ditched her Carrington Institute uniform, and was now in the cargo pants

and mismatched combination of T-shirts she'd favored when working with her father. She'd added a jacket as insulation against the cold, but as Steinberg watched her struggling at the wall, he realized that she hadn't really acquired a new wardrobe at all. The shirts were still too short, belly style, and he was positive that, were he closer, he would be able to see the bandages wrapping her middle, trying vainly to stabilize her ribs as she reached high. She heaved a small backpack up and over the wall, and the sound of her exertion, of the pain it was causing her, made it to his ears, even though he knew she was trying to hide it.

The thought of Joanna reaching, over and over again, for the top of the wall and of how much that had to hurt made Steinberg wince.

"Okay," he said. "You *really* have to stop doing that."

Joanna froze in mid reach, then dropped her arms and pivoted slowly to face him. Her expression was flat, no sign of guilt or embarrassment at having been caught. Maybe just the hint of annoyance that he had been the one to do it.

"Now I'm going to have to send someone around to get your pack," Steinberg said, approaching. "You are such the troublemaker."

"Don't bother, I'll pick it up on my way out."

"You're not going out, Jo. I'm taking you back to bed."

"Is that an offer, Mr. Steinberg?"

"You're hurt, Jo. You go out there looking to mix it up with CMO and God knows whoever else, you're only going to get hurt worse. You might even get dead."

She leaned back against the wall, folding her arms across her middle and fixing him with her deadeye stare. It was a good one, Steinberg had to admit. He'd known snipers who'd had thousand-yard-stares that didn't intimidate as much as Joanna Dark's.

"I'm waiting," Joanna said.

"For?"

"For the part where you tell me how this is different from any other time Carrington sends me out to do something. Of course it's dangerous, of course I can get killed. That's never stopped me, and come to think of it, it's never stopped you, either."

"It's different because this time the Old Man told you specifically to stay put."

"Then he should have tranqued me, because we both know that wasn't going to do it."

Steinberg started to retort, then stopped, thinking about what she'd just said.

Damn, he thought. *She's right. Carrington's doing it again. He's using her again.*

She caught the change in his expression, misread it.

"I'm going over, Jonathan. You can help me or you can get out of the way."

Steinberg shook his head slightly, coming closer, still in his own thoughts. It was the way Carrington worked, or at least how he worked with Joanna. Winding her up and turning her loose, manipulating her with a nudge here and a comment there. She was absolutely right; if Carrington truly hadn't wanted her to go out making trouble, he'd have made damn sure she couldn't. Which meant that he *was* doing it again, he was sending Jo out to draw fire.

She was still watching him, the same look of defiance on her face, and Steinberg had to wonder if she knew that she was being played. The anger at Carrington that he'd thought he'd misplaced five days earlier came thundering back. She was hurt, she was seriously injured. She'd been through one wringer already. To let her go through another one, so soon, it wasn't just wrong, it was practically criminal.

"Well?" Jo demanded. "You going to help me here or what?"

He was about to say that no, he damn well wasn't, he was about to tell her that Carrington was playing his games again, when a second thought struck him, and it hit hard enough to give him pause. Yes, Carrington was a manipulative bastard when he wanted to be, when he needed to be, but he wasn't, as far as Steinberg was concerned, an immoral man, nor was he a cruel man. He absolutely knew just how injured Joanna was, just how badly she needed time to heal, to recover.

But he'd wound her up all the same.

Dear Lord, Steinberg realized. *He really has no idea what's going on. Carrington really has no idea who's behind this at all.*

That scared him.

Steinberg had to admit that it scared him a lot, in fact.

"Where are you going?" he asked her.

"Right now, up and over. Then I'm going to Paddington to catch the express to Heathrow."

"And then?"

Joanna narrowed her eyes at him, suspicious. "Why?"

"What's the plan of attack here, Jo?"

She frowned, trying to fathom the reason behind the question. "Going after Core-Mantis. They're the obvious lead."

"Yeah, but how're you going to do it?"

"Oh, you know." She flashed him a grin, her teeth visible in the near-darkness. "The usual way."

Maybe I'm wrong, Steinberg thought. *Maybe I'm paranoid, maybe I'm being unfair to Carrington.*

"You're hurt, Jo. You go for the guns-a-blazing tactic, that could—correction, that *will*—backfire. You're at half-speed, if that."

"I would like to point out that my half-speed is better than your full speed, Mr. Steinberg."

"This isn't a contest. It's beyond serious out there. You leave, you may find it impossible to come back."

That seemed to worry her. "You think Carrington will fire me?"

"No, I think there might not be an Institute to come back to, Jo. It might just be a smoking crater patrolled by data-Dyne Shock Troopers."

The concern that had flooded her expression vanished, and she gave him a look that he suspected was most often seen directed at the village idiot. "Oh, that. C'mon, you can take them. You have before."

Steinberg found himself smiling without meaning to, had to fight it back down, but of course she had seen it, and her own grin was even brighter than before. Here they were, about to go to war with who knew how many hypercorps, and there was Joanna Dark saying, hey, easy, we can take them.

Joanna indicated the wall behind her with a turn of her head, then looked back at him. "C'mon, give me a hand."

"You're sure about this?"

"Jonathan, someone's out there using my face to start a fight. The only one who gets to do that is *me*. I am totally sure about this. It sure as hell is better than just waiting around her for dataDyne or Core-Mantis or whoever to come and attack us."

"Can't argue with that."

"I know. You want to make yourself useful? I'm going to need a contact back here, and obviously I can't go through the Ops Center."

"You want me to act as your controller again?"

"Well, yeah. You're not too bad at it, even if you almost got me killed last time."

"I *kept* you from getting killed last time, thank you," Steinberg said.

"If that's what lets you sleep at night."

Steinberg sighed, glanced back across the lake, at the floodlights illuminating the main campus buildings. He could just see the silhouettes of one of the anti-aircraft crews, manning their battery. He turned back to Jo, still watching him expectantly. He sighed again, and took the interface pad for the perimeter alarms from the breast pocket of his tactical vest.

"Command, this is Alpha," he said. "Shutting down grid delta-six, sensor check."

"Alpha, confirmed."

He tapped at the red-lined symbols glowing on his touch screen, waited for the icon representing delta-six to turn to green. Then he tucked the interface pad back in his pocket.

"All right," Steinberg said, coming forward to the wall and lacing his hands together as a step for Joanna to use. "Let's see what we can do."

"You're my guy," Jo told him, and with a grunt she stepped her right foot into his hands, then reached up for the wall and pulled herself to the top. "Talk to you soon."

Steinberg stepped back, opening his mouth for a last word, but she'd already gone over, then out of sight. He sighed for a third time, profoundly tired and profoundly worried, then keyed the receiver in his pocket, turning the sector's alarm grid back on.

"You might want to tie your boots," Steinberg said softly, and then he moved away, continuing his audit of the perimeter defenses.

Ted Reilly's Irish Bar
Durbin, South Africa
January 24th, 2021

Chun Fan entered the bar wearing her own face, and the handful of drunks already working their way through their mid-morning drinks barely paid her any mind. She doubted their reaction would have been any different had she entered wearing the shape of Joanna Dark, or even the shape of an eight-hundred-pound gorilla. She held for a moment just inside the doorway, savoring the coolness of the air, the respite from the summertime heat. It wasn't past eleven in the morning in Durbin, and the temperature was already rivaling that of summertime in Sichuan. She waited, letting her eyes adjust, taking in the room.

There were seven men present, six patrons and the barman, and the barman was apparently either so good at his job, or so bored by it, that he performed his duties while wearing a dataDyne "entertainMe" rig. He acknowledged Fan's entrance by turning his head her way briefly, and Fan wondered what she was sharing with his vision, what images were superimposed over her own. A sporting event, she suspected. Of the remaining six, five were far more concerned with the contents of their glasses than with the arrival of a somewhat short Chinese girl; the sixth, however, glanced up at her arrival, fixing her with a steely-eyed stare that seemed at once to appraise, condemn, and dismiss. Then he, too, returned his attention to his drink.

But it was enough for Fan to be sure he was the man she was after. He was dressed like an off-duty soldier, because that's what he was, or at least, that's what he wanted people to believe. In his midfifties, with a military haircut of salt and pepper, he looked to her eyes like a fit, if somewhat slender, American.

It was definitely him, but that didn't surprise her, because she'd had no doubt that he would be. The Continuity had been tracking former Marine colonel Leland Shaw, the Hawk Team commanding officer, for twenty-two days, now, and for the last five of them, he'd been here, in Durbin.

Fan hopped down the two steps from the entrance to the main floor, crossing to the bar. She felt giddy, the same sense of delighted excitement she'd shared with Ke-Ling back at the mansion still thrilling her. Things were going very well. Everything, everyone, was where they were supposed to be, doing what they were supposed to do. Her brothers and sisters, of course, because they knew the stakes of the game; Leland Shaw, drinking in a South African bar because he'd discovered that he was, beyond a doubt, a failure; the Bitch, now confirmed to still be cowering in New Zealand; Core-Mantis, methodically dismantling Beck-Yama exactly as the Continuity had advised them to do; even Daniel Carrington, still paralyzed by his confusion and his concerns.

And best of all, just as she'd arrived in South Africa, Shuang had called on Fan's d-PAL with an update on the real Joanna Dark.

"She just got on a Runyon-Adams commercial low-orbit

for Mexico City," Shuang said. "Zi got video of her as she went through security, then again as she boarded. Definitely going to Mexico, but we're not sure why. Carrington doesn't have an office there or anything."

"Core-Mantis does," Fan said.

"Oh. Right."

"She's traveling alone?"

Shuang nodded, adjusting the shoulders of her too-big dress. "And public transport, Fan! She's going solo, and that means that Carrington doesn't know she's going, right? Because if it was an op, she'd be using Institute transport, right? So she's got to be on her own."

"Maybe. Doesn't matter. You told Ke-Ling?"

"I told everyone!"

"I want her welcomed right, Shuang, just like we discussed, okay? Everyone on their best behavior. Did you find out what she likes to eat?"

Shuang's look of delight shifted to one of frustration. "It's hard! She eats, like, everything! Burgers and sushi and tofu and steak and, like, everything!"

"Make it steaks, then. The really good ones, the Kobe ones, okay? I'll call you when I'm done with the meeting. Love you."

"Love you, too!"

Shuang's face had vanished from the screen of the d-PAL, and Fan had tucked the tiny PDA back into the pocket of her jeans, then headed for Ted Reilly's.

|||||||||||||||||||

Fan bought a bottle of bourbon from the barman, who didn't seem to care that she was clearly underage, paying with her credit strip. Bottle in hand, she made her way to the rear of the bar, then flopped down opposite Leland Shaw in his booth.

Without looking up from his drink, Shaw said, "Taken."

Fan tilted her head, bending until she was almost resting her ear on the tabletop, trying to meet the man's eyes, and she had to hold it for half a second before he did, sparing her a glance. Fan grinned, and his expression didn't change, but the look in his eyes was nakedly hostile.

Straightening up, Fan wrestled with the wax seal at the top of her bottle, peeling it back to expose the stopper. She uncorked the bourbon, bent her head again to catch Shaw's eyes a second time, and when their gazes met again, she proceeded to top off his glass. Then she set the bottle between it and Shaw's half-filled ashtray and sat back.

"Always sit with your back to the wall, Colonel?"

"Find I live longer that way," Shaw said. He spoke slowly, but his words were clear, and Fan thought that if the man was drunk, he was doing a good job of covering it. He spoke with a slight twang, his accent from someplace deep in the American South. "And before you try to threaten or seduce or whatever me, little girl, you should check beneath the table."

Fan leaned forward slightly, excited. "Do you have a gun on me?"

Shaw blinked at her almost sleepily. "Couple ways you can find out. Being stupid is the quickest."

"Oh, no, that's not me, Colonel. I'm not stupid." Fan's smile grew. "What about you?"

Shaw's expression didn't change, but the hostility in his eyes flickered, then died of fatigue. After a moment, he brought up the hand he'd been holding beneath the tabletop, setting a P9P—the fancy tricked-out model with the titanium slide—beside his glass.

"I'm not looking for company," he said. "And you're too young for me even if I was."

"Well, not *company*, no. But maybe *a* company, yes? Some

nice corporate master to keep you and your Hawks on re-
tainer, to let you ease into the future you so richly deserve?"

The fatigue and boredom drained away, the hostility in
Shaw's expression returning.

"But you blew-blew-blew it, didn't you, Colonel Lee?"
Fan rested her elbows on the table, put her chin in her hands.
"You built the Hawk Teams as your meal ticket. Made a private army of specialized soldiers and then worked so super
hard to erase their existence, to keep everything they did de-
niable. Perfect for a hypercorp in trouble, just call Shaw and
the Hawks, they'll take care of it with no muss, no fuss, no
blowback, guaranteed rate of success, no failures, all that."

"That's right," Shaw said slowly.

"How's that been working out, Colonel? How's that record
looking these days? Offers for use of your services just rolling
in, are they?"

Shaw scowled, and Fan watched as his eyes moved to the
pistol lying beside the ashtray on the table, then back to her.

"You could," Fan agreed. "But it'd be the stupidest thing
you've ever done in your life if you did."

"Way you're talking, little girl, I'm willing to take that
chance."

"Yeah, but you're not thinking about your future, Colonel, and that's why I'm here, that's why I've taken the trouble to track you down. C'mon, now, use that military mind.
Girl walks into a bar just to find you, she's got to have a reason, an offer, right?"

"So far I'm hearing nothing but insults," Shaw said. "If I
wanted that, I'd remarry."

Fan laughed. "See? I knew I was right about you! I knew
you were the one I wanted!"

"For what?"

She lifted her chin from her hands, gestured wide. "To
help me run dataDyne, Colonel Shaw."

Now it was Colonel Leland Shaw's turn to laugh.

"Oh, that's good," he said. "That's rich, that's really . . . that's really rich, little girl. You almost had me going there, the talk, the manner, you had it all. Right up to the punch line."

He stopped laughing, his expression turning to a snarl.

"Now get the hell out of here before I *do* shoot you."

"And we're back to the part where that would be stupid, and you're not, right?" Fan lowered her arms, leaned back. "You've just had a run of bad luck, that's all. That thing in the Solomon Islands, that wasn't your fault. The job in Los Angeles, how could you know it would turn out so bad? Eleven of your men in the LA morgue, guess that kind of ruins the whole leave-no-traces thing, doesn't it? And one of your guys gone rogue, then getting caught and locked away in a Carrington interrogation box? Rotten luck, that's all."

"Rotten luck," Shaw said. "But luck doesn't wash with the hypercorps, good, bad, or otherwise, and especially not with dataDyne. They want results, and they want them made-to-order. Or they get someone else."

"But I want you."

"You're not dataDyne."

"I will be. I'm going to be the next CEO of dataDyne, Colonel Shaw. I'm going to replace Cassandra DeVries by the end of the month, and you're going to help me."

"No kidding? I'm going to retire to one of those private oil-rig communities in the North Sea."

"Those aren't all they're cracked up to be. One system failure in the stabilization drive and they sink like you wouldn't believe." Fan extended her hand to Shaw. "Zhang Fan, Colonel Shaw. Pleased to meet you."

He looked at the offered hand as if expecting it to hold a joy buzzer. "Nice name."

Fan exhaled, showing frustration for the first time, then lowered her hand. "I'm his daughter, Colonel."

"His daughter was Mai Hem."

"She wasn't his only one. She was just the one he let the world know about."

"You really expect me to believe you?"

"I don't see why you shouldn't."

Shaw just shook his head, reached for his drink. He drained half of it, winced, then set the glass back on the table. "Get out of here."

"I know why you took the Hovoro job, Colonel Shaw, the job in the Solomons that you did for Cassandra De-Vries."

"I did the job because dataDyne pays very well."

"You did the job because you were trying to buy your future," Fan said. "You were hoping to make a good impression, perhaps such a good one that dataDyne would offer you a position. You looked at DeVries and you thought that yeah, maybe she would be the new CEO, and wouldn't it be nice if she thought you were everything you said you were. Maybe you even thought that the new CEO would want a new director of CORPSEC, that you could end up in Anita Velez's job. That would've been nice, wouldn't it? A data-Dyne director's salary and no more combat ops from the back of a dropship in the middle of nowhere."

Shaw's mouth had turned sour. Fan watched as he took a second drink, drained his glass.

"You're fifty-four years old. You've got two ex-wives, and you're carrying over three point eight million dollars in debt right now, just to cover back pay and equipment for the Hawks. That future you were eyeing is in shambles. You're growing old, you're growing tired, and worst of all, you're getting slow. You need a way out. I'm offering you one."

Shaw looked into his empty glass, then set it back on the table. Without looking away from him, Fan refilled it from the bottle.

"You have a d-PAL?" she asked.

"Sure."

"Check your account at the Imperial Bank, Macao. Account number three-zero-zero-nine-four-nine-seven-two-eight-two-six—"

"You know the account number, yeah, you've made your point," Shaw snapped, shifting in his seat to pull his d-PAL from his back pocket. Fan listened to it as it chimed to life, waited while Shaw initiated the global connect, then IDed his way into his account at the Imperial Bank of Macao. He looked at the readout on the d-PAL's tiny screen, then back to Fan. "Jesus Christ."

"Eight point six million dollars, Colonel," Fan said. "I had the funds deposited on my order before I left China this morning. Eight point six million dollars is, incidentally, the annual salary for the dataDyne Director of CORPSEC. Do you see where I'm going with this?"

Shaw stared at the readout from the d-PAL for what, to Fan, seemed like a very long time. Then he shut the PDA off, resting it on the table beside his pistol, and shifted his stare to Fan.

"What do I have to do?" he asked.

"It's so easy, Colonel, you're going to love it."

"Somehow I doubt that."

"Cassandra DeVries is going to contact you within the next two to three days. She's going to want a meeting, and she's going to offer you a job. I want you to take the job."

"And what's this job going to be, Miss Zhang?"

"You're going to be asked to kill someone, Colonel, a young woman by the name of Joanna. You've dealt with her twice already, I think. Once in Hovoro, once in Los Angeles."

Shaw's eyes narrowed. "The redhead."

"Yes, that's her."

"That girl's a nightmare, Miss Zhang. That girl is responsible for taking my perfect record and throwing it in the crapper, as far as I'm concerned."

"That's because you haven't been properly briefed about how to handle her, Colonel."

"Killing her won't be easy."

"I don't want you to kill her. I want you to bring her to me."

"Simple as that?"

"Simple as that, Colonel."

He shook his head. "You think it'll be that easy? I've seen footage of this kid in action, even if you haven't. She dropped eleven of my men—*eleven* of them. Hell, she blew one of our dropships out of the sky by manually planting a shaped charge on it. While it was still flying. There's no way she'll come quietly."

"I'm sure she will."

"Why?"

"Because you have something she desperately wants. You have a connection to her late father."

Shaw's look turned from puzzled to curious.

"Her father was Jack Dark," Fan told him.

The curiosity shifted, almost to wonder.

"Son of a bitch," Shaw said. "Jack Dark had a kid?"

"It certainly appears that way." Fan leaned forward once more, hopeful and genuine. "Now let's talk about exactly what I want you to do, and how you're going to go about doing it."

dataDyne Executive Safehouse
37 km ENE of Nelson, New Zealand
January 24th, 2021

The latest argument with Velez had begun on the previous
morning, after Velez had given her an update on the attempt
to locate and neutralize Carrington's Joanna. Three data-
Dyne "elimination teams"—small squads composed of the
most elite Shock Troopers at Velez's disposal—were at perpetual readiness, one currently in Tokyo, one in Seattle, and
one staged in Paris. The one in Paris, Velez explained, was
there because she felt it was too risky to stage the team from
London, so close to the Carrington Institute.

That wasn't the cause of the argument, however. The
cause of the argument came from Cassandra's discovery that
Velez had refused to authorize a visit by DataFlow Special
Projects Director Dr. Edward Ventura, on the grounds that it
was a violation of security protocol.

Even given the short time she had been CEO, the refusal
had taken Cassandra by surprise, and she found it incompre-
hensible and annoying.

"I'm the bloody CEO, if I want someone to come and visit me, I expect them to do just that," she told Velez.

"And in virtually every case, you would be correct in that expectation, Madame Director. But in matters of security, I must exercise my own judgment, and it is my judgment that a visit from anyone—no matter how trusted—to this safehouse is an unnecessary risk."

"I want Ventura here, Anita. I want a progress report on AirFlow 2, and I want it now."

"You can arrange that via video conference."

"I don't want it by conference, obviously! I want it in person, and I want it first thing in the morning. Make it happen!"

"Madame Director—" Velez started to say, but by then Cassandra had turned and was striding past the Shock Troopers posted on the door to her office, down the hall. Cassandra heard the other woman swear under her breath in German, heard her rushing to catch up. "Madame Director, please."

"I don't want to have to argue about this, Anita! I've got three thousand things to do, this really shouldn't be one that takes this much time!"

Velez came alongside, interposing herself between Cassandra and the windows along the hall, blocking the exquisite view. Cassandra knew the move for what it was, an instinctive effort to protect her from any possible threat from outside, and in the past it wouldn't have bothered her, would have, in fact, been flattering. But given that the house was surrounded by countersnipers, missile platforms, and Shock Troopers patrolling in jump rigs, it was, instead, all the more annoying.

"May I say something?" Velez asked.

"Oh, please."

Velez frowned, framing her words, and Cassandra wondered what she was going to be criticized for this time. They came off the hall into the kitchen, and the two Troopers posted there snapped to rigid attention even as the chef and her assistant reacted to the entrance. Cassandra ignored them all, moving to the coffeemaker, grabbing the nearest mug. Like every piece of glassware, silverware, and flatware in the house, the mug sported the dataDyne double-D diamond, in this case lain onto the porcelain in multifaceted paint. When the light caught it, the logo seemed to alternately glow in gold, platinum, and blue.

"There's no coffee," Cassandra said, upon discovering the carafe empty. "There's no bloody coffee. Would it be too much to ask that there be, *please,* some bloody damn coffee!"

"Certainly, ma'am," the chef said, coming forward and sending her assistant scurrying toward the nearest pantry with the wave of a hand. The chef was in her late forties, perhaps, a little matronly, and her response was both solicitous and apologetic. "We'll have it brought to you right away."

"You don't need to bring it to me, you just need to have it *made* when I want it," Cassandra snapped, and it sounded remarkably catty to herself, and she caught it, caught the chef's deferential avoiding of her eyes, and had a horrible moment where she could see herself as everyone else in the room no doubt could. She saw herself, and she was positive that she was acting like a grade-A bitch.

She set the mug back down on the marble-topped counter, took a breath, then smiled at the chef. "I'm sorry. It's just . . . been a day, and it's hardly begun."

"No, that's all right, ma'am."

"What's your name?"

"Elizabeth Green," the chef said.

"If you could have some coffee brought up to my office, Miss Green, I would be very grateful," Cassandra said.

Then she turned around and headed out of the kitchen the same way she had entered, Velez again at her side.

"You were going to say something," Cassandra said, after a moment.

"I was, Madame Director, but I think, perhaps, you have just realized it yourself."

"That I'm acting like a bitch?"

Velez shook her head, not hearing the joke, or perhaps not wanting to validate it with an acknowledgement. "You are overworked, and you are overstressed. Both are results of the job, of course, but I am concerned that you are not helping yourself."

"Meaning what, Anita?"

"Meaning, Madame Director, that you are still attempting to run dataDyne as you ran DataFlow. You are attempting micromanage the corporation, and you are clearly being overwhelmed."

"If you're saying I'm not capable of—"

Velez stopped abruptly, turning to Cassandra, looking sincere in both her concern and her care. "No, Madame Director, I would never say that. It is no shortcoming on your part, and, if I may be frank, if anyone could master it all, it would be you. But no one person could, not even Master Li. His gift was that he was brilliant at delegating duties, that he unerringly positioned the right person for the right job at every stage. And that, Madame Director, is a lesson you must learn, for your own sake as much as dataDyne's."

"I do delegate," Cassandra said. "I delegate all the time, Anita—you're speaking nonsense."

"You delegate only in the most minor instances, yes. It is not enough. You must leave the running of Patmos to Miss Waterberg, Madame Director, and oversee the results. You must leave the running of Dun-Chow to Mr. Zefu. And you must leave the management of AirFlow 2 to Dr. Ventura, and trust that he will deliver what you have asked of him."

Cassandra tried to keep from scowling, resisted the urge to

once again tell Velez that she was wrong, that she knew how to delegate responsibilities just fine. But gazing past her shoulder, out the hall windows and down toward the beach and the water, she found herself remembering the last beach she'd walked upon, the LuxeLife resort in Hawaii, where the board of directors had finally come to the conclusion that Zhang Li would have to be replaced. She'd hated being at the resort, had stayed in her room almost the entire time she'd been there, working as if she'd never even left her office in Paris.

Right up to the moment she'd realized where she was and what she was doing, and had finally allowed herself to go swimming.

Is this who I'm going to become? Cassandra wondered. *An isolated, bitchy workaholic?*

"I take your point," she said to Velez. "I take your point, Anita, and I am trying. But AirFlow 2 is important to me, it's my legacy at DataFlow. Let Edward come here, please. Screen him however you like, how much you like, but I need to meet with him in person, just to see how it's going."

After a second, Velez nodded, even offering a small smile of encouragement.

"Of course, Madame Director. He'll be here first thing in the morning."

Ventura arrived during breakfast, which for Cassandra now consisted more and more often of a piece of fruit and perhaps a cup of yogurt, hastily eaten during opportune pauses in phone conversations. She was beginning to question the necessity of having a chef on staff, considering that the woman's abilities were so rarely put to the test.

The question was burning her, but Cassandra managed to keep her eagerness in check, giving Ventura time to settle. He'd flown in from Paris via Moscow and then Sydney,

Velez's proscribed route, an attempt to keep Cassandra's location secret. In Sydney, he'd been collected by a clutch of plainclothed Shock Troopers for the remainder of the journey to New Zealand. Ventura hadn't been actually blindfolded for the last leg of the trip, but it was an academic difference at best, since he'd ridden in an R-C/Bowman Tumbler with the windows removed from the passenger compartment.

As he stepped into her office, taking in the view from the windows even as he removed his coat and set down his laptop and component cases, Cassandra could see him attempting to puzzle it out. She saw no malice in it, only curiosity; had she been in his position, she certainly would have enjoyed the intellectual puzzle of trying to ascertain exactly where on Earth she had been deposited.

She let Ventura get settled, then directed him to the freshly drawn French press of coffee that Green's assistant had delivered only moments before. Ventura went to it eagerly, and Cassandra suspected that, between the project deadlines on AirFlow 2 and the travel time, he was probably tottering on the verge of exhaustion. While he prepared his cup, she shut down all of her open lines, issuing a blanket command to her secretarial staff that she would be unavailable for the next half an hour. Then she asked Velez to clear the room of Troopers, until the only people who remained were herself, Velez, and Ventura.

Finally, unable to contain her excitement any longer, she came around her desk, perching on the end of it and facing Ventura where he sat in one of the black leather office chairs arrayed before her.

"How's Arthur?" she asked.

"Very well, ma'am, he's doing very well. Do you want to see him now?"

With difficulty, Cassandra shook her head. "Soon, not

yet. I should hear the status report first, don't you think Edward? We're still on target for the rollout?"

"Version 2 will be ready for the switch-over at the end of the month, ma'am, as promised."

"I've got marketing on the verge of hysteria because they've nothing to go on. They're planning the unveiling to take place at the offices in Paris. I'll want you there."

Dr. Edward Ventura seemed to positively shine with pride. "It will be an honor."

"How are the packets coming? What's the completion?"

"Ninety-seven percent complete, ma'am. The last batch of modules are in debugging now, and I'll review them when I return to the office."

"You solved the problem you were having with the heuristic routines?" Cassandra twisted from where she sat without actually getting up, began rummaging through the sheafs and sheafs of papers on her desk. "I made some notes about that, actually, Edward, if you want to see them. Well, actually, I wrote some code, but you should feel free to take them as notes."

She turned back, offering him the papers, and Ventura awkwardly shifted his cup and saucer from one hand to the other, attempting to balance both while reaching for the papers. Cassandra had to come off the desk to give him a hand, taking the coffee and setting it on the table.

"Certainly, thank you, ma'am," Ventura said, taking the notes. "I'll look at them on the flight back."

She smiled at him, at his nervousness and her own foolishness. If Zhang Li had summoned her to China while she'd been at work on AirFlow version 1, she doubted she could have managed to be calm, either. If he'd then proceeded to give her notes on the software, she probably would have been even more uncomfortable than Ventura was.

"It's all right, Edward," Cassandra said, smiling. "I trust

you, I know it's going brilliantly. It's only that the project is very close to my heart."

Ventura, who had been trying to straighten the tangle of papers she'd handed him, relaxed. "I understand, ma'am."

Cassandra glanced over to where Velez was standing in the corner by the windows, caught the older woman's reflection off the glass. Velez met her eyes, nodding slightly, as if acknowledging Cassandra's efforts to cease micromanaging.

She put her attention back on Ventura and said, "And now, yes, I'd very much like to see Arthur."

Ventura set aside the notes, getting to his feet with hasty enthusiasm. He opened his laptop, quickly passing the security checks and setting it to boot, then moved to the component case and began removing the module segments. They were small, almost milky white cubes, as if made of glass and filled with clouds, each no larger than a fist, each capable of holding over a million terabytes of storage. Adapted from the same technology used in the quantum optical computers dataDyne used for its datacore storage, the modules had been specifically designed by Cassandra, Ventura, and others during Cassandra's final few months as the director of DataFlow. Then, the cost of merely one had been so staggering as to be almost prohibitive.

Once Cassandra had become CEO, though, she'd promptly increased the budget on the project.

Carefully, Ventura linked the cubes together in a daisy chain of quantum optical cabling, then connected the whole series to his laptop. While he worked, he spoke.

"There may be some transfer delay, ma'am. I'm linking him with the main cognition units in Paris, and I don't know how much packet loss we'll have as a result. The Outland interface has been giving us some trouble, as well; if it does go down, I'll have to issue commands via keyboard."

"I'm sure it will be fine, Edward."

"I just don't want you to be disappointed by any apparent lag times. Computationally, he's testing at a quarter-millionth of a second for the traffic routing routines, and that's even when we throw failures at him, or large scale natural disasters."

"I'm sure it will be fine," Cassandra repeated, and then let herself slip off the edge of her desk and to her feet, approaching Ventura and his laptop. "Almost ready?"

He nodded, and she thought she could sense in him the same anticipation and excitement that she was trying to master in herself. Ventura crouched onto his haunches, level with the laptop resting on the coffee table, and brought up his terminal interface. Fingers flying, he typed in a long series of code, and then executed the sequence.

For several seconds, nothing happened at all, other than the monitor on Ventura's laptop going blank. Then the screen flickered, and fresh code began scrolling madly past, far too fast for either of them to read, let alone interpret.

Ventura looked up at Cassandra, smiling with pride. "Go ahead."

Somewhat surprised at the nervousness she was feeling, Cassandra cleared her throat before speaking.

"Arthur, can you hear me?"

The voice came from the laptop's speakers, almost a whisper. "Yes."

"I'm Dr. DeVries, Arthur. Do you know me?"

"Yes."

"Who am I?"

"You are the chief executive officer of dataDyne, my parent."

Cassandra DeVries realized she was smiling so broadly her cheeks were beginning to hurt. She exchanged glances with Ventura, who was grinning back at her, just as delighted, just as proud.

"Arthur, do you know your function?" she asked.

"To monitor and maintain the safe, efficient, and speedy flow of all null-g traffic throughout the world."

"And how will you do this?"

"Direct them."

"How many will you direct?"

"According to the most recent data, seven hundred and seventy-three million, eight hundred and sixty-six thousand, six hundred and ninety-two null-g vehicles are equipped with dataDyne AirFlow.Net transponders."

"That's quite a lot, Arthur," Cassandra said. "Are you certain you can manage them all?"

"Capacity at standard cycle of use for one point two billion null-g vehicles equipped with dataDyne AirFlow.Net transponders."

"It's a big responsibility. How do you feel about that?"

"Parsing error."

Cassandra saw Ventura's smile falter as he looked at her, and he shook his head slightly. She nodded, understanding. Sentient though Arthur might appear, he wasn't truly a living thing, he wasn't an actual artificial intelligence.

"Arthur," Ventura said. "Do you recognize me?"

"You are Dr. Edward Ventura."

"That's correct, I am. I want you to do something, Arthur."

"Waiting."

"Please compose a poem for Dr. DeVries."

"Specify form."

"Short form, rhyming."

"Down black trees / please peas tease / around yet wheeze."

Ventura was watching for her reaction, and Cassandra couldn't help but feel her smile falter, feel the sadness in it.

So close, she thought. *So very close, but not quite. Almost sentient. Almost.*

"Thank you, Arthur," Cassandra said. "That will be all for now. You may resume learning."

"Thank you," the voice from the laptop said, and then the screen went dark once more, flickered, and returned to its desktop.

"There's no sense of self," Ventura said. "No matter how we run at it, there's no sense of self. Arthur's aware as an *entity*, but not as an individual. Consequently, he lacks imagination, which isn't the same as lacking innovation, because that's not the case at all. His problem-solving skills are phenomenal, to such an extent he's even started to avoid the basic traps."

"Pi," Cassandra said.

"Square root of negative one, yeah, like that."

Ventura closed the component case, latching it shut. "I have no doubts about his ability to manage the system. Arthur *is* AirFlow.Net version 2, he's already up and running. As far as that goes, all you need to do is present him to the public and tie him into the existing network, he'll do the rest. Everything else is honestly minor."

She nodded, staring past him, at the ocean beyond her window, feeling as surprised by her indefinable sadness as she had by her nervousness upon speaking to the computer. Calling the intelligence "Arthur," she realized, had probably been a mistake. Cassandra had meant it as an homage to her brother, a memoriam of a sort. But in so doing she had invested a personality in the machine that simply couldn't and wouldn't ever be there. Arthur DeVries was dead, and naming a semisentient AI Arthur just reinforced that point.

Ventura was standing in front of her desk, each of his cases in each of his hands, and Velez had moved in, ready to offer an escort to the door. He'd been saying something to her, but she'd missed it.

"I'm sorry, Edward, what was that?"

"I said I brought the code on the final module sets, if you want to review them, ma'am."

She looked past his shoulder, to Velez.

"No, Edward," Cassandra said. "I'll trust you to handle it. Have a safe trip home."

"Thank you, ma'am."

Velez escorted him to the door, and for a moment, Cassandra DeVries was alone, in silence.

Then she sighed, reinserted the earpiece for her phone, and began working through the seventy-three phone calls that had appeared on her call list during her meeting with Ventura.

CHAPTER

10

Core-Mantis OmniGlobal Regional
Supervisory and Administrative
Offices—Zona Rosa
Mexico City, Mexico
January 24th, 2021

Leaving London had been easy; deciding where to go was
the hard part.

Jo had left the Institute knowing that the quickest way to
her answers would be via Core-Mantis OmniGlobal and that
there were a number of ways she could go about acquiring
them, even if CMO proved reticent to share. Like every other
hypercorp, they had offices dotted all around the globe, with
hundreds of additional subsidiaries besides. There was an office in the Netherlands, she knew, and another in Prague, now
rumored by Institute intelligence to house a new quantum optical computer. There were branches throughout North and
South America, as well as Europe. Until recently, they'd held
nothing in Asia, though the impending fall of Beck-Yama was
about to change that, of course.

So Jo could pick an office, perhaps try to enter it covertly,
to gain her answers that way. It would be difficult, she knew,

especially given the wounds she was carrying. Without the Institute backing her with oversight and equipment, the task would be more difficult still. As far as that went, she had Steinberg and the gear she'd shoved in her pack, and that was it. Of the two, she wasn't certain which would actually prove the more useful—Steinberg sneaking around behind Carrington's back learning whatever he could, or the P9P pistol with its silencer and extra clips and the handful of other equipment she'd brought along with her.

The covert approach was certainly an option, even if it wasn't the most viable one.

Then there was the old-fashioned way, the way her father would have gone about it. The catch-and-release method, he liked to call it. Find the smallest fish in the pond you're currently searching, and proceed to bang his or her head against table, wall, floor, or other suitable surface until said fish gave up the name of the next, slightly larger fish in the pond. Repeat ad nauseum until either reaching your goal, or until running out of fish.

Catch and release. Bash and repeat.

It was tedious, it was slow, and it was labor intensive, since most of the fish had a tendency to wriggle, and a lot of them had the tendency to flee.

There was also a very good chance that the method wouldn't work in this instance. It was a fine technique for hunting down a skip who was hiding in a sea of perps. But getting information from hypercorp suits was always a different matter, because they would always have one thing they feared more than Joanna Dark, and that was their corporation itself. There was also the further complication that, in all likelihood, Jo would find herself facing CMO security at some point, and security would probably take a dim view of her interrogation techniques and would want to explain that displeasure to her. Probably using bullets.

The shape she was in, she didn't know how long she would last if it came to that.

So, in the end, the only real option was the most direct and, Jo supposed, the most civilized one.

She would go to CMO and she would ask them for information. Politely. Graciously.

She would even say "please."

||||||| ||| |||||

Jo decided on visiting Core-Mantis OmniGlobal's offices in Mexico City for several reasons. The first was that Mexico was considered, at least as far as the hypercorps were concerned, CMO's domain. They had established themselves in the country early on and had entrenched themselves quickly even as their operations had grown and spread throughout the rest of North America and Europe.

This went to the second reason, which was the fact that dataDyne—as yet—had no official presence in Mexico. Not for lack of trying, but between CMO's desire to keep data-Dyne out and dataDyne's demands for substantial revision and exemptions under current Mexican corporate law, no true progress had been made. It wouldn't last much longer, Jo knew; in the end, dataDyne would get their way, simply because they were bigger, and richer, and maybe even meaner than CMO.

The same could be said, after a fashion, of Beck-Yama. While the corporation was clearly drawing its final breaths, Jo knew that there were BYI people still actively seeking her; or, more precisely, they were actively seeking her doppelganger, which, in this instance, meant the same thing. Even if Beck-Yama InterNational wouldn't be a problem for much longer—and Jo, who had checked the news upon landing in Mexico City and seen that CMO had acquired and absorbed another three BYI subsidiaries, knew that they wouldn't be—there was no reason to risk it, not given the state she was in.

But the most important reason of all for coming to Mexico City was that Daniel Carrington had no presence there, either, and the last thing Jo wanted was some eager operative reporting back to London that Agent Dark had been seen walking the Zona Rosa. If that happened, Jo was sure the Old Man would blow a gasket, and then send Steinberg and maybe half a dozen others to bring her back to the Institute in London. Drugged and bound, if they had to.

So the choice was really made for her, as far as that went.

<hr />

From the airport, Jo took a null-g cab into Mexico City proper, straight to the Core-Mantis offices in the Zona Rosa. She gave the cabbie a hundred dollars and asked him to keep the meter running, then, leaving her jacket and backpack in the cab, she headed into the offices. She had no fear that the taxi would depart with her things, nor was she afraid of being robbed; asking the driver to take her to the Core-Mantis main office in town had the same effect as asking to be dropped off at the nearest police station. There was no way the cabbie would risk antagonizing CMO, even if he had no way of knowing that Jo wasn't one of their employees.

As for entering the offices light, Jo was positive that whatever security CMO had in place, it was going to be better than what she'd encountered at Heathrow. It was one of the things she was counting on, the fact that some command post or surveillance center buried deep inside the building would ensure that by the time she entered, she would not be seen as a threat.

It turned out that she'd made the right decision. Entering the lobby required passage through three separate checkpoints, and Jo was certain she was scanned at least that many times in addition to probing waves searching her for implanted electronics or other implements of espionage or sabotage. At the final checkpoint, she was steered into the visitor's line, where her ID was checked, and she was subjected to a thorough, but quick, pat down.

Once through the gauntlet, she headed across the lobby to the main desk, black-clad Core-Mantis security guards watching her advance every step of the way. Jo liked almost everything about the lobby, thinking that it was tasteful, very open, and generally welcoming. High windows allowed the sunlight in without condemning everyone inside to bake come the heat of summer. The floor, which she had expected to be of marble, was actually composed of tiles of Italian glass, and it gave the space a color and sense of vibrancy markedly different from any of the other hypercorp offices she had ever visited.

The only thing she didn't like about the lobby was the massive portrait of Shane Eddy, which seemed to cover most of one of the side walls. It was done in oil paints, or at least in something that was supposed to give the impression of an oil painting, almost classic in its styling. In it, Eddy posed with the CMO flag, standing at Tranquility Base, Earthrise visible in the background. As if to offset, or perhaps apologize, for the garishness of the piece, a stylized sculpture of the CMO logo hung from the opposite wall, almost to the same scale as the portrait.

Jo liked the sculpture, though something about it struck her as surprisingly feminine.

The young man working the front desk was very polite, very handsome, and didn't look that much older than Jo.

"May I help you?" he asked her in English.

"I do hope so," Jo said. "I'd like to speak with one of your employees, Portia de Carcareas."

The young man brought up the building directory on his terminal, saying, "Is she expecting you?"

"I'd be a little surprised if she was."

The man grinned, then abruptly changed it to a frown. "I can't seem to find a Carcareas in the directory. Perhaps I'm misspelling it?"

Jo spelled it out for him, and he tried again, gaining the same result.

"There's no Carcareas listed, I'm afraid." He smiled up at her, apologetic. "Are you sure you have the right office?"

"Actually, I'm not." Jo smiled right back at him. "That's part of my problem, I don't know which office she works out of."

"I'm not certain I can help you, then. It's against Core-Mantis OmniGlobal policy to give out information concerning personnel."

"Security," Jo said, commiserating.

"You know how it is."

"I do." She leaned forward slightly, making certain that, in doing so, at least three of the surveillance cameras she'd noted in the lobby could capture some really good pictures of her face. "Could you try this for me then? Contact your head of security for the building, and let them know that Joanna Dark is here, and that she'd very much like to arrange a meeting with Portia de Carcareas."

"That's . . . that's very irregular."

"Tell me about it," Jo said, and then crossed the lobby to the sitting area, taking a place on one of the four couches there. There were magazines, all of them issues of the CMO in-house publication, *Meritorious,* and she contented herself for almost ten minutes by leafing her way through them. All were filled with the standard hypercorp propaganda, though in one issue Jo discovered a photo spread documenting Shane Eddy's most recent journey to the Nepal Himalaya. It was, according to the accompanying article, the fifth time Eddy had achieved the summit of Mount Everest, and this time, he'd done it without the aid of Sherpas, using only

CMO-produced clothing and gear. Jo spent some time examining the photographs, trying to determine if they were fakes or not.

She was still undecided about them when she heard the clacking of heels on the tile, approaching her. Jo kept her attention on the magazine, making the very active decision to appear as nonthreatening as possible.

"You are Joanna Dark?"

Jo closed the magazine, setting it aside and looking up to see a tall and slender woman addressing her. She was African, tall and bald, with flawless skin so dark it seemed that her body turned to shadow inside her black CMO security uniform.

"Yes, I am," Jo said.

The woman studied her, as if unsure what to say next. She'd approached her alone, but Jo noted that the number of CMO guards in the lobby had increased, albeit subtly, as if preparing for a shift change. For the most part, the guards were all doing a good job of pretending to pay her no attention.

The woman said, "I'm Colonel Ainia Tachi-Amosa, commanding officer of the Fourth Division, Xiphos Company. I'm the regional director of security, Miss Dark."

"I'm honored."

The woman arched an eyebrow as if doubting Jo's sincerity. "Why are you looking for Miss Carcareas, Miss Dark?"

"I have some questions for her."

"And what is the nature of these inquiries, please?"

By way of an answer, Jo made a deliberate display of showing Ainia Tachi-Amosa her profile, first her left, then her right.

"Right face," Jo said. "Wrong person."

Colonel Tachi-Amosa stared at her, and Jo thought she looked confused for a moment, but then the woman nodded slightly. "Are you here as an agent of the Carrington Institute, Miss Dark? Or are you acting on your own accord?"

"Both, actually."

The colonel considered that, then said, "Perhaps you would be willing to discuss this in my office? You might be more comfortable."

Jo hesitated, conflicted. There was nothing overtly hostile about Colonel Tachi-Amosa, nothing that was striking her as an immediate threat, but going deeper into Core-Mantis hadn't been part of her plan. If her doppelganger was, in fact, a CMO agent working in disguise, it was conceivably a very dangerous thing for Jo to do.

The colonel waited, then added, "You were comprehensively scanned when you entered the building, Miss Dark. I know you are unarmed. I also know that your ribs must be giving you quite a bit of discomfort. My offer is sincere. We can speak more freely in my office, and in more comfort."

"I have a cab waiting," Jo said. "It has my bag in it."

"I can send someone to fetch it."

"There's a pistol in the bag, a P9P, and a datathief."

The colonel did the move with her eyebrow again, letting it rise, then fall, before saying, "You're very blunt, Miss Dark. I appreciate the candor. I will have the bag held for you at the desk here, with my word that it will not be opened."

Jo thought about that, thought that, once again, she was potentially being very foolish.

Then again, she told herself, *this is what you came here for, to talk. You'd be a fool to turn your back on the offer.*

Jo took a breath, then got to her feet. Her ribs positively hummed with pain, but she kept it off her face.

"Lead on," she said.

Most of Joanna's contact with Core-Mantis in the past had been peripheral, occurring at a distance. The closest she'd actually ever come to disrupting one of their operations had been during the mission in Los Angeles, and even then, it had been practically incidental. It wasn't because Core-Mantis didn't pose a threat—they were a hypercorp, and as far as Jo was concerned, that was enough to prove villainous intent. But compared to dataDyne, they were bush league, or had been until the last week.

Walking with Colonel Tachi-Amosa through the building, followed at a respectful distance by two uniformed guards, Jo could see that things were changing. There was a charge in the air, a palpable sense of energy and anticipation that seemed to flow out of each and every office they passed, that seemed to rise from every employee she saw. Twice while passing closed doors, Jo heard laughter coming from within, and it sounded genuine, and that both bewildered and surprised her.

She couldn't remember the last time she'd heard someone at the Institute laughing.

They reached Tachi-Amosa's office, the colonel dismissing the guards as she led Jo inside, directing her to a seat. It wasn't a small office, but, like the lobby, effort had been put into its design and layout, so that it felt both brighter and more spacious than it actually was. There was the requisite desk, relatively clean and not so large as to be ostentatious, and a compact seating area off to one side with a couch and easy chairs. Bookshelves covered one wall, cloth hardcovers with glossy jackets, and hanging opposite was a hi-res satellite map of Mexico. A second door was positioned in the wall near the desk, closed, and Jo guessed that being a colonel rated having your own bathroom. Behind the desk was a large window-monitor, showing multiple screens displaying all manner of data, including the ubiquitous stock ticker and talking-head newsfeed.

The colonel moved to her desk, pressing a key on the control surface, and the monitors faded away, the tint of the window increasing slightly. She pressed a second button, and for an instant, Jo heard an almost inaudible ascending whine, and then that sound, too, disappeared.

"Countermeasures," the colonel told her. "I hate eavesdroppers, and I don't want you to worry that this conversation is being overheard."

"You don't?" Jo didn't bother trying to not look puzzled. She had expected that everything she said or did, if not in the building then certainly in the colonel's office, would be placed on record somehow, someplace. "Why not?"

"Two reasons, honestly. The first is that it's unnecessary. If it's important, I'll remember it. The second is that I'd rather the official record be vague on this meeting." Tachi-Amosa made a general sweeping gesture with one hand, toward the seating area. "Make yourself comfortable. Have you eaten? Would you like something to drink?"

Jo shook her head, lowering herself into one of the easy chairs, and trying to figure out why Colonel Ainia Tachi-Amosa, commanding officer of the Fourth Division, Xiphos Company, was being so nice to her. The colonel watched as she sat, her expression neutral, then moved to take the chair opposite, so the two of them could speak facing each other.

"Now, Miss Dark," she said. "Why don't you tell me what you really want?"

"I want to speak to Portia de Carcareas."

"Why her, specifically?"

"Because I've only ever known the name of one other person who worked for CMO, and she's dead now."

"Did you kill her?"

Jo shook her head. The woman in question had taken her own life, and had done so out of despair and guilt. The guilt had come from being forced to betray the Institute. The despair had come from the realization that it would never end. CMO had been responsible for both.

They look pretty on the outside, she told herself. *But they're as bad as dataDyne, and don't you forget that, Joanna.*

"You guys did," Jo said.

Colonel Tachi-Amosa frowned. "We don't kill our own."

"I didn't say she was one of your own, colonel. I said she worked for you. Not by choice."

That earned a slight nod of understanding. "Espionage is not my arena."

"But counterespionage is?"

"Partly, yes."

"Is that why we're talking in your office, off the record?"

"In part. In part because I'm curious what your intentions are." The colonel leaned her long body forward, resting her arms on her thighs. "I've seen the intelligence, Miss Dark, I know the favors you've been doing for Core-Mantis. But you say you're still working for the Carrington Institute. Does that mean the things you've been doing, you've been doing at Daniel Carrington's direction?"

Oh bloody hell, Joanna thought. *She doesn't know. She doesn't know it wasn't me who killed Bricker and Matsuo.*

"I don't take orders very well," Jo said by way of an answer, and because it was the truth.

"I see."

The colonel straightened in her seat, watching Jo closely for several seconds, clearly thinking. Then she looked away, toward the map of Mexico, running the palm of her right hand across the shiny plane of her bald head. Finally, she sighed, apparently resolved, and faced Jo once more.

"I am not upper echelon, Miss Dark," Colonel Tachi-Amosa said, as if admitting to a personal shortcoming. "I do not have the authority to negotiate terms, or to give you any

guarantees regarding your future with Core-Mantis OmniGlobal whatsoever. I can—and am more than willing to—
protect you from Carrington if he attempts a retrieval. But I
simply do not have the power to negotiate things like ongoing personal security, position, salary, or benefits."

She paused, gauging Joanna's reaction, and Jo did her
very damnedest to keep her expression serious, even trying
to appear somber.

She thinks I'm defecting, Jo thought. *My injuries, she
thinks I sustained them escaping the Institute.*

"Maybe you should get somebody who *can* do those
things, Colonel," Jo said.

"Senior management is unavailable at the moment." The
colonel smiled thinly. "Ironically, as a result of your activities over the last week. They're all in Crete, overseeing the
dismantling of Zentek and the impending takeover of BYI."

"Then get Carcareas over here and let me talk to her."

"Miss Carcareas is unavailable right now."

"I want to talk to her," Jo said. "She's the one I'll deal
with, nobody else."

"We are trying to reach her, Miss Dark, I assure you," the
colonel said quickly. "But it may take some time before she
can get here."

Using the arms of the chair to assist her, Jo got to her feet,
and the colonel hastily followed suit. She could see the
worry on the other woman's face, the fear that she was going
to lose Jo.

"I want your private number," Jo told the colonel. "The
one for your ring-ring, not for the office, your private one."

"Miss Dark, I'm concerned for your safety if you leave
this building. If Carrington makes an attempt—"

"Then I'll deal with it the way I dealt with it before," Jo
snapped.

"Your injuries—"

"Are nothing compared to the other guy's."

The colonel paused, and Jo thought she saw the hint of a smile before she rattled of a fifteen-digit string of numbers. Jo repeated the sequence back, as quickly as it had come, and earned another arching of an eyebrow.

"Here's what's going to happen," Jo said, once she was sure she had the colonel's ring-ring number committed to memory. "I'm going to call you in twelve hours. You're going to answer. I'm going to tell you where Portia de Carcareas is to meet me, and I'm going to tell you when. You'll tell her. She'll meet me. Then, and only then, will I open my negotiations with Core-Mantis OmniGlobal."

Colonel Tachi-Amosa frowned again, but nodded her acceptance of the terms. "I can't convince you to stay here? At least to let us give you some medical attention?"

"Not unless you want to try doing it by force," Jo said. "But I don't think your superiors would like that very much, do you?"

"No," the colonel said. "No, they would not. Not given everything you've done for us already. They would view it as discourteous."

"So would I."

"I'll escort you out."

"Please."

The colonel led her to the door, back through the corridors and down once more to the lobby. She retrieved Jo's pack from where it had been held at the front desk, made a display of opening it for her and then setting out the contents, so Jo could make certain that nothing had been taken from it, that nothing had been added. Then Colonel Tachi-Amosa walked Jo the rest of the way out of the building, leaving her only as Joanna passed through the doors, wishing her a good day, and saying that she thought Jo was making the right choice.

"Welcome to Core-Mantis," the colonel said. "Welcome to the family."

||||||| ||| ||||||

SecureChat: Private Room 10029.29291.2992

>>*FLASHBLANK ENGAGED . . . INTRUSION LOCKOUT ENGAGED . . . CONNECTING.*

>>**ED_V_CODER** is **LOGGED ON** . . .

>>**CHRYSALIS BLOSSOM** is **LOGGED ON** . . .

>>**ED_V_CODER**: Hey, I need some more help. Got a minute?

>>**CHRYSALIS BLOSSOM**: Why is it all we ever talk about is work? :-p

>>**ED_V_CODER**: I'm in serious trouble here, CB.

>>**CHRYSALIS BLOSSOM**: Arthur throwing another tantrum? ;)

>>**ED_V_CODER**: It's the damned compiler again, I think. Every time it looks like I have the behavioral systems on line, the compiler dumps garbage code into the mix and Arthur blue-screens me. I'm at crunch-time now, CB, I'm on no sleep and pretty much all of the caffeine in Paris, and I've set myself up for a massive fall

>>**ED_V_CODER**: I ****really**** need some help!!!

>>**CHRYSALIS BLOSSOM**: Why not ask Cassandra?

>>**ED_V_CODER**: Can't. I'm good at this stuff, but next to her? I might as well be hand-coding websites, or writing in C+. She handed over some of her notes last time I saw her, and I *know* I should understand them and maybe--maybe!--I'm getting half of it. I'm not stoopid, but I've got nothing on this, I just can't track it to keep up

>>**CHRYSALIS BLOSSOM**: She's really that good, huh?

>>**ED_V_CODER**: Yes. She *really* is.

>>**CHRYSALIS BLOSSOM**: Then you should *really* tell her, don't you think? If she's the razor you say she is, she can solve the problem

>>**ED_V_CODER**: Can't do that. Not if I want to keep my job.

>>**CHRYSALIS BLOSSOM**: C'mon, she's not gonna fire you because you're stuck on something that maybe she's the only person in the world who understands it

>>**ED_V_CODER**: Maybe not for that. . . .

>>**CHRYSALIS BLOSSOM**: oh damn, baby, what'd you do?

>>**ED_V_CODER**: I had to demo for her yesterday, and I ended up coding a key-word module

>>**CHRYSALIS BLOSSOM**: You didn't!

>>**ED_V_CODER**: and then inserting it into the baseline to make it look like he was doing things that she totally expects

>>**CHRYSALIS BLOSSOM**: OK slow down

>>**ED_V_CODER**: him to be doing and that according to our timeline he *should* be doing but that for some damn reason I can't *make* him do!

>>**CHRYSALIS BLOSSOM**: . . .

>>**ED_V_CODER**: sorry.

>>**CHRYSALIS BLOSSOM**: You done?

>>**ED_V_CODER**: Yeah.

>>**CHRYSALIS BLOSSOM**: You *gotta* calm down, babe.

>>**ED_V_CODER**: I've got maybe 100 hours before Arthur has to do his thing, CB, I just lied to my boss, and I'm staring at a blue-screen. Calm is not in my vocab

>>**CHRYSALIS BLOSSOM**: LOL all right.

>>**ED_V_CODER**: Not to mention that it's performance evaluation time soon. If I don't get Arthur up and running, and do it without the boss's help, I might as well forget my shot at the bonus, the stock options, the promotion . . .

>>**CHRYSALIS BLOSSOM**: and of course, the yacht. Well, you promised me a trip to Capri, so I can't very well let the new boss fire you before I get my pleasure cruise, now can I?

>>**ED_V_CODER**: You're the queen. THANK YOU!

>>**CHRYSALIS BLOSSOM**: Okay, so hit me, codeman. What, specifically, is the problem?

>>**ED_V_CODER**: I *think* it's the behavioral sims. Arthur's not supposed to be fully sentient, but he should be able to make "reasonable extrapolations based on available data." Hell, Cassandra's the one who really understands this stuff, like I said, I can barely keep up. Conceptually, the project spec says that these simulated "humanlike" behavioral modes are supposed to make Arthur easy for nonprogrammers to work with, right? You just issue plain-language instructions and Arthur will parse them and then design and execute the necessary code.

>>**CHRYSALIS BLOSSOM**: Ah. So that's why all the secrecy. Interesting. With that code architecture on a larger scale, Arthur could streamline everything from educational systems to even something as vast as AirFlow, right?

>>**ED_V_CODER**: (Sigh.) You *know* I'm not supposed to talk about this.

>>**ED_V_CODER**: But yeah, that's basically it. Arthur's supposed to be the future of the company--and my ticket into upper management--but right now, he's an anchor around my neck

>>**CHRYSALIS BLOSSOM**: Can you send me the error logs?

>>**ED_V_CODER**: Sending now

[[[UPLOAD COMMENCING . . .]]]

[[[UPLOAD COMPLETED . . .]]]

>>**ED_V_CODER**: Okay, so check lines 10292.192 through 105501.201. Parameter input for instructions is being received and parsed, right?

>>**CHRYSALIS BLOSSOM**: Yeah, I see it. Then what?

>>**ED_V_CODER**: Arthur's either crashing when the instructions become too complex or just dumping garbage into his executables directory

>>**ED_V_CODER**: Like I said, I think it's a problem with the compiler.

>>**CHRYSALIS BLOSSOM**: Could be. Might also be in the security nodes, though. You corp guys armor everything, and it might be doing something silly, like treating the new code as a virus or worm. DataFlow security code is usually it's own worst enemy. Trust me. ;)

>>**CHRYSALIS BLOSSOM**: I think I might have a work-around, but you've got to let me poke around in the root structure for a few hours.

>>**ED_V_CODER**: I can get in real trouble if I let you do that.

>>**CHRYSALIS BLOSSOM**: And that would be more trouble that you're in now?

>>**ED_V_CODER**: (wincing) ouch

>>**CHRYSALIS BLOSSOM**: I'll kiss it all better, babe.

>>**CHRYSALIS BLOSSOM**: I promise: no one will ever know I was in there. Give me five hours in an access socket, and I'll plug the problem up. You get your promotion, I get my cruise to Capri . . .

>>**CHRYSALIS BLOSSOM**: actually, I think we'll *both* get something out of the cruise. ;)

>>**ED_V_CODER**: Okay. You're right.

>>**ED_V_CODER**: I'll send you the entry codes in a few minutes.

>>**ED_V_CODER**: And thanks. You're saving my life here, CB.

[[[CHAT TERMINATED / TRANSCRIPT FLASHBLANKED]]]

Carrington Institute
Rooms of Jonathan Steinberg
London, England
January 24th, 2021

The Institute had been on alert for six days now, and the strain of it was beginning to show everywhere Jonathan Steinberg looked. Walking the corridors of the Institute's main building, every conversation he overhead was spoken in hushed tones. Checking with Calvin Rogers that afternoon on the status of the Institute's small fleet of dropships, making certain they were ready and loaded in case Steinberg found himself having to deploy troops, he'd done it himself, speaking in a whisper until Rogers had put up a hand, frowning at him.

"It's just us in here, Jon," Rogers had said. "There's no need to whisper, man."

Tension was showing in other ways, too, and some of those ways were in danger of becoming problems. Twice Steinberg had put a stop to heated arguments between Institute guards, exhausted from their extended shifts, before they'd escalated to blows. The conflicts had been baseless, expressions of frustration and fear, and in each case easily resolved, but it worried him. Emotions were running high, and morale was beginning to deteriorate.

He did what he could, but the fact was, there wasn't much to be done. Until Carrington ordered Steinberg to have the defenses stand down, every one of his men and women were going to have to stay on alert. That meant long hours on post or patrol in the biting January cold; it meant shorter off-duty hours for sleep and meals; and it meant that the normal avenues of recreation were closed. No one was allowed to leave the Institute campus until Carrington gave the all-clear.

No one but Joanna, Steinberg corrected himself as he sat on his bed in his quarters, removing his boots. He'd returned to change his socks, to give his feet a chance to breathe again, and as he sat there, staring at his aching bare feet, he realized that sitting on the bed had been a very bad idea. It made him want to lie down, and he knew if he did that, he would want to sleep, and that was out of the question, at least for the moment.

With a grunt that made him feel older than he knew he actually was, Steinberg hoisted himself up and crossed to his dresser, searching for a new pair of socks. He was trying to get them on his feet while standing when his in-room terminal lit up, announcing the arrival of a text message. He abandoned the effort, crossed to where the small screen hung suspended on the wall, tapping it with an index finger.

Are you a big bad wolf looking for a good time? Contact littlelostlamb762@ fairytale-love.com for a chat that could change your life.

Steinberg blinked at the message, thinking that either Grimshaw's firewall wasn't everything it was supposed to be, or Joanna Dark had a very strange sense of humor.

With a sigh, he pulled out his desk chair and switched on the keyboard projector. Across the surface of his desk appeared a projected QWERTY keyboard, and Steinberg began typing on the desktop, fingers striking intangible keys. It took him two minutes to confirm that Fairytale-love.com existed, a site that billed itself as "discreet & sexxxy" with "the latest in 'LoveMatch VR' interactions, secure chatrooms for video or text messaging, and live girls."

Steinberg realized that he was going to have to actually join the site to go any further, and for a moment contemplated getting Grimshaw to hack his way in, just to avoid the deluge of spam that would come from doing so. Then he saw that littlelostlamb762 was actually online at that moment, and resolved himself to the inevitable change of e-mail address he was about to require.

Once he'd registered, he sent a personal message to littlelostlamb762, telling her that he was lonely and looking for a good time. Perhaps thirty seconds after that, he received an invitation to join a private chatroom, with video enabled. He accepted the request, watched the screen redraw and encrypt, and then he was looking at Joanna Dark, grinning at him broadly.

"*Baa,*" Jo said, her voice slightly distorted as it came through the speakers in his room. The video quality wasn't terrific, either, and Steinberg realized that Jo was using a private net kiosk for the communication. Wherever she was, it was still daylight, and apparently somewhere untouched by winter.

"You are a very strange girl," Steinberg told her.

"*You're one to talk, Mr. huffandpuff007,*" she retorted. "*What's the matter, was Big Bad Wolf taken?*"

"It's called Fairytale-love.com. Of course Big Bad Wolf was taken. Where are you?"

"*Mexico,*" Jo said.

"Smart."

She seemed pleased with the praise. "*Yeah, CMO was very helpful. I met with the colonel in charge of the region, a*" *woman named Tachi-Amosa, and she's arranging for me to meet Carcareas tomorrow morning in Veracruz for a little chat."*

"Carcareas?"

"During Initial Vector. The one I almost ran into back in New York."

"And she's agreed to meet with you?"

"CMO is under the impression that I've been doing them a lot of favors. They think I'm looking to switch sides. Didn't hurt that I apparently look like death warmed over and they think you're responsible for it."

"Me? What?"

"Well, maybe not you specifically, but Carrington generally. Stopping me from defecting, you know." On the screen, Joanna flashed him another grin, then glanced over her shoulder, looking at the passersby outside the kiosk. When she looked back, her expression was more serious, though Steinberg thought there was still some mirth in her eyes. *"I should make this quick. I shook the surveillance they put me under, but this is their town, so they may reacquire me anytime."*

Steinberg nodded. "What do you need me to do?"

"I'm assuming nothing's changed since I left?"

"No, the situation's the same. Last I heard, Beck-Yama's got maybe forty-eight hours left to live. We're still on alert. Not a peep from dataDyne, and the intrusion attempts seem to be done with for the moment."

"Huh." She seemed to think about that. *"What do you make of it?"*

"I don't make anything of it," Steinberg said. "Could be that whoever was trying to hack the system finally got frustrated with Grim's defenses. Could be that whoever was trying to hack the system wanted to get some sleep. God knows I do."

"Does that make sense to you? I mean, if the Institute's about to be hit, why suddenly stop trying to crack the system?"

"I'm not a programmer," Steinberg said. "I'm a ground-pounder, remember? Could be a dozen reasons why that I don't understand, not without having Grimshaw explain it to me. What do you need me to do, Jo?"

"I'm light," Jo said. *"Got the P9P and a datathief on me, that's pretty much it. No way to record this conversation with Carcareas tomorrow."*

"I'm not sure how I can help that."

"She's got a ring-ring, Jonathan. They're standard on CMO, they give them out with the corporate IDs. There's got to be a way that Grim can hack into it, maybe, something like that."

Steinberg tried not to look doubtful. "I don't know."

"Just talk to him, see if there's anything he can do, okay?" She glanced over her shoulder again. *"I've got to go. I'll be in touch."*

Before he could tell her to be careful, she'd cut the connection, and his monitor was now telling him that his credit account had been charged for the conversation. Steinberg reached up and switched off the projector for the keyboard, then tapped the monitor, putting it back to sleep. He pulled his fresh socks on, then his boots.

His computer was announcing the first wave of spam before he was out the door.

"Grim?"

"Mhhm?"

Steinberg looked at the hacker, sprawled in his underwear on his bed, and wondered if there was a way to wake him without actually needing to make physical contact. The odor in Grimshaw's quarters bore a disturbing resemblance to the one that now permeated the Ops Center.

"Grim, wake up."

Grimshaw moved slightly, rubbing his nose and repositioning so that his posterior canted upward, then resumed snoring.

Steinberg switched on the room lights, taking in the accumulation of detritus and paraphernalia that Grimshaw had decorated with. Posters of women in various stages of undress covered the walls. Most of the women were apparently computer-generated, though two were of Candee, who Steinberg knew wasn't a simulation but might as well have been. Stacks of computer magazines, paperback books, and d-PAL Reader data chips covered the floor, the desk, the bureau, sharing space with dirty laundry and a half-assembled model of *Carrington One,* the first null-g vehicle that Daniel Carrington had built as proof-of-concept. Toys were everywhere, including a legion of action figures. In the collection, Steinberg spotted at least three figures of the late Zhang Li's daughter, Mai Hem.

Leave it to the twisted old bastard to totemize his DeathMatch-star daughter for profit, he thought. Steinberg wondered how Joanna would react if she knew that Grim had tiny, variant replicas of the woman who had murdered her father in his room.

He turned back to Grimshaw, who had shifted again, still snoring steadily, and used the toe of his boot to nudge the man's side.

"Cassandra DeVries called," he said loudly. "She's offering you a job as her new Director of DataFlow and personal cabana boy."

Nothing.

The problem, Steinberg thought, *is that it's three in the morning and I really don't want to use the volume that's going to be required here.*

He glanced around the room, found an oversized novelty mug in the shape of an alien skull, and picked it up, examining the contents cautiously. The mug appeared to be empty but smelled strongly of maple syrup. Steinberg carried the mug into the bathroom, washed it out, and filled it with cold water from the tap. Then he returned to where Grimshaw was still sleeping and dumped the contents on the man's head.

Grimshaw awoke spluttering, eyes snapping wide. "Awake! I'm awake!"

"You are now," Steinberg agreed. "Keep it down."

Grimshaw blinked several times, then rubbed his eyes. He glanced down at himself, at the bed, and then to Steinberg, and the look he gave was that of a wounded child.

"You really didn't have to do that, Jon."

"No, I really did," Steinberg said.

"I haven't slept in three days. The Old Man said I could get some sleep." His expression changed suddenly, switching to alarm. "Shit, no, tell me they haven't started again."

"Not that I know of."

The relief on Grimshaw's face was enormous, until he realized that Steinberg had apparently woken him for no reason.

"Then I'm going back to bed," he said, then turned and realized his pillow, sheets, and most likely mattress were all now soaked. "Aw, c'mon, Jon."

"I need your help."

"I'll reset your password in the morning, man. Oh, c'mon . . . it's all wet."

"Let me rephrase," Steinberg said. "Jo needs your help."

That brought Grimshaw's attention back as if he'd been slapped. "Is she all right? She's recovering, right?"

"This is a secret, Grim, you understand what I'm telling you? The Old Man doesn't know about this, and he's not *going* to know, not from me, not from you."

"Dude, I don't know what you're talking about. What's going on with Jo?"

"She's in Mexico."

"Huh?"

"Buy a map, Grim. She went to make contact with Core-Mantis."

The alarm returned. "What the hell'd she go and do that for?"

"We figure CMO's the one profiting from the killings she's supposed to have committed. Look, I'll fill you in later, but right now she needs you to do something for her."

The alarm left again, now replaced by doubt, and Steinberg marveled at how clearly Grimshaw's face expressed everything he was thinking, everything he was feeling. If the man had to lie to Carrington's face, they were dead, he realized.

"I don't like going behind the Old Man's back, Jon," Grimshaw said. "When he finds out, he'll be pissed. You know what he's like when he's pissed."

"He's a little preoccupied right now, we'll be okay. Get your pants on."

"Why? Where are we going?"

"The computer center."

"Uh, Jon, it's called a network. If it's on the optical, I can access it from here."

Steinberg winced. "Right."

"What do you—what does *Jo* need me to do?"

"She's got a meet set with a CMO agent named Carcareas in about eight hours. She wants to be able to record the conversation, but she doesn't have the tech on her, and she's in CMO-controlled territory, so she can't find it herself. She was thinking you might be able to hack Carcareas's ring-ring."

Grimshaw ran a hand through his hair, then reached into the pile of magazines on the bedstand, finding his glasses. He put them on, frowning, then shook his head.

"Can't do it," he said. "Impossible."

"Joanna needs—"

"Jon, ring-ring's are passive-active devices, man. Unless you want to call this Carcareas chick and ask her to keep the damn thing on during the meeting with Jo, there's no way to hop that signal and record it, there's just no way to do it. It's like a light, it's either on or it's off. If I had the frequency, I could triangulate on it, sure, but I still wouldn't be able to hear anything unless it was actively being used. She has to have an open line to do what you're asking. Can't be done, sorry."

Grimshaw turned back to his bed, grumbled, and began attempting to reorganize his bedding to avoid the wet spot.

Steinberg considered, then said, "Jo asked for your help, Grim. There are three people who know she's not here right now. Her, me, and you. That's a lot of trust."

Still seated on his bed, Grimshaw turned back to him, pulling a face that was half resigned, half pleased. "Okay, okay, I get it. Let me think. What do we know about this CMO babe, this Carcareas?"

"She's one of their agents."

"Little more than that would be helpful."

"She's the one that Hayes met with in New York, during Initial Vector."

"Oh, right. That one was supposed to be some kind of major babe, yeah?" Grimshaw perked up, then rubbed at his eyes beneath his glasses. "Okay, so she's got to be upper-level, then, one of their key agents, not like that mole in LA was."

"I'd guess so."

"Then she's gonna be linked, she's going to have a ThroatLink." Grimshaw used the edge of his bedstand to help himself to his feet, flopped down again in his desk chair.

With one hand he pulled his monitor from where it hung against the wall, swinging it out on its arm, and with the other activated his IR keyboard. The screen lit up, showing a parade of dancing Candees gyrating in perpetual motion, and Steinberg had to bite back the urge to make a comment.

Grimshaw began tapping on the projected keys, hunting and pecking with a speed that would make Emily Partridge, in Carrington's office, green with envy.

"Cracked Core-Mantis's communication infrastructure about four, five weeks back," Grimshaw told Steinberg without looking away from his work. "Just to see if I could do it and hey, waddya know, I could, so I did. Left myself a back door into the system, just in case I wanted to return."

"Daniel know you did that? Or was this another one of your 'hobby excursions,' Grim?" Jon asked.

Grimshaw paused, a guilty look crossing his face. "Okay, so we both have secrets we need to keep from the Old Man. He catches me pleasure-hacking again, he's going to have me debugging intranet code for a month." His mouth curled in disgust. "In HTML."

"Your secret's safe with me." Steinberg struggled to keep the impatience out of his voice. "So you can just open up this back door, right?"

Grimshaw looked annoyed, like a teacher dealing with an unruly pupil who insisted on making rude noises in class. "You are *such* a grunt," he muttered. "The real question is whether or not the CMO data-hounds sniffed out my intrusion and left some traps behind or plugged the leak."

"And?"

Grimshaw's fingers flew in another flurry, and he squinted up at his monitor, then nodded. "And . . . no counterintrusion code, no sniffers, no code bombs. We got lucky. Okay, we're in. Spell 'Carcareas,' would you?"

Steinberg spelled it, and Grimshaw continued to type.

"Carcareas . . . okay . . . okay . . . there's no Carcareas listed here, Jon, she's not in the database."

"She has to be, she's a confirmed CMO agent."

"Then she's super-black or a commando or something like that, because she's not in here."

"That's their entire communications database?"

"Hell, yeah."

"Then she's in there."

Grimshaw threw up his hands, shoving his chair back. "You think you can find it, be my guest, soldier man."

Steinberg ignored the offer, turning around the room, thinking. His eye caught on one of the Mai Hems, a variant figure, still in its packaging.

"It's not her real name," Steinberg said. "It's her work name, not her real one. Is there a log of calls you can access?"

"Yeah, there is, but unless you know what we're looking for, it's going to be impossible to find what we want, man. CMO is kinda busy right now, what with the rape and pillage of Zentek and the impending same planned for Beck-Yama. Their network's singing like . . . like a really, really big choir, man."

The name, he thought. *What was the name she said?*

"Amosa," Steinberg told Grimshaw. "Tashi . . . no, Tachi-Amosa."

"Any idea how to spell that?"

"Jesus, I don't know, Grim. Sound it out."

"Touchy, touchy. So, who is he?"

" 'He' is the *woman* Jo met with, the one who's arranging the meeting with Carcareas. Colonel in charge of the region, something like that. She'll be ThroatLinked, too, won't she? We start checking her calls, maybe we can find Carcareas."

"That's a long shot."

"It's better than no shot at all," Steinberg said. "Get to work."

Grimshaw nodded slightly, turning his attention back to his keyboard. "You're gonna stay here while I do this?"

"That was my plan, yeah."

"Then make yourself useful."

"How do I do that?"

"You can start by changing the sheets on my bed, asshole," Grimshaw told him.

Portia de Carcareas arrived five minutes late for her meeting with Joanna Dark, and Jo suspected that her tardiness wasn't due to anything professional. It wasn't, for instance, enough time to perform a complete sweep of the area surrounding the café, of the Plaza Lerdo, the marble-tiled heart of Veracruz with its enormous fountain at the center. It wasn't even enough time to do an adequate walkthrough of the café itself, to secure an escape route or to spot potential backup that Jo might have brought with her.

No, Portia de Carcareas arrived five minutes late, Jo was certain, simply because she could afford to keep her waiting.

But she did arrive, entering the café with the easy grace of a woman who not only knew she was capable and smart and beautiful but who also knew that she was exceptionally dangerous. Watching Carcareas as she entered, Jo couldn't help but marvel at the woman's poise. To Jo, who knew herself as capable and smart and also exceptionally dangerous,

Carcareas's self-assurance was almost enviable. The fact that it still hurt to take deep breaths didn't help, either.

The woman veered right as soon as she entered, clearing the doorway and subtly placing her back to a wall, before removing her sunglasses and surveying the early morning crowd. She looked, at least to Jo, exactly the same as she had the last time she'd seen her, the only changes being to her wardrobe. The last time Jo had seen her had been in New York, at the Money Pit, a trendy Manhattan club-slash-restaurant that catered to hypercorp executives and the people who wished desperately to be like them. Carcareas had worn professional attire then, appropriate to a business-woman on the go, silk blouse and tailored trousers and perfectly applied makeup.

This time Carcareas had gone more casual but no less fashionable. She was wearing professionally faded and torn blue jeans that tucked into calf-high black leather boots, a washed-out black T-shirt that looked like it was cotton but was probably silk, and a loose-fitting coat that fell away from her shoulders with enough drape to hide any weapon on her hip that she might have brought to their meeting. A thin rope of pearls glowed against her skin, and the ring finger of each hand was adorned with simple bands, one of them a black-and-gold model ring-ring, the other an apparently plain circle of titanium.

Jo, on the other hand, was still in the same clothes she'd worn upon leaving the Institute. Her sand-colored cargo pants and her red Chuck Taylor All-Stars, the same ratty brown T-shirt with the red five-pointed star at its center that she'd had since she was sixteen. Looking at Carcareas, she had the sudden sense that, somehow, she'd managed to arrive for their meeting underdressed. No, not underdressed, exactly; that she'd dressed *wrong*. A café in the early morning in

Veracruz, and looking at Portia de Carcareas, now approaching Jo's table with a smile and a wave as if they were old friends, Jo realized why she felt the way she did.

Portia de Carcareas, without having said a word, made Jo feel immature. Made her feel like she was a girl and Carcareas was a woman, and that Jo had a very long way to go to cover the distance between them.

"Joanna?" Carcareas stood a couple feet off from the table, the smile warm, her manner cautious. "May I join you?"

"Free country."

"There's no such thing." Portia de Carcareas flashed a smile of perfectly white teeth, taking the offered seat. "But some of them are more affordable than others."

Jo shifted in her chair, glancing past the other woman, to the door and the view onto the plaza. Unlike Carcareas, Jo *had* swept the area before taking a table at the café. The sweep hadn't revealed anything more than the standard governmental surveillance, but Jo had planned egress routes just the same, as her father had taught her.

Carcareas peered at her with barely concealed curiosity.

"You seem to have been through quite the wringer of late."

Jo fought the urge to put a hand to her face, to check the scratches and lacerations still healing on her skin.

"Yeah," she said. "Someone made a point of telling me how I looked."

Carcareas chuckled, a breathless sound, then half-turned in her seat and motioned for the nearest server. "I'm going to have a coffee, I think. Should I order two?"

"I don't do caffeine."

"You poor dear, how do you manage to function this early in the morning?"

"I'm stubborn," Jo told her.

Carcareas ordered, waited for the server to depart, and then gave Jo another smile, appraising her without any attempt to conceal the fact that she was doing so. Jo sat through it with as much patience as she could muster. Carcareas's eyes were green, lustrous, and as Jo met them they seemed to shine even brighter.

"Knock it off," Jo said.

"Knock what off, exactly?"

"CMO got plenty of footage of me at the office in Mexico City. You don't need to add to it."

Carcareas's full lips parted in a smile, and then she closed her eyes for perhaps a half-second longer than one would if they were blinking before opening them again. Her eyes had changed color to brown, and the peculiar luster had gone.

"Happy?" Carcareas asked.

"Not hardly, but it's a start."

"Have you been having some bad days, Joanna?"

"More than you can count. But bad as they've been, the people responsible, they've had worse."

Carcareas made a clucking noise, shaking her head slightly. "So hostile. I'd have thought you'd be a little more . . . deferential if you were looking for shelter."

"I'm not looking for shelter," Jo said. "I'm not looking to defect."

"I know." Carcareas smiled with self-satisfaction, but held her silence as the server returned to deposit her *café con leche*. Then she added, "Though, if you'll pardon the unsolicited advice, you should certainly consider it."

"CMO's like all the rest." Jo knew she was veering off-topic, taking the conversation from where Carcareas wanted it to go down another path simply by saying that much. "You guys tart yourselves up nice on the outside, but you're no better than dataDyne or Beck-Yama at heart."

"Or Carrington?" Carcareas turned her cup of coffee in

its saucer with a light touch, letting her fingernails click against the porcelain. Her nails were polished the color of old blood.

"Carrington's different."

Carcareas shrugged, bringing her cup to her lips, blowing on the coffee before taking a sip. "How so? Because he takes care of you? We can take care of you, Joanna. We'd very much like to take care of you, in fact."

"We're not talking about this," Jo said, growing all the more frustrated with Carcareas because she was now frustrated with herself. "I didn't want to meet with you to talk about this."

"You're the one who brought it up," Carcareas said mildly as she set her cup back in its saucer. "But I'm happy to let the subject drop for now, if it makes you uncomfortable. If you're not interested in hearing what Core-Mantis OmniGlobal can offer you, what would you like to talk about instead?"

"I think you know. And I think you can figure that I'm pretty pissed off about it."

"You're telling me that you didn't kill Bricker or Matsuo, is that it?"

"I think you know," Jo said again.

Carcareas moved her cup in its saucer, turning it slowly so the handle was parallel with the edge of the table, the tip of her tongue just visible between her lips. Her now-brown eyes focused past Jo, into the middle distance, and Jo tried to suppress both her impatience and her frown. It was clear the other woman had lapsed into thought, that Jo had given her information Carcareas had been lacking, and that now she was trying to understand its significance.

For Jo, the conclusion was obvious. Whoever was out there impersonating her, either they weren't a CMO agent as she had suspected, or they were a CMO agent that Carcareas knew nothing about. Her instinct said it was the former, not the latter: Carcareas was clearly a high-level player for Core-Mantis—the difficulty in contacting her, the delay in arranging their meeting, proved that. Jo had the sneaking suspicion that the reason Colonel Tachi-Amosa had been unable to arrange her meeting with Carcareas any earlier than this morning was because, along with CMO's "senior management," Carcareas had been in Crete.

If that was the case, then Jo felt that there was very little going on at Core-Mantis OmniGlobal that Portia de Carcareas didn't know about.

"That's interesting," Carcareas said, finally. "So it wasn't you, and that means it wasn't Carrington helping us along."

"CMO didn't do it?"

Carcareas focused on her again, smiling softly. "Joanna, until you walked into our offices off Zona Rosa yesterday, Core-Mantis OmniGlobal had very little information about you."

"You had a mole in the Los Angeles office, Portia."

"And she gave us only the most basic information about you. And we must assume that what she had was sanitized by Carrington before you landed in LA."

"That could have been enough."

"Do you think so? Perhaps, given enough time. With Matsuo, maybe. But not with Bricker. It wasn't us, Joanna."

She said it softly, but there was conviction in it.

"You know who it was, though," Jo said. "Don't you?"

"I have a very strong suspicion, yes."

"Tell me."

"The Continuity."

"The Who?"

"The Continuity, Joanna," reaching for her coffee once more. Then she stopped, her hand almost touching the cup, and barely canted her head to the right. Jo had seen the gesture before, or at least, ones like it, and she knew what it meant. Carcareas had a ThroatLink, the Core-Mantis answer to the ubiquitous dataDyne "Second Ear" series of radios. Both were worn subcutaneously, but the ThroatLink was the more invasive, and in many ways, better product, with its mike implanted in the throat of the wearer and two leads that threaded along the base of the skull to transmit received sound via the bone to the inner ear.

Carcareas's eyes darted to Jo as she listened to whatever communication was being sent, then went back to her cup just as quickly.

Uh-oh, Jo thought, and she straightened in her seat and took a second look around the café as casually as she could manage it. The patrons seated at their tables had hardly changed since she had arrived, only three of them now gone, replaced by four men in their late sixties. Jo gave them an appraisal and didn't see anything that made her think she was missing something. She scanned the room in its entirety again and still didn't see anything to alarm her.

Then she noted that outside, in the plaza, the morning pedestrian traffic seemed to have altered its pattern. Her view through the windows was to the north, and since she had arrived, people had crossed the plaza from every direction constantly. Now, however, they seemed to be avoiding the western side.

Carcareas was whispering to her ThroatLink, speaking so softly that, even sitting opposite her, Jo couldn't overhear it. Jo shifted, wincing as if in more pain from her ribs than before, leaning back slightly. As she did, she freed the P9P from her waistband, keeping it hidden from view beneath the table.

"We should go," Carcareas told Jo abruptly. "We can finish this conversation elsewhere."

"I'm not going anywhere with you," Jo said, and she saw Carcareas stiffen slightly, knew that the woman had guessed what was going on quite literally under the table. "You can have Colonel Tachi and all of Xiphos Brigade out there for all I care, I'm *still* not going anywhere with you."

"Colonel Tachi-Amosa and Xiphos aren't outside, Joanna, but they are en route. Colonel Tachi-Amosa and Xiphos aren't your problem, or for that matter, mine."

"My problem is you," Jo said. "Your problem is that I've got a pistol pointed right at your Christmas basket."

"No, Joanna," Carcareas said, and her voice had taken on an edge as sharp as any knife. "Your problem is that there's a dataDyne hit squad setting up on the western side of the Plaza Lerdo right now."

Son of a bitch, Jo thought.

"What I am," Portia de Carcareas added, "is the solution."

dataDyne Executive Safehouse
37 km ENE of Nelson, New Zealand
January 25th, 2021

Velez didn't want Cassandra to watch the live feed coming into the command post of the operation in Veracruz, saying, "It is not something with which you should burden yourself."

"But I am burdened with it, Anita," Cassandra said. "I've authorized the taking of a life. I've authorized a murder. I should witness it."

"A life taken in self-defense is never a murder, Madame Director."

"This isn't self-defense," Cassandra said. "It's expedience."

The command post was buried fifty meters or so into the mountainside, and by the time Cassandra reached it with Velez, it seemed they had left New Zealand for another world entirely. She had expected a darkened room, ominous and even uncomfortable, but when the Shock Troopers had finished snapping to attention, had pulled back the reinforced steel door to allow her entry, what she stepped into felt familiar, and disconcertingly comfortable. It was like stepping into a computer lab, with dataDyne CORPSEC in the place of programmers, with Shock Troopers in the place of technicians.

When she stepped into the room, everyone present, even those clearly performing one task or another, stopped whatever they were doing and came to attention. She half-expected salutes to follow, though none did.

"As you were," Cassandra said, hoping desperately that the words didn't sound as awkward to them as they did to her.

As quickly as it had stopped, the activity resumed.

Velez guided her to a position near the center of the room, where they were joined by two men, each in CORPSEC uniform. Cassandra recognized the older of the two as Curtis Mack, the CORPSEC director of counterintelligence operations, one of Velez's immediate lieutenants. Her dealings with him since becoming CEO had been few, and never in person, limited to only three briefings delivered via video conference. He was in his late forties, perhaps, balding and clean shaven, and he wore glasses, and in every instance he had been polite and professional. As a result, Cassandra had no sense of him as a person whatsoever.

The other man, perhaps fifteen years Mack's junior, Cassandra had no memory of having met at all, and upon reaching them, he offered both her and Velez headsets, and she took that to mean he was Mack's assistant in one capacity or another. Cassandra took the offered set, making certain to make eye contact with the young man as she thanked him. When she did, the look on his face seemed at once pleased and terrified, and as he turned away, Cassandra wondered if she was truly so frightening as a result of her position, or her person. She turned to face Mack uncertain as to which she would have preferred.

"Ma'am," Mack said.

"Director Mack." As before, she made a point of meeting his eyes, this time offering a hand as well, which he took. She kept the handshake brief, tried to make it firm, knowing that he would judge her by its quality. "Nice to finally meet you in person. That business in the Amman offices got sorted out?"

"Yes, ma'am. He was revealed to be working for Core-Mantis, as we suspected. We flipped him, as you directed, gave him the designation: Sunburn. It was a wise decision, if I may say so, Madame Director. He's the source of our intelligence on this."

Cassandra gave an approving glance to Velez. "Really? Well done, Mr. Mack."

"Thank you, ma'am. According to Sunburn, the target attempted to make contact with a known CMO facilitator who goes by the name of Portia de Carcareas yesterday in Mexico City. Sunburn was able to obtain an image of the target from the security servers, and from that Director Velez was able to give confirmation. I understand that both you and the director have encountered the target before."

"Once. Might I see the image, Mr. Mack?"

Mack nodded, gestured to the young man who had handed over the headsets. He stepped hastily forward, offering a military-grade d-PAL to his superior. Mack tapped the screen twice in quick succession, then handed the device to Cassandra, who took it with her free hand.

The image was as perfectly clear and bright as if Cassandra was looking at Joanna through a window, the young woman speaking earnestly to someone out of the frame. It was such a good shot of her, in fact, that Cassandra wondered if the young woman had offered herself to the camera willingly, rather than in ignorance.

"We have a full name for her," Velez said softly at her

shoulder. "It may be an alias, but according to Sunburn, she presented herself as Joanna Dark."

Joanna Dark, Cassandra thought, still looking at the picture, thinking that the last two months had apparently been as rough on the young woman as they had been on Cassandra herself. The startling blue eyes stared out of a face marked with scratches and minor lacerations, and though she was smiling, Cassandra thought the girl looked very tired.

She handed the d-PAL back to Mack's assistant, saying, "Yes, that's her."

Mack gestured to one of the nearby monitors, tended by an Asian woman in CORPSEC uniform. "Working from the ID, and with the knowledge that the target was seeking a meeting with Carcareas, we were able to run a keyword search through the traffic coming out of CMO's Mexico City office. Their traffic is encrypted, of course, but given the priority of the mission, Director Velez granted authorization to connect with the quantum-optical at dataDyne Sydney. It wasn't until three this morning local before we were able to decode the relevant communications between CMO Mexico City and Carcareas.

"The long and the short of it is that we know where the target is, and we have a good idea of exactly how long she's going to be there. The strike team is staged, and they have confirmed that the target is on site and that Carcareas is with her at this moment."

"Carcareas came to meet her alone?"

"According to the intercept, those were the conditions of the meeting." Mack directed Cassandra's attention to the map displayed on one of the larger monitors nearby. According to the call-out glowing brightly beside the image, she was now looking at an aerial view of the central plaza in Veracruz, Mexico. Dots in red, amber, and green pulsed gently, marking positions. There were twelve of the green, but only one each of the red and amber, and those were positioned so close as to be touching, apparently in one of the buildings. The green had broken into two groups of six around the red and amber, with one group positioned to the north and west of them, along the edge of the plaza, the other directly to the south.

As she looked at the map, Cassandra could make out movement, the shapes of small figures as they moved around the fountain at the center of the plaza, and she realized that it wasn't a map at all. What she was viewing, she was viewing in real time. She stepped in closer, discovered that she could make out small details, see the shadows cast by the people as the moved in the early morning sunlight.

"This is a satellite image?" she asked Velez. "NSA?"

"Yes, Madame Director."

"Your friend Mr. Easton?"

Velez nodded slightly.

"Give him my compliments," Cassandra said, turning her attention back to the map. "Red is for the target? And amber is Carcareas?"

"Yes, ma'am," Mack said. "The green represents the strike team, now in two elements."

"Is there any way to hear what's being said?"

"No, ma'am. The meeting was already underway when the strike team arrived, making it impossible to plant a surveillance device in the café. Any attempt to close to establish line-of-sight necessary for an Audioscope feed would risk undue exposure and possibly cause the target to bolt the trap."

"I see, yes." Cassandra stared at the two dots, amber and red, wondering what it was they were saying to each other. It seemed so clear, now, what it was that Carrington was up to, what he was trying to do. He was strengthening Core-Mantis at the expense of Beck-Yama and Zentek, perhaps even forging an alliance with the hypercorp.

And once he has that, does he come after us? Cassandra thought. *Does he wait until CMO has digested its meals of Zentek and Beck-Yama and then come after us? Are they talking about it right now, this Joanna Dark and this Carcareas? Attack dataDyne now? Later?*

She remembered where she was, then—why she was in New Zealand, all of Velez's fears for her safety. Without meaning to, she found herself wondering if, at that very moment, Carcareas and Dark were talking about her, and how best to kill her, and the paranoia of it made a shiver race along her spine.

"Why is Carcareas marked in amber and not in red?" she asked.

Velez answered, "Red is reserved for target designation, Madame Director. Amber signifies third-party forces not specifically identified in our Rules of Engagement."

"I see. Yes, I do see." She ran a hand through her hair, considering. "Director Velez?"

"Madame Director?"

She turned to look at her, settling the headset over her ears as she did so. "I am hereby granting authorization by direct verbal command, as Chief Executive Officer and Director of dataDyne, to alter the designation on Carcareas from amber to red."

"As you say, Madame Director." Velez nodded slightly to Mack, and Cassandra turned back to the map in time to see the dot that was Portia de Carcareas change from amber to red. She could hear Mack's assistant speaking softly into his headset, heard him relaying the order to the strike team in the field.

On the map, Carcareas and Dark began to move in the direction of the plaza.

"Targets are going mobile," someone said.

Mack turned to Cassandra. "Madame Director?"

Staring at the two red dots, Cassandra de Vries found herself thinking of her brother, and the sadness in that moment threatened to overwhelm her.

Then she thought of Daniel Carrington.

Damn you for forcing me to do this, Daniel, she thought. *Damn you. And damn me with you.*

"Take them," she ordered.

Plaza Lerdo
Veracruz, Mexico
January 25th, 2021

"Stay close to me until we reach the exit," Portia de Carcareas said, rising from her chair. "There are two teams, one to the west, one south of our position. Once we enter the plaza, the southern team will attempt to come up and flank us."

"How do you know this?" Joanna hissed, following suit and concealing the P9P, still in her hand, beneath her jacket. "Where are you getting your intelligence?"

Carcareas shook her head, and as Jo watched, the woman's eyes changed color again, the brown washing away to an entirely unnatural, almost mirrorlike gray. She looked past Jo, then turned her head slowly from side to side, apparently focusing on nothing before looking back to her. With her right hand, she took a handful of Core-Mantis scrip and dropped it on the table; with her left, she brushed back the hem of her coat to rest her palm on the butt of a small automatic, riding in its pancake holster there.

Probably a CMO Rapier, Jo thought, which would suit Carcareas—small, elegant, and deadly.

"Ainia's at least three minutes out," she told Jo, her eyes reverting to their natural brown. "The southern team is moving to take entry positions, they're going to come in the back any moment. If we don't leave now, we're going to be caught in here like fish in a barrel. Our only chance is to break the trap and get to a place of cover where we can hold them off until Xiphos arrives."

"I don't trust you!"

Carcareas all but snarled at her. "Then it's mutual. I'm leaving now, Joanna. You either come with me, or you die here, and given the state you're in, that's liable to happen quite quickly. Don't be a fool, girl! I have the answers you want, you know that. The only way you'll get them is if we both can get out of here alive."

With that, Carcareas turned and began making her way toward the exit onto the plaza.

Muttering a curse, Jo moved to follow.

She'd just caught up with Carcareas at the doorway when the rear wall, only six feet from where Jo had been seated with her back to it, exploded inward. Masonry and timber spewed in their direction, debris and splinters pelting them, and Jo heard screaming from behind her; then a second explosion, even louder than the first, obliterated all other sounds, and she knew a flash-bang had followed the breaching charge. Carcareas seemed to have frozen, everything seemed to have slowed, and Jo felt the strange comfort she always felt when her perceptions would shift like this, when the world would dilate and the adrenaline would drop.

As much as she might hate it both before and afterward, the truth was that it was in moments like these that she finally found peace with herself. It was in moments like these that she knew who she was, because she knew what to do.

Pivoting in place, Jo brought the P9P to bear, firing off half of her clip with almost machine-gun speed at the group of armored men coming through the breach they'd made in the wall. The details of them seared into her mind as she fired, their bulletproof helmets, the dataDyne-issued CMP machine pistols in their hands, the MagSec pistols riding in holsters at their thighs, the almost imperceptible double-*d* diamonds engraved in the ceramic plating at the shoulders of their matte black body armor.

Her shots were true, all of them, the way they almost always were, and her bullets found their marks in the small pockets of exposed flesh between chin straps and body armor. Three of them fell, shot neatly through the neck, and she was charging forward, firing at the remainder before the ones still standing truly had time to process what she had done to them.

From the corner of her eye, Jo saw Carcareas twisting, her gun now held in both hands. One of the men still standing had his CMP up, had begun loosing a burst that punched a line like perforations in the wall, trying to track her as Jo threw herself into a slide. Then his aim went wild, arcing up as he fell back, and she watched as impact after impact appeared in a line on his armored torso, Carcareas pounding bullets into the man, buying Jo time.

Carcareas emptied the gun putting another man down, and the one remaining was stepping back, as if trying to reach the cover of the breach, while laying down a sheet of bullets. Jo turned the slide into a roll, dimly aware that she could feel her ribs moving in ways that they were never meant to. She tasted copper in her mouth, fresh blood, and wondered if that was because she'd been shot or because she'd torn something open once more.

Then she was out of her roll, coming up inside the last man's guard, and she caught the arm holding the CMP, trapped it as she turned her back into the man, forcing the weapon down, forcing her own finger over his on the trigger.

The CMP ripped another torrent of rounds at the floor, and she directed the last of them at the man's toes. Her hearing had cleared just enough that, with his mouth almost even with her ear, she could just about hear his scream of pain.

She twisted the CMP free of his grip, stepping forward and letting him fall back, then turned and cut a burst into his chest that made his body armor split and shatter. Then she moved the submachine gun to the man Carcareas had shot and dumped the rest of the clip into him to the same effect.

Turning back, she saw Carcareas coming toward her, shielding her own head, and it took Jo a moment to process why, what she was missing without the aid of her ears. Then the head of one of the patrons cowering on the floor burst apart, and at the same time a perfect lance of sunlight appeared in the wall from the direction of the northwest, and Jo understood there was at least one sniper who hadn't liked what she and Carcareas had just done.

Jo tossed the CMP in her hands to the other woman, then dropped low and began gathering the other five weapons. Two more shafts of light cut into the café in quick succession, one destroying a table, the other the left leg of one of the old men she had noted earlier. She felt the revulsion and outrage surging in her chest, strong enough to threaten the abandoning of sense.

Carcareas was shouting, the words filtering into Jo's hearing as if being thrust through mud.

"—stay here! They have at least one rocket launcher, they'll blast us to pieces."

Jo slapped the butt on one of the CMPs, activating its secondary mode. Instantly a detailed three-dimensional holographic duplicate of herself leapt forward a meter and a half from her position, in an identical pose. Carcareas's eyes, once again almost silvered gray, widened with understanding, and she repeated the move with the CMP Jo had tossed to her. The duplicate Carcareas leapt forward, mirroring her movements beside the holographic Jo.

"All of them!" Jo shouted to her. "We need to activate all of them!"

Each woman scrambled to take up the discarded CMPs, activating one after the other, and the holographs multiplied, jumbled, mixing with one another, each in perfect mimicry. They wouldn't last long, Jo knew; for the holographs to be convincing duplicates, they had to not only appear identical to their subjects, but they had to move and mimic them with absolute precision. That took power, a lot of power, and the batteries in the compact submachine guns wouldn't last long. Fifteen, maybe twenty more seconds at the most.

Jo slung one CMP over her shoulder by its strap, took the other two in each hand, and saw Carcareas doing the same. Both women scrambled to their feet, the field of duplicates doing likewise. Jo caught a glimpse of herself as one of the holographs, saw that there was blood leaking from the corner of her mouth. The pain in her side was dull, almost easy to ignore, and again she wondered how much hurt she was doing herself by moving in this way. When it was over, if she survived, she was sure she would be paying the price, that the ache her mind was dulling would erupt and that the agony of it would be thorough.

"Go!" Jo shouted, and her multiples mirrored the movements that came with her words perfectly, if not the sound of them. Carcareas, her now-silvered eyes shining, surged forward, and Jo sprinted along with her. Together, the two women and their six copies burst from the entrance of the café and into the sunlight of the Plaza Lerdo. As Jo cleared the doorway, heard the roar of the rocket on approach, she knew it hadn't been a moment too soon.

The explosion took her and Carcareas off their feet, sending them tumbling forward, a rain of shattered glass and blasted building pelting the marble-covered ground around them. Jo heard gunfire, watched as two of her duplicates vanished, their projection fields disrupted by rounds that would have found her head or heart. She rolled forward, felt the pain in her side sharpen, then abate as she lunged for the cover of the fountain at the center of the plaza. Carcareas dove in after her, the last of her holograms winking out as she came to a stop, and Jo realized that hers were gone, now, too, that it was truly just the two of them against dataDyne.

An abrupt and uncomfortable silence dropped onto the plaza, at first almost impossible for Jo to discern over the sounds of her and Carcareas's labored breathing. She belly-crawled forward, closer to the base of the fountain, and then, once she was certain it would give her protection from the west, turned her back to it, the CMPs still in her hands, to cover her left. Carcareas slid herself into position beside her, mirroring the pose to cover the right.

Jo realized she couldn't catch her breath, that there was blood dripping from her mouth and down onto her shirt.

"Were you hit?" Carcareas hissed. "Did they hit you?"

Jo shook her head, and suddenly the pain in her abdomen and chest surged, made her whimper before she could stop herself. She shoved herself back against the fountain with her feet, almost grinding her teeth as the intensity of the pain increased, building until she thought she would have to scream. The taste of her own blood filling her mouth threatened to make her gag.

"I think I'm kinda hurt," Jo managed to say.

Carcareas dropped the CMP she was holding in her left hand into her lap, then reached out and grabbed Joanna around her right bicep. A burning sensation leached into the muscle, Carcareas's grip tight, and Jo tried to pull away out of reflex. The burn spread through her arm, up into her shoulder, then abated, taking the pain Jo was feeling with it.

Carcareas released her grip, then showed her the palm of her hand, the tiny glistening spike that was folding itself back into the titanium ring she wore.

"Two cc's endomorphine," she whispered. "It won't fix you, but at least you won't feel any pain for a few minutes."

Jo nodded.

Carcareas flipped around, still staying low, focusing her Core-Mantis eyes in an attempt to see through the fountain.

"They're flanking," she whispered. "Three and three."

"Where's your colonel?"

Carcareas's lips moved in silence, speaking to her ThroatLink before answering Jo. "Ninety seconds. We're going to have to do this ourselves. Can you take the ones to the north?"

"Yes," Jo said, despite that fact that she wasn't at all certain she could. The endomorphine had banished all her pain, but in so doing, it had taken her ability to self-evaluate, and now she truly had no clue how injured she might be. There wouldn't be any way to tell what her body could and couldn't do until she tested it.

Carcareas looked to her, and Jo could see the woman was thinking the same thing, trying to conceal the doubt she was feeling. She nodded barely, then shifted again, taking the CMP back into her free hand. Jo brought her legs beneath her, tried to draw as deep a breath as she could without doing herself more harm, and found that the air came easy. She spat out a mouthful of watery blood, readjusted her grip on the two CMPs, and then launched herself forward, scanning the rooftops to the north.

When she broke cover, there were two of them visible, trying to move quickly from atop one building to another.

They had the same black body armor the group in the café had worn but carried long guns, instead of close-range room-sweepers. She felt dizzy, saw beads of light, as bright as the pearls Carcareas wore, dancing at the edges of her vision, and she heard someone shouting that they had a target, but between the swimming of her head and the expanse of the marble-floored plaza, the sound bounced about her crazily, and Jo couldn't discern its source.

Still sprinting forward, trying to reach the cover of a nearby building, Jo brought both CMPs up and to her left. The triggers resisted, then dropped, and she felt more than heard the weapons erupt, loosing a torrent of rounds at the two figures on the rooftop. She gave herself no chance in hell of doing any true damage to them, not with the range and the motion and the relative weakness of the CMPs' rounds, and so she was actually surprised when one of them staggered, then pitched forward, his legs giving out beneath him.

That was lucky, Jo thought, sliding into the shelter of a narrow doorway. Her vision was still dancing, quavering as if she was seeing everything through a heat haze. She could hear gunfire, the sound of rounds as they smacked into the building beside her, of ricochets sparking wildly from the floor of the plaza, but it all seemed distant and moving further away. She brought her right hand up, wiping her mouth with the back of it, and the blood that coated her skin was the bright red of a candied apple. She spat again, another mouthful of crimson.

The sound of something heavy and hard rang against the ground, crossed the distance of her hearing. Jo swore, diving out of the doorway, trying to outrun the grenade. A pair of invisible hands reached out to her in mid flight, she felt her lower body slewing in the air, and she came down wrong and hard, feeling the impact and not the pain of it. Jo half rolled, half sprawled, losing her grip on the CMPs in each hand. A broad smear of blood marked where she'd come down, as if drawn in an arc by a massive paintbrush, and she knew the grenade had peppered her, but she simply couldn't feel it.

With a cry, she flipped onto her back, catching the CMP still slung from her shoulder in her hands. Above her, trying to draw the laser-sight from a Fairchild submachine gun onto her forehead, another dataDyne assassin leaned over the edge of the roof. Jo fired on instinct, on her back and from the hip, and watched the man's face shield shatter, a mist of blood spattering it from within. He toppled forward, plummeted headfirst, and Jo found herself scrambling on her hands and feet for his body. A bullet slammed the ground beside her right hand, shooting shards of marble into her flesh, and she jerked her head as she felt something impact just beside her right eye.

Sniper round, she thought, and then was pulling herself over the body of the dead man, using him for cover as she stripped the Fairchild from his death grip. She exchanged her now-emptied CMP for the weapon, brought it up to her shoulder as another round tried to find her and missed, hitting the dead man instead and making his whole body rock.

Either the sniper was inexperienced or he was desperate, because he hadn't moved between shots, and Jo caught sight of him, saw the curve of his back as he tried to stay below cover while readying his next shot. She switched the Fairchild to single shot, snapping out its stock and then steadying it against her shoulder while blinking rapidly to clear her vision. At this range, the targeting beam was useless to her, but she trusted the sights. When the sniper started to rise again she fired three times in quick succession, and he dropped back, either dead or soon to be, Jo didn't know.

She felt a vibration, realized she had been feeling it for a few seconds and that it was growing in intensity. On the ground, pieces of shattered marble and splintered wood began to shiver, then dance, like water droplets on a hot stove. Dust was kicking into the air, and Jo brought a hand up to shield her eyes. When she lowered it again she could see the CMO dropship hovering perhaps ten meters over the plaza. Its troop doors were open on each side, and in them, manning the mounted guns, Core-Mantis soldiers in their black and gold. As she watched, the gun facing her direction opened up, firing at the rooftop above her. Spent brass fell from the gun, catching in the sunlight like pieces of gold, cascading into the plaza, splashing into the fountain.

The dropship turned in place, bringing its nose around to face her position, then lowered itself until it almost touched the ground. Soldiers leapt from each side before it came to a stop, and Jo lowered the Fairchild as two of them ran toward her. She got to her feet, putting out a hand to steady herself.

Then Jo fell forward, and when she hit the ground this time, it hurt, and she knew the last of the endomorphine was spent. There were hands at her arms, lifting her to her feet, and then she was being half-dragged toward the dropship, combat style. When Jo looked to where she'd hit the ground, she saw more of her blood, and she wondered idly how much of it she had left to lose, because it seemed that she had been losing an awful lot of it. When she looked for Carcareas, she still couldn't see her.

It was when they lifted her into the dropship that the pain came back at full speed, and Jo knew that this time she really would have screamed, except there was no air for her to scream with. She tried to inhale, and it felt like her lungs had been filled with barbed wire, and she choked instead, and that made the need for air all the greater. She tried again, and it was worse, and her vision truly began to swim, its edges filling with white noise, and she wondered how it could be that she felt like she was drowning when surrounded by nothing but air.

"Can't breathe," she managed to say.

She was moved onto a bench, on her back, and she felt the dropship shudder, taking to the air again. She turned her head, caught a glimpse of Carcareas on the bench opposite her, blood running freely down the side of the woman's face as a medic worked to stanch the flow. She met Jo's eyes, and her own seemed to have broken, one of them still silver-gray, the other unnaturally green, and her mouth was moving, trying to tell her something, but Jo couldn't hear her.

A man's hand pressed against her forehead, forced her head back, and she saw he had something in his hand, and she thought it looked a lot like a Tranq-7, the kind her father had used when they needed to sedate a bounty. A piece of ice dug into the side of her neck, seemed to eat at her skin like rot on a piece of fruit, and she realized she was losing consciousness, and she tried to fight it.

I'm good at fighting, Joanna Dark thought. *I'm good at fighting, I always win. I can beat this. I can still win.*

Then she dropped into oblivion.

Carrington Institute
Rooms of Stanley Peter Grimshaw
London, England
January 25th, 2021

"What the hell just happened?" Steinberg demanded. "What the hell happened to the feed?"

Grimshaw's fingers flew over his projected keyboard, his hunt-and-peck style as rapid-fire as ever, before stopping to readjust his eyeglasses and stare at his monitor. The screen, which had only moments before been a riot of colored horizontal threads that had jumped, shimmied, and pulsed, now displayed only a single flatline. Over the speakers linked to the computer, instead of Jo and Carcareas's voices, came only the gentle hiss of empty air.

"Did the hack go down?" Steinberg asked. "On the ThroatLink? Did you lose the ThroatLink?"

Grimshaw shook his head slightly, resumed typing in a flurry. It couldn't be over. Not after the magic Grim had worked to track down Carcareas's ThroatLink and tap in—cross-referencing thousands of communications between CMO operatives, until he uncovered the socket to

"Elena Iseli," the internal alias for the enigmatic Portia de Carcareas.

Steinberg stared at the monitor, trying to will the single line to split once more, to dance again with the sound of Joanna Dark's voice, distorted and crossed with static. It hadn't been easy to hear her, and it had been only marginally easier to make out Carcareas, herself, especially once the shooting had started, but there had been sound, they'd had the link.

And now it was gone, and even though he hated himself for it, the doubt had taken seed.

Steinberg continued to stare at the monitor and tried to put a name to what he was suddenly feeling. It was a peculiar sensation, similar in memory to others, but not quite like anything he had ever felt before. Like someone had shoved a balloon into his chest, then rapidly inflated it with ice. Like free-falling before letting his parachute open, except he was still standing in the middle of Grimshaw's cluttered and jumbled room in the Institute Residence Building. Like tumbling in a crashing car, back before null-g made gravity less of a problem.

It was not unlike what he'd felt the first time he'd ever gone into combat, the mix of pure terror and pure exhilaration that came before training and instinct took over.

And it was, he realized, an awful lot like heartbreak.

"She's not dead, Grim," Steinberg said. "She's not. You've got to get the feed back."

Grimshaw gave up at the keyboard, shoved himself back in his chair. He was agitated, clearly, and there was a stress in his voice when he spoke that Steinberg took, at first, to be a shared fear for Joanna.

"The link's dead, Jon. There's no signal at all, there's nothing."

"You're sure?"

"Of course I'm sure. It's not *broadcasting*, do you get it? It's a dead link, which means Carcareas's probably dead, too."

"I don't give a rat's ass about Carcareas. We've got to get Jo back."

Grimshaw turned in his seat, and his expression surprised Steinberg with the depth of its fear.

"She's not dead, Grim," Steinberg said again, trying to reassure him. "You've never seen Jo in the field. I have. A dataDyne hit team, even in her condition, she would've found a way out of it, especially if she knew CMO backup was on the way. She's not dead."

Grimshaw shook his head rapidly, as if to say that Steinberg was wrong, that Steinberg was missing the point altogether. Then he rose from his chair and started past the other man for the door.

"What the hell are you doing?" Steinberg moved, putting himself between the hacker and the exit. "We're not done, Grim! We've got to get her back, we've got to find out where she is."

Grimshaw continued forward, trying to dodge around Steinberg, clearly agitated. Steinberg stepped back, blocking the doorway entirely.

"Jon, get out of my way, man! We've got to talk to the Old Man!"

"Are you out of your mind?" Steinberg asked. "What the hell's gotten into you? Jo needs our help! Sit the hell back down, Grim, start hacking Tachi-Amosa's ThroatLink, something!"

"It doesn't matter!" Grimshaw tried for the door again, this time actually reaching out for the knob, then jerking his hand back as Steinberg knocked it out of the way. The look on his face was bordering on hysteria. "There's nothing we can do! We have to tell the Old Man! We have to tell him what we've learned!"

This isn't about Jo, Steinberg realized. *He's spooked by something else entirely.*

"We're not going to the Old Man," Steinberg said.

Then the door behind them opened, and from the look on Grimshaw's face, Steinberg knew who it was.

"No need," Daniel Carrington said. "The Old Man has come to you."

Carrington made them accompany him back across the Institute grounds to his office before letting either of them speak. Steinberg suspected there were two reasons for this, both of which he understood, but only one of which he felt was necessary. The first was that Carrington most likely found Grimshaw's personal quarters distasteful, and Steinberg couldn't fault him for that. The man wasn't prudish—and if what Jo had said about Carrington's prior relationship with Cassandra DeVries was to be believed, he was probably quite the opposite—but he was certainly reserved. Dressing down his chief programmer as well as his head of operations while surrounded by the cheesecake that adorned Grimshaw's walls would have probably made him uncomfortable, not to mention diminished his authority.

That was Steinberg's guess, at any rate.

The second reason was far more practical. By making them wait, Carrington was letting both Steinberg and Grimshaw soak in their own juices, so to speak. To Steinberg, who understood the tactic, it made little difference. Grimshaw was another matter. Throughout their walk, Steinberg heard the hacker muttering to himself, and it didn't sound good at all. By the time they'd actually reached Carrington's office, Steinberg was beginning to wonder if Grimshaw wasn't in danger of losing it altogether.

Carrington rested his walking stick against the side of his desk, then took his time coming around to his seat and settling in. He didn't offer either of them chairs, and when Grimshaw went for one, he was stopped with a growl.

"I didn't say you could sit, Stanley," Carrington hissed.

Grimshaw looked like he'd been slapped, and it wasn't solely due to the reprimand. To Steinberg's knowledge, Daniel Carrington had never used Grimshaw's Christian name before.

Carrington leveled his gaze at Steinberg, the bags under his eyes heavy and dark, making the glare all the more potent. For several seconds he didn't speak, and Steinberg waited it out. Beside him, Grimshaw shuffled, staring at his feet.

"Where is she now?" Carrington said, softly.

"We don't know," Steinberg said.

"You don't know."

"We lost her. We were trying to reacquire her when you interrupted us."

One of Carrington's bushy eyebrows crept slowly higher at Steinberg's choice of words.

"Oh," Carrington said, just as quietly as before. "I interrupted you, did I? Under siege for seven days, you let Joanna walk out of here to raise all sorts of Cain in the world, but I interrupted you."

Steinberg bit back his immediate response, then decided to hell with it, the worst the man could do was fire him.

"That is what you wanted her to do, sir, isn't it?"

Carrington's other eyebrow crept up to match the first before both of them fell once more to their accustomed positions. "You presume an awful lot, Jonathan. An awful lot."

Steinberg thought about that for a moment, and it seemed to him that he actually didn't presume much at all, but he thought keeping that to himself might be the wiser course. Beside him, Grimshaw was still staring at the floor, now worrying the carpet with the toe of his left sneaker. His breathing was growing more rapid, and Steinberg wondered if the hacker wasn't about to have a panic attack, or worse.

"Where did you lose her?" Carrington asked.

"Veracruz, Mexico," Steinberg said. "She'd made contact with a high-level CMO operative, name of Elena Iseli, previously known to us as Portia de Carcareas."

"The woman from New York."

"Yes, sir."

"Iseli is her real name, then?"

"Yes, sir. We were able to capture audio off of most the conversation, but there was a complication before things really got started. A dataDyne hit team arrived on the scene. I think it's pretty clear the target was Agent Dark, and not Iseli. There was an intense exchange of fire, to what result we don't know. Iseli called in CMO backup to cover exfil for herself and Agent Dark—they're *very* interested in Jo, sir, I'm not sure exactly why. They'd broken the ambush and were pinned down when the feed on the ThroatLink cut out. We have no intelligence on the resolution of the fight. It's possible that Iseli is dead."

Steinberg expected Carrington to ask about Joanna, then, about her status before the feed had died, but he didn't. Instead, he asked, "And what did Agent Dark learn?"

Steinberg needed a second, felt the familiar surge of anger that was becoming the requisite emotion in all conversations with Carrington regarding Joanna Dark.

"CMO claims they're not responsible for the deaths of Bricker and Matsuo," Steinberg said. "It sounded like Iseli honestly believed that Jo had done them gratis, as an attempt to earn CMO favor for a possible defection."

For the first time, the quiet anger that had been simmering in Carrington's expression seemed to drain away, and he moved his eyes from where they'd been fixed on Steinberg's to a position past the man's shoulder, focusing on the opposite wall. He blinked slowly, almost sleepily.

"Not Core-Mantis," Carrington whispered, and it was

clear that he was talking more to himself than to Steinberg or Grimshaw, that he was thinking aloud. "Not Core-Mantis, and there's no gain for dataDyne, either. Yet Core-Mantis benefits. Who's backing them? Who's responsible?"

Grimshaw spoke, without looking up, blurting, "Continuity."

The word had an immediate and electrifying effect on Carrington, made him sit bolt upright in his chair and come forward in his seat all at once. To Steinberg, who had heard Iseli mention it, the reaction was bewildering. It was as if Grimshaw had said "trout" or "mauve" or something equally nonsensical.

"Are you sure?" Carrington said.

Grimshaw wiped at his nose, forced himself to look up and meet his employer's eyes, and Steinberg, out of his own periphery, saw that the fear Grimshaw had been carrying earlier now bore a striking resemblance to outright panic. The hacker nodded, then nodded again, more vigorously.

"We recorded the conversation, we have it, I can play it for you," Grimshaw said, and then the words started tumbling out of him in a rush. "Jo asked her who was behind it, who was doing it, and Iseli, she said 'The Continuity' and then we lost the rest of it, because there was an incoming transmission from CMO direct to Iseli, they were warning her that dataDyne was on the ground and Iseli responded but we heard it, boss, we—"

"Play it for me," Carrington snapped, pulling himself from his seat by the edge of his desk, grabbing his walking stick once more.

Grimshaw balked, then lurched forward, taking the vacated seat. He searched for a moment for a means to switch on the interface projector, then realized that Carrington was old-fashioned enough to still be using a standard computer keyboard.

The sounds of the café in Veracruz filtered into the room, surrounding Steinberg, the audio fully three-dimensional and immersive, even with the static and distortion from the hacked feed. Murmured voices speaking in Spanish, barely audible, and the sound of crockery clinking together.

Then Joanna's voice, as if she were standing just within Steinberg's reach, her peculiar mutt of an accent gentle, even if her tone was insistent.

"You know who it was, though. Don't you?"

Iseli's answer came as if she was standing behind him. *"I have a very strong suspicion, yes."*

"Tell me."

There was a pause, a rise in the ambient noise before it fell away again as the audio stream in the ThroatLink compensated for Iseli's voice.

"The Continuity."

Grimshaw was staring at Carrington, where the big man now stood beside his desk, leaning on his walking stick, his eyes closed. If he had a reaction to the words, Steinberg missed it.

"The who?"

"The Continuity, Joanna . . ."

A new voice broke in, another woman's, the sound fully immersive, surrounding Steinberg but oddly modulated, as if layering itself between the ambient sound of the café and Iseli's voice.

"Xiphos Command, Molpadia Alpha, confirm," the woman said.

"Alpha, I've asked not to be interrupt—"

"Molpadia Alpha, be advised, dataDyne assassination forces confirmed converging on your location. We are en route, ETA two m—"

"That's enough," Carrington said, and the sounds surrounding them disappeared, and the office fell into silence once more. Carrington planted his stick, then used it to help him make his way to the windows at the wall opposite his desk. The glass registered his approach, shifted from translucent to opaque. Outside, the lights on the Institute remained predominantly dark, and the light dome thrown into the sky by London was all the more vibrant as a result. Steinberg had to resist the urge to tell the Old Man that maybe standing that close to a window wasn't a good idea, given the circumstances. Then again, if the Continuity—whoever the hell they were—were to attack them with something that could penetrate the reinforced concrete and ballistic multilayered glass, where any of them stood in the room wouldn't much matter.

Still seated at Carrington's desk, Grimshaw spoke, his voice subdued. "It makes sense, now. Doesn't it? If it's the Continuity, if they . . . if they're real, then it all makes sense."

"They're real, Grim," Carrington said. "They've always been real."

Steinberg watched as Grimshaw visibly shivered.

"What the hell is the Continuity?" Steinberg asked.

Neither Grimshaw nor Carrington immediately answered. Standing at the window, the Old Man closed his eyes, his brow furrowing, and for several moments remained that way, long enough that Steinberg began to wonder if he'd even been heard. But before he could ask his question again, Carrington spoke up.

"We're going offline," he declared. "The whole of the Institute, every campus."

Technophobe though he was, Steinberg found himself stunned with the enormity of the declaration. "You can't be serious."

"No, it's the only choice we have." Carrington pivoted on his stick, turning to back to them. "If the system's been compromised, we must take steps."

"I'm not the tech guy, I know that, but I also know that taking the whole network offline while we're under siege is pretty much handing the keys over to dataDyne or whoever it is we're facing."

"Then console yourself with the fact that it isn't, at least for the moment, dataDyne that is our problem." Carrington moved to the desk, putting his attention on Grimshaw. "Get to the Ops Center, have Communications send a flash signal to all campuses, director eyes only, most secret and immediate precedence, on my authorization, understood? You're going to need to coordinate with all of them, Grim, every campus, every machine. I want then all offline, and then I want them purged."

Grimshaw looked like he was going to be ill. "Even the optical?"

"Especially the optical, Grim. Then find yourself a clean machine—and I mean a *clean* one—and start coding. We need a bot and we need it fast, something we can get to every campus that they can introduce into their systems to sniff out any unauthorized codes, snappers, traps, or bombs. It has to be a damn good one, you understand me, lad? It has to be the best bot you've ever coded, because if just one line of Continuity survives this and we reinitialize the network, we'll be even worse off than we are now."

"We take the network down, how are we going to distribute the 'bot?" Grimshaw asked.

Carrington motioned with his head toward Steinberg. "Hand delivery. Now go. I'll want to see your work in three hours."

Grimshaw nodded, rising hastily, and literally ran from the room.

Carrington was looking at Steinberg, his expression unreadable.

"What's the Continuity? What the hell is going on?"

Carrington moved away from the desk, settled himself

heavily onto one of the couches in his office. He shifted the stick from his left to his right hand, set it to lean beside him.

"Is Joanna alive?" he asked.

"My gut says yes, absolutely," Steinberg answered without hesitating. "You want facts, I've got none for you, and with the network going down, I'm not going to be able to get you any without heading to Mexico myself."

"You're staying here."

"If she's hurt—"

"Then she'll have to deal with it herself. We have other problems, Jon, and on a much grander scale."

"I understand that, I've got that, even if I don't know the how or the why of it. Are you going to tell me what the Continuity is, Daniel, or do I have to chase down Grim and beat it out of him?"

The Old Man ran a hand over his beard, scratched at his chin. "Information warfare isn't nearly as new a concept as many people would like to believe, Jonathan. While people like yourself go out and pound the ground, as you're so fond of saying, there have always been others seeking to intercept, corrupt, and destroy the flow of information on a battlefield."

"Yes, it's called espionage."

"No," Carrington raised a finger, admonishing. "Not like this. This is more than that, Jonathan. As our world has become more networked, more dependent on machines and computers to relay commands, so to has the art of war. DataDyne's playbook doesn't begin with an information attack because it's easy or because it's convenient. It begins with one because it's necessary for anything else to follow. You strike the brain, and thus leave the heart exposed and unable to defend itself."

"They're hackers."

"Of a sort, but the word in this case is misleading, because it implies a dilettante's devotion to the art that fails to recognize the true threat, and because it implies an amateurish status. The Continuity, as I understand it, grows out of a Chinese military defense strategy established about twenty years ago, a team of experts who were devoted to information disruption and system corruption. They were called Titan Rain, amongst other things."

"Never heard of them."

"Few people did, much more's the pity. The Continuity arises out of them, but not from them, because unlike Titan Rain, the Continuity *is* a dataDyne product, in the same way that, say, Mai Hem and Friedrich Murray were dataDyne products. What little is known—and very little is known, Jon, the information I have is more supposition and rumor than fact—is that during the early teens, Zhang Li made a concerted effort to seek out and recruit the best and brightest of the new wave of hackers."

"Hackers? Not programmers?"

Carrington nodded slightly in approval. "Yes, it's a significant distinction. Hackers are, for the most part, a young group, they're not tempered by the social restraint and mores that maturity brings to bear. A programmer, you put up a sign reading 'do not enter,' they'll abide by it; a hacker will look for the quickest way inside. Grim's the same, and I believe it's a result of his age as much as his intellect.

"Zhang Li, reportedly, believed it as well. He went young. He went as young as he could. In many cases he purchased children outright from their families, or acquired them in other ways, and he secreted them away somewhere—no one knows where—and indulged them. Created a fantasy world for these children where their every desire was fulfilled, where their whims were answered without pause, hesitation, or reproach. The only discipline was the one he imposed, as was the only praise. He was their Santa Claus, and he was their Fagin.

"And in exchange for this, they were his Titan Rain. You

remember the *Karatakus* tanker disaster in Singapore, back in 2012?"

Steinberg nodded. "Liquid natural-gas tanker smashed into the harbor and exploded."

"Nearly a quarter of a million people dead," Carrington said. "That was the Continuity, Jon. They took control not only of the tanker's guidance system, but also the port and emergency response networks. They piloted the ship in at thirty-three knots."

"Why?"

"Two reasons, as I understand it. The *Karatakus* was owned by Gardener-Jordan LNG, and dataDyne had been looking to acquire the concern for quite some time, at that point, to no avail. That quickly changed in the wake of the crash."

"And the second reason?" Steinberg asked, even though he had a sickening feeling he already knew the answer.

"Because they could, Jon."

"I was afraid you'd say that."

Carrington looked to the door, the way Grimshaw had gone minutes earlier. "Grim's one of the best I've ever encountered. He's better than me, an accolade I do not hand out lightly, and he's almost as good as Cassandra DeVries, who is, without a doubt, the most gifted programmer I have ever met in a very long life with computers."

The Old Man settled his gaze back on Steinberg.

"Believe me when I say they make all three of us together look like children playing with counting sticks, Jon. If the system can be accessed, they can access it, it's honestly as simple as that. We've been wondering how Zentek fell so quickly, how it is that Beck-Yama is only hours away from becoming another subsidiary of CMO, this is how. The Continuity, Jon. They got inside each, they've been feeding information to CMO."

"But they're dataDyne's—"

Carrington shook his head, almost angrily. "No, no they're not, Jon, you're not listening to me. If what I've heard is true, they're Zhang Li's, and that's very different, because Zhang Li is dead, and they know that. Their loyalty was to him and only him. While they still may serve dataDyne, it's only due to deference to Zhang Li's memory, no other reason."

"Iseli said the Continuity was responsible for impersonating Jo. That doesn't sound like the group you're describing."

"Perhaps." Carrington frowned, then used his stick to get to his feet. "It doesn't matter. Joanna's problems are separate from our own. She did her job."

"Meaning she did exactly what you wanted her to do."

"I sense the note of disapproval in your voice." Carrington stopped by the door, waiting for Steinberg to join him. "Let's get moving. When the network goes down we're going to be like a baby in a crib, and I want to make certain no wolf comes knocking at the gate. Double the perimeter guard, and get one of the dropships up for overflight, with the others on standby."

"Why do you manipulate her like this?" Steinberg asked. "When you could have simply told her what it is you wanted her to do? You know she would have done it, she would have done it without hesitating."

"Do you truly think so?" Carrington asked.

"Yes."

"Then you'll forgive me for saying this, Jonathan, but you don't know Joanna as well as you think."

"Or maybe you don't."

That gave Carrington pause, but only for a moment.

"Assuming she gets back alive," he said, "one of us can ask her."

dataDyne Executive Safehouse
37 km ENE of Nelson, New Zealand
January 25th, 2021

"Entirely unacceptable," Cassandra told Anita Velez, furiously. "Entirely and absolutely unacceptable."

Velez didn't speak, the line of her mouth so tight that she'd driven the blood from her already pale lips.

"Twelve of our people—of *my* people—dead," Cassandra said, coming around the desk in her temporary office. She could feel herself shaking even as she moved, as if the fury she was feeling had invested every cell of her body.

Velez didn't move, not even to track her approach.

"Twelve *more* dataDyne employees," Cassandra said, moving in front of her, lowering her voice. "With mothers and fathers and sons and daughters and lovers and friends, and they're dead, Anita. Lying on rooftops and in alleyways in Veracruz, Mexico. Lying with bullet holes through their chests and shrapnel through their brains and their limbs broken and their blood shed. Lying in Core-Mantis OmniGlobal–controlled territory, so we can't even get their bodies back."

She fell silent for a moment, feeling her heart pounding in her chest.

"And for what?" Cassandra added, quietly. "For nothing, Anita. For nothing at all."

Velez stayed silent.

"You may speak."

Velez glanced from the middle-distance, met Cassandra's eyes, then looked away again. "I accept full responsibility for the failure of the operation, Madame Director."

"You bloody well should. How could it have gone so wrong, Anita? How in the world did this happen?"

"We made a tactical error."

" 'We'?"

"Director Mack and myself," Velez said. "We correctly identified the CMO response team's point of origin, but not its approach vector. As a result, the extraction vehicle for the dataDyne team was not properly staged to provide stand-off cover."

"Where is Director Mack now?"

"I believe he is preparing his resignation, Madame Director."

Cassandra turned away from Velez, back toward her desk. Message indicators blinked on her screen, three of them already marked as urgent, another six upgrading to immediate. She put a hand to her forehead, tried to massage out the tension headache that was squeezing her temples as if they were held in a set of oversized pliers.

"Who will you replace him with?" Cassandra asked.

"Madame Director?"

She turned back to look at Velez, saw that the woman still hadn't moved, and waved a hand at her, dismissing the pose. Velez relaxed almost reluctantly. "Who are you replacing Mack with?" Cassandra repeated.

"That will be your decision, Madame Director, not mine."

"It's your division, it's CORPSEC."

"The director of counterintelligence operations must be appointed by the CEO, Madame Director."

"As if I don't have enough to do? Who came up with that damn rule?"

"Master Li, Madame Director."

"Why the hell did he do that?"

"To prevent CORPSEC from gaining power to such an extent that the division might subvert or otherwise take over the corporation."

Cassandra stared at Velez, blinked. "He was afraid of a coup?"

"Master Li was . . . a cautious man."

He was a bloody loon, Cassandra DeVries thought.

"Fine, wonderful. And I suppose under that logic it would make no sense at all for me to consult you regarding the filling of the position, correct? Even though it's your area of expertise and not my own."

"That is correct, Madame Director."

"Fine." Cassandra took her chair, reached for her mug of coffee, and found the contents cold. She set the mug back down. "And in the meantime, Joanna Dark and her friends at CMO are still out there, still determining how best to murder me."

"We will reacquire the target, Madame Director, I assure you." Velez spoke with almost uncharacteristic softness. "We will reacquire the target, and I will personally make certain that neither she, nor anyone else, poses a threat to you or dataDyne."

"You're going to do it yourself, is that it, Anita?"

Velez met her eyes again, this time holding the look. "If you will permit me to continue as your director of corporate security, Madame Director, I swear I will."

Cassandra flicked her fingers across the keyboard in front

of her, cycling through the messages that had arrived, thinking. All three of the urgents were from the marketing and media division, begging for her attention regarding the rollout of AirFlow 2. Two of them concerned the actual staging of the event: reminded her that a rehearsal had yet to be scheduled and that they were rapidly running out of time. The third queried her wardrobe and when she would be free for a makeover.

There was nothing from Dr. Ventura, no update on Arthur's progress.

Cassandra looked back to Velez, who was still waiting for a response.

"No," Cassandra said. "You'll come with me back to Paris."

Velez looked as if Cassandra had just asked her to eat the oil glands off of a rotten skunk. "Madame Director, I cannot—"

"You really don't want to tell me what you can and cannot allow at this point, Anita. Not after that fiasco this morning. I'm going back to Paris, I have to start prepping the rollout, I've got marketing climbing down my back, and I've heard nothing from Ventura since he returned to DataFlow. I've been here long enough."

"I do not believe it is safe for you to return home, Madame Director."

"Are you saying you can't protect me, Anita?"

"It would be easier—"

"I'm not interested in easy at this point. I'm interested in what can be done. Are you saying you *can't* protect me?"

"No, Madame Director, not at all. Only that I will be unable to do both that and pursue the target in question at the same time."

"I've got a solution for you, then. Contact Colonel Shaw, have him meet me in Paris."

The color that had leached from Velez's face at the start of their conversation returned, flushing her fair skin almost to red. "I think that would be remarkably ill-advised, Madame Director. I think that would be, if I may say so, approaching folly. Their record of late has not been distinguished, not between their failures in both Hovoro and Los Angeles."

"You feel they shouldn't be given another chance?"

"Failure should not be rewarded."

"I'm sure former-Director Mack agrees with you," Cassandra said. "I want more men on the field, and Shaw can bring the Hawks to bear. We're approaching rollout, Anita, and I don't want to have to worry that I'm going to be shot while unveiling Arthur to the world."

"But Colonel Shaw—"

"Is getting a last chance," Cassandra DeVries said. "Just like you are."

She flew back to Paris late that night, paradoxically arriving early the same morning, and went directly from the data-Dyne hangar at De Gaulle to her offices via motorcade, Velez riding with her the entire time. It was just past six in the morning when she reached DataFlow, and the building was mercifully silent, only the skeleton night shift working the upper offices. She dropped her bags, told Velez that she expected to meet with Shaw in exactly one hour and fifteen minutes.

"I'll be back shortly," Cassandra said.

"Where are you going?"

"The lab. Just to check on progress."

"I'll accompany you."

Cassandra stopped, trying to hide her annoyance. She supposed that she could issue a direct order, that she could simply tell Velez to leave her—for the time being, at least—

the hell alone. But as she watched the older woman move to catch up with her in the hallway, saw the same fatigue on her face that Cassandra was feeling herself, it seemed like a spiteful thing to do. She was angry about the failure in Veracruz, guilty about the deaths of the men and women working for dataDyne, but in truth, her ire was directed more at Joanna Dark and, by extension, Daniel Carrington, than at Mack and Velez for their failure.

She supposed, if she were a different CEO, that she would have demanded Velez's resignation as she had accepted Mack's. Certainly, if Zhang Li were still in charge, he would have done no less—and, Cassandra was coming to suspect, probably a great deal more. The corporate culture of dataDyne expected as much, really; failure was, as Velez herself had said, not something to be rewarded.

Yet she hadn't asked for Velez's resignation, had, in fact, not even truly considered asking for it, though she had known that Velez would offer it if requested. The woman had all but done so.

Riding together in the lift down to the AI lab, Cassandra knew why she hadn't. It wasn't simply that Anita Velez was her friend, or at least the closest thing to one she was likely to have for a long time. It was that Anita Velez was her *only* friend, at this point. There just wasn't anyone else. Whether by duty or by choice, Anita Velez had remained the only constant in Cassandra DeVries's rapidly changing life.

And Cassandra didn't want to be alone.

Dr. Ventura was in the lab when they arrived, working at his private terminal outside the quantum optical chamber, lit by the tower of white light that emanated from the datacore. He didn't hear them enter, and Cassandra was grateful for that, because it gave her a chance to look around unmolested for once, Velez's shadowing notwithstanding.

She approached the glass wall surrounding the datacore first. It was an old habit, and Cassandra supposed it was as close to allowing the spiritual into her life as she ever came, to stand in the cast of its brilliant white light, to look down at the spinning heart of illumination and feel swept away, if just for a moment, by the raw power inherent in the machine. Billions of terabytes processed per millionth of seconds, how could she not feel that this was her cathedral, how could she not feel moved? This was the pinnacle of modern computing; there was nowhere else to go to find a machine that could do more, and do it faster.

Which, following that logic, meant that Cassandra De-Vries was committing a heresy of a sort, she supposed. Because that's what Arthur was, what she wanted Arthur to be. The *next* stage—not the present but the future. Carrington had changed the world with null-g, and Cassandra had helped to make that change a true one with AirFlow.Net. But an artificial intelligence, a *truly* thinking, sentient machine—that would make null-g look like canned beer. It would change everything.

Resting her forehead against the glass, the brilliance of the core burning against her retinas despite her closed eyes, she could see it, see how it could work, how it *would* work. The beauty of it, and its simplicity. A machine that would understand not only what was said to it, but what was *not*. A machine that would empathize, that would *care*. A machine that would *think,* on its own, by itself. A machine with a *soul,* and if she could make it happen, if she could do it right, a machine with a soul that was pure.

A machine that would shame me for what I have done, Cassandra DeVries thought.

She could see it. Not Arthur, not yet, she knew that. But soon. The machine that would be Arthur's brother or sister, Arthur's son or daughter. And Cassandra would help him do it, not for the sake of vanity, not to etch her name in history.

She would do it for the same reasons she had written Air-Flow.Net. She would do it to make the world a better place.

Velez touched her elbow lightly, pulling Cassandra back from the reverie, and she straightened, stepping back from the observation wall. Ventura apparently hadn't seen them yet, still bent to his terminal. Cassandra moved closer, examining the work that had been left out on lab tables and desks, the stacks of code and memory modules. Ventura continued to type, and she couldn't help but smile at that. There had been times herself when she'd become so lost in the code that the very building could have collapsed around her, and she would only have noticed because the power had gone out.

"Edward?"

Ventura's head came up as if caught in a noose, his expression almost comical in its surprise and alarm, and Cassandra had to bite her own tongue to keep from laughing at him. He put out both hands, as if to steady himself, sending his keyboard clattering from the desk even as he stumbled to his feet. At her shoulder, Anita Velez made a small sound, part disapproving, part curious.

"Ma'am." Ventura bent, scooped up the keyboard, settling it awkwardly back at his desk. "Ma'am, sorry, I . . . I didn't realize you were back."

"Just got in. I apologize, Edward, I didn't mean to surprise you like that."

"No, no, it's all right. I just . . ." Ventura gestured at his monitor, then abruptly leaned forward, striking a couple of keys, frowning. ". . . I was distracted, as you can see."

"I've been known to get the same way."

Ventura nodded, responding to her smile, then glanced

over to where Velez was now examining the contents of a nearby desk. He looked back to Cassandra, waiting, and when it became apparent that she'd rattled him so much that he wasn't about to offer, she sighed and gave him the cue.

"And how's Arthur?" Cassandra asked, gently.

"Good, he's good. Ninety-nine percent. We finished the last of the modules just after midnight, I sent everyone else home. Fighting with a bug in the Outland interface, it's the one I told you about last time, he's getting confused with verbal instructions. There's a lost line in there, something, I've been looking for it since two, maybe three this morning."

"Can I help?" Cassandra asked. "An extra pair of eyes, even if they're not fresh, might do some good."

Velez cleared her throat before Ventura could answer, and Cassandra glanced to her, saw that the woman was subtly indicating her wristwatch. Cassandra nodded, smiled apologetically at Ventura.

"Spoke too soon, I'm afraid," she said. "I've a meeting to attend, it seems. Probably should get myself cleaned up before it, as well. I can only imagine I look quite the fright."

"Oh, no, ma'am," Ventura said. "You look beautiful."

Cassandra laughed. "That's very kind, even if it's both untrue and unnecessary, Edward. Let me know when you have the interface back up and running, all right? We can route Arthur into my office, he and I can have another chat."

"Yes, ma'am, absolutely."

"And you might want to see about getting cleaned up yourself. You look like you haven't slept in days."

Ventura reflexively smoothed his necktie, then tightened the knot at his neck. "You know how it gets."

"That I do." She turned to Velez, saw that the other woman was watching Ventura with what Cassandra took to be an amused smile. "Let's head back, shall we?"

"Certainly, Madame Director."

"Edward?"

"Yes, ma'am?"

"Tell Arthur I'm looking forward to talking to him again."

"I will, ma'am."

<hr>

She used her private washroom to shower, thinking she would have to dress in the same clothes she'd been wearing, only to discover that a new suit had been laid out for her by one of her personal assistants. As was becoming expected, everything fit perfectly, from the lingerie to the new shoes.

Cassandra emerged to find Velez waiting where she had left her, but with the addition of a fresh pot of coffee and a brightly polished green apple. Cassandra took the coffee gratefully.

She'd finished half the cup and taken the apple when Velez said, "I wish to remind you of our conversation about the need to delegate."

"This is about Arthur."

"I recognize that the project means a great deal to you, Madame Director. But I feel it is both inappropriate and unnecessary for you to extend as much time and attention as you have done to Dr. Ventura. His job is to bring the project *you* have authorized to completion in whatever way necessary. You have all but told him that you are on call for him should he need your assistance."

"I've done no such thing," Cassandra said. She moved to her desk, taking a bite of the apple.

"You offered your assistance in debugging the code."

"That was a courtesy."

"And if he had accepted the offer, Madame Director? Would you have canceled your meetings for the day?"

"You're being absurd."

"I am merely illustrating my point."

Suddenly annoyed, Cassandra said, "Anita, let it go."

"Of course."

She took her seat behind her desk, flipped on the sequence of holographic projectors, then went through the ordeal of logging into her account. Velez checked her watch again, then moved toward the coffee service, pouring herself a cup.

"It does mean a great deal to me," Cassandra said, suddenly. "That doesn't mean my interest in Arthur is solely personal."

Velez nodded slightly, as if to say that she was waiting to hear the rest.

"It's professional, as well. However much it means to me personally, it means much more to dataDyne. AirFlow 2 has to succeed, Anita, or else we lose everything we've gained in AirFlow.Net. Upgrades are a tricky business: they fill the public with uncertainty and doubt, and if they don't work as designed or as promised, it can cause tremendous damage. We don't want to lose the AirFlow share to CMO or Carrington."

"No," Velez said, slowly. "Of course, you are correct."

"All right."

The holograph to her left shimmered, redrew, and her appointment secretary appeared. *"Madame Director, your eight-forty has arrived."*

"Send him in, please, Adrianna."

"Yes, ma'am."

Velez set her empty cup back on the service, moving to the door. "I have a few things I should look into, Madame Director. I trust you do not mind if I am not present for your meeting with the colonel?"

"What sort of things?"

"Regarding your safety now that you have returned to Paris."

Cassandra frowned, wondering if Velez was being petulant, then dismissed the thought just as quickly. Petulance
was an indulgence, and nothing about Anita Velez indulged.

"I'll be back to escort you home," Velez said.

"I'll expect you then."

She watched Velez leave the office, passing Colonel Leland
Shaw as he entered without saying a word. Cassandra got to
her feet, moved to shake the colonel's hand.

Then she told him exactly what she wanted him and his
Hawk Teams to do to Joanna Dark.

Core-Mantis OmniGlobal Health and
Healing Facility (Executive Branch)
Benghazi, Libya
January 27th, 2021

Jo opened her eyes to a world painted white. The ceiling and the four-bladed fan spinning lazily on its housing above her—both white. The bed and the sheet and the pillow and the hospital half-dress she found herself wearing—all white. The floor tiled in white, and the walls, including the windowsill and frame.

But outside the window, visible through the white curtains that fluttered on a warm and salted breeze, she saw a slash of blue, and pushing up onto her elbow for a better view, she knew it was the Mediterranean as much from the hue of the water as the smell of it in the air. Her father had shown her the Med not too many years before, chasing a bounty from Moscow to Vienna to Marseille and then, finally, to Tunis. He'd promised her a vacation after they'd made the skip, turned him in.

She couldn't remember the name of the bounty, Jo realized. It had been that insignificant. But she could remember that they hadn't gone swimming. The bounty in tow, they'd headed straight back to the US, to exchange their prize for cash.

Her throat hurt, too dry, and when she ran her tongue over her lips, they felt like straw. She swallowed, and the pain diminished, and she decided to try sitting fully upright, just to see if it could be managed, and to see if there was anything that she might drink.

She managed, but not without effort. Along her abdomen, around her torso especially, there was a constant, dull ache, but nothing that was impossible to endure. She could breathe, too, and she knew that was important, because she had a dim memory of not being able to, and that hadn't been pleasant at all. Yes, she still hurt, but at least it wasn't as bad as it had been in . . . in . . .

Oh, bloody hell, Jo thought.

It would come back to her, she knew it would, but for the moment she was drawing nothing, a big fat zero. She was registering aches and pains throughout her body, some of them she knew as older than others, but it was difficult to tell which was which. Her abdomen itched, and she put her right hand against her belly and saw that her hand had been bandaged, wrapped tightly in white gauze that kept her three middle fingers in a splint. Beneath the wafer-thin cotton of her hospital gown, she could make out the edges of an artificial skin patch.

Where I got shot, she remembered. *During the job in Los Angeles. I was shot in Los Angeles. Dr. Hwang patched it up, and then I tore it all to hell, and Dr. Cordell patched it up, and I tore it all to hell again.*

Who patched it up this time?

She swallowed again, felt something burn at the back of her throat. There was a stand beside the bed, with a pitcher and a cup, and she reached for the pitcher with her left, and had to hold her breath during the stretch. As she took hold of the pitcher, she caught sight of the status monitor built into the wall beside the headboard, listing her name and her vitals, her blood pressure and respirations and oxygen saturation. Then she saw the shining black and gold disk mounted on the wall, directly above the bed.

Core-Mantis OmniGlobal. I'm at a Core-Mantis facility, somewhere on the Mediterranean.

She'd never heard of a CMO medical facility placed on the Med—at least, not that she could recall.

"This," she said aloud, her voice croaking like a frog in a steam bath, "might be a very bad thing."

Her memory had returned fully by the time Portia de Carcareas came to see her, bearing a fresh pitcher of water in one hand and a shopping bag with the CMO logo on it in the other. She set the bag at the foot of the bed, hanging it off the footboard by its handle, then refilled Jo's cup before setting the pitcher on the stand.

Jo watched her without comment, and without any real sense of malice, trying to determine what she now thought of the woman. It was confusing to Jo, because her philosophy thus far had been to simply hate everyone and everything that was hypercorp or hypercorp affiliated, with the sole, grudging exception of those things Carrington, and with the worst of her ire reserved for dataDyne. By all logic, at least according to her own ethic, that put CMO squarely in the "hate them but not as much as those bastards at dataDyne" camp.

It would have been easy for Carcareas to have abandoned her in Veracruz, Jo knew, to have left Jo to face the dataDyne hit squad all on her own, with nothing but a wounded body and a P9P to fight them with. If Carcareas had done so, the best case scenario would have had Jo waking up in a data-Dyne super-black facility someplace where no one would ever hear her screaming, and the worst case would have been her never waking up at all.

But Carcareas hadn't. She'd done quite the opposite, in fact, and from the square of black that now covered Carcareas's left eye and the Nüe-Skin that shone all along her left cheek and neck, Jo knew she'd paid a price for it.

"It's the twenty-seventh," Carcareas said to her as she handed over the refilled cup of water. "You've been unconscious for just over two days, all time zones considered."

Jo nodded, pushing herself back in the bed with a grimace, then using the headboard to prop herself up.

"How are you feeling?"

"Mixed," Jo said, honestly, after taking another sip of water. "Parts of me feel better than others."

"Dr. Shattari and Dr. Mezzara were the two who worked on you," Carcareas said. "They were more than a little amazed at the state you were in. It looks like you've been shot multiple times in the same place."

"Just the once."

"You keep tearing the wound open, I'm told. You had the start of an infection, as well, but they put a stop to that. You'd also fractured another rib and managed to puncture your left lung. Luckily, it's the sort of injury that sounds much worse than it actually is, at least, if it's properly treated, which I am pleased to say it was. It also goes a long way to explaining that awful sound you were making in the Plaza Lerdo in lieu of actually breathing. You sounded like you were gargling with sand, dear."

"I hadn't noticed."

"Endomorphine will do that. I am sorry, Joanna, I'm afraid that might have been my fault. It dulls the pain receptors so much you can't tell when you're hurting yourself and when you're not."

"I'm alive, you're alive. Figure we're square."

Carcareas smiled, then patted Jo on the forearm before getting to her feet.

"There's a lav just out the door, with a shower and a bath. New clothes in the bag there on the end of your bed, everything should fit. When you feel up to it we can talk further. There's a lot to discuss, I think."

"Portia," Jo said.

"Hmm?"

"I'm not joining CMO. Just so we're clear on that. I appreciate all of this, but I'm not signing up."

Carcareas's smile was smaller, but seemed just as sincere as before. "So you keep saying."

"I just don't want a misunderstanding here."

"There's no misunderstanding, Joanna."

"It's just that it's never going to happen."

"Never say never, dear," Carcareas told her. "It's a very long time, and a lot can happen on the way to reaching it."

After dozing again for what felt like only a short while, Jo got up and took the bag Carcareas had left with her out the door and across the hall to the bathroom. When she left her room, she expected to see security in the hall, some sign of surveillance or other observation, if not specifically on her, then at least in the vicinity. What she saw was only a long white corridor with windows on each end, doors identical to the one she'd just closed behind her, and the only person she saw was a blond Caucasian woman working at a desk about halfway down on the right. The woman looked up and smiled at her when Jo emerged, then went back to whatever it was she had been doing. Somewhere unseen, someone was playing opera.

Jo stepped into the bathroom and found herself surprised by both its size and appointments. In addition to the shower Carcareas had promised and the expected amenities, there was a free-standing bathtub, a whirlpool, a steam room, and a sauna. It was, Jo realized, less of a washroom than the sort of place one might find at a spa. She half expected to see a door leading to mineral springs or mud baths.

She took her time getting cleaned up, as much to keep from aggravating her wounds as to take stock of them. Her middle had been bound tightly with Nüe-Skin tape, and it seemed to be doing its job, holding her ribs in place. She couldn't see any sign of where her skin might have been penetrated in order to repair the damage to her lung. The bullet wound in her abdomen was now covered in Nüe-Skin as well, though this piece was semitranslucent, and through the bandage Jo could see the angriness of her skin where it had been punctured and then repeatedly torn.

After the shower, she tried getting dressed and discovered that it was difficult to manage with only one hand. She unwrapped the bandage around her right, freeing her fingers, and when she flexed them the pain was so minor as to be inconsequential beside all her other injuries. It made dressing much faster, and it reassured her that she could shoot with her right, should she need to.

As for the clothes that Carcareas had brought her, Jo wasn't certain what she thought of them. They were black, pants in leather, shirt in linen, and Jo thought they were more the kind of thing that Carcareas would have chosen for herself. Jo wondered if that had been a calculation on the other woman's part, a way of saying that they were alike, or that they could be. The shoes were actually boots, also black, also leather, that rose just over the ankles, and without any heel to speak of.

Jo checked herself in the mirror after she'd finished dressing, leaning in to examine the scratches still healing on her cheeks and brow. All had been filled with Nüe-Skin, and most were disappearing nicely.

Then she saw the bruising at her neck, thin lines of almost-gray running along either side of the trachea.

The blond at the desk directed Jo to where Carcareas was waiting, on a deck outside. They were only two, perhaps three stories up, and it afforded a fine view of the water. The breeze was gentle, and the sun warm but not oppressive. When Jo looked to the sides, she could see low-roofed buildings, whitewashed, and make out half a dozen minarets further away, in the city, and she understood that to mean they were in Northern Africa, rather than in southern Europe.

Carcareas was working on a laptop at a large wooden patio table with a wide green umbrella to provide shade from the sun. On the table were also a pack of cigarettes, a pitcher of juice, and a bowl of fruit.

Jo walked over, taking her time, feeling the sunlight gathering on the variety of black fabrics she was now wearing. Her first instinct was to be shrill, to play it the way her father would have done, with muscle and volume, but she knew, already, that doing so would backfire. She was halfway to Carcareas when she realized that she'd been right about the clothing, as well, that they were wearing almost identical outfits, the sole difference being that Carcareas's shirt was white.

"It's all fresh," Carcareas told her. "Help yourself. You must be starving."

"I want it taken out," Jo said. She said it calmly, like an adult would.

Carcareas glanced up from her work on her laptop, and her brow almost furrowed for a moment. Then she went back to her work, saying, "I'm sure you do."

"I'm not joking, Portia, I want the ThroatLink taken out, and I want it taken out now. I didn't ask for it, I didn't want it, and you had no right inserting it."

"No."

Jo stared, feeling the anger rumble, threatening to erupt. "Did you do anything else? Give me new eyes, for instance?"

"And replace those lovely baby blues of yours? That *would* be a crime." Carcareas closed the laptop, then indicated the seats around the table with a sweep of her hand. "Sit down, Joanna."

"You didn't answer my question."

"Sit down and I shall."

Fighting her every urge to be contrary, Jo took a seat.

"You ought to eat something."

"You cut me open and put a piece of tech inside my *body*, Portia, and you did it without my permission. You put a damn *bug* in me! So you'll cut me a little slack if I'm feeling a bit too, oh, I don't know, *violated*, to eat anything you might offer me."

Carcareas's expression shifted subtly, and for a moment Jo didn't know what she was reading there, if it was regret or fatigue or something else altogether.

"You're right," she said, after a moment. "It was—it *is*— a violation. But it's one that can be undone with relative ease, and one that I think is warranted, considering what you want from us."

"If it's so easy to undo, let's handle it right now."

Carcareas shook her head slightly. "No, Joanna, not yet.

Who knows? If you decided you like working for us, you may wish to keep it."

"I'm not a fan of body modification."

"You mean aside from multiple piercings and a tattoo or two."

"I have one tattoo, and it's different, and you know that, so don't go all coy with me."

Carcareas considered, then nodded. "No, you're correct. I won't make light of it again. The situation with the ThroatLink is this, Joanna. With it, we'll be able to monitor your movements and your status, we'll be able to overhear any conversation you have. We also neglected to provide you with the means to open communications, or to select the band and frequency. So you're very correct when you call it a bug. That's exactly what it is."

For a moment, Jo said nothing, mostly because the only things she could think to say were the kinds of things Jack Dark would have said at that moment. Then he would have followed his words with action, most likely bouncing Carcareas's head repeatedly off of any conveniently available hard surface.

Probably a bad idea to do that, Jo thought.

But it took almost a minute to suppress the urge, to calm her racing heart and suppress the sense of outrage she was feeling.

When she finally felt she could speak without using every profanity she'd ever heard in all of her travels, she said, "We were interrupted in Veracruz."

"Yes."

"I'd like to continue that conversation now. I'd like to know who's been using my face to commit murder."

"They're called the Continuity," Portia de Carcareas said. Then she told Jo the rest.

It took almost forty-five minutes for Carcareas to lay it all out, at least as she professed to understand it, and for Jo to have her most immediate questions answered. During the conversation, Jo relented and helped herself to the fruit in the bowl and most of the juice in the pitcher, and before they were finished a young man came out onto the deck and served them each a plate of grilled swordfish on a bed of couscous, along with a bottle of white wine. Jo passed on the wine but ate the fish.

"I've been to Zhang Li's mansion," Jo said when Carcareas finally had finished. "The youngest people I saw there were the concubines and that bitch Mai Hem."

"My understanding is that they moved in after his disappearance."

"And they approached CMO about Zentek and Beck-Yama?"

"They approached us about Zentek, made the offer to use their unique services."

"This Fan chick, she's the one who made the offer?"

"Chun Fan, yes. She's the one I've dealt with in every instance. I believe she's their leader, at least nominally. She certainly speaks for them."

"And you guys didn't think it was suspicious? CMO didn't think it was odd that Zhang Li's information assassins were offering their services to dataDyne's competition?"

Carcareas turned her wineglass by its stem, smiling. "Of course we did, Joanna. But the offer was a hard one to refuse. And thus far, they have done everything they've promised to do."

"So how do I figure into this?" Jo twisted in the chair, trying to ease the stiffness she was now feeling around her middle. "I mean, did Fan come to you and say, hey, we'll deliver Zentek and whack Georg Bricker as a bonus while making it look like Carrington did it?"

"Your name never came up."

"Excuse me?" Jo stared, incredulous. "You expect me to believe that?"

"Yes, actually, I do. Either that, or you're far more egotistical than you've led me to believe." Carcareas sipped her wine, resettled the glass on the table. "As I told you when we first met, we had very little in the way of information about you prior to your introduction to Colonel Tachi-Amosa in Mexico City. While we certainly benefited from the appearance that Carrington—via you—aided us in our takeover of Zentek, actually taking steps to do so was never discussed by anyone at CMO, nor did I broach the matter with Fan or any other member of the Continuity. We barely knew who you were, Joanna. Even if we had wanted to frame Carrington, it never would have occurred to us to do so by using a doppelganger of you."

"You're telling me that the Continuity killed Bricker on their own, that his death wasn't part of the deal?"

"Not a specified part, no. CMO paid the Continuity to help facilitate the hostile takeover of Zentek. That's all."

"Someone else from CMO proposed it to the Continuity, then," Jo said. "One of your peers or bosses or something, they told them to use me."

"Joanna, I am the only one who was authorized to deal with the Continuity. Your name simply never came up."

"But that doesn't make sense!" Jo said, loudly, and then immediately regretted doing so as her chest once again reminded her that it was still in recovery.

"Of course it does. You're being singled out by the Continuity." Carcareas turned her wineglass again, raised her eyes from it to meet Jo's. "Why would they do that, I wonder?"

Jo thought about that, thought about what she could tell Carcareas versus what she should tell her. Zhang Li's death was still a closely guarded secret by the Institute, and there was reason to believe—even now—that dataDyne itself didn't know what had truly become of their founder. Sharing that intelligence with Core-Mantis OmniGlobal seemed like a foolish thing to do, as did explaining that Zhang hadn't been the only member of the Li family to die at Jo's hands.

It's revenge, Jo realized. *They know, somehow, the Continuity knows what I did, that I killed Zhang Li and Mai Hem. Their sister and their father, both.*

"No ideas?" Carcareas asked.

"None that I'm inclined to share, no."

"I adore your bluntness," Carcareas said with a laugh. "You have no idea how refreshing it is."

"Is that why you've been so helpful? Healing me up and telling me all this, because you like me?"

"You remind me of someone, Jo, let's leave it at that."

"Let's not. Tell me who."

"Me, of course. And, as I've already stated several times, I truly believe that you would be not only a great asset to CMO, but that you would find life much more to your liking working with us than working for a man like Daniel Carrington."

"I like working for Daniel Carrington," Jo said.

"You like working for a madman, then?"

"I beg your pardon?"

"He's insane, Jo, surely you've seen it. While the rest of the world goes about its business barely noticing the hypercorps, Carrington does everything in his power to push the battles between us into the open. His hatred of dataDyne in particular is well known and well documented. Why would he do that?"

"Because the hypercorps are evil and he understands that."

"Oh, please. You're betraying your age. Hypercorps are *business,* Joanna, and business can have both positive and negative effects. Saying that all the hypercorps are evil, or that hypercorps are inherently evil, is as fatuous and simplistic as saying that all politicians are corrupt. Speaking for myself and for Core-Mantis—something which, I hope you'll agree, I can do with some authority—we do far more good than harm in the world."

"But the harm you do, the good you do, that's incidental," Jo said. "You're not in it to do good. You're in it to make money."

"There's nothing wrong with turning a profit."

"There is if you do it off the blood and suffering of others."

"And that's what the hypercorps do, that's what your saying?"

"Yes."

"Then you include Carrington in that, I assume."

"What? No, the Institute isn't a hyper—"

"Joanna, two doctors had you in surgery for almost four hours, and that wasn't to implant the ThroatLink. So I ask you, on whose blood and suffering does Carrington profit?"

Jo said nothing, found herself staring at her empty plate, the remains of her late lunch. Unbidden, she could hear her father's voice, his admonitions and warnings about Carrington. Even when times had been rough, when bounties had been hard to come by, Jack Dark had avoided working for, working with, Daniel Carrington.

Don't trust him, he'd told her. *Don't trust Daniel Carrington.*

Not for the first time, Joanna found herself wondering how it was that she had come to do just that, and to do it in so short a time. Wondering that, the sense that she had failed her father returned, or rather, made itself known again, because Jo knew it had never truly left her.

"Never mind," Carcareas said after a moment. "We're off

topic again, and I've obviously upset you, and that's not something I wished to do. We'll speak no more about it."

"You're wrong," Jo said. "About Carrington."

"Perhaps I am. But if I extend you that, then perhaps you might consider that you're wrong about Core-Mantis. Something to think about, at any rate."

Jo pushed her plate away. "When can I leave here?"

"Whenever you like, though I think doing so might be a mistake. DataDyne, for whatever reason, clearly wants you dead, Joanna. If you're planning on going after the Continuity, you're going to be moving through territory thick with their security forces. You're not liable to get very far."

"I didn't say I was going after the Continuity."

"And we're back to being coy. Of course you are, Joanna. That's why we inserted the ThroatLink, and that's why I'm more than willing to help you."

"So you *don't* trust them."

"I told you, we never did. What the Continuity did to Zentek and Beck-Yama, may they both rest in pieces, they can certainly do to us. That's the problem with mercenaries; they're always for sale."

"You think I'm going to do this for Core-Mantis?"

"No, dear, you're going to do it because you wish to live, and that's now what this is about. The Continuity has set you up, the same as they did Carrington. It's no coincidence that dataDyne has you in their sights. The hit team in Veracruz was an elite unit, and there for you and you alone. I was entirely incidental, I'm sure. Which means that, as far as dataDyne is concerned, you're a threat, and they're going to keep coming after you until they're sure you're not one any longer."

Jo frowned, trying to find a hole in the logic, and realizing in short order that there wasn't one. By making it appear as if she had murdered not just Bricker but also Matsuo, the

Continuity had made sure that dataDyne would notice her. DeVries knew her as one of Carrington's agents. The only possible conclusion the CEO of dataDyne could have made was that Jo had been acting under Carrington's orders, and that certainly made it look like Carrington was in league with CMO.

"Can you get me into China?" Jo asked.

"No," Carcareas said. "What Mexico is to Core-Mantis, China is to dataDyne, Joanna. There's no way we could effectively insert you into country without being compromised."

"Then I'm going to have to do it myself," Joanna said.

"Yes," Portia de Carcareas agreed. "You are."

Home of Former dataDyne CEO
Zhang Li (Deceased)
38km SW Li Xian, Sichuan Province
People's Republic of China
January 27th, 2021

"Where is she now?" Fan asked her eldest brother.

"Working her way east," Ke-Ling told her. "She's in Turkey, just arrived in Ankara. I can give you the exact street address, if you want."

"You can do that?"

Ke-Ling spun around in his chair, making a full seven-twenty, raising his arms above his head, before finishing and sliding his chair back from the console where he and four of their other siblings had been working. At the end of the room, their brother Wen, all of eleven years old, burst into peals of laughter, wildly amused by his sibling's antics.

Ke grinned at Wen, then at Fan.

"Those dumb bitches at Core-Mantis, they put a ThroatLink in her," Ke-Ling told his sister, reaching out and grabbing her around the waist with both arms. Fan laughed, not fighting him, and fell gleefully into his lap. "There's nowhere she can go we can't find her, Fan. There's nothing she can say we won't hear."

"How are we doing on the Bitch?" Fan asked, squirming as her brother tried to tickle her. "Cut it out!"

"Rock solid. The last module's in place, and your boy-toy at DataFlow is so crunched he can't even tell what code's his and what isn't anymore. As long as she's too busy to take a look at it, there's no way anyone will tell the difference."

Fan twisted, tickling Ke-Ling in return, forcing him to free her from his grip. On her feet again, she began hopping up and down on her toes, the sudden feeling of excitement almost too much to bear. She closed her eyes, tried to envision the time line in her mind. Today was the twenty-seventh; the unveiling of Arthur would be on the thirtieth. If everything was to work the way they wanted, that meant they needed Jo-Jo here no later than the evening of the twenty-eighth, to give both her and Fan the time they would need for the Chrysalis change.

She opened her eyes again. "Good."

"Mostly good," Ke-Ling said. "I told you that Carrington took his servers offline, the whole network?"

"Yes, you did."

"They're back up, now, and they're clean. They found all the puncture wounds we left, Fan, every single one of them."

"Moscow?"

"Plugged."

"Vancouver?"

"Plugged."

"Should I ask about London?"

"They're all plugged. That fat-ass Grimshaw got his game together on this one."

Fan chewed on her lip, thinking, then bit down hard enough to start a trickle of blood flowing into her mouth. "So they know it was us."

"That's what I'm thinking."

Fan rolled her tongue around, tasting the tang of copper. "Jo-Jo been in touch with them?"

"Not sure she's going to. She knows CMO linked her, so anything she says to them, they're gonna hear."

"She doesn't have to call them, Ke-Ke. She can use a kiosk."

"She does that, we'll know. You want us to intercept?"

"I want to know what she tells them, but more importantly, I want to know what they tell her. How much they know."

Ke-Ling turned in his chair, calling out for Wen to come and join them. The boy hopped off his seat and hurried over, pulling at the waistband of his pants as he did so, trying to keep them from falling to his knees.

"You should wear pants that fit," Fan admonished him. "What would father say if he saw you like that?"

"These are cool," Wen told her, matter-of-factly.

"Get Quon and Ping-Ping," Ke-Ling told him. "Tell them I want to see them right now, okay? It's about Jo-Jo."

Wen grinned and nodded, then ran out of the room.

"He's going to break his neck," Fan said.

"Then maybe he'll get pants that fit."

Fan giggled, then lapsed into further thought, closing her eyes once more. The only variable left was Jo-Jo. She was a player in the drama, and they needed her at the mansion. They needed to fete her, to reward her for the kindness she had done Fan and her siblings by killing Mai Hem. Then she needed to be punished for the murder of their father. The thought of finally being able to do both was enough to make Fan want to burst with anticipation.

Her only regret was that Joanna Dark would never see dataDyne crumble, and that was a pity. Fan would have liked to show Jo-Jo the death of dataDyne. She was sure her archenemy, her soul mate, would have shared all Fan's joy at the sight of it, at the collapse of Zhang Li's kingdom. Whether or not Jo-Jo would have appreciated that the rest of the world would follow in its wake, Fan was unsure.

It would all fall down, it would all burn. Everything would burn.

But Joanna Dark wouldn't get to see any of it, because Joanna Dark would be dead.

Fan turned back to Ke-Ling and planted a chaste kiss on his mouth, this one far more chaste than the last had been.

"Get me Jo-Jo's current address," she told her brother. "And then get me a line to Colonel Shaw."

Carrington Institute
Rooms of Jonathan Steinberg
London, England
January 27th, 2021

Jonathan Steinberg knew he was tired because, when his monitor woke up with its insistent chiming, he had been dreaming about being asleep.

And that, Jon, is some seriously screwed up action, he thought as he rolled out of his bed and stumbled toward the monitor on the wall. The room was pitch-dark, the windows opaque, and he suspected it was early evening outside in the world, but he didn't know, and he didn't want to. If it was still early evening, that meant he'd been asleep for all of an hour, and if he'd been asleep for all of an hour and someone was calling to get him out of bed, clearly they had forgotten that he was a man who knew how to kill people in a variety of interesting and creative ways.

Steinberg slapped at the monitor, trying to silence its incessant chirping, missed, and knocked the photograph of his Afghanistan unit off its shelf. He had enough wherewithal to catch it with his free hand, though just barely, and not until it was resettled safely on his shelf did he try to activate the monitor a second time.

It came alive with his touch, and suddenly he was looking at Jo, and aware of three things all at once. First, that she was alive and he was very happy that was the case. Second, that she looked better than she had the last time he'd seen her, and that surprised him.

And third, that he was standing in his underwear.

It was the third thing that he expected her to comment upon, but she didn't. She didn't say anything, in fact, just cracked open a great big grin and seemed to be struggling with herself to not actually burst into laughter. The digital tag in the upper corner of the screen, Steinberg noted, said that she was calling from a public kiosk in Ankara, Turkey, where night had fully fallen onto snow-covered streets.

"Hey," Steinberg said. "Nice to see you're all right. We were starting to get worried about—"

Jo nodded, put a finger to her lips. Then she reached out of shot, presumably into her lap, and brought up a small pad of paper. She indicated the paper, indicated her eyes, then indicated his. Then she looked at him expectantly. Steinberg nodded, and she flipped open the pad, then showed him what she had written on the first page.

CMO PATCHED ME UP. THROATLINKED ME. CAN HEAR EVERYTHING I SAY, EVERYTHING I HEAR.

KNOW WHO'S BEHIND IT. CONTINUITY. GOING TO CHINA TO TAKE CARE OF THE PROBLEM, BUT CANNOT MANAGE TRANSPORT—TOO MUCH DD HEAT, THEY'RE TRYING TO KILL ME AGAIN.

Before he could stop himself, Steinberg said, "So what else is new?"

Jo grinned, shaking her head, then quickly scribbled on the pad, adding:

THIS TIME THEY REALLY MEAN IT. HIT SQUADS, THE WHOLE DEAL. NEED TO AVOID THEM.

Steinberg nodded, then looked at her, waiting for the next message. She returned the look with a similar look of expectation. Steinberg shrugged. Jo made a gesture of annoyance, flipped to a new page, writing quickly before showing it to him.

WRITE IT DOWN, DUMBASS.

Then she lowered the paper and put the words—and especially the last part—into her expression.

Write it down? Steinberg thought, turning and beginning to search through his desk for anything that resembled either paper or a pen. *On what? Who uses paper these days?*

The desk yielded nothing he could use, due in no small part to the fact that there was very little in it to begin with. He tried to find his d-PAL, realized he'd thrown it away in a fit of anti-dataDyne fury a couple of months back, then began searching through his bureau, then his closet. Each time he glanced back to the monitor, Jo was still there, watching him with a mixture of growing annoyance and impatience. Finally, she held up the notepad again.

GO GET SOME!!!

Steinberg nodded, held up his hand, splaying his fingers and mouthing the words "Five minutes, be right back."

Then he ran from the room in search of paper and something to write with, still in his underwear, and certain that

Joanna Dark, watching his departure on a net kiosk in Ankara, would have laughed her ass off if she hadn't been so worried about not making a sound.

He tried Grimshaw's room first, remembering the stacks of paperbacks and magazines, and discovered that the door was locked and that there was no way for him to get through it. Then he tried three other doors on the residence, including Joanna's, and found them all locked, too.

Paper, paper, he thought. *Who on this damn estate has paper?*

He left the residence, sprinting outside into the last sunlight of the day, and feeling the winter cold assault every bit of his exposed skin. One of his troopers, walking past, caught sight of him and hooted, and was promptly joined by another two troopers, as well as three of the Institute personnel currently making their way between buildings. He earned howls, wolf whistles, and laughter.

At least it's good for morale, Steinberg told himself.

His feet had begun to sting by the time he reached the Main Building, and he slipped on the marble floor of the entryway as he came inside, barely caught himself before falling, then passed the elevator and went for the stairs, taking them two and three at a time. He passed other employees, and they stared, and they laughed, and he knew he was cutting a hell of a figure, but it was too late to do anything about that now.

Partridge was working at her desk in Carrington's outer office when he burst through the door, and she looked up to see him rushing toward her. She screamed, bolting to her feet and backing away, all at once. Steinberg hoped the scream was in surprise rather than, say, horror.

"Paper!" Steinberg said. "Pen! Pencil!"

"Mr. Steinberg!" Partridge said, trying to recompose herself. She was a young woman, pretty and very proper, the perfect accent to Carrington's somewhat old-world-style office. "The Institute has a dress code! Mr. Carrington does not appreciate—"

Steinberg went for the desk, began rummaging through the sheets and sheets that were piled there, looking for something that was blank or, at the least, not readily apparent as being important. "I need something to write on! I need a pad of paper!"

"Get back!" Partridge said, shooing him with a hand. "You're messing everything about, just . . . just stand back. Cover yourself, please."

Steinberg backed off from the desk, glanced over his shoulder, back to Partridge, and then over his shoulder again, realizing that there were at least four people crowded in the doorway, watching the interaction. He looked down at himself, confirmed that his underwear was still on and still clean, then looked back to his audience.

"Don't you people have work to do?" he asked.

They shook their heads.

"Here," Partridge said, offering him a pad of A4 paper with one hand and a pen with the other. She extended each of her arms fully, barely bending, as if afraid of getting too close to him.

Steinberg took the pen and the pad.

"Thanks, Emily. Tell the Old Man I need him to meet me in my room right away."

"It's Miss Partridge," she said tightly. "You might want to dress before he joins you."

"Yeah, we don't want him getting the wrong idea about us," Steinberg agreed. "Tell him to hurry."

Partridge huffed, then reached for the intercom as Steinberg headed out the door, sprinting back the way he had come. He was coming off the stairs when he realized he was hearing the sounds of applause following him.

Jo was still on the monitor when he returned, looking thoroughly annoyed. She had a new message already written for him, and as soon as Steinberg came through the door, she held it up.

YOU ARE *SUCH A GRUNT!*

Steinberg nodded, writing hastily.

AND YOU LOVE ME FOR IT. HOLD ON COUPLE MORE MINUTES. WAITING FOR OLD MAN.

Jo nodded, then glanced around herself in the kiosk. Past her, outside the kiosk, Steinberg could see the bustle of Ankara's streets, the nightlife growing more vibrant despite the apparent cold. Wherever she was in the city, she'd picked about as busy a location for the call as she could have done, and Steinberg wondered if that had been a good idea or a bad one. Turkey was not safe territory by any stretch of the imagination.

He thought for a moment, then wrote a new note, holding it up for her.

LIKE THE NEW LOOK. YOU HEAVY OR LIGHT?

She smiled, scribbling.

COURTESY CMO. THEY GAVE ME LOAD-OUT. COVERED.

Steinberg nodded, set down the pad and the pen, then proceeded to pull on the pair of pants that had been hanging over the back of his desk chair. Jo watched, made a big show of pouting as he fixed his belt, then dropped the act altogether as the door into Steinberg's room opened.

"Jonathan, what the hell—" Carrington said as he entered, but Steinberg moved quickly and got a hand over the man's mouth before he could say more. It was probably too late; if CMO was listening, they had a vocal track of Carrington on file somewhere anyway. It wouldn't take them long to match it to what they'd just heard.

"Jo," Steinberg whispered in Carrington's ear. "She's been ThroatLinked by CMO. Anything she says or hears, they get it, too."

Steinberg moved back, letting his hand slip, and Carrington nodded. He was flushed, too, and breathing heavily, and Steinberg wondered if the Old Man had sprinted the length and breadth of the Institute campus, just as he had. Carrington moved further into the room, resting heavily on his cane, looking at Jo on the screen. She smiled at him, Steinberg thought perhaps sheepishly, and Carrington moved closer to the monitor. Then he gestured for Jo to do the same, and after a second to interpret the hand gesture, she leaned forward in the kiosk, giving the camera a close-up of her eyes.

Oh, Christ, Steinberg thought. *I didn't even think of that, I didn't even think that they might've done her eyes, too.*

Carrington stared at Jo in close-up for several seconds longer, then nodded brusquely and turned to face Steinberg, motioning him closer. On the screen, Jo sat back in the kiosk.

"Give me the bullet," Carrington whispered.

"Not much so far," Steinberg responded, speaking again in the Old Man's ear. He smelled, Steinberg realized, of rosewater and sandalwood. "She was lifted by CMO out of Veracruz. DataDyne sent a hit squad after her, it looks like CMO gave her backup. They patched her up, turned her loose again, don't know the details. She's in Ankara, as you can see. She knows about the Continuity, and she's planning on continuing into China, presumably to wherever it is they're located."

Carrington nodded again, barely, then reached for the pad Steinberg had been using and began to write on it at some length.

CONTINUITY = C.

AM AWARE OF THEIR PARTICIPATION. CAN YOU CONFIRM C BEHIND CMO TAKEOVERS OF Z AND BYI? FURTHER, CAN YOU CONFIRM C RESPONSIBLE FOR IMPERSONATION OF YOU?

FINALLY, CONFIRM FOLLOWING HYPOTHESIS—CMO DEALING WITH C RESULTS IN Z AND BYI TAKEOVERS. NOW CMO FEARS C WILL DO THE SAME TO THEM. USING YOU TO PRE-EMPT POSSIBLE C ACTION AS DESCRIBED?

Jo nodded, not bothering to use her pad.

Steinberg watched as Carrington scratched at his beard, thinking. Then he wrote again, this time much more quickly.

WHY C INTEREST IN SINGLING YOU OUT? WHY C APPARENTLY TARGETTING DD?

Jo shook her head, then bent her attention to the pad in her lap. While she wrote, Steinberg found his shirt and pulled it on.

THINK C KNOWS I DID ZL AND DAUGHTER. THINK THEY WANT PAYBACK. DD—NO IDEA. NO INFORMATION FROM CMO ON THAT TOPIC.

DIFFERENT PROBLEM—HOW TO GET TO ZL HOME WITHOUT DD PUTTING LOTS OF HOLES IN ME?

She lowered her pad, shrugging again, and Steinberg couldn't help but grin at her. Despite the new outfit—and he had to admit that he liked it on her, liked the maturity it projected, even the hint of sophistication—the gesture was pure, vintage Jo.

Carrington was writing again, and when he showed the message to Jo, she looked surprised, and perhaps a little concerned. When Steinberg saw it, he understood why.

NO ACTION AT PRESENT. CALL AGAIN +3 HOURS. FURTHER ORDERS THEN.

Then Carrington reached out to the monitor and killed the connection.

"You don't want her going to China?" Steinberg asked.

"No, it's not that. Obviously the Continuity needs to be taken care of, one way or another, and I suspect telling Joanna that I'd rather she left them alone will have the same amount of success as my telling her that she was confined to the Institute grounds. Though this time I would mean it."

"Then what is it?"

"It still doesn't make sense, Jon," Carrington said, grumpily tossing the pad and the pen onto the desk. "The heart of it, the big picture, we're still not seeing it. And I'm becoming more and more convinced that it's something very big, indeed."

"I'm not the planner, here, I'm not the idea guy," Steinberg said, lacing up his boots. "But it seems to me that we've been ignoring the obvious question."

"Which would be?"

"What's dataDyne's stake in all of this?"

"They don't have one, that's the point."

"Sure they do. They *always* do, Daniel."

Carrington grumbled, then moved for the door, waiting for Steinberg. Steinberg finished lacing his other boot, grabbed his jacket, then joined him.

"Where are we going?"

"Ops," Carrington said. "Maybe Grim's turned something up."

Steinberg waited until they'd left the Residence and had started across the campus before speaking again, making the request he'd been preparing.

"I want to go out to Ankara, back Jo up," Steinberg said.

"No, Jon, I need you here."

"She looks better, but it's cosmetic, Daniel. CMO had her out of commission for over twenty-four hours, at least, and that wasn't just to link her. She was in sorry shape before she left here, she's in worse shape now, I guarantee it, even if it doesn't look that way."

"I don't disagree with your assessment, Jon, but I'm not letting you leave here, not until we can stand down."

"There's been no attack, there's been nothing. I think it's time to lower our guard a bit."

Carrington looked at him, frowning. "DataDyne put a hit squad after her, Jon."

"Yeah, I know."

"Not Shock Troopers, not CORPSEC—this wasn't their defensive protocol, do you hear what I'm saying? Jo has been targeted for elimination. Think about that, and think about who gives that order, and why."

"It would have to come from DeVries."

"That's right. Which means DeVries has determined that we are now such a threat as to authorize a full covert action. They're going after Jo now. Do you think it's likely they're going to stop once they get her, if they get her?"

"No," Steinberg said, after a moment. "No, that wouldn't make sense, would it. If she's an enemy who needs to be removed, then so are we."

"Exactly. In my humble opinion, the only reason we've not had dataDyne at the gates already is that they're too occupied with other things at the moment. They're worried about CMO arriving in territory they previously shared only with BYI and Zentek, and they're worried about the unveiling of AirFlow 2. But you can be certain—certain, Jon—that once they've got those ducks in order, they *will* be coming here, and they'll be coming here in force."

"So we let Jo go after the Continuity alone, is that it?"

"Can we get her into China without her being detected?"

Steinberg considered for a moment, but not long. "Yeah, it can be done. It would have to be from the north—Jo would have to use Institute assets out of Russia. I could co-ordinate with Vaklav on the Moscow campus, make it happen."

"Then that's what you should do. Put it together, and when she calls back, give her the details and tell her—or write to her, I suppose—that I am authorizing her to eliminate the Continuity at her discretion."

"Is that an order or simply permission?"

They reached the Ops Center, stopping now outside its doors. Carrington planted his stick, looking at Steinberg with curiosity. "And the distinction would be what, exactly, Jon?"

"If it's permission, her sense of self-preservation might kick in," Steinberg said. "If it's an order, she'll die to complete it."

Carrington chuckled, as if amused.

"You can tell her it's an order, Jonathan," Carrington said.

It took less than two hours to coordinate with the Moscow campus, Steinberg liaising with Vaklav Dugarova to arrange a location where the Russian could meet Jo and to come up with a means of insertion into China. It wasn't by any means foolproof, but by the time they were done, Steinberg was confident that the plan had a reasonable chance of success. Jo would make it into China, and, if all went well, Vaklav would be there to get her out again.

He went back to his room and sat at his desk, writing out the plan as neatly and carefully and clearly as he could manage. That took him close to another twenty minutes, which brought him right up to the edge of the allotted three hours. Steinberg reached out for his monitor, swinging it clear of the wall, and waited for Jo to call.

She never called back.

DataFlow Corporate Headquarters
Presentation Hall A
17 Rue de la Baume
Paris, France
January 27th, 2021

Cassandra DeVries stood behind the podium on the stage of the enormous presentation hall, lit by the stage lights, and let herself be picked apart by the army of ants called the dataDyne media relations and public affairs division.

"If you could turn your head to the left a little, please, ma'am."

"Like this?"

"No, a little further . . . no, that's too much, ma'am—there! Yes, like that."

There was murmuring from the audience, the flash of several d-PALs and laptops as they were switched on and updated. Most, if not all, of the lights on the stage seemed to be pointed directly into her eyes, and Cassandra had to squint to make out even the barest silhouettes. She resisted the urge to sigh. Of the many things she was discovering that she hated about being CEO, this was in danger of becoming the worst, and considering that she was living in fear for her life, that was saying something.

According to the display built into the podium, it was two minutes to eleven o'clock at night, which meant Cassandra had been standing onstage in the presentation hall for just shy of four hours. That was in addition to the last day and a half that she'd spent in what Michael Long and his PR cronies condescendingly referred to as "media preparation": rehearsals and practice Q&As and mock interviews and— God help her—camera tests. Outside the building the media tents were being erected, the decorations were going up. The Parisian foot traffic along the avenue outside the DataFlow offices had been closed earlier that afternoon, diverted to neighboring streets in an attempt both to provide a security buffer and to allow the frenzy of work to continue more smoothly. A no-fly zone was also now in effect, covering a quarter-mile radius around the location. Construction workers, painters, and caterers from dataDyne subsidiaries around the world were toiling late into the night, preparing both building and grounds for the event.

Attendance for the AirFlow 2 release was expected to top fifty thousand, with the media making up only a part of that number. There would be politicians and dignitaries and pop stars and directors from every one of dataDyne's divisions. There would be not one, not two, but three separate rock concerts, two fireworks displays, and at least one formal black-tie dinner, all of which would commence tomorrow evening and conclude, finally, on Saturday night, the thirtieth, with Arthur's unveiling to the world.

It was a dog-and-pony show of a like and scope to make Cassandra DeVries's stomach churn, and it gave her far greater insight into the thinking and personality of her predecessor than she'd have ever thought possible. Zhang Li had hated personal publicity, had eschewed the public life almost entirely with the sole exception of the DeathMatch broadcasts from his home in China, and even those featured his daughter far more than they had him. He had refused to make public appearances, to offer even the barest media comment, leaving such things to the media relations division.

And no wonder, Cassandra thought. *If this was what he was in for, no wonder he never went outside.*

The fact was that the whole display turned Cassandra's stomach, from the garish demonstrations of dataDyne's wealth and power to the snobbish condescension of the publicity people who could readily find fault in everything and everyone except themselves. She'd never in her life been so consistently and repeatedly subjected to passive-aggressive insults, and she was the bloody chief executive officer of dataDyne.

That was the most infuriating thing to her, and the longer she stood uselessly on a stage being picked apart bit by bit, the more certain she became that the people in the audience who claimed to want to help her, to want to help dataDyne, wanted precisely the opposite. The media relations organization had once been run by Takahata Sato, now director of dataDyne's ServAuto Robotics division. Sato, along with Friedrich Murray and Amanda Waterberg, had been in contention for the CEO position along with Cassandra. As far as Cassandra was concerned, that meant that media relations was run by Sato-loyalists, led by the man Sato had appointed to succeed him, a suntanned and arrogant American named Michael Long.

Cassandra believed in running dataDyne as she had run DataFlow, as a meritocracy. The best would rise to positions of authority and responsibility as a result of their ingenuity, discipline, and hard work. Results would speak for themselves. It seemed the proper—if not the only—way to run any business, let alone dataDyne.

It also seemed that she was in the minority on this point and that Zhang Li himself had disagreed with the thesis. Under his leadership, promotion in dataDyne was a matter of politicking and cronyism, accomplished less through what one did than through who one knew and what one could then offer them in exchange. It was a divisive, and in Cassandra's opinion, ultimately destructive way to run a company, the technique of a king who wished his princes to squabble amongst themselves rather than to unite and, potentially, dethrone their regent.

The more time she spent as CEO, the more Cassandra felt she was both discovering and understanding her predecessor. Like many of the decisions Zhang Li had made, it was one based on fear, a terror of losing control. Fear, it seemed, had been a huge factor in Zhang Li's life.

It also meant that her style of leadership was in opposition to the status quo. It meant that she threatened people like Takahata Sato and Michael Long.

Four hours spent standing here, a day and a half lost to this nonsense, lost from the business of running dataDyne, and for what? To promote AirFlow 2?

No, Cassandra thought. *They don't care about dataDyne, and they don't care about Arthur.*

This is their revenge. Their petty, meaningless, selfish revenge. And I've had about enough of it.

The murmured conversation from her hidden critics continued, with Cassandra the obvious topic of conversation. She took the opportunity to glance off toward stage left, where the newest of her personal assistants was standing by, a young woman by the name of Gabrielle Shephard. Cassandra caught her eye and mouthed the word "water," and her assistant quickly came onstage with a bottle in one hand, d-PAL in the other.

"I have a message from Colonel Shaw for you, Madame Director," Gabrielle whispered as she handed the bottle over. "The message is, quote, have target located, en route to handle matter personally. Will report positive result before oh-eight-hundred hours tomorrow, your local. End quote. I'm not quite sure what it means, ma'am."

Cassandra drained half the bottle before answering. "Don't worry about it, Gabi. Thank you."

"Do you need anything else, ma'am? I have some aspirin, and I can have dinner brought for you as soon as you'd like."

"I'm all right for now, thank you."

The young woman looked pained. "There are . . . I'm afraid there are *several* other messages for you, if you have a moment. Director Waterberg at Patmos has been trying to reach you, as has Director Hesch at Ellison Electronic Security. Director Hesch has been calling hourly, ma'am, he's very concerned about the collapse of Beck-Yama and CMO's assumption of their holdings along the Pacific Rim."

Cassandra handed the bottle back, rubbed at her right temple with two fingers. "I'll call him as soon as I get free."

From the audience, someone called out, "Excuse me! You! Get off the stage!"

Gabrielle stiffened slightly, and Cassandra nodded to her, and the young woman backed away with a dignity that Cassandra wished she could find in herself at the moment.

"You moved, ma'am," someone else in the audience told Cassandra. "Please, lift your head, yes, like that. Just like you were before. Thank you. Please, *please,* Madame Director, just try to stand still, okay? We don't want to be here all day."

"I don't like that glare off her nose," a woman said. "Look at her nose, it looks like a beak."

"We can powder it. What I don't like is the wardrobe, it's way too twenty-ten."

"I thought that was her thing, that she liked retro. How else can you explain what she's been wearing?"

"She can like retro all she wants, but this is the future, boys and girls, this is the bright new tomorrow, and she can't present the future looking like she's pining for the past."

"Excuse me," Cassandra said.

"What's with the hair? Can we get extensions for her hair? Or a weave?"

"You think it's too short?"

"Short? It looks positively butch, we *have* to fix that."

"Excuse me," Cassandra repeated, louder.

"Can we bring up four, seven, and fourteen? Just to do something about the shadows."

The lights on the stage intensified, and, as a result, Cassandra's headache grew to keep pace.

"Oh, good lord, that won't work. Her chest is too flat. The way the lights are hitting it, throw in her hair, she looks like a boy. Is that what we want? We want the world to think that dataDyne is run by a little blond boy? I mean, really."

There were a couple of laughs from the darkness, hastily stifled.

"Excuse—"

"All right, ma'am, are you still with us here? Sorry about that. We're going to have wardrobe come up with something else for you. What's your bra size? You're a thirty-four C?"

"I beg your pardon?" Cassandra asked.

"Dammit, Michael! You made her move her head!"

Squinting against the lights, Cassandra could make out Michael Long, his d-PAL in hand, his earpiece glowing a gentle green. "Please, ma'am, don't move your head, all right? You've got to stop fidgeting, you're like a puppy, I swear, all right? We're trying to make you beautiful, here. You've got to help us out."

"I think that is what I'm doing," Cassandra said evenly.

"Well, yes, I can see how you would *think* that's what you're doing, but every time you move you're actually not doing that. We have to get this right, and we're on a tight schedule here, and I think you'll agree that you don't want to unveil AirFlow 2 to the whole *world* while looking like you just tumbled out of a wrestling ring with half a dozen gorillas."

Cassandra nodded, barely, then said, "All right, bring up the lights."

"I'm sorry, ma'am, we're not finish—"

"Yes, we are. Bring up the lights, now."

There was a pause, an abrupt stillness from her hidden audience. Somewhere behind and above her she heard the reverberation of a switch being thrown, and the stage lights remained on, but the house lights joined them. In the audience, roughly clustered at the center of the second and third rows, the media affairs and public relations representatives stared back at her. Most of them were seated, but Long stood with three others at the center, two women and another man, and like the rest of the group, their expressions offered all manner of opinion about Cassandra, but nothing that remotely approached respect.

I am the CEO and Director of dataDyne, Cassandra DeVries reminded herself. *I am the head of the most powerful corporation the world has ever seen.*

"You've had how long to put this together, Director Long?" she asked, coming off the podium and toward the lip of the stage.

"We've been working out the final details for the last six weeks." Long checked his d-PAL, then added, "Of course, we could have gotten more accomplished if you'd made yourself available to us sooner."

Cassandra nodded again, ever so slightly. "I see. This is my fault, then? This burgeoning fiasco?"

Long smiled, shaking his head. "No, ma'am, we'll get you sorted out. You just have to trust me, you just have to work with me."

"Not anymore I don't," Cassandra said. "You're fired."

With satisfaction, Cassandra realized that the fidgeting had stopped. Long blinked at her, as if he hadn't quite heard her.

"I'm . . . what?"

"Fired," Cassandra said. "Get out. Now."

"But . . . Madame Director, you're not thinking. I'm your director of media . . . I mean, AirFlow 2 launches the day after tomorrow, you can't possibly . . ."

Cassandra slapped her forehead lightly, as if struck by sudden insight. "Oh, right, I *need* you and your people! Is that it, Michael? Is that what you're trying, in your insipid, tongue-tied, and vacuous way, to tell me?"

Long's cheeks, Cassandra noted, seemed to be growing redder, even despite the man's artificial tan. "Yes, ma'am, that's correct. You can't change out the team this close to the—"

"And that's what grants you permission to repeatedly insult and humiliate me, is that it? Because I can't do anything about it?"

Long closed his mouth. Past him, the cluster of PR flacks squirmed uncomfortably.

"I want an answer, Director Long."

"You can't . . . you can't switch the team now. You do, the rollout will be a disaster. You can't do it."

"Watch me," Cassandra said, and then she turned to face stage left and was pleased to see that Gabrielle had already emerged onto the stage, standing ready with her d-PAL in hand. "Gabi, contact Anita, tell her I need CORPSEC down here right now."

"At once, Madame Director."

Cassandra jumped off the edge of the stage, smoothed her skit, and looked to Long again. "Your d-PAL, corporate ID, and laptop. Set them on the stage, please."

"You—"

"Now!" Cassandra shouted, loud enough that her voice filled the auditorium.

Long came forward, depositing each item beside her on the edge of the stage.

Cassandra pointed to her right. "Stand there until CORPSEC arrives to escort you from the premises."

She watched as Long did as she'd ordered, then turned her attention to the rest of the group. "Which of you were hired by Mr. Long?"

Roughly half of the hands went up, all of them hesitantly.

"You're fired," Cassandra told them. "IDs, d-PALs, laptops. Now."

She waited until they had followed her order and had moved to join Long. There was some grumbling, but it stopped as CORPSEC burst into the hall, led by six Shock Troopers and Anita Velez. They had come running, and the Shock Troopers had activated the laser sights on their submachine guns, and when the thin red beams found Long and his cronies, they froze as if suddenly encased in ice.

"Madame Director?" Velez called out urgently.

"It's all right, Anita."

Velez gestured with her left hand, taking in the room, and Cassandra saw that she held her sidearm in the other. Holstering her weapon, Velez asked, "Is there a problem?"

Cassandra held up a hand, indicating she wished Velez and the others to wait, then looked at the remainder of the PR group. There were twelve left, all of them looking at her with fear in their eyes, and Cassandra DeVries discovered, to her surprise, that the reaction pleased her. She wondered if that meant she was becoming petty, and then decided that she didn't much care. She was the CEO of dataDyne, and if they wouldn't grant her the respect she was due, they sure as hell would grant her the fear.

"Which of you were hired by Mr. Sato?" she asked them.

It took more time for the hands to go up this time, probably, Cassandra suspected, because they were trying to determine if they could get away with lying. It didn't take them long to realize that they couldn't. Of the twelve, nine put hands into the air.

"You're fired as well," Cassandra told them. "You know the drill, put your things on the stage."

She looked to Velez, still standing at the back of the auditorium with the Shock Troopers and CORPSEC guards.

"Anita, please make certain that all of these people are escorted from the premises. Make certain that they are divested of any company materials that they cannot prove they acquired through their own personal expenditures. If any of them is still here in ten minutes, have them arrested for trespassing. If any of them resists you, you have my permission to use whatever force is required to remove them."

Velez nodded, and Cassandra watched as the woman spoke to the Shock Troopers and CORPSEC guards around her. They came down the aisle together, Velez pulling off to join Cassandra as the others gathered the group and marched them out of the auditorium.

"You three, come here," Cassandra told the ones who remained. "Gabrielle?"

The young woman knelt at the edge of the stage. "Yes, Madame Director?"

"Do you have any management or publicity experience, Gabi?"

"Some. A little."

"Good."

She turned to the three who had approached, all of them standing nervously and desperately trying to decide if looking at Cassandra or away from her was the safest thing to do.

"This is Gabrielle Shephard," Cassandra told them. "She's the new director of media relations and public affairs. You answer to her, and she answers to me."

There were hasty nods of understanding, murmurs of "yes, ma'am" and "yes, Madame Director."

"Gabi?"

The young woman nodded, eyes wide. "Madame Director?"

"Get to work," Cassandra told her, and then strode from the auditorium, Velez following at her heels.

<hr>

"I need a minute of your time, Madame Director," Velez said as they were moving through the lobby on the way back to Cassandra's office. DataFlow personnel parted on each side to allow them to pass. The sounds of construction echoed all around them.

Cassandra didn't slow down, passing two Shock Troopers who snapped to attention without acknowledging them. "You have until I reach my desk."

"I think there's a problem with Arthur."

She stopped, looking at Velez. They'd reached her personal elevator, and Velez pressed the call button with one hand, sliding her ID card through the reader with her other, all the while meeting Cassandra's gaze.

"What kind of problem?"

"I'm . . . unsure. There's been unusual activity in the servers out of the AI lab, I've been unable to trace it."

The elevator arrived, its doors swishing apart. Cassandra entered, waited for Velez to follow and repeat the procedure with button and keycard. The lift began its ascent.

"Have you talked to Dr. Ventura?"

"He's been unavailable, Madame Director."

"Arthur has to be presented the day after tomorrow, I'm not surprised."

Velez didn't say anything.

"This server activity," Cassandra said. "How does it relate to Arthur?"

"I'm not certain that it does, Madame Director. But given the sensitivity of the project, I felt it should be brought to your attention."

A sudden surge annoyance flooded Cassandra. "Anita, you're the one who's been riding me to delegate more authority. Are you now asking me to cancel the God-knows-how-many appointments that have backlogged over the last day and a half to review Arthur's code? Is that what you're asking me to do?"

"No, Madame Director—"

The lift came to a stop, and Cassandra stepped out even before the doors had finished opening, into her outer office. Three of the four desks were still manned, even at this late hour, with Gabrielle's the only empty one. Her secretaries all got to their feet, two reaching for their d-PALs, the third hastily gathering up what looked to be a dangerously unstable mountain of paperwork. All of them looked exhausted, though all of them were also doing their best to hide that fact.

"Welcome back, Madame Director," they chorused.

"Get Director Hesch on holo, wake him up if you have to," Cassandra said, not caring which of them did it as long as it was done. She went through the double doors into her office, making a beeline for the desk and removing her suit coat as she did so, tossing it into one of the easy chairs in the sitting area that she never, ever seemed to have the time to actually enjoy. At her desk, she started the login sequence for her laptop, then began switching on the holograph projectors. Two of the secretaries had followed her in, already laying out paperwork and offering d-PALs for her attention.

She looked up and saw that Velez was still standing there, waiting.

"Well?" Cassandra demanded.

Velez looked momentarily flustered. "I'm unsure how you wish me to proceed."

"Arthur works, Anita," Cassandra said. "If you have a problem, if you have concerns, then bring them to Dr. Ventura."

"As I said—"

"I don't have time for this!"

Velez straightened, then nodded curtly. "Very well."

"Is that all?"

"I understand that Colonel Shaw has acquired the target."

"That's my understanding also. I'm pleased that at least someone around here is able to do what I asked them to without my needing to hold their hand while they bloody do it."

Velez didn't say anything for a moment, then nodded again, as curtly as before. "Am I to assume you will not be returning to your residence tonight?"

"Correct, I'll be spending the night here."

"Then I will check in with you first thing in the morning."

"If you think you can manage it, Anita, yes, that would fine," Cassandra DeVries said. "Otherwise I can ask Colonel Shaw to do it, if you'd rather."

Without another word, Velez left the office.

Then Cassandra was on conference with Director Hesch of Ellison Electronic Security, discussing CMO's threat to their security systems market share, and all thoughts of Arthur, Velez, and Colonel Shaw were forgotten, washed away in the needs of dataDyne.

Hotel English Guest House
Ankara, Turkey
January 27th, 2021

A week ago, Turkey had been disputed territory, with Zentek, Beck-Yama, and dataDyne all holding offices in parts of the country, each hypercorp attempting to lay the greatest claim to the nation and its resources. Now, though, Jo could see the signs of change, the coming battle between CMO and data-Dyne that would be fought over the prize. Not yet, but soon, after CMO had digested its recent meals and consolidated its acquisitions, after dataDyne had taken the measure of its new opposition and decided the best means of eliminating it.

In the meantime, dataDyne was using the lull to bolster its defenses, to entrench itself, and there were signs of the hyper-corp's attentions everywhere. No matter where she looked, it seemed to Jo that she was seeing the double-*d* diamond. That she hadn't attracted their attention yet was due in equal parts to luck, skill, and the fact that she had Portia de Carcareas riding in her head, telling her where to go and what to avoid.

Jo hated the ThroatLink, hated that she had no control over whether it was switched on or off. She hated the invasion of her privacy, that she had to watch every word she said, everyone she spoke to. Bad enough that she hadn't been able to actually speak to Jonathan, to let him hear her voice, to assure him that he was all right and give him grief about his black briefs. Bad enough she hadn't been able to ask Carrington if she'd done what he'd wanted all along, if his admonition to remain at the Institute had been just his way of getting her to go where he'd wanted.

After she'd concluded the call, Jo had left the kiosk behind, stepping out into the biting Ankara cold, trudging her way through the ice-crusted snow in search of someplace warm where she could wait for three hours before calling back. She'd stopped in the shelter between two buildings to dig around in the small black duffel bag she carried, removing from within a heavy overcoat, also black. There were weapons inside as well, provided—like everything else—by Carcareas. Two pistols—one of them a Rapier with a shortened barrel, almost identical to the one Carcareas had carried in Veracruz, the other one a Hussar, larger and meaner and consequently less concealable—and a compact submachine gun, the Avatar. All the weapons were proprietary CMO, and Jo wasn't terribly familiar with any of them, but that didn't much bother her; they were guns, and Joanna Dark had yet to meet a gun she couldn't make shoot straight.

"Do you like your presents?" Carcareas asked softly.

It was a disturbing, even unnerving sensation, as if the woman's voice was a whisper that could be felt more than heard. It made the sound a tactile experience, made Jo feel that Carcareas was literally inside her head, reading her mind.

"You're my imaginary friend," Jo answered quietly. "You're the tooth fairy."

"I think you'll prefer the Rapier, Jo, though you should lock the Hussar to your biosigns as soon as you get the

*chance. You don't want someone taking it from you and us-
ing it against you."*

"Fine. Soon as I find a place to hide out for a bit, I'll do
just that."

Silence fell, matching the descending darkness, and Jo
hoisted the duffel and started back onto the street, thinking
that Carcareas had left her again. But as she reached the end
of the block and turned, the woman's voice came back, gentle and sure.

*"Not that way, go right. North side of the block, do you
see it? The Hotel English, it's a small boutique hotel, quite
lovely. There's a small bar and a restaurant, as well, and you
won't be disturbed there."*

"Been to Ankara before, have you?"

*"Quite a few times. The winters are dreadful, but the
food is nice."*

Begrudgingly, Jo changed direction, reversing and then
crossing the street. The hotel façade was discreet and far
more European than Jo had expected, and stepping inside
she could see why the hotel was named as it was. The décor
was vaguely Edwardian, with red velvet wallpapering and a
thick oriental carpet covering the floor of the lobby. A small,
round man worked alone at the registration desk, and he
watched her entrance with polite interest, directed her to the
bar when she asked.

It was quiet inside, and empty but for the bartender and a
single patron who seemed intent on monopolizing most of
his attention. Jo asked if it would be possible to get some hot
tea, and in short order she had a glass and a pot and a seat at
a table in the back.

"You don't drink alcohol, either?"

"Never developed a taste for it. It's like caffeine, I don't
like things that make me not trust myself."

"Interesting. I often consider caffeine a necessary tool in this line of work."

"Why do you care what I eat or drink?"

"Curiosity."

Jo moved the duffel onto the bench beside her, opening it again and keeping it out of the bartender's line of sight. She checked the Hussar without pulling it free, saw that it had been chambered in .45 ACP. She flipped open the panel along the handgrip, pressed her thumb into the exposed recess, and waited. After three seconds, the pistol vibrated in her hand, and she knew that it was now keyed to her biosigns and that, until reset by a gunsmith, it would refuse to fire for anyone but her. She slipped the weapon into her overcoat pocket, feeling better for having done so. Between that and the Rapier tucked at the small of her back, she felt confident that firepower wouldn't be an immediate problem should she have to face dataDyne again.

Then she remembered the two snipers and the rocket launcher and the six CMPs she'd dealt with in Veracruz, and for a fleeting moment she considered trying to move the Avatar to the cover of her overcoat, as well. But that was ill-advised and probably paranoid. Much more hardware and she'd be clanking with every step.

She checked her watch, sipped her tea, and then checked her watch again and saw that she still had two hours and forty-three minutes to go before she was supposed to call Jonathan back. Jo sighed, and then immediately wished she hadn't, because Portia took it as an invitation to begin chatting with her again.

"I've been doing some research, Joanna," Carcareas whispered in her bones. *"Would you like to know what I've been researching?"*

"Profit margins?"

"Jack Dark."

Jo felt her jaw clench and wondered if the leads from the ThroatLink could register it as a sound. If so, she hoped it was an unpleasant one.

"Very interesting man, your father. Oddly, I can find nothing about your mother."

"Portia," Jo warned. "You want to be very careful what you say next."

"But I mean it in all sincerity, Joanna," Carcareas said, quickly. *"I assure you, I find him a fascinating man. I would have dearly loved to have met him. Born in New York, twenty-fourth of April, 1969, his early education is unremarkable but for his skill in athletics. Did you know he still holds the record at his high school for the most yards rushed during a single football season? Refused college, including several scholarships, to enlist in the United States Marine Corps. Serves two tours before joining Force Recon. Deployments to Guantanamo, Tokyo, Rwanda, Kuwait, Singapore . . . then he left. Do you know why he left, Joanna?"*

There was heat building in her cheeks, she could feel it. "No."

"It's odd, that's all. Honorably discharged, then joins the Detroit Police Department. Heads up the antinarcotic task force for couple of years there, but I'm sure you remember that; you would have been, what, seven, eight?"

"I was twelve, and this conversation is finished."

"I'm upsetting you."

"You are, yes, actually. As if that wasn't the point."

"But it isn't the point."

"Then why the hell did you bring it up?"

Carcareas paused. *"You don't seem to truly comprehend how remarkable a young woman you are. I find that extraordinary."*

"I don't comprehend it because I don't especially believe it."

"But it's so clear. Certainly Carrington knows it. I know

it. DataDyne knows it, too, why else would they be trying so hard to kill you?"

"And this has what to do with my father, exactly?" Jo asked, angrily.

"Someone's responsible for making you into who you are. If it isn't him, then I'm at a loss for suspects. The Force Recon information explains an awful lot about you, actually, especially if he imparted that training to you in any small way, and I think it's clear that he did. How old were you when he first taught you to fight?"

Jo refused to respond, checking her watch again. All of six minutes had passed since the last time she'd checked it.

"Oh, come along, Joanna, answer the question, indulge me."

"It's kind of hard to concentrate on the room with you yammering in my skull."

"There's nothing to concentrate on, you're perfectly safe. Indulge me. How old were you when he started teaching you how to fight?"

Jo drank her tea, feeling the heat of the glass against her lips, almost painful in its intensity. The ache in her ribs was growing more acute, as well, and she wondered if that was a stress reaction, her body sharing the discomfort of her mind and her heart.

"Seven," Jo said. "I spent a lot of time in the hospital as a kid, I had some pretty severe spinal damage. It wasn't until I was five that I could really walk. He had to wait until he was sure I'd recovered before he could start training me."

Carcareas said nothing for a couple of seconds, and Jo imagined she was taking notes, then thought that was silly, because in all likelihood Carcareas was simply recording their conversation. It would be someone else's job to take notes from it later.

It probably wasn't wise sharing information with her, Jo

knew. Even if Carcareas was doing a good job of sounding interested in Jo—or, perhaps, even *was* truly interested in Jo—ultimately, it was an intelligence-gathering job for Core-Mantis. The smartest thing to do would be to simply shut up and endure the prattling in her head until Carcareas finally grew tired of not having her questions answered.

That was the smart thing to do, but Jo didn't actually want to do it. On a purely operational level, she wasn't giving Carcareas anything the woman wouldn't be able to ultimately divine from other sources, that was already clear. Carcareas had found the information about Jo's father; it wouldn't take long to find what little remained in the public record about Joanna herself, up until the point that Grimshaw had sanitized her life. The hospital stay, that was public record. Everything was public record, really, up until almost a year ago, at which point Joanna Dark had ceased to exist in any official capacity at all.

That's how it was working for Carrington. Everyone at the Institute, from Rogers in the motor pool to Potts in the armory, none of them were officially employed by Daniel Carrington. They drew regular paychecks from shell corporations and holding companies, funds deposited into accounts in false names. Working for Carrington, you were a ghost.

Carcareas already knew she worked for Carrington. Filling in a little of the backstory couldn't do any harm at this point, could it?

Jo realized she was justifying the conversation to herself, trying to come up with a reason to allow it to continue. She knew why, as well; she honestly couldn't recall the last time anyone had asked about her *as a person*. What she liked or didn't like, for instance. Where she'd grown up. What she thought about this music or that video.

The best she'd ever gotten out of anybody at the Institute, including Jonathan, was a "How are you feeling?" And it was only ever Jonathan who had made her think he was asking about her for more than operational concerns. Not even Carrington, with his grandfatherly bearing and paternal smile, had ever asked Jo about . . . well, being Jo.

"Seven," Carcareas said, her voice so soft it was barely audible, as if she was the voice of Joanna's conscience and not a woman sitting some thousand miles away with a headset and a laptop. "That's very young for that kind of training."

"Shaolin monks begin training apprentices at the age of five. It's not that young."

"But the Shaolin don't begin training them to fight at five, Joanna. They begin teaching them their philosophy at five, the rudiments of physical training. That's not what happened in your case, is it? Or do I misunderstand?"

"No," Jo said. "No, it was young, you're right."

"And you started shooting at the same age?"

"All of it started at pretty much the same age, yeah."

"What was that like?"

Jo paused, looking into her half-empty glass of tea, then out at the bar. The one patron she had noted was picking up his coat, moving to leave, and the bartender had turned his attention to his d-PAL, holding it in both hands. Jo could tell just from his stance that he was playing some sort of game on it.

"I loved it," Jo said. "Every minute of it."

Carcareas sounded less surprised than genuinely curious. "Because you were spending time with your father?"

"Yeah."

And because that was how I knew he loved me, she added to herself. Even if he never did know how to say it.

For a long time, Carcareas said nothing. Jo finished her tea, checked her watch yet again, and saw she had two hours and twelve minutes left to go. She looked up, thinking to order another pot of tea, and watched as a new customer entered the bar. He was an older man, perhaps in his midfifties, and as he unbuttoned his overcoat his eyes ran the room, settling briefly on Joanna before continuing on their way to find the bartender. She heard the new arrival ask for a beer, watched the bartender leave his d-PAL on the bar to fetch the order. The man glanced back at Jo, nodded slightly, as if acknowledging her presence, then turned his attention away again.

Jo let her hand find the grip of the Avatar, still in the duffel bag. He was too old to be hypercorp muscle, at least from the look of him, but something about the man set off alarms with her. It was in his bearing, the squared shoulders and the way he leaned as he tipped his beer. All of it seemed to say not only that he knew how to take care of himself but that he had no problem demonstrating the fact to anyone who might wish to doubt him.

"Might be trouble," Jo said to Carcareas, so quietly she couldn't hear the words herself even as she spoke them.

"*DataDyne?*" Carcareas asked, concerned. "*We've been monitoring their Ankara transmissions, there's nothing indicating a hit team is—*"

"He's coming over," Jo said, and she raised her gaze to watch as the man and his beer approached her table. With his free hand, he was digging into his trouser pocket, at the front, and he kept his eyes on her while he did it, as if trying to assure her that whatever he was reaching for was nothing she should be alarmed by. His eyes were blue, watery, and she could make out a legion of creases on his sunburned face. His hair had more gray in it than black. He stopped a few feet off, giving her space, then pulled his hand free from his pocket and placed what he was now holding on the table between them.

It was a coin, a large one, perhaps twice the size and thickness of an American half-dollar. Slightly tarnished, but in the low light of the bar it still shown gold, and Jo could see without touching it the globe, anchor, and eagle emblem of the United States Marine Corps embossed on its center, the words "Semper Fidelis" beneath them. She reached out, then stopped herself, checking the man with her eyes, and he nodded, so she continued, picking it up and giving it a closer examination.

"*Joanna?*" Carcareas asked softly.

"I've seen this before," Jo said softly, turning the coin in her hand. On its reverse face were printed a set of paratroopers wings, and above them, what appeared to be a diving mask with air hoses running to it. "It's a challenge coin."

"By tradition, you'd have to produce your own now, or else buy a round of drinks."

"I don't have one," Jo said.

"Your father did. He had one just like that."

"And how do you know that?"

"Because your father was Jack Dark, and I was his commanding officer," the man said. "My name is Leland Shaw."

Carcareas had gone utterly silent.

"The leader of the Hawk Teams," Jo said. "You work for dataDyne."

"That's right."

Well, here it is, Jo thought. *You're done. There's no way you're taking a whole group of Hawks, not in the shape you're in. Fighting one of them nearly killed you, and there's no way the colonel came here alone.*

The thought should have frightened her, but it didn't. What it made Joanna feel, instead, was ashamed, because looking at the coin in her hand, she couldn't help but think that her father would have been disgusted by the whole situation. She'd let herself be trapped, she'd let herself be lulled into a false sense of security.

I never should have come in here, Jo thought bitterly. *Stu-*

pid. Should have kept moving. Instead, I trapped myself. Stupid. Stupid stupid stupid.

Shaw was saying something to her, and she'd missed it, but Carcareas hadn't, apparently, because along her bones she heard the woman say, *"He's lying."*

"I'm sorry, what?" Jo asked.

"I'm here to help you," Shaw said.

"You're going to help me?"

"You were spotted four hours ago when you arrived via CMO transport," Shaw told her. "DataDyne has not one, but two hit teams converging on this location, and we've been retained to act as the third, just in case it goes wrong. We've got to get you out of here, and we've got to get you out of here now."

"I'm checking his story," Carcareas told her. *"It's possible something slipped past us, that you were spotted on arrival."*

Jo didn't know whether to laugh or to simply start shooting. "Are you kidding me, Colonel? You're dataDyne's bitch, the Hawk Teams dance on the double-*d* string. Tell me another one."

"You're the daughter of a brother Marine," Shaw said. "You're the daughter of a man I stood beside in combat when hell and bullets were flying. I may take contracts from dataDyne, but that doesn't mean I'm not a Marine, still. And if your father taught you anything, young lady, then I'm sure he taught you that even the worst Marine son of a bitch is worth more than the best that the rest of the world has to offer."

"Macho bullshit," Carcareas murmured.

"If you're really his daughter, you know it's true," Shaw said. "And if you're really worthy of calling yourself Jack Dark's kid, you'll come with me now, because it means you'll live."

Jo hesitated, looking down and speaking with the barest breath to the ThroatLink. "He on the level, here?"

"We're still trying to confirm, Jo. But I find it hard to believe that dataDyne would have hit teams on the ground that we did not know about."

"You also didn't know they were in Veracruz until just before they hit us."

"I'm not certain this is analogous. I think going with him might be very dangerous."

Shaw was waiting for her, his hand outstretched.

Either way, Jo thought, *this is going to turn out badly.*

"All right," she told Shaw. "I'll come with you."

There was a vehicle waiting for them outside, a retrofitted null-g van, and Shaw helped Jo into the back, following her inside. There were two of his Hawks in the vehicle, with a third at the wheel, and they nodded acknowledgments to her and the colonel upon their arrival but said nothing as the van took to the air.

"Where are we going?" Jo asked.

"We've got a staging ground near the airfield," Shaw told her. "From there we can help you go wherever you want."

"Why are you doing this?" Jo asked him. "Why are you helping me?"

"I told you. Even the worst Marine is still a Marine. Jack was a friend, I owe him this."

"Did you know him well?"

"For a while I knew him very well. For a while we were like brothers."

"It's just that I don't remember him ever mentioning you."

Shaw looked at her, curious. "It was a long time ago,

young lady. And Jack was never the kind to talk about the things he did, the things he saw."

She nodded slightly, accepting that. Her father had really never talked to her about his time in the service, only that he had served, and that he'd gone in proud to do so. He'd never told her why he'd left.

The van tilted, losing altitude, and Joanna felt the shift of the engines as the null-g switched modes to land. There was a dull creak as the vehicle touched down, and Shaw moved past her in the narrow space, to the rear doors, pushing them open.

"This way," he told her.

Jo got up to follow him, the two Hawks who had ridden along in the back rose as well, and she caught the flash of something metallic in one of their hands. Without stopping to think about what she was doing or why she was doing it, Jo pivoted to face them while throwing herself backward through the open rear doors, in the direction Shaw had gone. The air above her sang as shots from two Tranq-7s skimmed past, close enough that she was certain she could feel the pellets caressing her skin.

She slammed into Shaw square in the back with her own, and they went down together even as she drew her pistols, the Rapier coming to life in her left, the Hussar in her right. She fired twice from each weapon, not bothering to count the hits, rolling off of Shaw and flipping herself back to her feet. She heard Carcareas calling out to her, and her skull seemed to vibrate with the woman's voice in her head.

Jo dove forward, toward the side of the van, and she fully expected not only the rattle of gunfire to follow her movements but the slam of the rounds as they found her body. The wound at her side tore open again, feeling like someone had taken a saw to her middle. She was already short of breath.

She came out of the roll as four more shots missed her by fractions, tranquilizer pellets bursting against the side of the vehicle, creating tacky spots of green and blue.

They want me alive, Jo realized, and then fired a double-tap from the Hussar at the Hawk who had made the mistake of trying to follow her roll around the vehicle. She hit him in the head with each shot, and he flopped back, and that earned the gunfire she'd been expecting, and somewhere around her a chorus of automatic rifles opened up. Rounds sparked against the side of the van, smashing through metal and shattering glass.

"No live rounds!" Shaw was shouting. "Alive! Tranqs or hand-to-hand only!"

Behind her, from the front of the van, Jo heard the driver's door open. She twisted from the hips to track the driver, and her ribs erupted in agony, pulled too far, too fast. He heard her, dove for the ground, and when she fired, she astonished herself by missing.

Then something tore into the side of her neck, made her head jerk, and she realized that someone had grabbed hold of her from behind, had taken her by the hair and was jerking her off of her feet. She fired both pistols blindly, down at the ground, and the grip released and a man screamed as his feet turned to shattered bone and powder. Jo turned into him, pushing the barrel of the Hussar into his crotch, firing twice more. The man collapsed, howling and gurgling.

Carcareas was still calling her name, but she sounded funny all of the sudden, and as Jo looked for another target, a way to escape, she realized why. One of the Tranqs had hit her, was making the world slide as if she stood on on the deck of a storm-tossed ship. She struggled forward, her lungs burning, and then her vision exploded white. She staggered back and fell to one knee, feeling the start of a nosebleed, and she knew that she'd been hit in the face. She tried to get up and found she was face-to-face with Leland Shaw. He stabbed her in the chest with the barrel of his gun, and she felt the little air she still had bursting from her mouth, and she fell again, this time onto her back. She heard, rather than felt, the guns in her hands skitter away across the concrete, knew she had lost them.

Shaw dropped with her, keeping the pressure up, the barrel of the gun an agony between her breasts.

"Jack Dark?" Leland Shaw said, his voice swimming through her head, mixing with Carcareas's desperate cries for Joanna to respond. "Jack Dark was a son of a bitch, little girl."

Then he pulled the trigger twice in quick succession. Joanna had just enough time to be grateful that Shaw was using a Tranq-7 and not a true firearm before time, firearms, and Leland Shaw all ceased to matter to her.

Then she laughed, or tried to, because she knew that Leland Shaw, the lying sack of shit that he was, had told the truth about one thing.

Jack Dark *had* been a son of a bitch.

dataDyne
Your life, our hands

FOR IMMEDIATE RELEASE TO ALL APPROVED NEWS OUTLETS AND DATADYNE FIRSTLOOK™ NEWSFEED SUBSCRIBERS.

BE THERE WHEN THE LIGHTNING STRIKES TWICE . . .

29 January 2021–30 January 2021

YOU ARE CORDIALLY INVITED to the public unveiling of the next generation of DataFlow service software, the hotly anticipated AirFlow.Net Version 2.0. Credentialed invitees can participate in the largest, most anticipated product rollout in dataDyne history. (Events will also be simulcast on all dataDyne-sponsored news and entertainment networks.)

Join us for twenty-four hours of spectacle and celebration amid the splendor and beauty of Paris, France*. Special events include**:

29 JANUARY
12:00 PM
Commencement of Festivities, featuring DeathMatch VR superstars Nolan "Headshot" Ross, Brian "Killzone" Maeda, and Kristine "Princess Die" Hatch.

1:00 PM
DeathMatch VR Gold Match Tournament (sponsored by Royce-Chamberlain/Bowman Motors).

6:00 PM
Tournament End Ceremonies—Featuring musical guests Empire X, Killcount, and Copper Jacket.

8:00 PM
Catered Dinner and Open Bar (accredited guests only). Menu to include a selection of French, Greek, and Northern Italian dishes, cooked to order by celebrity media chef André Legrande and Grande Catering.

30 JANUARY
12:00 AM
Midnight Screening of director Stephen Ross's science-fiction extravaganza *Farthest Stars* (starring Rick Swift and Julie Jewel).

2:30 AM
Afterparty, hosted in the dataDyne Corporate Banquet Facility.

8:00 AM
Directors' Champagne Breakfast. Don't miss product demonstrations and upcoming releases from several dataDyne subsidiaries, including Royce-Chamberlain/Bowman Motors, ServAuto Robotics, and Frontline Military Technologies.

12:00 PM
The Presentation Ceremony and Activation of AirFlow.Net 2.0 by dataDyne CEO CASSANDRA DEVRIES.

SOURCE:

FROM THE OFFICE OF GABRIELLE SHEPHARD,
DIRECTOR OF MEDIA RELATIONS AND PUBLIC AFFAIRS
DATADYNE CORPORATION

---

*All visitors must present ID at all times and are subject to invasive and noninvasive security screenings. Presentation of this invitation indicates compliance with all dataDyne corporate security procedures and a waiver of dataDyne liability.

**All times are Paris local and are subject to change without notice.

Information contained within this release is © 2021 dataDyne Corporation and subsidiaries and may not be released except through approved distribution channels, per International Corporate Copyright laws. For more information contact the office of the Director of Media Relations and Public Affairs/dataDyne Corporation at gshephard@dataDyne.mediarel.node.public.

DataFlow Corporate Headquarters
Office of dataDyne Chief Executive
Officer Mlle. Cassandra DeVries
17 Rue de la Baume
Paris, France
January 28th, 2021

The video was gritty, battlefield quality, colors oversaturated and slightly off. It had been shot from the harness camera worn by one of the Hawks under Colonel Shaw's command, and even computer stabilization didn't help much to keep the image leveled or centered on its subject. But it showed enough, and it showed Cassandra DeVries what she believed she had wanted to see.

"This was outside of Ankara, just prior to midnight last night, Madame Director," Colonel Shaw told her. "Acting on intelligence from sources in the Turkish military, we were able to locate the target leaving central Ankara. Based on the information we gathered, I ordered an ambush of the target at the location you can see here, a private airstrip just east of the city."

Cassandra nodded her understanding, then wiped at the

sleep still in the corners of her eyes, not looking away from the small monitor the colonel had set on her desk. She felt sore, mostly in the lower back, a result of the two hours of sleep she'd managed to steal on her office couch. Someone— Velez, probably—had brought her coffee, and she took a sip from the mug while watching the video.

On the screen, dressed in black, with a pistol in each hand, Joanna Dark rolled and rose, firing each weapon. The camera skewed, as if its wearer was moving to avoid fire, and Cassandra was looking at a wall, then the ground, her view panning quickly over a dead Hawk lying in his own blood, clutching at his privates. Then the picture steadied, and she saw the barrel of an assault rifle being aimed by the Hawk wearing the camera, saw him sighting Joanna Dark as the woman spun and dove again, her mouth open. Cassandra imagined she was shouting invective and obscenities. The cameraman fired, missing her barely, and Dark spun away again, toward the end of the vehicle she had been using for cover.

The image jumped, bobbing crazily, and Cassandra assumed that the Hawk wearing the camera was scurrying for a new position. When he found the young woman again, it was in time to see Colonel Shaw shooting her in the chest at extremely close range. Dark staggered, falling back, and Shaw dropped to his knees on top of her, and Cassandra could see that he had rammed his pistol squarely into the woman's torso. Dark's body jerked once, then a second time, her mouth opening again, and despite herself, Cassandra found herself imagining the agony of having round after round tearing through her thorax, bursting organs and rending veins.

She's so young, Cassandra thought. *She's just a girl.*

The camera steadied, moved closer to where Dark now lay motionless on the ground. Shaw was getting to his feet, and at the edges of the frame, other Hawks were moving in, the barrels of their weapons canted down at the body on the ground. Shaw moved half out of panel, and Cassandra saw the colonel's hand appear in the shot, a glint of light off the barrel of his pistol. He fired once more into the woman's head, and her body spasmed with the impact of the round, and as Cassandra watched, a pool of too-bright blood rolled out from beneath the girl's broken head.

Then the screen went dark.

"Mission complete," Colonel Shaw said.

Cassandra nodded, forced herself to look away from the dead screen to where Shaw was standing in front of her, at the desk. The man looked crisp and clean, his uniform fresh, and his expression somber. Behind her, she heard Velez move from where she had stood to watch the video with her, coming along the side of the desk.

"How did you dispose of the body?" Velez asked Colonel Shaw.

"Standard procedure," Shaw said. He kept his eyes on Cassandra as he answered. "We loaded the corpse into the vehicle visible in the video, then sanitized the location with incendiaries."

"Her weapons, they weren't Carrington issue."

"Core-Mantis OmniGlobal," Shaw said.

"What happened to the audio?"

"A malfunction on the recording track."

Cassandra looked at Velez, curious, then at Shaw. "Did she say anything? Before she died?"

"Nothing worth repeating, no, ma'am," Shaw told her. "Certainly not in polite company."

Cassandra nodded again, took a sip of her coffee, and found she couldn't taste it at all. Velez was watching her, now, and her expression was clearly troubled, but why, Cassandra couldn't tell.

"Why was she at the airfield?" Velez asked Shaw, suddenly. "Where was she heading?"

Shaw reached into his uniform, pulling a long plastic envelope from an inside pocket. He held it out for Cassandra, and she saw Velez's frown deepen to a positive scowl for a moment before the other woman regained control of her expression. Cassandra took the envelope. Blood had soaked one edge of it, now dried to a reddish brown.

"We found that on the body," Shaw told Cassandra. "If I may say so, ma'am, I think we neutralized her just in time."

Velez moved back to the desk, watching as Cassandra unfastened the clasp on the envelope and emptied the contents onto her desk. There were four sheets of paper, all of them neatly folded, and Cassandra laid them out side-by-side, examining them. She was surprised to see that one of the sheets was a photograph of herself, a copy of the standard publicity headshot that had been taken just after she'd been named CEO and that was widely used in print and electronic media. The second and third sheets were maps: one of the Paris neighborhood surrounding DataFlow, and the other the floor plan of Presentation Hall A and the area immediately surrounding it. Notations had been made on both in black ink, lines drawn with arrows and other symbols. The floor plan had additional notations, as well, numbers that, to Cassandra, made no sense at all.

The fourth sheet was a copy of the event schedule for the thirtieth, with the noon unveiling of AirFlow 2 underlined.

"What do these numbers mean?" Cassandra asked quietly, indicating the figures on the floor plan.

Shaw answered before Velez could, saying, "It's a firing solution, ma'am."

"A firing solution?"

"Snipers prepare them if given the opportunity. It saves them time when they're in the field. She probably prepared them using the floor plan."

"This is classified," Cassandra said, looking to Velez.

"The floor plan is a classified document, it has never been released to the public. How did she come to have it in her possession?"

Velez had been staring at Shaw, her expression as tight and disapproving as ever, and she took a moment before responding to the question.

"It's a very good question, Madame Director," Velez said. "I'll look into it at once."

"I didn't ask if you would look into it, Anita, I asked how it happened."

Velez's jaw tightened, and Cassandra supposed that was because she didn't care for being scolded in front of Colonel Shaw.

"I don't know, Madame Director."

"Obviously not." Cassandra looked at the four pages on the desk in front of her, then pushed her chair back from the desk and got to her feet. "Colonel Shaw?"

"Ma'am?"

"How many Hawks do you have with you here in Paris?"

"Seventeen, ma'am. I can have another twelve here within three hours."

"Please do so. I'd like you to assume security oversight for the AirFlow 2 rollout, effective immediately. That gives you very little time—the event begins tomorrow morning. Liaise with Director Shephard, please. You will, of course, be compensated."

"Yes, ma'am," Shaw said, and leaving the display monitor and the envelope on her desk, he pivoted on a toe and quickly covered the distance to the door, exiting briskly.

Velez was staring at her, her expression caught between outrage and humiliation. Cassandra met the look without sympathy. After a second, Velez looked away.

"Say it," Cassandra ordered.

Velez shook her head slightly, her brow furrowing.

"Say what you want to say, Anita."

"Very well." Velez met her gaze again, keeping her voice level. "I am the Director of Corporate Security, not Colonel Shaw. By giving him authority over the rollout, you compromise me and my position, and you create a situation within CORPSEC that could lead to further confusion and even greater danger."

Cassandra slammed her palm down onto the pages still resting on her desk, hard enough to topple the portable video display Shaw had used. "They were going to kill me! Carrington was preparing to send that little bitch here to put a bullet through my head at the unveiling, Anita! In front of the press, in front of the world, they were going to blow my brains out! And you think I'm making a mistake?"

"Shaw has an agenda—"

"Of course he does, you think I don't know that? I know his financials, I know he's looking for a permanent position with dataDyne! And frankly, as far as I'm concerned, he just passed his audition with flying colors! He just stopped a plot to end my life, Anita, and that's more than you've managed to do in the last week!"

"How did he find her?" Velez demanded, raising her voice in anger for the first time that Cassandra could remember. "We'd been searching for Dark ever since she escaped us in Veracruz, a priority target, but he suddenly finds her in Ankara after less than two days of searching?"

"I don't care how he did it, he did it, and that's what matters!"

"But it doesn't make sense!"

Cassandra picked up the copy of the event schedule, crumpling it in her fist as she showed it to Velez. "Where did she get this? Where did she get the floor plan, Anita?"

Velez hesitated, then shook her head.

"You can't tell me, can you?" Cassandra said. "You don't know. It could have been leaked, it could have been pulled off a server, it could have been delivered by a spy. You don't know."

"No, Madame Director."

She threw the paper back down on her desk, glaring at Velez. The other woman said nothing.

Cassandra drew a breath, steeling herself, saw Velez react, the momentary widening of her eyes. She was a smart woman, Cassandra knew. There was no doubt she hadn't seen this coming.

"Madame Director," Velez said softly. "You cannot trust Leland Shaw."

"We're not talking about Colonel Shaw any longer," Cassandra said, matching her tone to Velez's. "Now we're talking about you, Anita. I think you'll agree, you haven't distinguished yourself over the past week."

Velez hesitated, then shook her head ever-so-slightly, forced to concede the point.

"You're correct about the situation within CORPSEC," Cassandra said. "Putting Shaw in charge of the event security does compromise your position."

Velez met her eyes, waiting for the rest.

"I'd like your resignation on my desk before lunch," Cassandra said.

"You don't want to do this." Velez's voice remained soft.

"I don't see as I have much choice. Either you give me your resignation, or I fire you."

"This is a mistake." Velez moved closer. "You're making a terrible mistake, Madame Director."

"I rather think I'm correcting one."

"There's something going on, I don't know what it is, but the signs are everywhere. Veracruz, Ankara, Zentek, Beck-

Yama, Core-Mantis, Carrington, even Shaw, I'm sure they're part of it, all of them."

"I need your d-PAL and your ID. Your sidearm, I believe, you own yourself."

"Cassandra, please!"

"We're done, Anita. DataDyne and I both thank you for your service."

Then she held out her hand, and waited for Anita Velez, who had been her friend, to tender her resignation.

```
>>COM NODE: 128.2981.9291 >> FLASH ENCRYPT
>>TRANSMISSION, INCOMING_SATELLITE: AERIE-914
>>TRANSCRIPT BEGINS . . .
```

COMMUNICATIONS OFFICER: HAWK NEST TO HAWK LEADER. COLONEL, I HAVE A CALL FOR YOU ON THE SECURE NET, IT'S ON THE SCRAMBLER.

SHAW: MACKENZIE? WHAT THE HELL ARE YOU TALKING ABOUT? THERE'S NOTHING RUNNING RIGHT NOW.

CO: I CAN'T EXPLAIN IT, SIR. BUT IT'S GOT YOUR PASS CODE AND WAVE SIGNAL. SHALL I PATCH IT THROUGH?

SHAW: . . . AFFIRMATIVE, LIEUTENANT.

CO: HAWK NEST TO SIGNAL DELTA DELTA ZERO THREE FIVE, YOU ARE SECURE WITH HAWK LEADER, GO AHEAD.

X: COLONEL! HOW'D THE VIDEO WORK OUT?

SHAW: . . . WHY ARE YOU CALLING ME?

X: A COUPLE OF REASONS, ACTUALLY. THE FIRST IS TO THANK YOU—AGAIN—FOR THE SPLENDID JOB YOU DID IN DELIVERING THE PACKAGE. A LITTLE BROKEN, BUT ENTIRELY SERVICEABLE. JUST AS I'D HOPED.

SHAW: YOU'RE WELCOME.

X: SECOND, OF COURSE, IS TO CONGRATULATE YOU ON YOUR NEW JOB. I LIKE TO THINK THAT I HAD A SMALL PART IN MAKING THAT HAPPEN FOR YOU, OF COURSE, WITH THE VIDEO AND ALL, BUT IT'S YOUR TRIUMPH AND YOU SHOULD BE PROUD. THINGS ARE WORKING OUT JUST AS I SAID THEY WOULD, AREN'T THEY?

SHAW: YES. YES, THEY ARE.

X: WHICH BRINGS ME TO THE REASON I'M CALLING. ARE YOU STILL ABOARD WITH WHAT WE DISCUSSED?

SHAW: WE ARE.

X: I'M GLAD TO HEAR YOU SAY THAT. I'M ASSUMING YOU'RE

SAYING IT BECAUSE YOU'RE HAPPY WITH THE ARRANGEMENT, RATHER THAN, SAY, BECAUSE YOU'RE AFRAID WE MIGHT TELL A CERTAIN SOMEONE THAT THE WOMAN SHE THINKS YOU KILLED YOU DIDN'T KILL AT ALL. I'D HATE TO THINK THAT WAS WHY YOU WERE BEING SO ACCOMMODATING AND EVERYTHING.

SHAW: I'M AWARE OF THE POSITION I'M IN. YOU CAN RELY ON ME FOR MY CONTINUED SUPPORT.

X: [LAUGHS] OH, I AM SO GLAD YOU SAID THAT, COLONEL! YOU HAVE NO IDEA HOW GLAD I AM! I KNEW I WAS RIGHT ABOUT YOU! DIDN'T I SAY THAT WHEN WE FIRST MET? AND I WAS RIGHT, I KNEW YOU WOULD BE PERFECT. WE'RE GO-ING TO HAVE A GREAT FUTURE TOGETHER!

SHAW: I HOPE SO.

X: THERE'S ONLY ONE MORE THING I NEED YOU TO DO TO MAKE SURE THAT FUTURE COMES ABOUT, NOW. WE HAVE TO REMOVE THE WOMAN WHO IS SITTING IN MY CHAIR, SO TO SPEAK, YOU FOLLOW ME?

SHAW: . . .

X: COLONEL? COLONEL, DON'T GO ALL SQUEAMISH ON ME.

SHAW: WE DIDN'T DISCUSS THIS.

X: WELL, ACTUALLY, COLONEL, YES, WE DID. NOT IN SO MANY WORDS, BUT WHEN I TOLD YOU THAT I WOULD BE TAKING OVER, THAT IMPLICITLY ASSUMED THE REMOVAL OF THE CUR-RENT CEO, DON'T YOU THINK?

SHAW: . . .

X: [SIGHS] YOU DON'T WANT TO BACK OUT ON ME NOW, COL-ONEL. YOU REALLY DON'T.

SHAW: I'M NOT THINKING ABOUT BACKING OUT, I'M THINKING ABOUT HOW TO DO IT.

X: DON'T BOTHER, I'VE ALREADY WORKED IT OUT FOR YOU. YOU'RE MOVING YOUR HAWKS IN AS SECURITY FOR THE EVENT TOMORROW, YES?

SHAW: THAT'S RIGHT. BUT IF YOU'RE THINKING OF DOING IT THERE, I'LL TELL YOU RIGHT NOW IT'S A BAD IDEA. THERE ARE GOING TO BE A LOT OF PEOPLE ATTENDING, A LOT OF WITNESS—

X: NO, NO, NO, HUSH, NOW. IT'S NOT GOING TO WORK LIKE THAT.

SHAW: THEN HOW IS IT GOING TO WORK?

X: YOU'RE TAKING OVER FOR VELEZ, THAT MEANS YOU'RE HER PERSONAL PROTECTION. CORRECT?

SHAW: YES.

X: WHEN SHE TAKES THE STAGE ON THE THIRTIETH, FOR THE UNVEILING, YOU'RE GOING TO BE THERE, AREN'T YOU?

SHAW: YES.

X: THEN THAT'LL BE ALL IT TAKES. ONCE SHE TURNS THE MA-

CHINE ON, EVERYTHING ELSE WILL TAKE CARE OF ITSELF. IT'LL LOOK LIKE AN ACCIDENT, YOU DON'T EVEN HAVE TO WORRY ABOUT IT.

SHAW: IN FRONT OF THE AUDIENCE?

X: IT'S ABOUT THE MACHINE, COLONEL. SHE HAS TO TURN IT ON.

SHAW: I DON'T UNDERSTAND.

X: YOU DON'T NEED TO. ALL YOU NEED TO DO IS MAKE SURE SHE ACTIVATES AIRFLOW 2, ON TIME, ON SCHEDULE, AND ALL ACCORDING TO HER PLAN. THAT'S ALL. THAT'S IT.

SHAW: THAT'S ALL?

X: THAT'S ALL, COLONEL. BUT—AND THIS IS IMPORTANT—SHE MUST ACTIVATE THE SYSTEM. IF SHE DOESN'T, ALL OF THIS IS FOR NOTHING. I END UP WITH NOTHING, WHICH MEANS YOU END UP WITH NOTHING. BECAUSE—AND I DON'T WANT YOU TO THINK THIS IS A THREAT, BECAUSE, REALLY, IT ISN'T, IT'S JUST THE TRUTH—IF THIS FALLS APART, I SWEAR TO YOU THAT I WILL MAKE SURE YOUR CURRENT BOSS FINDS OUT HOW YOU LIED TO HER. I'VE GOT THE ORIGINAL FOOTAGE, COLONEL, BEFORE WE DOCTORED IT FOR YOU, DON'T FORGET THAT.

SHAW: TRUST ME, I HAVEN'T.

X: THEN WE HAVE AN UNDERSTANDING?

SHAW: YES.

X: WHAT DO YOU NEED TO DO? TELL ME.

SHAW: I NEED TO MAKE CERTAIN SHE ACTIVATES AIRFLOW 2.

X: NO MATTER WHAT, COLONEL.

SHAW: NO MATTER WHAT, YES. AND THEN WHAT HAPPENS . . . ? . . . HELLO?

SHAW: DAMMIT, MACKENZIE, COME BACK.

CO: SIR?

SHAW: WIPE THE TRANSCRIPT, INCLUDING THE RECORDINGS, LIEUTENANT. THIS CONVERSATION NEVER HAPPENED.

CO: . . . WHAT CONVERSATION WOULD THAT BE, THEN, SIR?

>>COM RECORD PURGE >> DELTA ONE ZERO FIVE AUTHORIZATION
>>RECORD DELETED.

Home of Former dataDyne CEO
Zhang Li (Deceased)
38km SW Li Xian, Sichuan Province
People's Republic of China
January 29th, 2021

There was a girl looking at her when Joanna Dark opened her eyes. The girl was Chinese, perhaps her age, perhaps a little younger, with a broad, pleasant face and a smile so genuine and so happy that Jo's first thought was that things couldn't be that bad at all.

They were in a bedroom somewhere, Jo realized, and she was on, rather than in, the bed. It seemed like a nice room, comfortable and tidy but without much by way of decoration. A pair of crossed hook-swords hung on one wall, and on the dresser, Jo could make out the shape of a framed photograph, shrouded with a black veil. A bright pink and blue teddy bear, easily half Jo's height, sat in one corner, beside the chair the girl was sitting in.

"Move slowly," the girl said, and Jo realized she was speaking in Mandarin. "You're still quite injured. Here, let me help."

She left the chair, crossing to where Jo lay, offering a hand, and after a second, Jo accepted it and the aid in sitting up. Her ribs ached as they had before, but she wasn't having any difficulty breathing, at least as far as she could tell. Her abdomen, on the other hand, still sang with pain, and when Jo gingerly turned to rest her feet on the flagstone floor, there was a new sensation of both tightness and burning.

The girl released her hand, stepping back, the smile as gentle and loving as before.

"My name's Fan," the girl said. "And you're Joanna."

Jo ran a hand through her hair, pushing her forelock back, out of her eyes, nodding. Everything felt heavy, sluggish, and her head still throbbed with the remnants of the tranquilizers that Shaw had pushed into her blood. Once more, her mouth felt like someone had used it as an ashtray. Jo rubbed her eyes, then took another look at Fan.

The girl was continuing to smile at her. She had shoulder-length black hair, cut roughly at the edges, not unlike the style that Jo wore herself. Her clothes, too, seemed to be a mirror of what she was wearing, black pants and a black T-shirt and black ankle-high boots.

"Where am I?" Jo asked. Her voice sounded rough, disused.

"You're in China," Fan answered. "At the home of Master Li. You're safe, don't worry."

"The mansion?"

Fan nodded, still smiling.

"You're the Continuity?"

"One of them, yes. I'm the eldest, actually. Do you want to speak in English? I can speak in English if you'd like."

"I don't . . . I don't really care."

"You're confused. That's okay, I'd be confused. The colonel used enough Tranq to put down a stampede of elephants, I'm afraid. I was actually getting a little worried that he'd used too much, that your respiratory system might collapse. You're not well, are you? I mean, you've been through quite a lot lately."

"Yeah, it's been a rough week," Jo said, looking Fan over again. "Fan."

"Yes, that's right."

"You're the one who's been impersonating me?"

Fan giggled, looking down at herself, her clothing, then back to Jo. "That obvious, huh?"

"Kind of."

"Are you asking if I'm the one who killed Bricker and Matsuo while wearing your skin?"

"Are you?"

"Yup."

"Why?"

"Well, because they had to die, Jo, I mean, c'mon. That's obvious, right?"

"No," Jo said, shaking her head slightly and feeling it ache as if her brain was sloshing about freely inside her skull. "Why me?"

Fan's expression lit with understanding. "Oh, that's easy. You haven't figured that out?"

"Put it down to the Tranq. I'm a little slow at the moment."

"No, that makes sense. Well, it's obvious. We wanted you to come here, my brothers and sisters and I. And we had to keep dataDyne and Carrington and all the rest falling over themselves while we got everything ready. It's worked out really well. You wouldn't believe how well it's worked out, actually."

"You *wanted* me to come here?"

"Yeah. That's why we had Shaw grab you. Saved time, and that way we didn't have to worry that dataDyne would fill you full of holes before you arrived."

The turn of phrase stuck with Jo, the same one she'd written on her pad while communicating with Steinberg and Carrington. That wasn't a coincidence, she realized, though maybe it had been a slip of Fan's tongue to use it.

"You've been tracking me," Jo said. "All along."

"It's not that hard to do if you know how, Jo-Jo. Once Iseli had the ThroatLink put in you, it was even easier."

"I'm sorry, 'Iseli'?"

"Oh, right, yeah. You know her as Carcareas. Her real name is Elena Iseli."

"You guys take it out? The ThroatLink, I mean. Is that why I'm not hearing her in my head?"

"No, it'll come out in a bit, probably. Maybe." Fan brought her shoulders up in an elaborate shrug, laughed. "None of us has ever tried Chrysalis with implants, so I don't know what'll happen, honestly. Might get rejected, might get ejected, for that matter. Or it might just be integrated into the rest of the shift. We'll find out, won't we?"

"I'm sorry, I don't understand."

"You will." Fan held out her hands to Jo. "Come on, I'll explain it as we go along. You've got to meet the rest. We're having a party."

"I'm not sure . . ." Jo closed her eyes, feeling another wave of the receding tranquilizer passing through her, making her feel momentarily nauseated. ". . . I'm not sure I'm up for a party, Fan."

She felt Fan's hands closing around her wrists, the grip firm but kind. After a moment to let the nausea pass, Jo got to her feet, Fan helping her.

"You will be," Fan told her. "It's in your honor, after all."

She was led to a brightly lit banquet hall that had clearly been used by Zhang Li to entertain his honored guests. The table was large enough to seat fifty, carved from a slab of redwood and polished until its surface shone like blood-colored glass. Bright and intricately woven tapestries hung from the walls, and pieces of sculpture, both abstract and archaic, stood on pedestals at regular intervals. Light shone from crystal sconces on the walls and from three massive chandeliers that hung high above the center of the hall.

In collision with this refinement were obviously newer decorations. Multicolored streamers of crepe billowed from where they'd been taped to the walls, criss-crossing the breadth of the room. Bundles of helium balloons, green, yellow, orange, and red, bobbed and swayed on their anchors at the table, attached to the backs of several of the chairs. Low-wattage party lasers sent beams dancing across every surface, cycling through every color in the visible spectrum one after another. Where the beams met crystal, the light burst into miniature suns.

Above it all, at the back of the hall, amateurishly painted on a large swatch of white fabric—Jo wondered if it wasn't a bedsheet—was a homemade banner, reading, "Welcome Joanna!"

That would have been enough to make her stop where she stood, except that, when Fan lead her through the doors, the room erupted in noise and music. From all around the table, boys and girls jumped up from where they'd been seated, some of them standing in their chairs, some taking the floor. They wore party hats, and alternately waved or blew on noisemakers, and as one they all called her name.

"Joanna!"

Dumbfounded, Jo looked to Fan, saw that the young woman was smiling broadly, looking right back at her with expectant delight.

"Welcome to the Continuity, Mai-Killer," Fan said.

The noise turned to applause, hands and feet pounding on the table, on the floor, the boys and girls—Jo was certain there wasn't a single one of them older than herself, and from the first look it seemed safe to say that most were perhaps just half that—cheering and clapping for her arrival. Two young men, seated side-by-side, blew kisses to her, and one of the girls suddenly surged out of her seat and sprinted toward her, a bouquet of flowers in her hands. The flowers were roses, red and white, and Jo took them awkwardly, and the girl backed away bowing before turning fully and racing back to her seat.

I'm out of my mind, Jo thought. *I'm feverish, that must be it. The gunshot wound, it's infected and I'm feverish and this is not happening.*

Fan reached out, taking her by the elbow gently, and began guiding her through the room, passing along the left-hand side of the table. The applause continued, everyone turning to watch as she and Fan passed. Jo could see that a feast of a sort had been prepared and laid out already, plates and plates heaped with cookies and pastries and cakes and chocolates, bowls full of steaming noodles and broth. There were pieces of fried chicken and roasted duck, layers upon layers of steaks. Bottles of radically different shapes and sizes held drinks, what looked like everything from water to vintage champagne.

They reached the head of the table, where three places had been set, side-by-side, only one of them occupied: it held a young Chinese man, perhaps a year or two younger than Fan. He stood like the rest, applauding with them, the same look of delight on his face. When Jo and Fan finally reached him, he stopped clapping long enough to reach over and pull out the high-backed chair marking the seat of honor, offering it to Joanna. All the more certain that she was hallucinating,

Joanna took it, placing her bouquet of flowers on the table beside her setting.

Fan held up a hand and the applause died, though it seemed in no hurry to do so. Then she bent her head to speak in Joanna's ear, saying, "You really ought to say something to them."

Jo looked at Fan, feeling an odd surge of panic.

I don't know what the hell I'm doing here, she thought. *What the hell am I supposed to say to them?*

Fan's smile was brimming with encouragement.

Jo took her feet again, wincing slightly at the twinge from her ribs. She cleared her throat, saw thirty sets of eyes looking to hers with anticipation and expectation.

"Thank you," Jo said. "You honor me."

There was a roar of approval from the table, the clattering of cutlery and more applause. More kisses were blown her way.

At her right, Fan reached out for the wineglass placed at her setting, lifting it into the air. All around the table, boys and girls followed suit.

"To Joanna Dark," Fan said. "The killer of most-vile sister, Zhang Mai, joins us at last!"

Cheering, glasses raised to the ceiling, but before anyone could drink, Fan held out her free hand, and the table went silent.

"To Joanna Dark," Fan said. "The killer of most-revered father, Zhang Li, joins us at last."

All at once, and as abruptly as turning off a light, the mood at the table shifted, growing palpably darker. The smiles vanished altogether, and Joanna now found thirty sets of eyes boring into her with more hatred than she had imagined possible from faces so young. It was absolute, and it was vicious, and for a second Jo wondered if the table wouldn't try to attack her en masse at that moment, if they wouldn't come at her with their chopsticks and steak knives and salad forks and try to end her life there and then.

Fan turned to face her, the smile gone, all evidence of previous kindness banished.

"You murdered our father, Joanna Dark. We are what he left behind. We are his children. We are the Continuity."

"He murdered mine," Jo said before she could think that, perhaps, it would be better to not say anything at all.

"No," Fan said. "His bitch-slut daughter did. But it doesn't matter. Everyone here knows what it's like to lose their father. We understand that grief. We understand that rage."

Jo said nothing, staring at Fan. The size of the hall made the silence all that more oppressive, all that more heavy.

Fan held the glass out for a moment longer, then turned back to face the rest of the table. She drank, and the boys and girls all followed suit. With ceremony as grave as her words, Fan set her glass back onto the table.

Then she laughed, a peal of delight, and said, "Let's eat!"

The one seated to Jo's right was named Ke-Ling, and he was apparently the second-eldest child. He talked incessantly as he ate, almost babbling with excitement, telling Jo that he was a fan of hers, that he had watched the recording of the DeathMatch VR battle she had fought with Mai Hem exactly 317 times, the last of which had been that very afternoon.

Fan, for the most part, stayed silent, except to ask Jo why she wasn't eating.

"Not that hungry."

"You really ought to eat something, Jo-Jo. You're going to need your strength."

That was an opening, but before Jo could ask why she would need her strength, three of the youngest kids at the table came up to Fan, bearing garlands of flowers for her, Jo, and Ke-Ling. Down at the far end of the table, a boy of perhaps fifteen was using a machete to slice pieces of a seven-layer cake. A couple of the others were throwing food back and forth at each other.

"Stop it!" Fan barked at them. "Manners!"

The children obediently settled back into their seats, and then, after the briefest of pauses, began yammering again.

"Why am I here?" Jo asked Fan.

Fan considered, then abruptly reached out and touched Jo's cheek, brushing her hair back from where it had fallen over one eye. Jo had to fight the urge to clear the hand, to get it out of her face. Doing anything that would start a fight seemed like a very bad idea, especially given how she was feeling and the current environment.

"Yes," Fan said, deciding. "All right."

She rose from her seat, dropping her hand and then smoothly drawing a Falcon 2 pistol from where she'd apparently been carrying it tucked into the waistband of her pants. It was a quick move, fast enough that Jo didn't realize what Fan had done until the young woman had the gun in her hand, and before Jo could move Fan was pointing the pistol at the ceiling. She fired twice, quickly, and the rounds sang off the stone above them, and the hall went deadly silent.

"Jo-Jo has asked why she's here," Fan said. "Who wants to tell her?"

Almost every hand at the table went up, with the exception of Ke-Ling's, at Jo's right. Ke-Ling served himself a second helping of fried duck.

"Shuang, you may answer."

Roughly halfway down, on the left, a young girl stood up. She was wearing a concubine's dress, one of the ones that Jo had seen on Zhang Li's kept women during her last visit to the mansion, but it clearly didn't belong to the child, and she seemed to disappear within its folds.

"You are our friend," Shuang said. "And it is right to honor our friends."

"And why is she our friend?" Fan prompted.

Shuang looked to Fan, then to Joanna. "Because you killed Zhang Mai, called Mai Hem. You killed the daughter who dishonored our father and our family. So it is right that we should give you thanks, and that we should honor you."

"That is the first part," Fan said with approval. "Who wishes to answer the second?"

The same hands rose, even as Shuang resumed her seat at the table.

"Tai-Hua."

The boy who stood looked to be perhaps sixteen, maybe a little older. He grinned as he got to his feet, wiping his face with a napkin, before addressing Joanna.

"You are our enemy, because you killed our father. You stole his immortality, and by doing so, you corrupted his dream, the dream that was dataDyne. You corrupted it, and gave control of it to the Bitch. You are the killer of Zhang Li, and you must answer for that."

"So this is my last meal?" Jo asked Fan. "We hit dessert and then you shoot me?"

Fan giggled, and all around the table, the boys and girls gathered there picked up the sound, echoing and augmenting it.

"No, Jo-Jo. If this was about an execution, we'd have done it days ago. We could have. We could have let the dataDyne hit team in Veracruz succeed, for instance, instead of warning the Xiphos Brigade that they were there. We could have pointed dataDyne your way in Ankara, instead of making sure it was only Shaw who knew you were there. We could have killed you a million times, a million ways, all with the press of a key, with a line of code. But we didn't. You're not here to be simply executed."

"But you want revenge."

"We do, that's correct. But we also want what's *right*. And I want what you denied me."

Somewhere down the table, a voice spoke up, was quickly hushed. Cutlery clinked, then went still.

"I've never met you before, Fan," Jo said. "How could I have denied you anything?"

"You killed Zhang Mai, Jo-Jo. Her death was mine. I was to become the favored daughter, I was to replace her in the eyes of our father. But you killed her, and then you killed him. You took my destiny from me. Now you will return it."

"How? I can't bring Master Li back to life."

"We will fight, the way you and Mai Hem should have fought, Jo-Jo. We will fight the way our father intended, the way DeathMatch was always meant to be fought."

"I did that once," Jo said. "I'm not a big fan of it."

"We will fight the way our father meant for us to fight," Fan continued, as if she hadn't heard. "You and I, in the DeathMatch arena. No safeties this time. No third-party bots turning statues to life. No external hacks to give either of us unauthorized weaponry. No last-second disconnects to save your life or mine should one of us fall. We will fight the way our father intended, and we will fight to the death, with the world watching."

"You're going to broadcast it?"

"Of course. DeathMatch was always meant to be a spectator sport. To have it be anything else is to dishonor our father's name, just as the Bitch dishonors it by attempting to be him."

"DeVries."

"The Bitch, yes," Fan said.

Jo glanced down at her still-empty plate, then out at the faces surrounding the table, watching and listening. She still felt dizzy, slightly light-headed. She looked at her hands, both of them bruised, the Nüe-Skin beginning to flake away.

"You'll dishonor your father's name anyway," Jo said to Fan. "When I defeated Mai Hem, I was at full speed, at full strength, just as you are now. But I'm not, Fan. I'm hurt. I've got broken ribs and a hole in my side that's gone infected. I've got bruises that have bruises. Defeating me won't be a triumph. It won't bring honor. It'll bring exactly the opposite."

Fan smiled, gently.

Then she turned the Falcon in her hand, dug its barrel against the left side of her own belly, and pulled the trigger. There was a muffled report, the shot buried in her flesh, and an immediate, wet, thunk came from behind her as the round passed through and into the chair, a mist of blood trailing.

No one at the table moved.

Fan moaned softly, as if in the throes of ecstasy, and carefully pulled the gun from where she'd pressed it to her body. Blood and gunpowder peppered her hand. She pointed the barrel at Jo.

"Now we'll be even," Fan said with a sigh. "Ke-Ke, take her to be prepared."

Before Jo could wonder what that meant, she felt something cold and hard being pressed to the base of her skull, saw the children all around the table quickly getting to their feet. Ke-Ling took hold of her shoulder with his free hand, pulling her out of the chair, and there were many more guns pointed at her now, and she knew that if there'd been a chance of getting away from this madness at all, it was gone now.

With no idea where they were going or what would happen next, Joanna was marched from the banquet hall into the bowels of Zhang Li's dead mansion, toward the labs.

"The Change always hurts," she heard Fan calling after her. "Try to enjoy it."

>DATADYNE ARCHIVE
>>AUTHORIZATION: ZHANG LI ALPHA
>>>SUBDIR: UNCONVENTIONAL ARCHAEOLOGICAL RESEARCH PROJECTS, CODENAMED "GRAAL."

NODE: 12973_291 > Encrypt 1
FROM: FIELD 1<Sage, Dr. David, project GRAAL field lead>
TO: CEO 1 <Zhang Li, dataDyne CEO>
RE: Unusual field samples from project site ASCENSION
Message dated: 14 February 2019
Message reads:

Master Li—
  Preliminary lab analysis of the biologicals recovered from project site AS-CENSION has been completed. In general the results and biomatter source are inconclusive; at this time, this department lacks suitable material for baseline comparisons.

Initial Findings:
Sample contains a small amount of nanoconstructs, of organic composi-tion, originally found near the Tunguska, Siberia dig site. Sample taken by field team BRAVO, with appropriate decontamination and artifact-preservation protocols.
  Sample found inside small (8 cm high by 4 cm wide) artifact, apparently of stone, adorned with glyphs consistent with those recovered from the FU-SION, NEXUS, and ALLIANCE dig sites.
  In lab tests, we have found that these nanomachines, which we are code-naming CHRYSALIS, possess a unique property. If exposed to an exist-ing biosignature (through standard neural lacing, similar to DeathMatch VR biometrics monitoring and synchronization, q.v.), they can—if properly implemented—mimic in another host that same biosignature, for limited periods of time.
  In essence, sir, the nanomachines can allow, in lab animals, a test rab-bit to transform into, for example, a test rat. The transformation is com-plete and profound—body mass, physical characteristics, even minor injuries, all seem to pass from one host to another.
  This process is not without pain—test animals appeared to be under great physical strain, and several of the smaller subjects did not survive.

The process also appears to be "dosage" specific—smaller exposure to CHRYSALIS reduces the length of time that the altered form can be maintained. Currently, experiments are under way to determine how to prolong the period of transformation; human trials may begin as soon as eight months from now.

Currently, transformation times last only 3–5 hours. With proper study, I believe we can extend that period to as much as 24–48 hours (though I anticipate this will cause considerably more pain and physical stress to the host).

NODE:	12973_291 > Encrypt 1

NODE: 12973_291 > Encrypt 1
FROM: FIELD 1 <Sage, Dr. David, project GRAAL field lead>
TO: CEO 1 <Zhang Li, dataDyne CEO>
RE: CHRYSALIS project update
Message dated: 14 March 2019
Message reads:

Master Li:

Per your directive, I have discontinued all safety protocols and have begun, albeit reluctantly, to launch human trials.

As many of the test subjects provided by procurement are somewhat damaged, the results are promising but not as successful as might be expected with proper study, safety precautions, and research.

Currently, the CHRYSALIS transformation is a four-stage process, outlined below.

- Step one: Programming of nanomachines.
- Step two: Implantation of the nanomachines into the individual being "transformed."
- After initial implantation, it takes 2–4 hours for the host to be fully transformed. The more profound the transformation (i.e., alterations of body mass, height, etc.), the more painful the process. There is a significant chance at this stage for the host to suffer from profound neurological and cardiac stress.
- Step three: Transformation. This can be maintained, given the size of dosage and concentration, for 2–18 hours; longer periods of time, but no more than 48 hours, require a longer incubation period for the nanomachines, larger dosage, and a longer, more painful transformation. In testing, some neurotoxins have disrupted the transformation to a limited degree, for periods of up to 30 seconds (after which the nanomachines react and restore the subject to the transformation template).

- Step four: Reversion. Similar to the transformation stage, and quite painful, as the nanomachines "repair" their alterations—which causes similar body stress to the host. Pain, fatigue, dehydration, and other debilitation is common.

Finally, sir, I must respectfully request that, in order to maximize chances of success for this project, additional safety measures be implemented. While this will adversely affect the rather aggressive schedule required by your office, it will improve our overall chances of success.

NODE: 12973_291 > Encrypt 1
From: FIELD 1 <Sage, Dr. David, project GRAAL field lead>
To: CEO 1 <Zhang Li, dataDyne CEO>
RE: CHRYSALIS project update
Message dated: 06 June 2019
Message reads:

Master Li:
   Per your directive, all CHRYSALIS materials have been packaged and delivered—via your personal security forces—to your research facility in China.
   Sadly, I must register my concern at this turn of events. While your desire to oversee the project yourself is commendable and understandable (particularly given the resources that have been devoted to the project), I am concerned that by removing myself and my team from the research efforts, the recovered samples may be damaged or destroyed.
   I respectfully implore you to reconsider.

NODE: 12973_291 > Encrypt 1-1-2
FROM: HAWK 1 <REDACTED>
TO: CEO 1 <Zhang Li, dataDyne CEO>
RE: MISSION ACCOMPLISHED
Message dated: 07 June 2019
Message reads:

Sir:
   All ASCENSCION researchers and personnel have been sanitized, per your orders. Authorities believe explosion was accidental.
   -S

CHAPTER

24

"I don't know about this, Jon," Calvin Rogers said.

Steinberg finished checking the rigging on his combat harness, then switched his attention to the Fairchild he'd taken from the armory without Potts's permission and—hopefully—without his notice as well. He popped the clip, checking the tension of the spring with his index finger, and, satisfied with what he found, began loading nine-millimeter rounds into place, one after the other.

"Jon—"

Still feeding the clip, Steinberg said, "I can't fly, Cal."

"I know that." Rogers checked over his shoulder, toward the entrance of the bay, and Steinberg guessed the pilot was trying to assure himself that they were still alone. Then Rogers glanced upward, and Steinberg figured that was to check if the security cameras were still in place and on. They were, but that wasn't a problem for the moment, since Steinberg had convinced Grim to ghost the image of Bay 2 onto

Bay 1 for the half an hour he had hoped it would take to get loaded and airborne.

"The Old Man can't see us, Calvin," Steinberg said. "It'll be all right."

"The Old Man'll sure as hell see us when we take off, though," Rogers said.

"Not if you do it real quiet."

"It doesn't matter if I have the bafflers on the jets or not, someone's gonna see it!"

Steinberg looked up from his loading for a moment. "It was a joke, Calvin."

"I don't want jokes, I want solutions. I want, what I really want, is to not do this. I don't think it's a good idea, Jon. I think we ought to wait."

The clip loaded, Steinberg fitted it to the Fairchild, slapping it into place, and got to his feet. He placed the submachine gun with his other weapons inside the dropship, then turned to face Rogers, standing beside the pilot's door.

"I'm done with waiting, Cal," Steinberg said. "We've been waiting for over a week, and for most of that time Joanna's been out there drawing fire for us. She was supposed to check in a day and a half ago: she didn't. She's wounded, she's alone, and I don't give a good God damn what the Old Man says anymore, we're going to Ankara, and we're going to find her."

"Look, Jon, I know how you feel about her, but—"

"What does that mean?"

Rogers looked uncomfortable. "The same way I feel about Emily, Jon, c'mon."

"No, not 'c'mon.' Explain it. You have a thing for Partridge, you think that means I have a thing for Jo?"

"I've seen how you look at her."

Steinberg moved alongside the dropship until he was standing directly in front of Rogers, looking down at him. "And how do I look at her, Calvin?"

"Jon, man, don't be like this. I know what you're feeling, but—"

"You have no idea what I'm feeling." It came out as a snarl, far more than Steinberg had intended, and Rogers flinched slightly. "This has nothing to do with how I feel about Jo, whatever that may be. This has to do with loyalty, Calvin. We don't leave our people hanging, we don't abandon them. If it was you out there, if you'd crashed in Ankara or wherever, you'd sure as hell be expecting me to come and get you. This has *nothing* to do with Jo. This is what we do, because we're the good guys, remember?"

"It's been almost forty hours since she checked in. We don't even know if she's alive."

"Grimshaw confirmed that her ThroatLink was still working as of this morning. If she was dead, it would be, too. He doesn't know where she is, but he can tell she's still alive. So we go to Ankara, Calvin, and we start looking for her from there."

Rogers met his eyes, then nodded, once, but that was all it took, because Steinberg knew he meant it. It was one of the things he liked about Calvin Rogers; the man didn't waste his words, and the single nod was all it took. He was in.

As if to prove it, Rogers turned and started to pull himself into the cockpit of the dropship. Steinberg reversed back toward the troop doors, was about to climb inside himself, when the radio on his belt squawked.

"Commander Steinberg, Romeo Two, respond."

Steinberg hesitated. He'd kept the radio on more to make certain that, if the Old Man found out what he and Rogers was up to, he'd have some warning. He hadn't counted on any of his people trying to raise him directly. Romeo Two, along with Romeos One, Three, Four, Five, and Six, were responsible for the front gate, the most direct and public access to the Institute campus.

"Commander Steinberg, Romeo Two, please respond."

"Hold on a second, Calvin," Steinberg said, and hopped back down from the dropship, pulling the radio from his belt. "Romeo, go ahead."

"Sir, we need you at Alpha."

"Why?"

"There's . . . there's someone here asking for you, sir." There was a pause, the hiss of static indicating that the line was open, the guard trying to formulate what to say next. "She, uh . . . she says you know her."

Rogers had swung himself about in the cockpit, his legs dangling out of the ship, looking at him curiously, and Steinberg found he was sharing the sentiment. None of the girls he'd ever met in London knew what he really did for a living, or where he lived. If he ever went home with anyone—and God knew he couldn't remember the last time he'd had that much time or that much luck—it was to their place, never to his.

"Sir?"

"She give a name?"

"She says her name is, uh . . . Verez? She says you know her, sir. At least in passing."

"Verez?" Steinberg repeated.

"I'm sorry sir, no, it's Velez. Anita Velez."

"Don't let her leave," Steinberg said, and he ran for the gate.

"I assume I will get my clothes back?" Anita Velez asked, adjusting the bathrobe that Daniel Carrington had provided for her. It had been a grudging courtesy, and Steinberg suspected that, if he could have gotten away with it, Carrington wouldn't have bothered. But he was a man of manners, if nothing else, and after all, Velez had come to them.

"No," Carrington rumbled. "You won't. We'll get you something else to wear."

"Sooner rather than later, then, if you please."

"I think we'd like some answers first."

"You interrogate everyone who comes bearing information in this fashion, Mr. Carrington? Mr. Steinberg? Or is this treatment reserved only for women?"

Steinberg shook his head, glancing to where the Old Man was sitting opposite Velez on the couches in his office. Carrington leaned forward, using his stick to support himself, and rested his chin on his hands. When he spoke, it was as low and threatening as a waking grizzly.

"The treatment is warranted both by the person and the situation. We've spent over a week preparing for the inevitable dataDyne attack, something your arrival conceivably presages. Further, we have reason to believe that either dataDyne or a dataDyne-affiliated force now has the ability to fabricate doppelgangers in one fashion or another, ones good enough to endure at least a close visual inspection. When I add to that, Miss Velez, the fact that you are the director of dataDyne CORPSEC and Dr. Cassandra DeVries's personal bodyguard, I believe you can understand why I would take every precaution before granting you a personal audience."

"But your scans satisfied you."

"Our examination of your clothing and your person yielded nothing, but that's not the same as saying that you've come to us clean."

Velez adjusted the bathrobe again, closing it further about her person. The slate blue eyes seemed to bore holes into Carrington, and when they flicked for a moment in Steinberg's way, he thought he could actually feel the hatred in the look.

If she hates us so much, why the hell is she here? he thought.

"I assure you that I have," Velez said. "As I told Mr. Steinberg when he had me handcuffed at the gate, I'm here because I need your help."

"Don't whine," Steinberg said. "You'd have done the same to me."

"I'd have shot you," Velez corrected.

"Well, there you go."

She looked to Carrington again. "I'm not here as a friend, I wouldn't insult any of us by pretending to be so. I am your enemy, but that does not mean that I cannot be honest with you, or sincere in my request. I need your help, Mr. Carrington."

"An even more extraordinary thing for me to believe without proof," Carrington remarked. "Perhaps you should begin to explain yourself, Director Velez."

"Former director," she said. "Cassandra—pardon me—Dr. DeVries relieved me from duty early yesterday morning."

Steinberg looked at Carrington, and from the look on the Old Man's face, saw that the news was as surprise to each of them.

"You've been replaced?" Steinberg asked.

"By Colonel Leland Shaw. I believe you know him."

"He's the Hawk Team leader."

"Yes, Jon," Carrington said, mildly annoyed. "I do know the name. Why?"

"Ostensibly because Colonel Shaw succeeded where I failed."

"Succeeded at what?"

Velez hesitated, looking away and frowning, and Steinberg tried to read the conflict in her face but couldn't make much of it. She was good at keeping blank, and the fact that he could tell she was struggling with what to say next—or, perhaps, how she was going to say it—was a triumph by itself.

"I regret to inform you that your agent, Joanna Dark, was

killed in action in Ankara just past midnight the day before yesterday."

Steinberg grinned. "No, she wasn't."

Both Velez and Carrington looked at him, Carrington with curiosity, Velez with something closer to reproach.

"I am afraid I saw the video, Mr. Steinberg," Velez said. "She was shot multiple times in the chest, then once through the head."

"Jon?" Carrington had arched an eyebrow, waiting for further explanation.

"Grim cracked the CMO communications relay, sir. He's been using it to track ThroatLink communications. The ThroatLink they put in Jo, it was still active as of this morning. If she was dead, it would be, too."

"Has he been able to pick up anything from it?"

"No, sir. The link she's on, it's reserved for their upper echelon operations, and heavily encrypted. We can track the signal, but the intercept comes through as garbage." He glanced at Velez, then decided that what he would say next was an open secret, if it was a secret at all. "Grim thinks that he could probably crack it if he could use the optical to break the encryption, but given the current situation, he didn't want to risk stealing any cycle time from the machine."

"I see," Carrington said, and he began to turn his attention back to Velez, then stopped and returned it to Steinberg. Mildly, almost sweetly, he asked, "You wouldn't know for how long Grim's had access to their communications, would you, Jon? When he might have decided, by himself and without my authorization or permission, to go joy-hacking an enemy hypercorp?"

"I wouldn't know anything about that, sir."

Carrington grunted, turning back to Velez. "Interesting that Colonel Shaw would want Cassandra to believe he had succeeded where you failed."

She nodded slightly, her brow creasing. "But it's yet more evidence of what I have suspected. And it makes me believe all the more that not only is dataDyne's life in danger, but Doctor DeVries's is as well."

"You're not going to find many people sympathetic to the future of dataDyne in this room, Ms. Velez," Steinberg said.

"Don't be an ass," she retorted. "Hate us to your heart's content, envy us as you must, but don't for a moment attempt to convince me that you do not understand what dataDyne means to the world. We employ over half a billion people in almost every country. We *are* the global economy. DataDyne's demise would be the demise of civilization as we know it, and that is no overstatement."

"Unless Core-Mantis OmniGlobal steps in to take your place," Carrington said.

"I have considered that," Velez said. "Certainly, that appears to be one way things could turn out. But it brings me to my point. Eight days ago, CMO was barely a threat worthy of our notice. Since then, they have toppled both Zentek and Beck-Yama, and they appear to have done so with your help."

"And that would be why Cassandra wanted Joanna dead?" Carrington asked.

"I urged her to authorize your assassination, as well," Velez responded. "If that makes you feel any better."

"My ego appreciates the attention, even if my heart feels otherwise. And if I tell you, Miss Velez, that the Institute had nothing to do with CMO's recent successes, what then? Would you accept that?"

"Possibly. It comes down to one question. It comes down to Arthur."

"Who's Arthur?" Steinberg asked.

Velez didn't answer, watching Carrington closely and making no secret of the fact that she was doing it. Whatever the question meant, apparently its weight was enormous, and Steinberg had the definite impression that how Carrington answered would either make or break the direction of the conversation that followed.

"Arthur," Carrington said. "Arthur is the name of Cassandra's brother. He died when she was eight, in an automobile accident. He was six years old, and, as you might imagine, his passing had a profound impact on her life."

"She told you," Velez said.

"We shared many things during the brief time we were together," Carrington said. "AirFlow.Net rose out of Arthur's death, a way to make certain that what she endured no one else would ever have to."

"That's Arthur?" Steinberg asked.

Carrington nodded.

"You're wrong," Velez said, and Steinberg was certain there was both relief and disappointment in her voice when she spoke. "Arthur is the name of AirFlow.Net version 2.0, Mr. Carrington. Arthur is what will be unveiled tomorrow at noon in Paris, and, within minutes of being introduced to the public, Arthur will take over the traffic control of all null-g vehicles fitted with dataDyne transponders, everywhere in the world."

"It's a software code name?" Steinberg said. "She named the software after her dead brother?"

Velez ignored him, staring at Carrington. "Do you see, Mr. Carrington? Of all the names, why she would give that one to AirFlow 2. Not to AirFlow 1, but the second generation, the next generation."

Carrington sat forward as if shocked. "No. No, Miss Velez, it's not possible, not yet. Even at its most advanced, we're at least two years away from harnessing the processing power required, and that's optimistic. Cassandra knows that, we discussed the problem inherent in artificial cognition many times. There are still literally thousands of problems to be solved. Even with her genius, it's simply not possible."

"You underestimate both her intellect and her passion, Mr. Carrington. I've seen it at work. The only thing Arthur lacks is a sense of self."

"What are we talking about?" Steinberg asked, now certain that he had, once again, missed the important part of the conversation, yet remaining just as certain that he'd been present for the whole thing. "What the hell's Arthur?"

"It's—" Carrington said, and then corrected himself, "—he's an AI, Jon. That's what you're saying, isn't it, Miss Velez? She's created an artificial intelligence to run Air-Flow 2."

"That is precisely what I am saying." Velez seemed to relax slightly, though only in her posture. The worry remained on her brow. "That you apparently knew nothing of it confirms what I have feared. There's another force at work, still hidden to me. The same force that has aided CMO. The same force that provided Shaw with the evidence required to remove me, and place him beside Dr. DeVries."

Carrington said nothing, sinking back against his couch and closing his eyes, diving deep into his thoughts. Velez's scowl returned, and since Carrington obviously couldn't see it, she pointed it at Steinberg, who shrugged.

"He's thinking."

"Then he should do it quickly. Dr. DeVries's life is in danger, I'm sure of it. And if he still feels anything for her at all, then I am asking him to forget about his hatred of dataDyne. I'm asking for his help to save her life."

"Not her life," Carrington murmured. "No. No, it's much bigger than that."

"What do you mean? Damn you, man, open your eyes!"

"You say he's not fully sentient. What does that mean?"

"There's no sense of self."

"Then there's no sense of conscience." Carrington sighed, almost sadly. "And now it all makes sense, Jon. All of it. The

Continuity. Zentek. Beck-Yama. CMO. We wanted to know why the Continuity would help CMO instead of helping dataDyne, and here's your answer. They don't care, because none of them will survive."

Velez looked from Steinberg to Carrington, the frustration and confusion on her face almost painful to behold. "What are you talking about? What is the Continuity?"

Carrington sat up, used his stick to rise from the couch. "It doesn't matter. Jon, she's going to need some clothes."

"We going somewhere?"

"To Paris. You'll need to bring troops. Miss Velez, can you muster any support on the ground there?"

"I would want to know why."

"Can you do it?"

"Shaw took over from me yesterday, I'm certain he hasn't had time to purge the division. There will be several deputy directors still loyal to me, yes. If you tell me why you need them."

"To stop Arthur," Carrington said. "He's going to destroy the world."

DataFlow Corporate Headquarters
12th Floor, Secured Wing, Arthur Lab 1
17 Rue de la Baume
Paris, France
January 30th, 2021

Dr. Edward Ventura was waiting for Cassandra in the lab, as she had asked him to be, when she arrived at twenty minutes to six in the morning with Colonel Shaw and Director of Media Relations Shephard in tow. Of the four of them, Cassandra hazarded that it was Shephard who looked the most rested, and she suspected that was due either to a judicious application of makeup, or a similarly judicious application of stimulants. For both their sakes, Cassandra hoped it was the former.

Ventura himself looked tired, bags heavy beneath his eyes, but he made a valiant effort to rally when he saw her enter, and she appreciated that. He'd already changed for the noon unveiling, and instead of his lab clothes was wearing a three-piece suit that was both elegantly tailored and apparently making him violently uncomfortable.

"Edward, thank you for being here," Cassandra said, offering him her hand. "I know it's an ungodly hour, but the schedule's so tight today that this was the only window I could find."

He smiled weakly, taking the offered hand, then releasing it as if even that might prove too taxing an effort. "It's fine, ma'am."

"You look positively done in. I hope you're taking a vacation as soon as this is over."

The smile brightened for a moment. "I'm thinking of taking a cruise."

"I think that's an excellent idea." Cassandra turned, indicating Shaw and Shephard. "This is Colonel Shaw, he's the new Director of CORPSEC, and this is Director Shephard, she's taken over for Mr. Long. She has your schedule for the day. I'll want you onstage with me at noon, as we discussed, and then you'll need to make yourself available for a couple hours after, for Q and A with the approved media outlets."

"I understand."

"Everything's ready?"

"Yes, ma'am. We've configured the interface so you'll actually have the box with you on the stage." Ventura turned, reached for one of the memory cubes on his desk. "It's not technically the control surface, you know, but it'll be a good visual, or at least that's what they tell me. Everything's been preestablished from here to tie Arthur into the air-traffic control network. All you have to do is give him the word."

He offered the cube to Cassandra, and she took it, as always momentarily surprised by its deceptive lack of weight. She turned it in her hand, then passed it back to Shephard.

"What's the procedure?" Cassandra asked Shephard, watching as Ventura stifled a yawn.

"We've taken the liberty of rigging an actual switch onstage," Shephard said, smiling with slight embarrassment. "Old-fashioned, but I think it's a nice visual. When you step onstage to give your presentation, we'll put a live image of the datacore up on the plasma behind you, so the audience can see it, and Arthur's voice will be piped through the speakers in the hall. It's up to you how to introduce him, what you want him to say. I suppose you can have him talk about anything."

"Just don't ask him to compose a poem," Ventura said.

Cassandra smiled. "No, I'm not sure his brand of doggerel will engender confidence."

Shephard continued. "I'd suggest you talk to him about AirFlow 2, obviously. Explain his parameters, let the audience hear exactly what he's designed to do and how he's going to do it. We have a countdown graphic prepared, and when you're ready to synchronize, just say so. We'll put it up on the screen. Count down, throw the switch, and AirFlow 2 will go online. We're trying to make it as easy as possible for the audience to follow."

"Simplicity is the goal." Cassandra peered closer at Ventura. "You really do look awful, Edward. Are you sure you're all right?"

"My stomach's giving me some trouble, ma'am," he admitted. "Stress, I think."

"I don't doubt it." Cassandra turned to Shephard. "Gabi, is Edward needed for anything this morning?"

Shephard consulted her d-PAL briskly. "No, Madame Director. Dr. Ventura's free until half past eleven, when he's to meet you backstage in Hall A."

"There you go, Edward," Cassandra said. "Head home, lie down for a few hours. I'll have Colonel Shaw send one of his men to collect you before you're needed here."

"Maybe I'll do that, ma'am."

"Not maybe."

"No, ma'am."

She smiled at him, and he returned it weakly. Then she turned to Shaw and Shephard and said, "Right, all of you, out. I want to be alone in here for a few minutes."

"You've breakfast shortly with Directors Waterberg, Hesch, and Kollinsky, ma'am," Shephard reminded her.

"Thank you, Gabi, I do recall. Now out, all of you."

Shephard headed for the door, and after a second, Ventura followed her, casting a glance back over his shoulder as if trying to determine if he had forgotten anything. Shaw remained exactly where he was.

"You, too," Cassandra told him.

"As your personal bodyguard, ma'am, I'm uncomfortable with the thought of leaving you alone."

"You're as bad as Anita was, Colonel. I'm perfectly safe here. Now, please, I'd like a moment or two by myself."

Shaw hemmed, then turned and followed in the direction of Shephard and Ventura. Cassandra watched him go, waited until the door had slid closed, until she was certain she was alone in the lab. Then she crossed to the observation glass that ringed the view of the datacore. As she had before, she rested her forehead against the wall, felt the glass cool against her skin, the press of the light from below visible even behind her closed eyes.

To her surprise, she began to weep, felt the tears beginning to spill out, felt her heart beginning to race and her pulse beginning to pound. For almost a minute she resisted, fought against the sudden intensity of the sorrow, and then she surrendered to it and began to sob.

It had been a long time in coming, she realized, especially after the events of the past nine days. It had been as hard and as bitter a time as she could ever remember, as bad as the days that had followed the death of her brother, and when she thought of that, she knew why, exactly, she was crying.

Grief, Cassandra thought. *Grief and mourning, the death of everything that I was.*

Because she knew she had changed, and she didn't know if she liked who she had become. But the woman Anita Velez had pulled from her bed nine days ago, the woman who had been wrapped in body armor and bustled all the way to New Zealand, that woman hadn't been the CEO of dataDyne, only a pretender. That woman had thought that Daniel Carrington still loved her, and that there was right and that there was wrong. That woman had believed that some prices were too high to pay, even for dataDyne and its survival. That woman, in the end, had believed in the value of friendship, and loyalty, and merit.

Since then, Cassandra DeVries had changed, and as she wiped her tears away with her fingers and fought to compose herself once more, she knew it more than ever. She had killed Friedrich Murray, but she understood now that it had been an act of self-defense. Killing Murray had spared dataDyne, and, as Anita Velez had said, Cassandra DeVries *was* dataDyne. She no longer felt guilt or even sorrow for what she had done.

The way she felt no guilt or sorrow over the death of Joanna Dark.

She *was* dataDyne, and anyone who threatened the corporation threatened her. Anyone who threatened her threatened the corporation.

Nine days ago, she had been a pretender to the throne.

Now she was the queen. For the first time since her appointment by the board, Cassandra DeVries believed and accepted it.

And she mourned for what she had lost.

She wiped her eyes once more and looked through the glass at the spinning white column that was the quantum optical datacore. Her cathedral and her god.

"Forgive me," Cassandra said. "For all my sins."

"Parsing error."

Cassandra turned, searching the lab. Several of the monitors at the various workstations were still on, dataDyne screensavers endlessly repeating the company motto, "Your life, our hands." She stepped away from the core, looking about.

"Arthur?" she asked. "Is that you?"

"Systems online."

She turned, following the direction of his voice, found herself heading in the direction of Ventura's desk. She came around, pulling out the chair, and saw the monitor was live, that Arthur's code was cascading past with the frightening speed she'd witnessed in New Zealand. His voice seemed to be emanating from the speakers on the desk.

"Do you know who I am, Arthur?"

"You are Dr. Cassandra DeVries, chief executive officer and director of dataDyne. You are my parent."

"That's right," she said softly. "It's nice to talk to you again."

Arthur didn't respond.

"It's customary to respond with the same sentiment," Cassandra said. "I say that it's nice to see you again, and you say that it's nice to see me, too."

"It's nice to see you, too," Arthur said.

"Are you ready for today, Arthur? Are you ready to go online?"

"All systems nominal set minus one."

"I'm sorry, what was that?"

"Repeating. All systems nominal set minus one."

"Define minus one, please."

"Parsing error."

Cassandra frowned, then reached out and pulled Ventura's keyboard drawer forward, so it was positioned over her lap. "Set diagnostic, Arthur."

"Setting. Query module."

"Outland interface. Run diagnostic."

"Outland interface, diagnostic initiated. Completed. Outland interface nominal."

"Arthur, define 'set minus one,' please."

There was a brief pause, barely noticeable, and Cassandra supposed that in every other situation, she would not have noticed it at all. But Arthur was, effectively, a quantum-optical computer, and with his processing speed there should have been no delay at all—at least, none that she could perceive.

"Parsing error."

She tried the same command, this time with the keyboard.

"Parsing error."

She tried again, still with the keyboard, issuing the command from the root structure.

"Parsing error."

After a moment of consideration, she began typing again. Her first instinct was to do a search for any line containing the command to set variable to minus one, but she realized that would take far too long and would most likely result in several thousand results, if not hundreds of thousands. Instead, she began a scan of the individual memory modules, searching through them by designation and trying to cross-reference them with the modules that were already installed, each of them labeled as a separate set.

There's one missing, she realized.

"Madame Director?"

She looked up from the terminal, saw that Shephard had stepped back into the lab.

"Madame Director, your breakfast is in three minutes. If we're late, we'll be behind all day."

"Just a moment, Gabi."

"I don't mean to press, Madame Director."

"I understand, I'll be right there."

Across the room, lit by the light of the core, she watched as the young woman nodded and backed out of the room.

"Arthur," Cassandra said. "I have to go now. I'll speak to you again soon."

"I'll speak to you again, soon."

"Arthur, I want you to do something for me. We're going to create a little program, just you and I."

"Understood."

"We're calling this program 'Anita,' and I'm the only one who will be allowed to execute it, is that understood? You will key this program to my voice, and my voice alone. Confirm, please."

"Program designated 'Anita,' execution limitation defined. Waiting for program parameters."

"On execution, purge all memory modules. Repeat and confirm."

"Program designated 'Anita,' execution limitation, activation by voice authorization only. Full purge, all memory modules."

"Thank you, Arthur." She rose from Ventura's desk. "One last thing."

"Waiting."

"Delete and purge transcript file of the last five minutes, please."

"Purging."

Cassandra DeVries moved for the doorway, where Director Shephard and Colonel Leland Shaw were now visible, waiting for her, wondering if Anita Velez hadn't been absolutely right.

Wondering if she hadn't made a terrible mistake.

Home of Former dataDyne CEO
Zhang Li (Deceased)
38km SW Li Xian, Sichuan Province
People's Republic of China
January 30th, 2021

It had hurt Jo more than anything she could ever have imagined, and in the end, when she had screamed, there had been no shame in it. Even as a child, even when she had been paralyzed for weeks, even months at a time, as surgeons and scientists had worked to repair the the defect in her spine, it was nothing compared to this.

She had screamed, and she had wept, and Chun Fan had stayed beside her through it all. She had held Jo's hand and mopped her brow, put the end of the straw in her mouth to give her water that felt like broken glass as it slid down her throat. She had stroked her hair, and told her she loved her, and that she knew it hurt, but that pain was something they both understood.

The agony of it had been so extreme that Jo hadn't really noticed the moment that Fan's attitude changed. She didn't really see the flaring hatred in the young woman's eyes, the contempt curling her lip. She didn't truly register the words the girl was saying to her, not until she began beating her around the head and chest.

"Whore!" Fan had called her. "Filthy, dirty, shameful whore! You failed him! You failed our father! Disgusting, foul bitch!"

And Jo had been in such pain already, the tears blurring her eyes and her whole being consumed with fire and ice, it hadn't mattered that it didn't make sense. She'd heard enough, heard the words *failure* and *father,* and that had only compounded her agonies. Even when Ke-Ling and three others had pulled Fan off of her, the woman still flailing, trying to scratch Jo's eyes out, it had meant nothing.

It had been the worst pain Joanna Dark had ever experienced.

Right up until the moment she looked in the mirror when it was all over, and saw the face of the woman who had murdered her father staring back at her.

She was still staring at her reflection when the door to the small lab opened, and Chun Fan returned, followed by Ke-Ling and the girl who had spoken at the banquet, Shuang. Shuang carried a bundle of clothes in her arms. Fan held a MagSec, and Ke-Ling a SuperDragon, the latest in dataDyne assault weapons. They didn't point the weapons at her, but they didn't have to, either, so Jo figured it wasn't because they were still trying to be polite.

Fan's lip curled in disgust at the sight of her standing in front of the mirror, barefoot and wearing only a simple white shift. Before Jo could think to move or speak, the young woman had cleared her throat, spitting in her direction. Jo got a hand up, catching the sputum on her palm.

"You're insane," Jo said, and she was appalled to discover that her voice, like her body, belonged to Mai Hem.

"Don't talk to me, whore," Fan said with such ferocity that Jo expected her to raise the pistol and start shooting right then. That she didn't she could only attribute to Ke-Ling, who stepped forward, interposing himself between the two women.

"Fan! Stop it!"

"I'm going to kill her, I'm going to—"

"Not yet! It's not ready yet, remember the plan! Remember the timing!"

Fan struggled visibly to regain control of herself, and then, as if by magic, the fury seething in her seemed to vanish altogether.

"Jo," she said. "Oh, Jo-Jo, I'm sorry. I'm . . . I'm sorry, you look just like her. I forget."

"What have you done to me?" Jo asked, and again it was Mai Hem's voice, and the fact that it was also hers and she couldn't avoid it threatened to make Jo scream. "What did you do to my body?"

"It's called Chrysalis," Ke-Ling said, stepping back to let Shuang move past, watching as the girl moved to the procedure table where Jo had been strapped for the duration of the transformation. Shuang began laying out the bundle in her arms carefully, and Jo saw she was putting out a set of clothes, everything from lingerie on up. "Our father discovered it while pursuing the Graal. His search brought him many such wonders."

"I want my body back!" Jo said. "You hated Mai Hem, you said so yourselves, why would you do this to me? If you want to kill me, kill me! Why make me look like her?"

"I told you," Fan said, and it sounded genuinely innocent. "You stole my destiny. This is how I get it back."

Jo stared at her, utterly at a loss.

"You killed Mai Hem," Fan explained. "I was supposed to do that. You killed our father. You have to die for that. Now, when I kill you, I can do both things at once, defeat Mai Hem and avenge Master Li. See?"

"You're crazy," Jo said again, her voice barely a whisper. "You're all absolutely off your nut."

"The change isn't permanent, silly," Fan said. "I mean, if it was, I'd still look like you, wouldn't I? It'll end in a day or so. Or after you die. Whichever works."

"No, this is sick," Jo said, and still her voice was Mai Hem's, and it was driving her mad, making her want to shriek, to tear at her throat, just to make it stop. "This is sick, this is . . . this is evil. You've turned me into the woman who murdered my Da!"

"But you're the woman who murdered *our* Da. I think that's only fair, don't you?"

A sob burst from her throat, the sound of Mai Hem's sorrow, and Jo had to turn away from Fan, fighting with everything she had to keep from letting the despair and grief and outrage from bursting forth. There was the sound of motion behind her, the shuffle of feet and the brush of silk on silk.

"It's okay to cry," Shuang told her. "We cried when we learned what you did."

Jo covered her face with her hands, feeling her whole body shaking.

"Get dressed in the clothes we brought," Ke-Ling said from behind her, his voice soft. "When you're ready, come to the door. Don't take too long."

There was the sound of more motion, footsteps heading toward the door. Jo heard the hiss and click as it slid back, and then Fan's voice as she left the room, saying, "I don't understand why she's so worked up. It's not like she killed her father. Mai Hem did that."

Then the door hissed closed, and she was alone again.

||||||||||||

The clothes, as Joanna feared, were Mai Hem's.

I can't wear these, she told herself. *I can't do it.*

But in the end, she did, because she knew that if she didn't, Fan would simply walk back into the lab and shoot her to death.

This time, when she saw herself in the mirror, she did weep.

||||||||||||

Ke-Ling, Shuang, and half a dozen other members of the Continuity walked her from the lab back to the main floor of the mansion, along corridors she had hoped she would never see again, to the grand entrance hall with its Death-Match arena. As they walked, more and more of Zhang Li's "children" fell in behind them, and Jo heard them muttering, mocking her.

But it's not me they're mocking, she thought. *It's Mai Hem. You're not Mai Hem. Don't forget that. Don't let yourself forget that. You're not the woman who murdered your father.*

She faltered, stopped abruptly, and heard the sound of Mai Hem's laughter.

You're not the woman who murdered your father.

"Keep moving, please," Ke-Ling said, pointing his Super-Dragon at her.

Jo put a hand to her mouth, nodding, trying desperately to stifle the giggles she felt welling inside her.

I am going mad, she thought. *One second I'm weeping, the next I'm hysterical.*

With difficulty, she managed to keep her silence, continued walking with the crowd of children who hated her. It was difficult, moving in Mai Hem's shell. The woman had been taller than Jo, her legs longer, and her choice in clothing hadn't made movement particularly easy, either. The heels on her boots had to be four inches, if not more, and more than once Jo was afraid she would fall and break her ankle.

And wouldn't that make for a short fight, she thought, and again had to fight the need to giggle.

They entered the grand hall, and it was just as Jo remembered it, to such an extent that she wondered if Fan and the others hadn't worked diligently to make it so, to recreate that night almost a year prior when she'd "killed" Mai Hem for the first time—locked in virtual combat for the dark amusement of Zhang Li. The DeathMatch beds were still in the same position, the large, heavily modified units unique to Zhang Li's particular version of the game. The commercial rigs sold by dataDyne were far smaller, designed for portability and ease of use, consisting only of a visor and a tangle of biofeedback sensors.

The beds were something else altogether, metallic cocoons that encased the player entirely, with millions of sensors built into every surface. The sensors not only detected the player's most minute muscle impulses for translation to the game's virtual reality, they also acted as feedback sensors, relaying corresponding sensation. At full intensity— and Joanna knew this from experience—they would inflict physical trauma that would replicate any virtual injury.

It was called DeathMatch for a reason, after all, and it wasn't because it made good copy. It was called DeathMatch because by Zhang Li's rules, if you lost, you died.

Fan was waiting for them in the center of the room. She had tied her hair back into a short ponytail and had changed into a black jumpsuit. Her shoes, Jo noted with some envy, were flat-soled sneakers.

"That one," Fan told her, indicating one of the beds.

"Not the one I used last time?"

"That's right, that one," Fan said. "Mai Hem's."

"Fan," Jo said. "I'm not Mai Hem, I'm Joanna. Joanna Dark."

"You sure look like Mai Hem," Fan said with a laugh. Then the laugh transformed into a snarl. "Get into the bed, now, you sick whore, or I'll kill you here."

Ke-Ling and three others all raised the weapons they were holding, settling their sights on Jo.

"What happens if I win?" Jo asked.

"You won't win. I've waited my life for this. You won't win."

"If I do," Jo asked. "If I win, what happens? Do I come out of the bed and get shot anyway?"

"No, you fight to live," Fan said. "Those are the stakes, as they always were for my father. You fight to live, or else you will not fight with your whole heart, with your whole being. If you win, you live. Get into the bed, Jo-Jo."

Taking a last look around the room, Jo moved to the bed and lay down inside the molded recess. The odd, blue-green biomemetic gel that made up the interior squished beneath her weight, parting to accommodate her, wrapping her body. One of the children, a boy, leaned in and began attaching the feedback leads to her temples and fingers.

Across from her, Jo watched as Fan took her position.

"Are we tied in?" Fan asked.

From somewhere in the room out of her line of sight, Jo heard a girl answering. "All set. Ready to broadcast on your command."

"What time is it in Paris?"

"Almost eleven o'clock," Ke-Ling said. "Arthur goes live in an hour."

"This won't take an hour." Fan grinned. "As soon as we start, upload the final packet."

"What happens at noon?" Jo asked.

Fan looked at her, and Jo realized that, once again, the insane young woman was seeing Mai Hem, and Mai Hem alone.

"Everything burns, whore," Fan said. "Everything burns. Cut us in."

There was a hiss of static, the bed vibrating slightly as the top began to lower into position. Through the speakers beneath her head, Jo heard the trademark DeathMatch music fading in, the prerecorded announcement that she had listened to so many times in the past. For a fleeting moment, she thought about the people all around the world, their computers, their d-PALs all suddenly thrumming with messages saying the same thing, that a true DeathMatch was about to begin, Zhang Li–style.

The bed closed with a hiss of escaping air as the seals locked into place, and for a second, Jo was wrapped in darkness.

I'm Joanna Dark, she thought. *I am Joanna Dark, I am not Mai Hem. And I can beat this bitch.*

The world flashed white, turned to a dot, and then unfolded like an origami box.

When it resolved, Chun Fan was waiting to kill her.

Carrington Institute VTOL
Chameleon Class Dropship #001
2,085 Feet, Level Flight
English Channel
January 30th, 2021

Anita Velez, riding in the troop compartment of the drop-ship opposite Steinberg, removed her headset and shouted at him over the din of the engines.

"There's a no-fly zone established that extends out a quarter of a mile from the DataFlow offices in all directions," she said. "But there is a park to the north of the offices, just over that distance, point two-eight miles, surrounding the Allée de la Comtesse de Ségur. My people will meet us there with vehicles, we can cover the rest of the distance quickly."

"How many of them will meet us?" Steinberg shouted back.

Velez shook her head, frustrated. "Only fifteen. Communications are being routed through the Hawk Teams, and I am afraid of what Shaw will do if he knows we are coming. I was able to contact only one of my deputies, but he is a good man, and he *will* be there. Once we reach DataFlow, I expect we will be able to muster more support."

"Any idea how many Hawks we'll be dealing with?"

"I am unsure, Mr. Steinberg. I would guess that Shaw has pulled his full complement to handle security, especially if he is, as we suspect, being duped into a coup attempt. According to my information, that could be as many as forty Hawks on the ground."

"And they're in close? All of them, they're on the close protection?"

"My information is that only half of the Hawks will be deployed within Hall A, the rest of them are on the perimeter. Shaw himself is on close-guard of Dr. DeVries. He is the priority target, Mr. Steinberg."

"Your priority target, Miss Velez, *not* mine. My job is to shut down Arthur before he can do what he was programmed to do."

Velez made a face, but nodded, and Steinberg couldn't fault her for it. He didn't much care for the woman, but he had to admit he respected her. She was a wolf, as far as he was concerned, and loyalty was something that counted for a lot in his book. If nothing else, Anita Velez was loyal.

Steinberg tapped the shoulder of the trooper riding beside him, a young black man named Dorsey that Steinberg had recruited from Los Angeles SWAT that past fall, motioned that he wanted the headset hanging beside him. Counting him and Steinberg, and omitting Calvin Rogers in the cockpit and Velez seated opposite, there were eight troopers aboard. If Velez was right about the numbers she could muster, the opening play would have to be done with serious precision to compensate for their lack of shooters.

Dorsey shifted a compact model Fairchild submachine gun into his lap, reached around, and handed the headset over. Steinberg settled the phones over his ears, adjusting the boom closer to his mouth, then pressed the transmit button on the cord.

"Papa Bear, Papa Bear, this is Goldilocks."

"Go ahead, Goldilocks," Carrington answered.

"Velez says she has fifteen, that's one-five, CORPSEC that will meet us on the ground. Estimates Hawk forces at forty, that's four-zero. Approach is overland, from the north."

"Understood."

"Sir," Steinberg said. "I need rules of engagement, here. We're going into a situation with media, dignitaries, civilians—there're a lot of people going to be on the ground. I have to know when we're weapons free."

"This has to be done clean, no collateral damage, Jon."

"We're in plainclothes with light load-out, as you ordered, P9Ps and the cut-down Fairchilds, suppressors for both. But even at the best of times those things make noise, sir. If we can create a distraction of some sort, set fire to a building or something—"

"I said no collateral damage, and I meant it. Best case scenario at this time has dataDyne taking a hit, and Velez is correct when she says that could have a profound impact in every part of the world."

"That's still better than the worst case scenario, sir."

"I agree. If it comes to that, you are weapons free. Arthur cannot—repeat—cannot go live."

Steinberg looked across to where Velez was seated, now wearing blue jeans and a black leather jacket hastily scavenged from one of his female troopers' locker at the Institute. It was inappropriate dress for the event, but going with plainclothes was a better option than marching into DataFlow wearing the Carrington colors. She'd taken the same weapons the rest of them had, was currently double-checking the fit of the silencer to her P9P. In addition to the pistol and the Fairchild, she'd taken a combat knife.

"Sir," Steinberg said, watching Velez as she worked. She didn't look up, and he hoped to God that meant that she couldn't hear him. "I need to know if I'm authorized to fire on Dr. DeVries."

There was a pause before Carrington responded. *"Negative, Jon."*

"If she's the one to throw the switch on this thing, sir—"

"I repeat, negative. You are not authorized to fire on Cassandra. If it comes to that, the world can burn, do you understand me?"

If it comes to that, the world damn well will, Steinberg thought. *And if it comes to that, I'm putting a bullet in her, I don't care if you're still in love with her or not.*

"Understood, sir," Steinberg said. "Goldilocks out."

<hr>

It was a truth that Steinberg had discovered early on during his career in the military: when things went to hell, they went to hell as fast as they possibly could.

"It's genius," Carrington had said as he'd led him and Velez from his office, moving as fast as his bulk and his leg would allow him. "A computer that can take plain language instruction, that can be told the result you desire and then self-propagate the programming necessary to achieve it. Cassandra and I discussed the possibility of such a machine often, but in theory only, never in practice. The difficulties in parsing speech alone are enormous, but to then implement such instructions as effective, nonbugged code, it becomes an astronomical undertaking."

"But she's done it?" Steinberg said. "That's Arthur?"

"So it would seem."

"Arthur is a limited AI," Velez said. "As I explained, he has no sense of self."

"But he can implement plain language direction, and that's why Cass is using him for AirFlow 2." They'd reached the elevator, and Carrington jabbed the call button with his thumb, then turned to face Velez. "The idea is that he can create his own programming to compensate for any variables in traffic, be they increases in volume, changes in direction, even alterations due to environmental factors. Tied into the global network, able to monitor every single null-g vehicle fitted with a dataDyne transponder—and that's almost all of them—Arthur would know, for instance, if an ambulance had been dispatched to an address in midtown Manhattan and could thus reroute corresponding traffic to allow for the fastest travel time."

"Yes," Velez said. "That's my understanding."

The elevator arrived, and Carrington lumbered inside, Steinberg and Velez following.

"Suppose Arthur decided, for whatever reason, that he didn't want to do that, Miss Velez," Carrington said. "What then?"

"The traffic pattern would remain the same."

"No, you're thinking about him as a machine, not as a *thinking* machine. No sense of self, no sense of conscience. Arthur doesn't wish to execute the command, what does he do?"

"He ignores it."

"Correct." Carrington looked to Steinberg. "Now consider the following. You're a group of children who are, for all intents and purposes, a cult. Your leader is Zhang Li. He gives you everything you could desire, everything you need. He is your alpha and your omega. And all he asks in return is that you program for him, you hack for him. Any machine anywhere, if he wants it, your job is to get it for him."

"I get anything I want?" Steinberg said.

"I'm Zhang Li," Carrington said, as the elevator came to a stop. "I can give it to you, so, yes, anything."

"I do whatever you ask," Steinberg said.

Velez, hustling alongside, shook her head. "I don't understand. What does any of this have to do with Master Li?"

Carrington ignored her, still speaking to Steinberg. "You do whatever I ask. Then I die. What happens to you?"

"Zhang Li is dead?" Velez asked. "You know this?"

"He's been dead for several months," Carrington said. "He's your reason for living, and he's gone. You're a cult of spoiled children, and your father is dead. What do you do?"

Steinberg shook his head.

"You do what spoiled children do when they don't get their way," Carrington said. "You break things."

"You mean Arthur."

"You're not thinking big enough, Jon, that's always been your problem. We're talking about Zhang Li, the founder of dataDyne."

"All right, you break dataDyne."

Carrington shook his head, annoyed. His cheeks, Steinberg had noted, had turned pink, and he was wheezing slightly from the exertion of the pace he'd set. They were crossing the grounds to the Main Building, now, and Steinberg assumed they were heading to the Ops Center.

"You break the world," Carrington said. "Because the world belonged to Zhang Li, or so he liked to believe."

"If they were his children, his cult, they would be loyal to dataDyne," Velez said, adamantly.

"Not everyone shares your sense of duty, Miss Velez. We're talking about children. They didn't know from dataDyne, they knew from Zhang Li, and they knew dataDyne was *his*. But it's not anymore, not as far as they're concerned. It's Cassandra's now, and they can't stand the thought of that. If Zhang Li can't have the world, no one can have it."

"I still don't see how—" Steinberg started to say.

"Arthur isn't an AI, Jon, he's a weapon of mass destruction." Carrington stopped, out of breath. "AirFlow.Net is ubiquitous, the world's largest computer network. But Arthur is about to be plugged into that network. He can control every vehicle with a dataDyne transponder. Imagine it. Imagine them crashing all at once."

Steinberg could, or at least thought he could, his mind suddenly filled with visions of null-g vehicle after null-g vehicle abruptly plummeting from the sky, crashing one after another into the ground. How many null-g vehicles were there? Millions of them, there had to be, maybe hundreds of millions of them—they were as omnipresent as the automobiles they'd replaced once were.

"Now," Carrington said, softly. "Imagine what they crash *into*, Jon. The White House. The Kremlin. Nuclear power plants. Oil refineries. Schools. Hospitals. Army bases. Missile silos. High-rises. Bridges. Homes."

"Jesus Christ," Steinberg said.

"Now imagine them doing it all at once," Carrington whispered. "All around the globe, in every nation."

"It's insanity," Velez said. "It's beyond insanity, it's nihilism."

"That is exactly what it is," Carrington agreed. "The end of all things. If Zhang Li can't have it, no one can."

||||||||||||||||||

They'd crossed the water and Steinberg felt the dropship descending slightly. He broke out of his harness, pulled himself to his feet, and moved to the open troop door on the port side. Looking down, he could see the city of Rouen rushing past beneath their feet. He stepped back, hating the height, then keyed the headset again.

"Calvin?"

"*Go ahead, Jon.*"

"Velez has a landing site for us, you want to come in from the north."

"Give it to me."

"Some park on the Allée de la Comtesse de something or other."

"The Comtesse de Ségur, yeah, I know the one."

"You do?"

"Emily was telling me about it."

"Ah."

"GPS says we'll be there in eight minutes."

Steinberg checked his watch. It was already seventeen past eleven in the morning. According to Velez, Arthur would be switched on at noon, or damn near close to it, at least.

"Faster would be good," he told Rogers, and then he went back to his seat on the bench and began affixing the suppressor to the end of his Fairchild, ordering the rest of his troopers to do the same.

There wasn't a doubt in his mind that they'd be needing them before the hour was up.

Home of Former dataDyne CEO
Zhang Li (Deceased)
38km SW Li Xian, Sichuan Province
People's Republic of China
January 30th, 2021

Jo found herself in trouble immediately.

The Arena had barely finished resolving before Chun Fan charged at her, sprinting across the smooth stone floor of the Arena with a shriek of rage, then leaping into the air with what, to Jo, was the obvious intention of putting the heel of her right shoe into the center of Joanna's throat. Jo snapped her hands up into a rising cross-block, once again appalled by the sight of Mai Hem's hot-pink lacquered fingernails as her own, and had just enough time to realize that Fan had feinted.

Instead of extending her right leg for the kick, the insane young woman was folding it back, beneath herself, and then her left shot out as if fired from a cannon. Jo tried to twist out of the blow, felt the heel of one of Mai Hem's useless boots snapping beneath her feet, and then felt ribs that had up until that point been behaving themselves explode in a riot of pain. The world vanished, as if some bug in the program made the

Arena, and Joanna, both cease to exist for a moment. Then she was back, and she knew she was lying on her back, because her view of Fan was from below the woman.

"You're already beaten," Fan hissed at her, still speaking Mandarin. Then, to make her point, she stomped on the bullet wound in Jo's abdomen.

Jo thought that her pain sounded just like Mai Hem's had when she had killed her for the second time.

Her vision swam, blurred, and what breath she was holding fled. She tried to get up, to use her legs, and the muscles in her belly and the pain in her ribs made it clear that doing so was going to be impossible, and then she was being kicked again, and she was certain that her ribs would never heal. Choking for lack of air, she rolled toward the source of the last kick, nearly flailing, and somehow caught Fan's leg before she could fire it off again. Jo kept rolling into it, trapping the leg and hoping against hope that Fan would be too stubborn to move, that she would let Jo break the joint.

Fan fell backward instead, dropping smoothly to the floor and pulling the leg free with the momentum. Jo was on her belly now and getting her hands beneath her, tracking the crazy young woman. Fan hadn't stopped, had gone from the fall into a backflip, and before Jo was even to her knees, the girl had planted herself back on her feet. Jo saw the shine of blood on Fan's jumpsuit, took meager comfort in the fact that, apparently, all the young woman's jumping around had torn open the wound in her belly, as well. Jo tried to brace for the next attack, knowing that if it was another kick to the ribs, the fight would be all but over.

Yet Fan didn't attack, instead bouncing lightly back on the balls of her feet, putting more distance between them.

"I could always beat you, Mai-Mai," Fan said. "Hand-to-hand, guns or knives, I've always owned you."

Jo coughed, saw cherry-red blood spattering lightly onto

the stone floor. Mai Hem's blood, her blood, it was the same. The battering she'd already taken had moved her off the center of the arena, toward the line of pillars that supported the platforms ringing the edge of the space. She put a hand out for support, got painfully to her feet, then almost fell again when she put her weight down on the broken heel of her right boot.

Fan was continuing to back away, putting the breadth of the Arena between them. From somewhere beyond the space came the sound of wind chimes, and suddenly small pockets of rippling air began to coalesce all about them.

The weapons were arriving. From the corner of Jo's eye, she saw a Falcon 2 pistol shimmer into existence, perhaps twenty feet from where she stood, near the base of another pillar. Above, on the platform, a ballistic vest came into existence, toppling as it fell over. Behind her, she heard the clatter of more metal, something heavier landing on the stone, a submachine gun or assault rifle. There was the distinctive sound of a blade ringing out, followed immediately by another one, as two combat knives dropped out of nothing and into their shared reality.

Fan smiled at her, and then, as quickly as she had before, went for the steps nearest where she was standing, racing up to the second level, opposite.

With effort, Jo pulled herself around the pillar, into the shadow cast by the platform above her. She waited half a second, then lurched forward, moving further into the darkness, until she reached the boundary wall. She cut to her right, turning, trying to keep the pillars between herself and the opposite platform, knowing that her ridiculous clothing was making her all the easier to spot, despite the shadows. She didn't see Fan, but she didn't need to; she knew what the other woman was doing, knew that the girl was taking her time to choose her weapon.

Jo used the wall at her back as support, reached down,

and pulled off her boots, first the left, then the right. The pain in her chest and belly was enough to make her eyes tear, and it took two tries to remove them both. She steadied herself, trying to keep her breathing shallow and rapid, then reached again, this time for the hem of her absurd half-and-half dress. It was made of silk, swathes of it opaque pink, other patches entirely translucent, designed to be almost, but not quite, entirely revealing. Hissing against the pain, she tore the edge of the dress, freeing her legs.

"Mai-Mai! Come out and play!"

Jo raised her head, trying to find the voice, found that she couldn't. It was the nature of the Arena, the way it bent sound, made it unreliable with echoes and reverberation. Nothing in the Arena was there to make the battle easy, that was part of its design. The open space at its center was a killing floor, there for hand-to-hand or a straight-up shoot out. The platforms existed to provide both cover and perches to shoot from. The whole location was designed for the contest, to make it brutal and to let the audience see as much of it as possible.

She stifled another cough, quietly spat out a second mouthful of blood, then looked around for a weapon. She caught the faint shine of metal to her right, perhaps twelve feet away, and started toward it, feeling the texture of the stone floor through her silk-stockinged feet.

A gun, Jo thought. *Just give me a gun.*

Then she saw what it was, and the despair she felt threatened to eclipse the pain. Painfully, Jo went to one knee and picked up the weapon. It was a wrist crossbow, the Javelin model, loaded with a five-quarrel magazine.

This is so *not fair,* she thought as she fastened it into place on her sleeve.

Somewhere in the Arena, she heard the heavy clack of a bolt being run back on a weapon. Too loud to be a Fairchild, maybe from an assault rifle, the FAC-16 or the Kangxi.

There was movement out of the corner of her eye, and Jo spun, heedless of what it did to her wounded belly, saw Fan landing lightly on the floor of the Arena, beyond the shelter of the platform. She was carrying two weapons, a CMP and the FAC-16, and as she righted herself, she dropped the CMP, preparing to bring the FAC up into a firing position with both her hands. She'd gone with the weapon Jo would have chosen herself, Jo realized.

Jo dropped left, firing twice from the Javelin, and just as she loosed the second quarrel, she realized she'd been had. Each of her shots passed harmlessly through the image of Fan, leaving the hologram unaffected.

Stupid! Stupid stupid stupid failure!

She should have seen that coming, she should have accounted for that. It was the same trick she'd used in Veracruz, it was the same thing her father had always warned her about, to take nothing for granted. And she'd fallen for it, and she had failed him. She had shamed him, she had brought dishonor on his house.

From her left, Fan opened up with the FAC, the rifle barking again and again, and Jo went into a shoulder roll, came out of it between two of the pillars. Bullets spat off the stone, sparking and whining. Without breaking stride, she ran forward with all the speed she could muster, out into the open center of the Arena. From somewhere behind her, she heard Fan shouting in glee.

"Run! Run away from me, you miserable cow!"

The Falcon 2 that she'd seen earlier was still on the ground, resting enticingly on the stone, and she knew it would hurt, but she knew she had to have that gun. The FAC opened up again, a second torrent of rounds chasing after her, and Fan was tracking her with the spray, and she prayed that the girl was aiming high. Jo shifted her balance to her heels, let her hips fall behind her legs, and the silk stockings covering her feet did what she knew they would, slipping on the stone even as they tore. She let herself fall into the slide, feeling the friction burn of the smooth stone along her bare thigh, hearing the rounds cutting the air over her head as she went down.

Then Jo had the Falcon in her hand, and she turned onto her belly even as she continued to slide, shouting out with the pain, trying to use it, and she saw Fan. The woman had taken a position beside one of the pillars, near where Jo had been hiding, using the stonework as a support. Jo fired twice, then twice more, and two of the shots hit the girl square in the sternum, and she staggered back but didn't drop, and Jo realized that Fan had taken the body armor, as well.

Her slide ended with her beneath the opposite platform from where she'd started, and instead of trying to regain her feet, she simply rolled behind the nearest pillar. Once she had her back to it, she used her legs to push herself upright. She was out of breath, and when she stopped moving, the pain hit her like a freight train.

She was going to lose, Jo realized. She was going to lose this fight. She was wounded, and Fan was faster, and, worse, Jo was beginning to realize that Fan knew all of her moves. Fan had been waiting for her to make a break for it, Fan had known that as soon as Jo had realized she'd been taken in by the hologram, she would leave her cover to find a new one.

"*Joanna?*" Portia de Carcareas said. "*Joanna, can you hear me?*"

She was so lost in her pain and her fear that she was certain it was her imagination.

"*Joanna, is that you? Are you fighting Chun Fan?*"

Jo edged to the side of the pillar, risked glancing around. She couldn't see Fan, guessed that, like herself, the other woman had retreated to the shadows beneath the companion platform.

"Portia?"

"*Is that you, Joanna? The one who looks like Mai Hem?*"

"They did something to me, they . . . *changed* me, Portia—"

"*You've got to calm down.*"

"They changed me, I can't . . . I'm hurt . . . I'm going to lose, Portia, I don't know what to—where were you?"

"*You're not going to lose, calm down. We lost your signal, the Continuity must have been jamming it. We got it back when they began broadcasting the battle.*"

From across the Arena, Jo heard a soft, electronic beep, and her blood went cold. She knew the sound, knew that Fan had swapped out her FAC for a new weapon, for the Plasma Rifle—an experimental weapon that could fire pulses of supercharged particles that acted like directed microwaves, melting flesh and sparking off metal. Worse, it possessed an effective camouflage system, a dataDyne-proprietary light-bending apparatus that rendered the user invisible, for as long as the battery would last.

Again, it was the choice Jo herself would have made, if she'd had the opportunity, if she'd been able to make the choice at all.

"*Jo,*" Portia de Carcareas said in her head. "*Listen to me. You're fighting* wrong, *you're not—*"

"Shhhh," Jo murmured. "She's coming. She's cloaked."

Carcareas went silent for a second, then said, "*Look to the right.*"

"You can see her?"

"*It's not much of a show if we can't see both the combatants, Joanna,*" Carcareas said. "*She's in a halo in the broadcast, and you look like hell, by the way. Here she comes.*"

Jo listened, trying to hear anything but the noise of her own ragged, broken breathing.

"*Now!*"

She pivoted from the pillar, turning to her right, the Falcon out and firing blindly. There was a shimmer from the edge of the platform, and then Fan appeared. She returned fire, leaping to her left, rolling onto the stairs. Jo ducked back to cover, tossing away the emptied pistol. She could hear Fan cursing as she ran past, overhead.

"There's a SuperDragon to your left, behind the second to last pillar on your side. You can't see it, it landed on its butt."

Jo moved, searching for the weapon, and found it where Carcareas had said it would be. The woman kept talking.

"Firepower won't help you, Joanna. She's going to beat you in a straight one-on-one, that's already clear."

"She knows all my moves." Jo checked the SuperDragon, saw that the clip was fully loaded but that the grenade launcher was empty. "I try another duck-and-cover, she'll put a bullet in my head."

"That's because she's fighting Joanna Dark. But you're not Joanna Dark."

"I am, I'm—"

"You're Mai Hem, Jo. Use that! Use—"

The transmission cut out with a screech of static that made Jo stagger, and she nearly lost her grip on the assault rifle. She was certain that her ears were now bleeding along with most of the rest of her.

From above, her voice echoing, Fan said, "No no no *no*, Jo-Jo! That's *cheating*, and there's *no* cheating this time! Not this time, no cheating! No disconnects!"

Joanna righted herself again, trying to banish the new pain that had seemed to gleefully join the rest. The sound of Fan switching out weapons echoed once more across the stone, the woman apparently swapping something heavy for something light. Jo checked the SuperDragon again, thinking that, as weapons went, she absolutely hated the assault rifle—bulky, ugly, inelegant. Given the opportunity, she would have cheerfully traded it for something accurate, something precise. Those were her weapons, that was the way she worked.

That was the way Joanna Dark worked.

Oh damn, she thought, and it made sense, then, such perfect sense. Carcareas had been right: Fan knew exactly how to fight Joanna Dark. Fan knew how to fight the way Jo fought—despite the woman's abundant madness, Fan fought like Jo. She fought smart.

But that had never been Mai Hem's thing. That had never been what had made Mai Hem the darling of DeathMatch. Mai Hem hadn't been smart, hadn't ever tried to be. She had been a show, she had been *the* show. People hadn't tuned into the public DeathMatch to watch the fights. They hadn't tuned into the exclusive pay-per-view blood tournaments. They had tuned in to watch Mai Hem—sexy, gaudy, over-the-top Mai Hem, who never used a Falcon if there was a MagSec handy, who never went with a sniper's rifle if she could find a rocket launcher. On more than one occasion, Jo had thought the woman had survived not because of skill or tactics but simply because she was so brazen and had exhibited such an utterly and completely insane disregard for her own safety.

The real question was, which of them was more crazy? Chun Fan or Mai Hem?

I am not Joanna Dark, Jo thought. *I am Mai Hem.*

Then she tucked the stock of the SuperDragon against her hip and crushed its trigger beneath her finger. The weapon came to life, erupting with a torrent of lead, and Jo swept the barrel back and forth, firing at nothing at all and at everything at once, and she heard Mai Hem's laugh, and, still firing, she began walking forward, out from the cover of the platform. The assault rifle went dry on her, and she tossed it aside, still walking forward, taking her time, and she saw the bead from a laser sight blur over the stone and knew that Fan had put the sights on her head. She half expected it to end right then, with a bullet through her brain, but it didn't come.

At the center of the Arena, Jo turned, raising her arms despite the pain that shot through her chest as she did so. Mai Hem's dress was sleeveless, all the better to show off her muscles, and Jo stretched the way she'd seen Mai Hem herself do so many times before, the way she'd done to give the audience at home an eyeful.

Fan, holding a Maas P9P in both hands, the beam from its laser sight bobbing slightly across Jo's vision, stared at her.

"Hacker girl," Jo said. "No wonder Father never let you play."

Fan's expression had been one of confusion, even astonishment, but now it melted into anger. "Shut up!"

Jo laughed, Mai Hem's distinctive, horrible laugh that seemed to be coming to her with more and more ease. "Make me."

Fan fired, missing, and Jo felt the round pass so close it burned along her scalp. It took everything she had not to flinch. She laughed again.

Fan jumped lightly down from the platform, readjusting her sights. With an elaborate sigh, Jo turned away, presenting her back as a target. It was madness to do it, utter madness, and again she expected the punch of the bullets, the sensation of her insides being crushed open by ballistic bricks. There was a MagSec resting on one of the steps nearby, and she began walking toward it as if she had all the time in the world.

"Turn around!" Fan shouted at her. "Turn around and look at me!"

Without stopping, Jo raised her left hand and gave her the middle finger.

Fan fired again, and this time the round went wider than before, smacking into the stone staircase and sending tiny shards flying through the air. The shot hit within inches of where the MagSec lay, and Jo reached out and took the pistol as if she hadn't noticed or, better, as if she didn't care. Still with her back to Fan, she made an elaborate show of examining the gun, picking it up in both hands and then holding it high, squinting along the barrel.

"Turn around! Turn!"

With another sigh, even more bored and heavy than the last, Jo turned around to look at Fan, letting the MagSec in her hand dangle beside her right thigh. The girl had followed her across the Arena, closing the distance between them to perhaps ten feet at the most. She still held the P9P in her hands, and now the targeting beam was swaying wildly, jumping back and forth, as if every time it found Joanna, some invisible force was making it slide away.

"You're not her!" Fan said. "She's dead! You're not her!"

Jo licked her lips slowly, as if wetting them for a kiss, and started walking forward.

"You're not her!" Fan screamed, and she fired three times in succession, and one of the rounds hit Jo, taking a bite out of her left shoulder.

Jo laughed, because that was exactly what Mai Hem would have done.

Then she was directly in front of Fan, and with an easy swipe, she brought the heavy barrel of the MagSec up, crossing her front, hitting Fan's hands and knocking the P9P out of the way. Before the girl could bring the gun back into line, Jo had the MagSec's barrel hovering in front of her face.

"You're not her." Fan's eyes shone with wild confusion and terror. "You're not her, you're Jo-Jo."

"I'm not her, no," Jo said. "But I sure as hell look like her, don't I?"

And then Jo did what Mai Hem would have done.

She pulled the trigger.

DataFlow Corporate Headquarters
Presentation Hall A
17 Rue de la Baume
Paris, France
January 30th, 2021

The hall, at capacity, could seat 7,675 people. With the addition of standing room, perhaps another two hundred could
be added to that number, but doing so risked blocking the
aisles and further risked bringing the ire of the fire marshal
down on the event. While the French government as a whole,
and the Parisian government specifically, had no desire to
antagonize or even annoy dataDyne, there was always the
chance that some overzealous public employee might take it
upon himself to cause trouble.

So the aisles in Hall A were being kept clear. The seats,
however, were all filled.

Cassandra DeVries peeked out at the audience from behind
the curtains at stage left and marveled at the number. It wasn't,
perhaps, that many people at all, not in the grand scheme of
things. She knew, for instance, that almost three times that
number were gathered outside at that very moment, crammed

into the media tents, watching the video relay from inside the hall. That was just outside, here in Paris. Around the world, there were similar media tents, similar halls and ballrooms, all of them filled with people, some of them media, some of them politicians, some of them simply lucky enough or important enough to have earned an invitation to the unveiling.

To say she had stage fright was putting it mildly. As far as Cassandra was concerned, she had stage terror.

"Would you like some water, ma'am?" Shephard asked. "Or some tea? It's good for your voice, I'm told."

Cassandra looked at the young woman with some alarm. "Is there something wrong with my voice?"

"No, Madame Director, not at all," Shephard said quickly. "You sound fine, I just wanted to know if there was anything I could get for you."

"I sound fine?"

"You sound like you always do, Madame Director. Honestly."

"I think I'm fine."

"It's okay to be nervous, ma'am. I certainly would be." Shephard gave her a reassuring smile. "If there's anything I can do?"

"Dr. Ventura hasn't arrived?"

"Not that I know of, no ma'am."

Cassandra turned, locating Colonel Shaw who was standing some fifteen feet away, near one of the A/V consoles along the backstage wall. He had his radio to his ear—there hadn't been time to fit him with a standard dataDyne subcutaneous—and he caught her glancing his way and acknowledged the look with a nod, then went back to his conversation.

He looks stressed, too, Cassandra thought. *The only one of us who doesn't is Shephard. At least my instincts about her were correct.*

Shaw lowered the radio, approaching. "Ma'am?"

"You sent someone to gather Dr. Ventura?"

"He should be here in three minutes, ma'am," Shaw said. "They're just landing now."

"Is something wrong?"

The colonel frowned, his eyes going toward the stage before coming back to hers. "No, ma'am, nothing for you to worry about. We're having some . . . communications problems with some of the exterior guard posts, that's all."

"They're warning house lights," Shephard interrupted. "The multimedia presentation is going to start."

Cassandra moved from where she had been speaking to Shaw, coming alongside Shephard once more, looking out at the stage. The rumble of noise from the house began to subside, the thousands of muted conversations all ending together. Behind her, Cassandra heard one of the access doors open, turned in time to see Edward Ventura entering, hastily smoothing his necktie. She held out a hand, beckoning him closer as Shaw moved to close the door behind him.

"Just in time, Edward," she whispered in his ear.

"Yes, ma'am. Sorry, I overslept."

Cassandra turned to face him, straightening the knot of his necktie. "It's all right, you're here now."

She thought the man was actually blushing.

From the speakers hidden behind the plasma screen and throughout the hall, the first notes of the dataDyne corporate anthem rang out. Cassandra saw Shephard smiling and wished that she'd had the presence of mind to ask her new director of media relations to forgo the use of the tune, though she understood why Shephard had made the decision to use it. The music was rousing—even, she supposed, inspiring—but she found the lyrics sentimental and saccharine, with its constant chorus of "Your life, our hands."

Cassandra leaned slightly to speak in Ventura's ear. "Edward, what does 'set minus one' mean?"

The young man glanced from where he'd been watching the video display that accompanied the corporate anthem on the plasma screen, giving her a puzzled look. "I'm sorry?"

"Set minus one," Cassandra whispered. "Arthur was listing it as an error when I spoke to him in the lab."

"His audio pickups were on? I thought I'd switched him off."

"Well, apparently you forgot. What does it mean? I couldn't find a reference to it, though admittedly I didn't have long to look."

Ventura frowned, thinking. "I'd think it's referring to one of the modules, a 'set.' Though any module with a negative integer would be unviable in the coding sequence—he would simply ignore it."

"I see," Cassandra said, and she forced herself to smile, and then to add, "Probably nothing, then. Don't worry about it."

Ventura nodded, turning his attention back to the stage. The anthem had ended, the prerecorded video segment beginning. On the screen, images of the various dataDyne subsidiaries and their products began flashing by while a paternal and reasonably witty narrator launched into a self-congratulatory monologue about the corporation and its remarkable success. In every nation, in every home, the narrator told the audience proudly, dataDyne was there, making life better.

Cassandra glanced back to Shaw, saw that the man was watching her from the post he'd taken at the door, once again speaking on his radio. With the lights now down, she had difficulty reading his expression, but it was becoming impossible to miss the tension in his posture.

Her mind went back to what Ventura had said, about the error being a reference to a module. A nonsequential module, she realized, one that would have to be triggered if it existed outside of the numerical sequence. Why had Arthur referenced it at all? It didn't make sense, it should never have come up.

She wondered if it was possible, just possible, that Arthur had been trying to tell her something.

Something . . . Cassandra thought. *Something is definitely wrong here.*

Not for the first time, she wished it was Anita Velez standing at the door, and not Leland Shaw.

The music changed, switching to a different cue, and now the images flashing by on the plasma screen were of vehicles. Automobiles first, and then, of course, *Carrington One,* followed quickly by a montage of the null-g transports that had followed in its wake. Royce-Chamberlain/Bowman Motors got the most attention, as was appropriate as a dataDyne subsidiary. The narrator was speaking in grand terms about how the world had shrunk, how the dream of flight was now beyond commonplace. The death of the traffic jam, the narrator exclaimed, the end of air pollution, but not the end of accidents.

The DataFlow logo appeared on the screen, the AirFlow.Net branding seal beneath it.

"DataDyne fixed that problem, too," the narrator was saying. "With the help of one of its most brilliant minds, Dr. Cassandra DeVries."

Suddenly, it was her face on the screen, a shot that Cassandra had never seen before, and she was certain it was a composite, something worked up in a lab somewhere, and not simply a photograph that she could not recall having posed for. She looked, she had to admit, stunning, so good that she could hardly recognize herself. Her eyes seemed to glow with intelligence, her smile to promise friendship and good hope to any who might ask for it. Her skin was flawless.

She wasn't certain if it was the photograph or the reaction from the hall that surprised her more, honestly, because the applause that accompanied the image was beyond thunderous. People were actually cheering, and a few were whistling while others shouted her name.

"Most eligible bachelorette in the world," Shephard whispered in her ear, seeing Cassandra's expression. "You shouldn't be surprised."

The narration was ending, music beginning to swell and the stage lights beginning to rise. Shephard was saying something else, smiling encouragement.

"Ladies and gentlemen," the narrator said. "Please welcome to the stage the chief executive officer and director of all dataDyne and its subsidiaries, Dr. Cassandra DeVries."

Then Shephard was pushing her gently forward, and Cassandra found herself crossing the stage to a standing ovation, applause so thick and loud it seemed to buffet her. From the corner of her eye, she saw a Caucasian man in a three-piece suit rush for the stage, a bouquet in his hand, and then be intercepted by two of Shaw's uniformed Hawks before he could reach her. Someone shouted that they loved her. Someone else asked if she would marry him.

She took the podium, noting the placement of the display stand beside it, its top covered with a sheet of black fabric. The lights that had so tormented her that last time she'd stood in Hall A were back, shining into her eyes. On the podium, beside the clock, the remarks that Shephard had prepared for her scrolled into position, projected at eye-level, to keep her from having to look down.

The applause continued, and after a moment, Cassandra understood that she would have to put a stop to it, rather than wait for it to run its course. She switched the display off on the podium, catching Shephard's surprised reaction from the corner of her eye, then smiled out at the audience and gestured for silence.

"Ladies and gentlemen," Cassandra DeVries said. "Allow me to introduce you to Arthur."

And with that, she pulled back the sheet and showed the world its first artificial intelligence.

DataFlow Corporate Headquarters
Presentation Hall A
17 Rue de la Baume
Paris, France
January 30th, 2021

Surprise makes all the difference in the world, Jonathan Steinberg thought. *Surprise, and betrayal.*

Then he slid his knife hard and fast into the side of the neck of the man who was standing post inside the south stairwell of Presentation Hall A, using his other hand to pull the Hawk's head back and toward him. Steinberg yanked the blade free, then punched with it a second time, hearing the wet gurgle of escaping air as blood and breath both fled the man's body in ways they were never meant to leave.

Silently, he lowered the man to the ground, then stepped back and motioned Velez and three of her CORPSEC guards forward. Velez advanced without bothering to look down, stepping over the corpse, but two of the guards couldn't manage the same, each of them looking down, and he saw the confusion and the fear in their eyes. As far as they knew, this was dataDyne versus dataDyne, and as much as they may have trusted Velez, Steinberg was certain that his presence wasn't helping matters.

Velez came back from where she'd been checking the stairwell, spoke quickly and quietly to him.

"It's eleven-fifty six," she said. "We cannot take or clear the hall in the time we have left, and Dr. DeVries is already onstage. I suggest you take your element this way, up and through the access along the hall. It will bring you in through the skies over stage left. I will take my element along the parallel track, descending to stage right. If you see Shaw, do not hesitate to kill him."

"What about your boss?"

"Do not concern yourself with Dr. DeVries," Velez said, and Steinberg couldn't mistake the warning in her voice. "If I see you take any action toward her, I will view it as hostile, is that understood?"

"She can't be allowed—"

"She will not be. Go, we don't have much time."

Steinberg wiped the knife clean, slid it back into its sheath at the small of his back, then moved the Fairchild from where it was hanging beneath his coat to his hands. He turned, extended his left hand, communicating orders to the Institute Troopers still waiting in cover inside the lobby. They'd already moved the four Hawks they'd had to down just to get that far, and wherever the bodies had been hidden, Steinberg hoped it would take more than four minutes before they were discovered.

With the Troopers at his heels, Steinberg began racing up the stairs, taking them two and three at a time. There was no way to do it quietly, and he only hoped that Shaw hadn't posted any guards at the top of the stairwell. With the men and women following him, he imagined they sounded like a stampede of cavalry.

Let's hope we arrive like them, too, he thought, bitterly.

The stairs ended at a landing with a closed access door marked "Authorized Personnel Only." Steinberg swapped the Fairchild for his P9P, double-checked the silencer, and then, confirming he still had his people at his back, shoved the door open.

Velez had been correct, the door did grant access to skies above the house, the scaffolding and criss-crossed beams designed to hold the stage lights. He also discovered that Shaw wasn't an idiot and that there was a Hawk positioned there, a rifle in his lap and a radio in his hand. The man turned, reacting, and before he could say or do anything more, Steinberg had fired twice, scoring two head shots at close range.

The Hawk dropped his radio, toppling backward onto the scaffolding where he'd been seated. Then he began to list, and Steinberg swore, dropping his pistol and diving forward, through the narrow door. He missed the man with his first grab, just as he started to roll free, and desperately grabbed at him again, managing to catch hold of the Hawk's pant leg at the last moment.

Which maybe wasn't such a good idea, because the Hawk had turned to true deadweight, perhaps 210 pounds of it, and gravity wanted the body as much as Steinberg did. He felt himself sliding forward suddenly as the rest of the man's body fell free of the scaffolding, and then Steinberg was jerked through the door after him. For a horrible moment he could see the scene as if in some twisted black comedy, the dead Hawk about to plummet from the skies to the house below, splattering blood and brain on the gathered media, and Steinberg following immediately in the dead man's wake, adding insult to injury.

His body stopped short, the arrest jarring, and Steinberg nearly lost his grip on the Hawk even as he felt hands on his own boots and legs, trying to pull him back to safety. He hissed with the exertion, desperate not to lose his hold on the dead man, feeling the sweat in his hands mixing with the ballistic fabric of the Hawk's trousers. Then he was being pulled back, and new hands reached past him, taking hold of the Hawk, and together he and the dead man tumbled back to the safety of the landing.

Dorsey helped him to his feet, saying, "Nice save, sir."

"Yeah, you too," he said, picking up his discarded pistol. "You guys stay here, make sure nobody comes up behind me."

"Yes, sir."

Steinberg started out onto the skies, working his way precariously over the packed house to the stage. DeVries's voice seemed to come from all around him, almost deafening this close to the speakers. On the stage, he could see the woman, lit by the house lights, standing at the podium, and beside her, on a stand, a small cube that seemed to glow with internal light, and resting beside it what looked to him like a large button or switch of some kind.

"And how many vehicles are there with dataDyne transponders, Arthur?" she was asking.

The voice that responded was androgynous, almost empty of inflection. "At this moment, there are seven hundred seventy-three million, eight hundred sixty-nine thousand, nine hundred seventeen null-g vehicles equipped with dataDyne AirFlow.Net transponders."

Beneath him, in their seats, Steinberg heard the audience gasp in appreciation. Whether that was of Arthur's ability to answer or the sheer number of vehicles, he didn't know, and he didn't much care. All he could think about was that seven hundred seventy-three million of anything crashing all at once was almost beyond his capacity to imagine. He thought about that, and he thought about the fact that if he fell off of this stupid, tiny, thin little rail he was trying to walk along without making noise, it would be a very stupid and very painful way to die.

But at least it'd be over quick, he thought.

"That's an extraordinary amount of vehicles," DeVries was saying. "DataDyne must make quite a good product if we've sold that many of them, wouldn't you agree?"

"DataDyne products," Arthur said, "are the best in the world."

Laughter rose up from below, and on the massive screen at the back of the stage, Steinberg could see the close-up of DeVries smiling, her eyes shining in mirth. He glanced to his left, could just make out Velez making her way along the skies, parallel to him.

"So, Arthur," DeVries said. "Can you tell us, please, your function? Your purpose?"

"To monitor and maintain the safe, efficient, and speedy flow of all null-g traffic throughout the world."

"When will you do this?"

"From activation until deactivation."

"You mean you'll never rest?"

"Parsing error."

On the stage, DeVries looked from the cube she had been speaking to out at the audience. "Arthur is very literal, you see. He doesn't need to rest, so the question has no meaning to him."

There were murmurs of understanding, even approval.

"I'll ask it a different way," DeVries said. "Arthur, will you ever require downtime for maintenance?"

"No."

"Why not?"

"This is a self-diagnostic, closed system. Maintenance routines are executed once per every one million computational processes."

Steinberg had reached the stage, crossing over the lip and now looking directly down on the cluster of figures standing out of sight of the audience. He could make out three of them, possibly a man and a woman standing together, and maybe another man, but it was difficult to tell from the angle and the lighting.

"How frequently does that diagnostic run in real time, Arthur?"

"At peak capacity, diagnostics run once every point eight-seven-eighth of a second."

There was another gasp from the audience.

"What happens if you discover an error?"

"I repair the error."

A smattering of applause, and now Steinberg had reached the ladder that ran from the skies down to the back of the stage. He checked over his shoulder, saw that Velez was perhaps ten seconds behind him. Looking down, he tried again to identify the figures he was seeing, thinking that one of them had to be Shaw. Dorsey was right behind him, waiting.

"Now, ladies and gentlemen," DeVries was saying. "Allow me to introduce the man who can, by all rights, call himself Arthur's father. Please join me in welcoming Dr. Edward Ventura, DataFlow's head of artificial intelligence and very soon to become the new director of DataFlow itself."

A new round of applause, and Steinberg watched as the man standing closer to the stage, the one who had been standing beside the woman, hesitantly ventured out from behind the curtain. DeVries had turned to welcome him, beckoning him forward.

Shaw, Steinberg thought as he watched the remaining man, and he swung himself out onto the ladder. Then, gripping it by the rails rather than by the rungs, he began a rapid slide down to the rear of the stage, trying to keep his eyes on the man he was certain was Leland Shaw as he descended. Shaw was moving, suddenly, approaching the woman still standing out of sight, watching the events on the stage. Steinberg could hear DeVries speaking again, and then a man's voice, presumably Ventura's. There was laughter from the audience.

Steinberg hit the ground hard, his hands aching with the friction burn of his descent. Shaw was speaking to the woman still, a radio in his hand, and that was when Steinberg realized it was all about to go wrong. The radio was the tell: Shaw had to know he was down men, that there were hostiles inside his perimeter. He saw the gun in the man's other hand, another P9P, and Steinberg realized it was the custom model with the titanium slide, and he had enough time to at least admire the man's choice in weaponry before Shaw shot him twice in the chest.

It wasn't the first time he'd been shot, but, as the rounds smashed into his body armor and cracked his ribs, sending him to the floor and his pistol skittering away into the darkness, Jonathan Steinberg wondered if it wasn't going to be his last.

"Something's just occurred to me," DeVries said from the stage. "Something I'm sure the more paranoid of our audience out there has already considered. What would we do if someone hacked Arthur, Edward? How would we respond to that?"

Wincing, Steinberg rolled to his left, trying to free the Fairchild from its harness beneath his coat. Shaw had grabbed the woman, pulling her in front of him as a shield with one hand, ramming the barrel of his still smoking pistol against the side of her neck, his expression bordering on panic. Steinberg fumbled the Fairchild into his hands, coming up to his knee, wishing to God that he was, for one moment and despite the miserable baggage that it would entail, Joanna Dark.

Because if he were Joanna Dark, he wouldn't be afraid to take the shot, he would have been certain that he would hit

Shaw and not the pretty young woman who was now struggling against the man's grip, eyes snapped wide open in terror. If he were Joanna Dark, Steinberg thought, he wouldn't
have been shot in the first place.

"It's not possible, Madame Director," Ventura was saying, voice full of pride. "Arthur is self-aware, even if he isn't
fully sentient. He would detect any unauthorized access of
his memory modules, any corruption or shift in his code."

Steinberg thumbed the burst selector down from full-auto
to three-round burst, tried to get to his feet while keeping the
sights on Shaw. The woman had stopped struggling. Shaw
glanced toward the stage, then back again before Steinberg
could react. Steinberg didn't like what he was reading in the
man's expression. Shaw was scared. Shaw was on the verge
of panic.

Bad, very bad, Steinberg thought. *He panics, and this becomes a bloodbath.*

"*Unauthorized* access," DeVries said. "What about *authorized* access, Edward?"

"No one with the proper authorization would do such a
thing, Madame Director."

"No, I don't suppose they would. After all, it's their lives
in our hands, isn't it?"

A ripple of laughter from the audience, but nervous, now,
as if somehow they'd sensed the sudden tension that seemed
to be coming from the stage.

"Well, I suppose we should give them what they've been
waiting for, don't you agree, Edward? Would you like to
handle the countdown or the switch?"

"Oh, I think you should throw the switch, Madame Director. After all, it's your company."

Laughter again, more of it, the moment of tension passing.

Shaw had started to move, but away from the stage, not
toward it, and Steinberg felt his own panic rising. If he broke

toward the stage to try to stop DeVries, he had no doubt that Shaw would fire on him and keep firing until the Hawk leader was sure he'd done it right. But if Steinberg didn't move, if he didn't stop DeVries, Arthur would go live.

The countdown had started, the audience joining Ventura as he called out the numbers, growing louder with each one.

"Five!"

Steinberg shifted to his right, toward the stage, and Shaw compensated, backing away, still pulling his hostage with him. He wished to hell he knew where Velez was. He wished to hell he hadn't balked, had just fired when he'd first had the opportunity.

"Four!"

Shaw had his back against the wall now, his eyes dancing between Steinberg and the stage.

"Three!"

I'm going to hell for this, Steinberg thought, and he whipped the Fairchild up, but Shaw was moving, too, and the woman was stumbling forward, suddenly free.

"Two!"

Steinberg fired, the suppressed shots sounding like the ripping of wet paper, and he saw his rounds hitting metal, the face of the access door as Shaw ducked and tumbled through it. The woman had hit the ground, was scrambling to get out of the way.

"One!"

Steinberg turned, lunging toward the edge of the curtain, to the stage, and he knew he wasn't going to make it, that he had failed. He knew the world was going to end, and in the adrenaline agony of the moment, he wondered if, wherever Jo was, she was in a null-g vehicle, if her death would be quick or lingering.

He hoped it would be quick. She deserved that much.

"Anita," DeVries said.

Steinberg skidded to a stop, the Fairchild in his hand, finally getting a view of the stage, where Ventura and DeVries were standing around the little cube. From the way she'd said it, the inflection and the tone, he fully expected to see Velez on the stage with them, being addressed by her former employer. But she wasn't there, it was only DeVries and Ventura, and DeVries was stepping back from the switch, leaving it untouched.

Then Anita Velez, bleeding from a cut on her cheek and tucking her pistol beneath her jacket, stepped out from the opposite side of the stage.

"Madame Director?"

DeVries turned to face her, and if she was surprised by the other woman's arrival, Steinberg couldn't tell.

"Please have the hall evacuated," DeVries said. "And take Dr. Ventura into custody."

"At once, Madame Director."

DeVries turned to the audience, brushing past a stunned Ventura. CORPSEC was already rushing onto the stage.

"I'm afraid we're experiencing some technical difficulties," DeVries said. "Thank you all for coming."

Then she headed off the stage, coming toward Steinberg, her expression a mask of quiet fury. He stepped back to let her pass, and he thought she might acknowledge his presence, but she didn't break stride. He watched as DeVries went to the woman Shaw had taken hostage, helping her to her feet. From the house, Steinberg could hear the murmuring of the crowd, their confusion turning to anger.

"When did you know?" Steinberg asked.

DeVries looked from the young woman to him, and her eyes flashed with fury. "Ventura's answer was the wrong one. 'No one with proper authorization would do such a thing.' That was a denial, not a statement of fact. This is dataDyne. Of *course* they would."

"Nice company you've got here, ma'am."

"Mr. Steinberg," Cassandra DeVries said. "You and any other Carrington Institute operatives you have in your company have precisely three minutes to leave dataDyne property, or I'll have you shot."

And then, wrapping an arm around the shaken young woman's shoulder, DeVries headed off, into the shadows.

"You're welcome," Steinberg said.

Calebasée Café
18 Boulevard Allegre
Fort-de-France, Martinique
March 11th, 2021

"He's staying at the Squash Hotel," Anita Velez told Joanna Dark and Jonathan Steinberg. "On the Boulevard de la Mame. Room 412."

"And right now?" Joanna asked.

Velez used her head to indicate the building behind her. "Inside. Alone. Finishing his dessert."

Jo adjusted her sunglasses, glancing past Velez at the entrance to the restaurant. A table of patrons seated out front burst into laughter at something their waiter had said. Past them, she could see through the open windows to the interior, and at the rear she thought she could make out a figure seated with his back to the wall.

"Thanks," Steinberg told Velez.

The woman considered the word, as if Steinberg had uttered something profound, then ran a hand down the front of her tan linen suit, drawing herself up to full height. It put her almost a full head taller than Jo, and when she looked down at her and then Steinberg, the expression wasn't quite one of disapproval, but it was close.

"If you do not wish to do this, I will handle the matter myself," Anita Velez said.

"We've got it," Jo told her. "Don't worry. You can tell your boss we're covered."

"This is the only favor we shall ever do for you, or Carrington." She moved her look to Steinberg. "I offer this in exchange for your aid in my time of need. But do not mistake it. We are enemies."

"Then you better leave," Steinberg told her. "Before I decide to do something about that."

Anita Velez almost smiled, then turned away and quickly disappeared in the crowd of tourists milling on the boulevard.

They watched her go, waiting until they were certain she was gone, before Steinberg asked, "How do you want to do this?"

"We'll wait until nightfall," Jo said. "We've waited this long. Another six hours won't hurt."

It had been a long road to recovery for Joanna Dark, almost six weeks, and three of them had been in the Institute's sick bay in London, tended by a very strict Dr. Cordell. In addition to the infection in her abdomen, the two bullet wounds, the three broken ribs, the one punctured lung, and the half-dozen other injuries she couldn't be bothered to list, there had been the system shock incumbent in the Chrysalis reversion. Some kind of bizarre, experimental nanotech, Cordell had said, nothing unusual from Zhang Li, who had no hesitation to launch unethical and dangerous product testing.

Then followed an exploratory surgery followed by a second procedure to actually remove the Core-Mantis OmniGlobal ThroatLink.

She almost missed the ThroatLink, missed having Carcareas in her head. But then she would think about the way CMO had used her, the way their dropships had descended on Zhang Li's mansion even as she had stumbled from the DeathMatch bed. The way the women—and they'd all been women, Jo could tell that, even behind their suits of basalt-black body armor and full face shields—had shot every last one of Zhang Li's children, his Continuity. She could remember screaming at them to stop, not having enough air to do it, and then there'd been Colonel Tachi-Amosa, and Jo had been tranquilized yet again.

When she'd woken up, she'd been alone in a hotel room in Moscow, and her body had once again been her own. She'd rolled off the bed, promptly vomited, and then managed to call the Institute in London to tell them where she was. A man from the Moscow campus, Vaklav Dugarova, had come to fetch her, had flown with her all the way back to London.

It hadn't been until almost a full week later that she'd gotten the whole story from Steinberg, what had happened in Paris, how the world had almost come to its end.

"What were they like?" he'd asked her, meaning the Continuity.

"They were kids," Jo had told him. "They were kids who had lost the only thing that ever mattered to them."

"Zhang Li."

"No." Jo had shaken her head, lying in the sick bay bed, trying to get Jonathan to understand. "Someone who loved them."

"Weird way to show it."

And Jo had nodded, and Steinberg had left, and she had

thought that maybe he was right about that. But she didn't know.

Her own father hadn't done much better, after all.

||||||||||||||||||

It took more than six hours. It was closer to ten, almost midnight when Leland Shaw unlocked the door and stepped into his hotel room, and in the interim, Joanna Dark had had plenty of time to think as she had waited for him in the dark. Mostly, she thought about her father; sometimes, though, she thought about what she was there to do, and whether or not she could actually bring herself to do it.

At her request, Grim had gone digging, scouring US Department of Defense records. Shaw had done a good job vanishing himself, but it had been incomplete, and in the end, Grimshaw had confirmed for Joanna that Leland Shaw and Jack Dark had, in fact, served together in the United States Marine Corps, both as members of Force Recon. He had even been able to confirm that Shaw had been her father's commanding officer for a short time.

But that was all that Grimshaw had been able to learn. Not what had passed between the two men. Not why Jack Dark had left the Marines. Only that Leland Shaw hadn't been lying when he'd told Joanna that her father had stood beside him in combat.

A fellow Marine, Jo thought. *Who knew my father better than I ever did.*

Shaw entered clumsily, and she could smell the rum on his breath and the sweat on his skin as he moved past without seeing her, switching on the lights and drunkenly veering in the direction of his bed. He was having trouble getting his jacket off, and she wondered how drunk he was, and whether it was enough to buy him a break.

She decided it wasn't.

He'd removed his coat and his shoes, had set his holster with its titanium-slide P9P on the dresser, when Jo detached herself from where she'd been standing, pressed against the wall, and came forward. He saw the movement coming, mostly because she wasn't trying to be particularly fast or particularly stealthy anymore, and he made a halfhearted lunge for his gun, but it was clear he lacked commitment. Jo kicked him in the side, sent him off the bed and onto the floor, and only then did she draw her own gun.

"Wondering when you'd show up," Shaw said, rubbing his side and beginning to sit up.

Jo pulled her silencer from her jacket pocket, began screwing it into place at the end of the Falcon. "Don't get up, Colonel."

Shaw blinked at her rapidly, then ran his hand across his eyes.

"Figured it'd be you or Velez. I was kind of hoping it'd be Velez."

With a final twist, Jo released the silencer, then racked the slide on her pistol. "You think she'd be easier on you?"

"She wouldn't have taken it personally."

"You're wrong," Jo said. "She would have taken it even more personally than I do. That's the problem with professionals, Colonel, we're all alike. We take our jobs very seriously."

She pointed the pistol at Shaw's head.

"God, kid . . . we can work something out."

"I don't think we can."

"I knew your dad!" The words came out quickly, in a blurt. "I served with him for years! Mogadishu, did he ever tell you about Mogadishu? Or Tokyo? Did he ever tell you about the time we took the plane in Madagascar? Or the time he got drunk in Thailand, nearly got arrested for public indecency, and I had to bail him out? Did he tell you any of those things?"

Jo readjusted her aim. "No."

"I know things, Joanna! I know things about your dad! I'll share them with you!"

"In exchange for your life?"

Shaw's nod was vigorous, his eyes almost glassy. "Yes! Anything you want to know about him, I'll tell you!"

Jo shook her head. "Do you know what they did to me, Colonel Shaw? Do you know how badly they hurt me? What they turned me into? Do you have the faintest idea?"

He looked at her blankly, either the alcohol or his fear or his ignorance conspiring to keep him from answering.

"You gave them the daughter of a brother Marine, Colonel, and you expect mercy?"

"I can tell you things about him!"

"I already know enough," Jo said, and she shot him three times, twice in the chest and once in the head. She unscrewed the silencer and dropped it back into her pocket, then slid the Falcon back into position at the small of her back. After a moment, she crouched down on one knee and began going through his pockets, and after perhaps fifteen seconds, she found what she was looking for.

She got back to her feet, staring at the challenge coin, then slipped that into a pocket as well.

"My father was a son of a bitch," Joanna Dark told Leland Shaw. "Just like you."

She left the lights on when she left the room.

FOR IMMEDIATE RELEASE TO ALL APPROVED NEWS OUTLETS

FROM: Gabrielle Shephard, Media Relations and Public Affairs Division

Product Rollout Update

There has been a great deal of understandable interest in the culmination of DataFlow's recent product rollout celebrations for AirFlow.Net 2.0, and the scheduled, but regrettable, interruption of the final ceremonies. To help allay consumer fears and to dispel some of the fog of misinformation that has arisen (notably on competitor newsfeeds), I'd like to take this opportunity to clarify the events of 30 January 2021.

Rest assured that DataFlow, and dataDyne, are committed to excellence in our products, and even more, to consumer safety. The final activation of AirFlow.Net 2.0 was temporarily postponed, due to a minor programming error that was detected in the system's signal-processing apparatus.

This malfunction is in no way associated with AirFlow.Net 2.0—the error was localized in a third-party relay that had been mistakenly installed by contractors who were setting up the conference facility in Paris. Consumers and shareholders should be pleased that it was the diagnostic routines for AirFlow.Net 2.0 that detected the error and self-halted the demonstration, as part of the system's overall safety programming.

Any reports that the AirFlow.Net 2.0 system is nonfunctional are wild speculation. A secondary rollout (initially scheduled for deployment in the Asia/Pacific Rim region) will go ahead as planned, with worldwide implementation within 90 days, per the existing product release calendar.

It should also be noted that the public events surrounding the AirFlow.Net 2.0 launch were a spectacular success, with concerts and DeathMatch VR tournaments crowning the ratings, and adding a great deal of dataDyne brand equity to our already successful entertainMe™ networks. We at dataDyne wish to thank our loyal customers for their continued support.

Gabrielle Shephard
Vice President, Media Relations and Public Affairs Division
dataDyne Corporation

World Financial Times-Independent

Core-Mantis Omniglobal on the Rise

Clash With dataDyne Inevitable?

By Pieter von Beck, Staff Writer, *World Financial Times-Independent*
London (FT-I)

The world financial markets have taken a keen interest of late in the sudden and unprecedented growth in prominent hypercorporation Core-Mantis OmniGlobal *(WORLDAQ: CMO)*, and it's attendant rise in market share.

In the wake of the collapse of Zentek and its absorption into CMO (and the subsequent destabilization of rival Beck-Yama InterNational), CMO has climbed into prominence, and has already begun to challenge dataDyne Corporation in several of dataDyne's *(WORLDAQ: DD)* key markets (notably in China, as CMO's newest forays into consumer body-modification and fashion, augmented by a revitalized Zentek line of ZeeWear™, have just launched in Beijing to great success).

Industry analysts insist that dataDyne is still the reigning powerhouse, with massive market penetration, broad diversification, vertically integrated product categories, and streamlined overhead, though Joseph Bishop, director and chief financial analyst of Bishop Financial Strategies, Ltd., indicates that dataDyne is by no means secure. "They are the longest-established player for these kinds of stakes," Bishop said, "but they do appear somewhat weakened. Dr. Cassandra DeVries and her much touted AirFlow.Net 2.0 rollout was disappointing—and it had a disastrous effect on DataFlow stock values, which dropped nearly 20 percent within 48 hours of the aborted product launch."

Still, others are quick to point out that a less-than-stellar software debut has not hampered other software pioneers, and that DeVries and dataDyne have a strong track record for delivering quality products.

Core-Mantis OmniGlobal CEO Shane Eddy, however, was quick to leap into the fray. "CMO has long had an interest in the personal null-g vehicle market, and our product teams are working hard to deliver SafeFlight 1.0 within the next fiscal year. Finally, consumers will have the freedom to choose how best their safety can be governed while traveling."

With the move into Chinese markets and the surprise announcement of a direct competitor to the venerable AirFlow.Net product line, the battle between Core-Mantis OmniGlobal and dataDyne is far from over.

TECHFEED > SCIENCE NEWSFLASH

NULL-G PIONEER DANIEL CARRINGTON ADDRESSES AERONAUTICS ASSEMBLY

By Alicia Brattin, TECHFEED Aeronautics Correspondent

Dateline: London

Null-g pioneer and founder of the Carrington Institute, Daniel Carrington, addressed the 23rd Annual International Aeronautics and Aerospace Conclave in London this afternoon. Carrington, a respected engineer and scientist, and the creator of the open-source technology that powers the modern personal aviation industry, gave the keynote address for the Conclave.

Citing the need for continued innovation, and the stifling effects of corporate oversight, he called for "constant vigilance. The new breed of global hypercorporation is interested merely in the bottom line, in the capture and containment of large percentages of 'market share.'

"It is our job to make sure that they never forget that their 'market share' is composed of a vital, irreplaceable commodity: human beings. We, as scientists, as the innovators and creators who make the technology they so gleefully adapt, package, and fling into the marketplace, look upon—and will continue to look upon—their precious markets with better eyes than those they grow as fashion accessories.

"We must never let them forget that they are a delivery system for beneficial technology, a means to an end. We, as the creators of that technology, must never let them forget that our goal is the betterment of mankind, not larger numbers on the ledger sheet. Nor should we forget our responsibility to shepherd that technology. It is a matter of pure responsibility, to ensure that what we create is not perverted into something harmful, that it is not turned into mere widgets and meaningless candyfloss, endlessly repackaged, refined, and regurgitated.

"We must ensure they never forget that we will watch what they do with our better eyes, with our hearts and consciences locked on the singular goal of making the world a better place, and the bottom line be damned."

Carrington's speech was met with some criticism from the scientists in attendance, many employees of larger hypercorporations such as dataDyne and Core-Mantis OmniGlobal. Dr. Michelle Ballantine of the Runyon-Adams Aerospace Research Division said, "Carrington's own organization includes an industrial and manufacturing arm. It seems unusual that he would be so outspoken about the negatives of corporate control of research and technology distribution, while he himself competes directly with such organizations. That doesn't sit particularly well with me, or my company."

Carrington himself was apparently unsurprised at the sour reaction to his address, but continued, "To that end, as the creator of the null-g technology that has had an undeniable impact on the world economy, I feel it is my responsibility to closely monitor the recent developments in the aviation safety community. The failed launch of AirFlow.Net 2.0 [from dataDyne subsidiary DataFlow] and the sudden rush to launch SafeFlight 1.0 [from Core-Mantis OmniGlobal] should concern us all, and I pledge to closely monitor the progress of both projects, to ensure that the gift of flight is not tarnished by monopolistic corporate practices."